FOREVER THEIRS

A MFM SMALL TOWN SUSPENSE NOVEL

ANCHOR BAY
BOOK 1

KENNEDY L. MITCHELL

To those of us who have been hurt and betrayed by someone who said they loved you.
Keep moving forward, because we deserve better.

PROLOGUE
UNKNOWN

It was a shame, really. If I was a better person, someone with the ability to experience regret or guilt, I might feel somewhat sorry for the terrified woman who was running for her life.

Away from me.

But instead of those annoying emotions so-called normal people suffered through, a thrill thrummed through my veins as I stalked Caroline as she pushed through the overgrown underbrush and weaved between the thick and thin white tree trunks that blocked out the rays from the seemingly ever-present sun this time of year in Alaska.

Decomposing leaves, which were just now drying out from the thick layers of snow that covered this area until last month, crunched while loose rocks rolled beneath the thick soles of my worn hiking boots as I moved through the trees, careful to not lose sight of the reason for this little outing, which pulled me away from my valuable work. The crisp mountain air filled my lungs with every deep inhale, the temperature just warm enough that my breath didn't fog with each exhale. Why this nosy-ass woman took on her own investigation and notice every fucking thing around Anchor Bay, who knew, but I was certain she would pay the costly consequences for her actions.

Another pathetic sob and scream for help carried through the thin, cool air, making my lips quirk upward in a genuine smile that only the hunt could bring to my face—a far cry from the fake mask I wore when in town, even with my family.

Her cries pierced the quiet like that of a shrieking eagle, but it didn't matter. No one would hear her, no matter how long or loud she screamed for someone to save her. We were too far from the main trail, miles from anyone who would care that I was slowly stalking the terrified woman with terrible intentions in mind once I caught her. She knew no one would be close enough to help her, considering the in-depth knowledge of the area needed for her role as an extreme hiking guide with that damn company in Anchor Bay, Uplift Adventure and Rescue.

But the noise was really starting to annoy me. This deadly predicament she found herself in was her fault—well, hers and Brandon Taylor's. She came out here alone, looking for clues and following a hunch on what happened to all the women who had gone missing on the Soul Trail. If neither had poked around where they didn't belong, then Caroline here probably wouldn't be minutes from her untimely death.

Well, maybe death.

She glanced a frantic, wild-eyed look over her shoulder. Her long blonde hair whipped in the wind, almost concealing the fear flickering in her blue eyes. I licked my lips, imagining her at my whim, her pain-filled cries and sobs vibrating off the walls of the bunker. I had yet to decide what to do with her after I caught her, considering this was an unexpected hiccup in the day. Thank fuck I was out checking on the livestock, ensuring they were ready for shipment, or Caroline could've found them and ruined all my hard work.

Too much effort, time, blood, and sweat had gone into restarting the trade business that faltered after Dad's death until I came along to let one nosy little bitch ruin it all.

Nosy, yes, but oh so pretty with those tears streaming down her round face.

Shoving both hands into the cargo pants side pockets, I picked up my lazy pace to keep her in sight. When she glanced back again the toe of Caroline's boot caught on something, causing her to stumble closer to the side of a steep slope. I didn't even attempt to hide my low, amused chuckle that escaped as she tipped forward, gravity taking over to send her tumbling to the bottom of the shallow ravine.

Careful with my footing so I didn't stumble like she did, I moved down the slope, loose dirt rolling with every cautious step. This was the perfect opportunity to overtake her while she was stunned from the fall. I had enjoyed the quick, thrilling hunt, like I always did, but it was time to end the chase and get back to work. Though, if I were honest, which I rarely was, the loads of money made from selling the women I procured was great, but this part—the hunting of a weaker and unassuming prey—excited me and was by far my favorite part of the skin trade. It made me eager to identify and target the next unsuspecting victim quicker and quicker between each acquisition to feel that high again.

But it was the insistent urge that put me and the whole damn operation on that fucker Brandon's radar in the first place. If I had the time to pause and take a break from it for a while, let the suspicions and building cases die down like

Dad did, maybe I could've avoided the shit storm I was currently skirting.

A few feet away, Caroline's limp body shifted along the loose dirt, and a pain-filled groan vibrated through the air, barely audible over my approaching footsteps.

Palms to the soft earth, she pushed herself up until both arms gave out, making her face-plant back into the soil. I lingered, the toe of my boots almost touching hers, and scanned her small, fit frame. Her white-blonde hair was now streaked brown, dirt caked on the normally silky strands from an earlier fall and the roll down the slope. Deep crimson oozed from a thick gash on her cheek, but even that didn't take away from her natural beauty. For longer than I could remember, I had found Caroline attractive and made it a point to weave myself into her life while also watching from the shadows for my own enjoyment—not to hunt and capture her, like the others.

I reached a gloved hand down and adjusted myself, the scene before me too erotic for someone like me not to be hard as fuck.

A guttural groan filled the quiet as she shoved off the ground just enough to flop onto her back. Whimpering with every labored breath, face pinched in delicious pain, Caroline blinked her dirt-coated lashes open, allowing her to see my face, clearly identify me, for the first time since the chase started.

"What... what?" It was like I could see the wheels slowly turning as she pieced it all together. The moment it clicked, just noticing I was not there to save her or offer support. Her bloodshot eyes widened. "I don't—"

With a huff I waved her off, not having the energy to explain the deranged complexities that spurred my actions and desires. "Don't try to make sense of it. Just accept that this is it." I cocked my head to the side as I continued to study her petite face. "Or it will be eventually, if not now."

"Why?" she croaked, nails digging into the ground as she attempted to push her exhausted body farther away from me.

"Why what?" I snarled, already annoyed by her pathetic, whiny voice. Hopefully, she wouldn't be this talkative later. Words weren't needed for what I planned to do with her. It had been a while since I kept an acquisition for myself. And this one was special. Her stumbling into my operation was a unexpected gift I shouldn't pass up. "And if you want to place blame, well, this is all your doing, Caroline. If you had just listened when I repeatedly suggested that you leave the missing girls and hiker cases alone. But no, you had to keep fucking digging, and look where that got you."

"You." Her voice trembled as she put more effort into backing away. Like that would do anything. She was mine now—until I grew bored with her like the others. Which, based on my past, I would, but thankfully, I had many different ways to dispose of her once I did.

I nodded with a smirk and tossed both arms out wide. "Me."

"But... but I... we trusted you," she accused before breaking down.

I rolled my eyes at her sobs and croaked cries for someone to save her.

Time to end this.

For now.

With an annoyed sigh, I whipped the gun from where it was tucked into the back of my pants and pointed the barrel at her chest. Pale, almost translucent lips popped open; blue eyes widened with fear as her scream cracked through the midday air, only to be covered by the boom of the gun firing.

Lowering the weapon to my side, I stared at her still form, debating if I had time to start the fun now or later. A quick glance at my watch had me cursing under my breath. There wasn't enough time to play *and* get her secured before my shift at work.

I had to get the area cleaned up so no one would suspect a woman lost her freedom here, then head into town to pretend to be the one thing I absolutely wasn't.

A good guy.

1

ASPEN

This could quite possibly be the biggest mistake of my life.

Or my best idea ever.

My already nauseous stomach rolled, bile creeping up the back of my throat with every wave that slammed against the small boat. Wait. Was something this size considered a boat or a ship? What was the difference between the two?

Fuck if I knew or cared about the floating vessel's classification at the moment. My focus was split between not throwing up and berating myself for forgoing that preventive Dramamine or emergency Xanax before boarding, despite debating the need for either or both. When booking this rash, totally unplanned, somewhat extremely careless adventure, I had three options. A tiny seaplane—no, thank you—the ancient charter bus from the airport to Anchor Bay, which would take over three hours—hard pass—or boat. This was a more direct route, aside from the plane, and I assumed the boat trip would be more fun, making it an exciting way to start the trip.

I chose wrong.

Seemed to be a running theme in my life as of late.

With both palms pressed against my stomach to help quell the sloshing, I twisted around on the hard plastic seat and eyed the man behind the massive chrome wheel. But if he noticed my pleading stare for him to slow down, he didn't give a flying fuck, because his gaze stayed locked out front, actively ignoring me.

Fine.

Blowing out a calming breath, I swiveled back around to face the front, port side?—I should really have done a little more research on watercrafts to keep from spewing the cheap white wine I downed on the turbulent flight here. This trip was supposed to be relaxing, helping me to forget about the asshole and the horrible job I left behind in Seattle. A break from my lonely reality in the peaceful serenity of Mother Nature.

Peaceful, my ass.

"How much longer?" I shouted to be heard over the roar of the motor and the slam of the waves against the hull. I mentally raised my fist, super proud of myself for knowing that one.

"Soon enough," grumbled the guy as he shifted his stance to turn his body away from where I sat.

Rude.

It was fine. I was fine.

Everything was fucking fine.

If I said it a few more times, maybe my rattled nerves and racing heart would believe me. Though I couldn't blame all my tension on the boat ride, the somewhat-hot asshole, or the bumpy flight. Yesterday, I'd essentially up and walked away from the little life I'd built in Seattle over the last five years. A great life, I guess, from the outside looking in.

Which, even from the inside, wasn't that bad.

I had a stable, highly sought-after job as an adventure photographer with an acclaimed outdoor magazine, even though it had turned into less of what I loved and more into following James Peoples around, making sure he had the perfect shots and pictures as he demanded and knew I could provide.

The man himself wasn't rude or mean and didn't do anything I didn't want to happen, even though when things did turn physical between us, it was because he needed something from me, or I had threatened to leave because I was over helping him chase his dream instead of my own. The man I fell into infatuation with and then slowly fell out of it over the years wasn't a narcissist who made me walk on eggshells or physically hurt me. We were the power duo everyone in the outdoor-loving world watched from the sidelines, thinking we had it all. The duo I hated being a part of a little more every day that I saw him shift from extreme outdoor adventurer to... whatever the hell he had become with his rise of fame.

James also never promised me a relationship, though he liked to lead me on or flirt so I'd do his bidding and ensure his photos were perfect. We had this toxic thing between us that I couldn't seem to find my way out of... until yesterday morning.

When I walked in on him eating out our editor on the conference room table.

Full on, him on his knees with his face between her thighs and her legs wrapped around his head. That had been a shock, considering one, he hated going down on women—or so he said in the past—and two, because, well, I was suddenly smacked in the face with the fact that I wasn't the only one he was leading on or keeping in the wings for when he "needed" me. There was something about hearing another woman moan the name of the man who you had given up so much for and followed around the world for three years that made you reconsider things.

Between blinks, I realized following him around and documenting his career made *him* happy, not me.

Helping him from the sidelines to become a household name made *him* happy, not me.

Dropping everything when he called because he "needed me" made *him* happy, not me.

The few instances of mediocre sex were something to look forward to and put up with all the other bullshit for, weren't they?

Okay, even I knew the last one was a lie. But not every guy was amazing in bed or had a dick that could make you moan just by looking at it. James was adventurous, exciting, and enthralling. Every guy wanted to be him, and every woman wanted to be with him. He knew how to play that card, manipulating people to get what he wanted.

Including our editor.

Realizing all that while backing out of the conference room so I could pour bleach into my eyes was like a punch to the gut while a dull knife dug into my heart.

He used me.

And I allowed it.

The fucker never wanted *me*. He only wanted what I could do for his career by taking the best shots, finding the most fantastic and unknown destinations, and dropping everything when he needed me, like a clingy little puppy desperate for an ounce of attention.

"Fuck my life," I muttered under my breath. "The bastard turned me into a touch-starved puppy. Awesome."

So, instead of confronting the asshole like an adult, I'd

marched to my desk, grabbed what personal belongings I could from my cubicle, and stormed out. Not that anyone followed. James was too busy eating Barbara's cunt to notice me catching him or leaving.

Barbara, though... oh, she saw me. And winked.

Clue number one that the devouring happening on the polished mahogany wood wasn't a first-time offense. She didn't look surprised to see me or that concerned.

No, she looked like the cat who ate the canary.

Or the cat who was getting eaten?

Fuck my life.

Face in both palms, I inhaled deeply, the stench of fish and saltwater filling my nose. I was fine. What was most shocking was that I actually *was* fine. There were no tears or hurt lingering from what I saw and left behind. That should be a major sign that maybe I wasn't as happy in the little life I'd carved out in Seattle after all. The second sign was a very unsuspected emotion.

Relief.

Profound relief that I was finally done and out of that toxic web that I had helped weave. Though I didn't realize it at the time, all I was doing was trapping myself in a life I didn't want or love.

I was so damn relieved that I'd finally cut all ties with that dumbass. Three years of working side by side together, and I was relieved that it was done. The web was demolished, and I was free to sprint far, far away to the one little town in Alaska that had been on my bucket list for far too long.

"This is a new start," I said out loud. "A new me."

"Good for you."

Instead of responding to the surly driver—erm, captain, maybe—I flipped him the bird over my shoulder and pressed a hot cheek to the cold glass. This was my new start at twenty-eight years old. Where maybe I could excavate the parts of me I used to love, remember the areas of life I was passionate about, and bring them back to the surface. And this resort in Anchor Bay was the best place for me to do just that. The Nest was all about helping you find inner peace through isolation and living among Mother Nature.

Hopefully, Mother Nature would take pity on me and was kinder than that ho Fate.

I must have nodded off at some point, because the next thing I knew, the boat's engines were more of a purr than a roar, and the rocking motion was not nearly as seasick inducing. Licking my dry lips and wiping at the corners for drool, I blinked away the sleep coating my eyes and sat up straight, back cracking with the quick movement.

"We're here," a deep voice rumbled, reminding me I wasn't alone.

With my back turned, I rolled my eyes to the cloudy sky. I bit my tongue to keep from snapping at the grumpy asshole. Pretty sure the approaching bustling dock filled with boats of all sizes and adorable, small, brightly painted buildings indicated that we were finally here.

Once, a long time ago, it was a place for hopeful gold miners to strike it rich, but now, it was a tiny Alaskan town that had been revitalized and turned into a secret gem for nature lovers and extreme sports lovers alike. Though the town itself was small, the population less than a thousand, it was the starting point to many trails, amazing salmon fishing, and, in the winter, all kinds of various snow-centered activities.

Anchor Bay.

Place of my unforeseen dreams and holder of all my hopes.

No pressure, town, but I need a lot from you.

Without a word, the grumpy guy secured the boat to the dock and motioned for me to disembark. I stood on unsteady legs from the gentle rocking motion, looping the strap of my weighed-down satchel over my head. The driver attempted to take it from me when I first boarded the boat to secure it with the rest of my luggage, but I'd refused to let it out of my sight. Between the top-of-the-line laptop with all the editing software, my camera, and various lenses I almost needed to sell an organ to purchase, everything inside was too valuable to allow someone else to handle it.

My feet hit the sturdy wooden dock, which groaned beneath my weight, and a few grumbling fishermen dodged me as I paused, giving myself a second to take it all in.

So, this was it. A chance to step away from reality, and the life I hated yet forced myself to live day after day for the last few years, and find myself again.

The two overstuffed duffel bags crammed full of all my hiking gear and anything else that was clean at the time of my rushed packing were slapped to the damp planks by my feet.

"Your ride will be here soon. You can meet him in that parking lot."

Narrowing my eyes, I stared up at the massive asshole. "What is your problem? Did I do or say something that pissed you off, or are you always this damn moody?"

He crossed his thick arms over his chest and widened his stance as if preparing for a fight. With an arrogant look, he stared down at me, not saying a word.

"Really, Lang." The voice at my back had the man shifting his glare over my shoulder. "Making the resort guests feel all warm and fuzzy with your stimulating conversation skills, I see."

With a huffed laugh, I turned to find a man heading our way wearing a wide, inviting, and somewhat mischievous grin.

"Sorry about Langston," he said, pausing in front of me. "He's grouchy on the best day, but before he left to pick you up, a certain someone got under his skin—"

"Knock it off, Aiden," the burly man behind me practically growled. "Grab her stuff and get going. We have a meeting in an hour that we'll both be late for if you don't hurry the fuck up."

"Charming," I scoffed.

"Don't take offense," the Aiden guy fake whispered as he grabbed the two Army green duffel bags I brought along for this adventure and lifted them like they weighed nothing. "He just needs to get laid." With a dramatic wink in Langston's direction, Aiden stepped around me. "If you're ready to get your adventure started—" He adjusted his hold on the thick straps and inclined his head down the dock. "—then let's go."

"Aspen. Aspen Carter," I whispered, my mind still reeling as I took in the sights. And I wasn't just in awe of the colorful wooden buildings lined up along the shore, raised high above the water by sturdy stilts, or the groups of fishermen laughing and working all around me. Despite my new and breathtaking surroundings, I couldn't stop my gaze from slipping back to the stupidly hot man.

Classically handsome, almost pretty features fit perfectly on his heart-shaped face. A scar bisected his right eyebrow, which added to his good looks rather than took away from them. Light brown hair streaked with natural golden highlights fell across his forehead, which he constantly had to flip out of the way. It looked soft and perfect to run my fingers through. His caramel-colored eyes seemed to sparkle anytime our gazes clashed, almost as if he liked what he saw just as much as I did. Though that was probably wishful thinking, my desperate loneliness creating something that wasn't there. Because why would he like what he saw? I wasn't anything special. Average height, average build, dark brown eyes that were a little too big for my face, and thick wild almost-black hair, which was currently tied up in a knot that I wasn't sure I'd ever untangle. He was far out of my league.

"Well, Aspen, I'm Aiden. Welcome to Anchor Bay." With the end of my duffel, he urged me in the direction he came from, gently tapping it against my thigh. The solid wood planks were slick beneath the soles of my hiking boots, making each step slow and cautious to keep from falling on my ass or slipping right into the bay. "The resort's SUV is in the parking lot. We'll get your stuff loaded up and head that way. It's not far, twenty minutes or so."

"You work for the resort?" I asked while maneuvering around a thick coiled rope lying in the middle of our path.

"Not technically. I work for a local adventure and rescue company, Uplift Adventure and Rescue. I had just dropped off a couple back at the resort after their motorbike expedition when the owner asked me to help out. We're a tight-knit community around here, so it wasn't a problem. We support each other however we need to, even if that's saving unsuspecting victims from Langston's grumpy ass. Sorry again about him. He's had a stick up his ass the last few weeks."

I hummed a noncommittal response, not sure how to respond, too stuck on how he described the community in Anchor Bay. A tight-knit community sounded glorious, even though I knew it came with its own set of challenges. Back in Seattle, there was no community, not even within the magazine I worked for. Many times, when traveling with

James and the TV production crew, I felt utterly alone. It was odd that on individual assignments that sent me deep into the mountains or hikes where I wouldn't see anyone for days, I never felt lonely. Yet in a city full of people, surrounded by bodies and those I knew personally, the ache of loneliness was sometimes so heavy it felt hard to take a full breath.

"Are you meeting someone here?" Aiden asked, drawing me out of my depressing thoughts.

"Nope," I said with a smile. "Just me and my camera for an entire week."

"Ah, you're a photographer." I nodded. "Well, people come from all around the world to capture the sights Alaska has to offer. I'm sure you'll find plenty to photograph."

Right now, I just wanted to snap every aspect of the adorable town. Maybe all remote Alaskan villages were as cute as this one, but there was a vibrancy that pulsed off the people who passed along the dock and shone off the bright buildings that made me think this place was unique, special even.

"That's us." I trailed behind Aiden, actively trying to keep my attention off his firm ass and not stare at the way his corded arms flexed and moved, stretching the cuffs of his snug T-shirt while carrying my heavy luggage toward an older safari-type Land Rover with The Nest's logo stamped on the hood. "Go ahead and hop in. I'm sure you're ready to get out of the wind. I'll load these two bags really quick."

The mention of the cool breeze rushing off the water had me wrapping both arms around myself like that would ward off the chill. For mid-May, it was still cold to me, even with the afternoon sun attempting to break through the clouds. I had heard that the weather this time of year was notorious for changing on a dime. After climbing into the stiff seat and slamming the passenger door behind me, I secured the seat belt. Fingers tingling from the cold, I rubbed both hands together and blew bursts of hot air between them.

Good thing I packed for the various weather possibilities, or my first stop would be the outfitting store at the resort, where the prices would no doubt be ten times the cost back home.

Home.

Was that even what my tiny apartment back in Seattle was?

Maybe I should just give up the big-city life, admit that Mom was right, and head home to Utah, where my family still lived. Mom would welcome me home after reminding me how she told me photography wasn't a sound career choice, and Dad, well, he'd just put me to work on the ranch, grateful to have an extra set of hands and not really caring why I was home, just glad that I was.

But I didn't want to go home. I didn't want to admit defeat just yet. I had enough money saved up to get through a few months without the steady income of a paycheck. That should be plenty of time to grab some amazing shots I could sell online.

The SUV jostled, pulling my gaze from the baby blue-painted coffee shop, as Aiden lumbered behind the wheel and slammed his door shut. After turning the key and firing up the engine, he shifted in the seat to face me.

"All set?" I offered a reluctant nod. His lips pressed in a tight line before responding. "That's not super convincing, Aspen."

I should not love the way his deep voice sounded when he said my name.

Clearing my throat, I forced a smile. "Yes, I'm ready."

"Ready for...?" he asked, running a hand across his lips as he studied me with a curious look in his searching eyes. It took me a second to realize he was seriously asking me, as if he could tell I was lost, just winging this whole adventure, which I totally was.

I blew out a breath, my smile turning genuine. "Everything, I guess. For a fresh start, a new adventure, and a new me."

A dimple popped on each cheek as Aiden's smile grew. "Well, then, it's a good thing you chose Anchor Bay."

"Why is that?"

"Because that's why we all came here."

I arched a brow. "And you found it here in Alaska?"

His eyes sparkled. "Anchor Bay, yeah. Every damn day, Aspen. Every damn day is something new and exciting, and, after meeting you, I know today will be no different. You're going to shake things up around here. I can see it now."

With that, he shoved the gearshift into First and pulled out of the parking spot.

Brows furrowed, I studied his profile as we exited the lot, only turning to look out the window as we drove down the main street.

What in the hell did he mean by that?

I wouldn't bring anything new or exciting to the table. It was probably a line he told all the resort guests.

Yeah, that had to be it.

Which really sucked, because I desperately wanted it to be true.

2

AIDEN

The drive to the resort was quiet, though I didn't mind, which was odd for me. I hated silence. It allowed my mind to wander, for all the mistakes I'd made and thousands of past regrets to force their way to the forefront of my mind, making me relive them over and over again.

Yet with the woman sitting in the passenger seat, who was as unique as her name, I didn't need to ramble on about the town's history or make casual, meaningless conversation to keep the uncomfortable silence away like normal. I felt at peace. Something that, lately, even downtime with Miles couldn't create. Maybe because most of my regrets and mistakes revolved around my best friend.

How we were still friends after everything was 100 percent due to his forgiveness and understanding.

"Do you have a lot of hikes and things like that planned while you're here?" I asked, shooting a look at Aspen out of the corner of my eye.

Fuck, she was gorgeous. Not in a flashy, look-at-me kind of way. Her beauty seemed to radiate from the inside out.

The way her dark gaze kept sliding my way signaled that she thought I was attractive too.

Or she was worried I was a serial killer ready to make a skin suit out of her soft, fair skin. I wasn't, but considering the mysterious deaths and disappearances that had happened in the last year, maybe she should be more wary of strangers.

A bolt of worry had my stomach twisting at just the thought of Aspen in danger, all because she chose Anchor Bay for her vacation. The idea of her going out into the woods, hiking on the long, treacherous trails alone, had me gripping the wheel harder than necessary.

"Nothing yet." Leaning to the side, she pressed her head against the window. "This was kind of a last-minute decision, so I have no plans. Though I'd love some suggestions on close trailheads and the best trails with views."

"Most people spend months planning out their trip to Alaska, or at least need that long to gather all the gear required for the climate and terrain."

She shrugged. "I've worked for a fairly popular outdoor magazine for the last five years, so I already had all the hiking gear and recently did research on Anchor Bay as a place for us to spotlight. It was easy to throw everything into a bag and leave. I just needed to leave him and my job fast, so no time to plan out exactly what I'd be doing here the next several days."

My ears perked up.

"Leave *him*?" Fuck, was I crushing on some heartbroken woman who came here to heal?

She cringed and shot me a reluctant look. "Yeah, sorry for that slip. You don't want to hear about the life and drama I'm here to escape."

Normally, I'd agree with her, but I uncharacteristically

wanted—no, *needed*—to know more about this beautifully sad woman sitting beside me. I inhaled deeply, forcing more of her sweet scent into my lungs, and held the full breath, hoping to imprint it deep inside me. Her casually gorgeous style, yummy scent, and the calming tones of her voice were drawing me deeper into her orbit, and there was nothing I could do to stop it.

Not that I wanted to. Because for the first time in way too fucking long, I felt something other than the heavy weight of my guilt pressing on my chest or my mind spinning with anxious thoughts about past mistakes I couldn't change.

"Sure, I do." When she shot me an incredulous glance from the passenger seat, I couldn't help but chuckle. "We've got about fifteen minutes until we get to the resort for you to tell me all about it." *And don't leave off in the middle of the story if you're still with "him." Or are still in love with him.*

Fuck, don't let her still be in love with him.

I gave my head a hard shake to dislodge that thought. What the actual fuck was all this about? Who cared if she was still in love with him? It wasn't like I'd have a shot with her. She wasn't from our community and didn't understand the unique relationships we preferred.

Unless she was into sharing too.

I swallowed a groan that vibrated in my chest just thinking about this woman between me and Miles.

"Well, let's see here," she said.

I cleared my throat in hopes of dislodging those erotic thoughts so I could focus on her.

"When I left home to pursue my passion in nature photography, my mother said it was a waste of time, telling me I would fail and probably end up alone with a hundred cats. My dad wasn't really supportive of my 'illogical career decision' either, but his opinion didn't have anything to do with my wanting to pursue photography. He was more pissed that he was losing a ranch hand."

I arched a brow at that, which made her smile.

"Surprised? I grew up helping my dad, doing whatever needed to be done. We mostly raised cattle, plus a few goats that my mom made Dad buy—oh, and the chickens, of course."

"Of course," I said with a smile.

"After submitting my pictures to different media outlets, I landed an internship at this magazine in Seattle. After a couple of years of proving myself, they decided to pair me up with James Peoples. If you don't know his name, he—"

My scoff cut her off. "I know who James Peoples is. He used to be this badass extreme sports and exploring guy until he—"

"Became a household name and decided he liked the celebrity life as a fake explorer for a TV show instead of being hungry, dirty, and exhausted somewhere out in the middle of nowhere for a magazine article?" I nodded and pressed my lips together to keep from interrupting. "Yeah, I saw that awful transition happen right in front of me. James Peoples... that's the *him* of my depressing story."

"Oh."

Not the most intelligent response, but it was all my brain could come up with after that bomb. Because damn, James Peoples was *the* adventure guy for years, and I guess still was, just more mainstream with his TV show. Some of his tips and tricks to survive in various climates were some I still used today when out on rescue missions. I had heard his new fame caused him to water down his survival suggestions, and now everything out of his mouth was about his sponsors or himself.

"So, after three years of following him around, and me

just now realizing he led me on and used me for my talent, yesterday, I went into a meeting with James and our editor to talk about doing an article on Anchor Bay only to find him—" She groaned into her palms. "—in a compromising position with our editor."

"What a fucknugget," I snapped. "Who does that?"

"James fucking Peoples?"

I shot her a half smile. "Assholes, that's who. Please tell me he's now missing one, if not both, of his tiny balls."

"How did you know they were tiny?" she responded with an almost smile.

"The bigger the ego, the smaller the balls. It's science."

"Hmm, science might be different up here in Alaska."

"It is. It's much, much better."

Now her smile grew genuine, so wide the corners of her eyes crinkled. I reluctantly pulled my gaze away from Aspen and back to the road to keep from running into a five-foot-tall snow wall left behind by the plows this past winter.

"It does seem that way already," she mused while staring at the gorgeous views out the window. "Better, that is. There's always been something about the outdoors, the peace that settles deep inside you, that has spoken to me. But this place, after doing some research on the resort and town, there was this insistent pull. Almost like it was calling me home." She shot me a wince. "That sounds strange, doesn't it?"

My thick hair shifted with my quick headshake. "Not to those of us who live here and came here for that exact reason."

"I've wanted to come here since the initial research I did several months ago, but we couldn't fit it into James's busy appearance schedule, and he didn't want me coming here with anyone else from the magazine—"

"What the hell? Why not?" I snapped.

She shrugged. "I mean, we were... whatever we were—practically a team after doing so many trips and editorials together."

My hands tightened around the steering wheel. "That shouldn't give him the right to dictate where you go and who you go with. It was your job, for one, and two, no one owns you."

She turned in her seat and stared point-blank at me. "What? Explain more of that thought process."

I cleared my throat and shifted uncomfortably. "If you trusted the person you'd be working alongside, male or female, then why shouldn't you have been able to go if your editor allowed it, no matter what that fucker James said? Obviously, if there were other red flags about the coworker, that would warrant some concern, but it seems like he was more focused on keeping you at his side for selfish reasons rather than your safety. If he was a real partner, he would've dropped everything to go with you or encouraged you to go without him, knowing it was what you wanted."

Her jaw dropped. Eyes wide, she blinked at me, not uttering a single word. My stomach cramped and my heart raced, worried I'd just fucked this up—whatever *this* was—by opening my damn mouth.

Out of nowhere, she lunged across the console and slammed a palm against my bicep. I cursed at the unexpected assault, even though it didn't actually hurt.

"You are so right!" Aspen exclaimed, hitting me again. "Holy fuck, you are so right. He didn't want me around the other guys at the magazine, yet he was messing around with Barbara behind my back. And we were never really a couple, even though he liked to make me feel like we were," she grumbled at the end.

What a leeching fucker. Probably led her on, kept her waiting in the wings for when he was lonely or needed her for something. I fucking hated users.

"And Barbara is...?"

"My editor. Well, former editor, since I emailed her my resignation letter this morning."

"Good for you. Look at you, taking a spontaneous trip to Alaska and starting a new chapter in your life. This calls for drinks."

She beamed a megawatt smile and clapped her hands. "Yes. That's exactly what I need. Alcohol to celebrate my 170-pound weight loss." I shot her a confused look. "I'm talking about the relationship, losing the weight of James's jealous, self-centered, egotistical ass from my daily life."

"And how do you feel?"

Please don't say sad.

Please don't say regretful.

Please say horny.

She released a heavy sigh and slumped back against the seat. "Relieved. Free. Not sad. I should feel sad, right?"

I shrugged. "No one can tell you how you're supposed to feel, Aspen. You're the one who lived the life, felt the strain and effects of the toxic relationship you were in with him."

"Are you a driver *and* a therapist?" she asked, hitting my shoulder again.

"Nope, just someone who has made his own mistakes and has fucked up enough to know everyone is different. How we handle life is based on our past. Only someone single-minded would ever put expectations or boundaries around how someone should feel."

"Yep," she said, popping the *P*. "Totally an undercover therapist." Rummaging through the bag at her feet, she pulled out an expensive-looking camera. "And I've decided, starting right now, I'm going to document this new me—this new chapter, as you called it."

Raising it to her face, she pointed it at me. Before I could protest, several clicks sounded through the SUV. Lowering the camera, she studied the small screen with a soft smile.

Fuck it. If taking random and terrible pictures of me made her smile like that, then she could waste the battery on me.

Though I should probably tell her I photograph best naked.

Too soon?

As we crested the hill, the resort came into view. Smiling to myself, I slowed so I could gauge her reaction. It wasn't fancy by any means, but that wasn't what the resort was for. The Nest was built for those who wanted to enjoy nature and experience it during the day or on short camping trips but have a warm, soft bed in a private cottage to come back to. Just outside Anchor Bay was a trailhead that started a long and dangerous trail that led to Kenai Fjords National Park, so a lot of people stayed at the resort before backpacking for days along the trail or as a reward after the long hike if they started in the park and headed our way.

Twenty-three cabins were spaced around the main part of the resort that housed the restaurant, bar, small outfitting shop, and reception desk, which was where I guided the SUV as we wove through the expansive property.

"This is exactly how I pictured it," Aspen said, snapping pictures of the cabins as we passed. "It's perfect. Just what I needed."

Pulling up in front of the doors that would lead to the check-in desk, I put the SUV in Park and leaned against the driver's door.

"Head in there"—I pointed just over her shoulder—

"and get checked in. They'll give you a key to your cottage, and I can drive you and your gear over so you don't have to haul it. There are bikes you can borrow from the front desk—they have a shit ton—if you want to go into town. We try to manage our environmental impact, so most people take their bikes around instead of cars if the weather is nice. Meaning anytime it's above freezing."

With a hesitant nod, she reached for the door handle and paused. "Do you think I'm insane?"

I huffed a laugh. "Why would I think that?"

"I somewhat ended a toxic relationship yesterday, packed up my stuff, and flew to Alaska. It's kind of like I'm running away."

"Or running toward the life you were meant to live. Don't overthink it, Aspen. Sometimes we need a reset in life. You're one of the lucky ones who figured out you needed to make a change before too many years were wasted being unhappy."

"Are you talking from experience?" she whispered.

I swallowed hard and broke off her intense stare. "My life reset came at the expense of someone I love nearly dying. After that, a lot of things shifted into perspective for me. Which is why I'm here. It's not a flashy life full of material things, but I'm happy. The community I live in, they're my family. Dysfunctional as shit, but what family isn't?"

Chewing on her lower lip, she just nodded and shoved open the door.

"Everything will work out, Aspen," I assured her.

"But what if it doesn't?" she responded over her shoulder.

"Then you'll have a lifetime of memories to look back on from your time here." I shot her a cocky smirk. "I'll make sure of it."

With a choked laugh and flushed cheeks, she shook her head and climbed out of the SUV, slamming the door shut behind her.

That wasn't a no...

So maybe we had a chance to have some fun while she was here.

We as in me, Aspen, and Miles.

All I had to do was get them both on board, and maybe this would be a week none of us would ever forget.

3

MILES

Stepping into the conference room, I scanned the few faces of the people already here for the company meeting. Uplift Adventure and Rescue had over twenty people working there, either as guides, rescue teams, or various support staff. I counted only a handful in the makeshift conference room, which was about normal.

Keeping to the wall, I made my way around the long table toward the back of the room, dodging the few chairs not tucked under. Catching someone's eye, I hitched my chin, acknowledging our temporary hire, Hudson. Temporary, as in he moved here for one reason, which would hopefully be wrapped up quickly. He was a detective back in LA, served as a SEAL with Uplift's owner, Brandon Taylor, and was recently brought here by Brandon to help investigate the uptick in unsolved deaths along the trails and several missing female hikers.

Beside him stood Oliver Johnson, our small town's deputy sheriff, whose father, the sheriff, wasn't too happy about his son's eager acceptance of outside help in the unsolved cases.

Which was suspect as fuck if you asked me.

As I lowered into the metal folding chair, Baylee and Liam both smiled my way from across the table, which I returned. The two had recently started dating, which was fine with everyone, even Brandon, the owner. Baylee was a kind, gentle soul who was left devastated after the loss of her high school sweetheart and fiancé. She deserved everything that could make her smile again, and if our broody cowboy, Liam Wilson, could do that, then they had my support.

I arched a brow at Langston as he fell into the metal seat beside me, grumbling under his breath. I swore the ground shook beneath his heavy weight, and that was saying a lot, considering I wasn't a small guy with my solid six-foot-three frame. Lang was Uplift's captain of all things that float, so any adventures involving the water were his specialty.

The grumpy fuck shot me the finger and slouched down in his seat like an upset toddler. I fought the twitch of my lips, knowing full well what got my coworker all riled up. He was never outgoing, but his persistent grouchiness started when the company hired the new scheduling coordinator and social media guru, Juno Jones, who arrived last month.

The sexual tension between the two was almost laughable. Toss West, our genius mechanic and Langston's friend with benefits, into the mix, and the rest of us had stockpiled popcorn to watch them avoid their attraction to each other. At some point, it would bubble over, and I, for one, couldn't wait. Maybe then Langston would pull the oar out of his ass and go back to being his regular irritable self instead of an all-around asshole.

"Your buddy is an instigating bastard," Langston griped as he watched Juno step into the room.

"Guess he's taking tips from you in that department," I said, unable to hide my smirk. "What did he do this time?"

"I called him out on being a grumpy dickwad to a new resort guest." A heavy hand slapped my shoulder as the man in question folded into the chair to my left.

"You wouldn't have cared if you weren't trying to get into her pants," Langston snarked, his gaze still locked on Juno as she talked with Hudson and Oliver. His glare darkened when her laugh sounded around the room at something Oliver said.

Fuck, the man had it bad, and he had no damn clue.

At the perkiness in my best friend's tone, I shifted in my seat to face Aiden and angled my head, studying his face. He was in way too good a mood, considering he normally hated making resort guest runs and complained about it afterward. But instead of being pissy, Aiden looked happy— ecstatic even, if that wide smile was any indication of his real mood.

"He's wrong," Aiden said, reaching across me to shove Langston's shoulder. "It's not just about getting in her pants." His smile fell. "She's fucking amazing, man. The whole package, and there's just something different about her, Miles. Whatever the fuck it is pulled me in the moment we met. I swear I could see her fitting in great here."

I swallowed hard and nodded, trying not to let my disappointment show. If he wanted to pursue a woman on his own, he could. Just because I needed our unusual setup didn't mean I would hold my friend back if he wanted this woman. And if she could chase away the demons he constantly fought, which seemed to have faded at the moment, then I was on board.

His light brown eyes searched my face, lips dipping into

a deeper frown, telling me I didn't do a great job of hiding my disappointment in knowing our past fun was done.

"Fitting in great with *us*, Miles." I just nodded as relief flooded my veins and turned my attention across the table. "Don't worry. You'll see what I'm talking about tonight. I bet even you won't be able to resist her pull."

My neck cracked from how quickly I snapped my head around, eyes wide. The asshole just chuckled and slapped me on the back instead of explaining what he meant.

"What are you talking about?" I said through gritted teeth. "What about tonight?"

An uneasy feeling grew in my gut at the mischievous smile that tugged at his lips. The bastard had gotten me into too much damn trouble after that look.

"Tonight, *we*, as in you and me, are taking her out for drinks at Dave's."

"Why?" *Sigh.* I could tell he was excited, but fuck, he knew we didn't mess around with guests. It was either locals, which were few and far between, who were okay with our specific needs or going to Anchorage. The hard-and-fast rule was created three months ago after a resort guest we messed around with grew concerningly clingy and outstayed her welcome here in Anchor Bay. After that shit show, we decided never again. "You know the rule. Or do you want a repeat of Jessica Scroggins?"

Aiden visibly shuddered and checked over both shoulders like she might pop up out of thin air. Which, to his credit, wasn't too far off. The woman had followed us both around, appearing everywhere we went for a month after her trip to Anchor Bay was supposed to end. It was when we got home to our cottage after a four-day camping excursion and found it trashed that we finally did something about her stalking.

"She's not like that, man—"

"What's put that dopey look on your face?" Ethan, our survivalist expert and trainer, said as he swiveled a chair around and straddled it, laying both arms over the back. "Did you finally see that bird you've been talking nonstop about?"

"There is no reason to make fun of me because I'm an ornithophile," Aiden said with a smirk, knowing full well we hated it when he used that term. Which, of course, made my best friend use it in conversation any chance he could.

"Don't admit that out loud with an officer of the law in the room," Oliver, laughed from where he leaned against the wall. "Keep your kinks to yourself, Aiden."

"What are you doing here?" I asked over Aiden and Ethan bantering back and forth.

"I asked him to attend the meeting with us." Everyone stopped talking when Hudson stood. With Brandon away, checking out that potential new site in Montana, he'd put his old SEAL buddy, Hudson, as lead. I would say I resented the idea of us needing supervision, but sometimes it felt like Brandon ran a daycare instead of an adventure and rescue company staffed mostly with his military buddies and other veterans.

Like me.

Just thinking about my time in the service had the scarred skin on my back pulling uncomfortably. I shifted in the seat, trying and failing to hide the pain-filled grimace from my best friend. I waved off the concerned look he shot me and turned my focus back to Hudson.

"The remains of another male hiker were found early this morning on this side of the Soul Trail." Muffled curses filled the room. Not wanting to miss a single detail, I leaned forward, resting both forearms on the long wooden table. It wasn't much of a meeting room, but since we only used it once a week, Brandon didn't see the need to make it pretty. "The remains are on the way to the coroner in Anchorage now. We won't know anything official for several days, but I assume he'll be like the others."

"What the fuck is going on out there?" Ethan snapped, his anger-filled gaze locked on the single window as if monitoring for danger. "This is the third male this year alone. That's not counting the female remains and those still missing."

We all waited, breaths held, for Hudson to respond.

"With Hudson's experience and my authority"—Oliver's worried eyes flicked between Juno and Baylee—"we'll figure this out. I'm working with the law enforcement rangers inside the national park to make sure we haven't missed any victims, but that's going to take some time. Until then, I don't want anyone going out alone."

Baylee held up both hands. "You won't hear any pushback from me."

Liam looked at her with concern and hugged her even tighter to his side.

"Or me," Juno piped up while tying her blonde ringlets into a high ponytail.

"Shocking," Langston muttered under his breath. I rammed an elbow into his side, hoping to hit his damn reset button.

"That goes for everyone in here." Hudson scanned the room, lips pulling down in a frown. "Where is Caroline?"

"She mentioned being gone for a day or two," I offered, remembering the odd conversation from yesterday. "Something about wanting to find a more challenging location for our more skilled rock-climbing clients."

Hudson nodded but seemed hesitant. "Wish she

would've come to me first, but nothing we can do about it now. Considering we believe women are the targets, we want you to be extra careful out there when female clients are involved. Even if they just booked a day hiking trip, Brandon and I want at least two of you out there with them." He ran a hand over his short dark hair. "We don't know how deep this goes yet. But we will. With my past experience as a detective and Oliver's knowledge of the area and people, we will get this solved."

I had no doubt he'd put all his energy into solving the mystery of what was going on in our town and along the trail, considering he had some skin in the game. When Brandon asked him to come help out, Hudson brought his wife and their young daughter up too. If women in Anchor Bay were in danger, so was his wife.

"Just wait until you meet her," Aiden whispered after leaning in close. "You'll see what I'm talking about. She's different."

"All right," Juno said with a loud clap, gaining everyone's attention. "Now that we're all caught up on the creepy shit going on around here, let's talk about this week's schedule. It's a fairly light week since we're transitioning from the snow adventures and fewer rescues to the summer activities..."

As she went down the list of excursions and who would lead, I zoned out, considering I'd already memorized the schedule and where I was needed. Everyone had their own specialty, so anytime something was put on the books, we knew who would take that reservation. Aiden and I were responsible for the motorbike and snowmobile trips, along with any snow-related rescues. As a retired SEAL, being out in the wilderness, surviving on what little we brought or foraged for was second nature.

"And you're never going to believe who she left behind in Seattle," Aiden said out of the side of his mouth with a smirk.

"I'm not going to ask how you already know all this." I chuckled. When he just kept staring at me, I sighed and pinched the bridge of my nose. "Fine. Who did she leave?"

"James fucking Peoples."

I huffed a humorless laugh. "That pretend survivalist shithead?" Aiden nodded. "And why should I care about that? Or her, for that matter? Come on, Aiden, you know better—"

A knowing grin tugged at his lips, cutting me off.

Fuck. That wasn't good.

For me, at least.

"You should care about this new guest because she's someone special... someone you've heard of." I continued to glare at my friend, urging him to get to the fucking point. "Her photos, those pages you ripped out of magazines, are still somewhere in your room."

I blinked at him, trying to catch up with the conversation, when suddenly it clicked.

"You're telling me Aspen Carter is this guest you're going on about?" Aiden gave me a smug nod and crossed both arms over his chest, leaning back in the metal chair until it rocked precariously on two legs. "Are you fucking with me?"

That smirk fell. "I wouldn't do that to you, Moose." My lip twitched at the nickname that came from my time as a SEAL. "I know what those pictures meant to you while you served, what they gave you."

Hope.

That was what those amazing photos in the outdoor magazine my mom occasionally sent had given me. Some nights bunkered down in a foxhole, waiting until the perfect moment to strike our target, I'd stare at the glossy pages ripped from the spine. I'd smooth out the wrinkles on my thigh and stare at the breathtaking landscape she'd captured on film. It reminded me of what I was protecting, of what I was sacrificing years of my life for.

I'd never seen a picture of her, but I was already halfway in love with the unknown woman because of her talent and clear love and awe of nature.

Which was a huge fucking problem since she was now here. In Anchor Bay.

And I was going to have drinks with her and Aiden tonight.

"You can thank me later," he murmured and then turned his attention back to Juno.

I continued to stare at his profile, debating whether he was right or not. Meeting her for drinks was one thing, but I knew Aiden had deeper intentions with the woman than just a few cocktails. Which was where the problem was in his plan.

I wasn't sure I'd recover if the woman I almost idolized for her brilliant talent turned away in disgust when she saw my battle-scarred body. Ran away when she realized how broken I truly was—more on the inside than out.

So, no, this couldn't happen, no matter what Aiden wanted.

I had to protect myself.

Because if that flicker of hope died inside... that would shred what was left of me.

4

ASPEN

Crisp, clean air flowed through my nose as I inhaled deeply and held it until it burned in my lungs, then slowly released it through pursed lips. Over and over, I repeated the calming exercise while sitting on the hard composite wood planks of the back porch, gazing out at the gorgeous view of several snow-covered mountain peaks that glinted in the bright afternoon sun. Or was it early evening? With no phone or watch to monitor the time and a desperate need to unplug, plus the nearly sixteen hours of sunlight during this time of year, it made it difficult to know exactly how long I'd been sitting here, lost in thought.

The short nighttime hours would make getting enough sleep here tough, but it also had its benefits. Longer days and more hours of natural light than back home meant additional time out on the trails and in the mountains taking pictures.

With a content sigh, I plucked the Uplift Adventure and Rescue brochure—the one Aiden made sure I had several copies of after he helped carry my bags into the cabin—off the porch beside me and scanned the offerings.

"Ugh, how is a girl supposed to choose?" I groused to myself and flipped back to the first section to review all the options again.

Everything looked fun and amazing, and there were way too many great options to pick from. I wanted to book every single one, but there was no way, considering I only had seven days in Anchor Bay before having to go back to my shit-show life. A heavy weight settled in my chest, making me work for each inhale. With the heel of my hand pressed to my sternum, I rubbed to dispel the building pressure created by just thinking about Seattle.

What the hell will my life look like after this spontaneous trip is over?

There was no way I could, or would want to, go back to the magazine after my abrupt and unprofessional exit. Hell, even the thought of returning to that big city filled with pollution, surrounded by strangers, and the soul-eating loneliness I felt every day made my heart race with anxiety. That wasn't living. It was barely surviving, just going through the motions.

I didn't want to go back, not when being here for less than half a day showed me there was so much more out there. A happier life, one where I didn't dread waking up in the mornings to do it all over again.

This was my chance to reset the trajectory of my future, just like what Aiden called this random, crazy trip, and he couldn't have been more right. Sitting on the back porch of the very basic single-occupancy cabin, staring out at the mountains, with the clean air rustling my hair, caressing my skin, and filling my lungs, settled me in a way I hadn't felt in too long.

This place just felt right. As if I was exactly where I was meant to be.

A soft knock on the cottage door had me unfolding my pretzeled legs and standing with a groan. On the way to answer the door, I glanced at the wall clock. The corners of my lips pulled up into a giddy smirk. Aiden was five minutes early for the celebratory drinks we planned before he left earlier, and somehow, I knew that wasn't the norm for him. With his easygoing nature, I had a feeling he was the type of person who ran a few minutes late wherever he went.

I wrapped my fingers around the doorknob, giving it a quick twist and slowly easing open the heavy wood, verifying through the three-inch crack that it was in fact Aiden waiting on the other side before opening the door all the way. Holy hell, the man was beyond gorgeous. He'd changed into a basic deep green T-shirt that hugged his chest and arms, paired with dark-washed jeans, and he seemed to have at least tried to fix his floppy hair to keep it out of his eyes.

At well over six feet, he gazed down at me, and the wide, all-white-teeth smile that was on his face slowly dipped into a frown.

My stomach flipped. Shit, was he disappointed with what he saw? I looked down at my soft green sweater, jeans, and boots. Maybe I should've put in more effort, like brushing my hair or putting on some lip gloss.

"I didn't hear a lock disengage before you opened the door." I blinked up at him, not understanding the odd, confusing statement. He was right, but who the hell paid attention to that kind of detail? I must have forgotten to lock it after he left, as I was in too much of a hurry to lose myself on the back porch. "Does that mean it wasn't locked?"

"Forgot to, I guess." I shrugged, somewhat relieved his frown was because of the lock situation, not because of how I was dressed or looked. "It's fine. I'm fairly certain bears haven't figured out how to turn doorknobs," I said, tongue in cheek, not understanding the big deal. The Nest wasn't secured by high fences or anything, but with the way they spread out the guest cottages and were so far from town, I wasn't concerned about some random person walking in on me, unlike back in Seattle.

"It's not bears I'm concerned about, Aspen," Aiden said, his voice tight.

The few rogue hairs that had escaped my messy bun drifted across my face as I cocked my head. "Then what should I be worried about?"

Lips in a tight line, he glanced over his shoulder, a muscle along his jaw twitching as he worked it back and forth. "Just from now on, lock it for me, okay? The town might look small and inviting, but not everyone is on the up-and-up like me and my best friend, Miles, who you'll get to meet here in a few. He's meeting us at Dave's."

I nervously chewed on my lower lip and tightened my grip on the edge of the door. "All right, yeah. That sounds okay, I guess. You're sure I'll be safe with you and your friend? Me going out in a town I've never been to for drinks with two guys who I don't even know the last names of sounds like the start of every horror film or episode of *Dateline*."

He snorted an incredulous laugh. "You will be perfectly safe with us, but you made a valid point." Reaching into his back pocket, he pulled a slender leather wallet free, flipped it open, and thumbed out his driver's license before handing it to me. Holding the stiff plastic close, I scanned his photo, annoyed that the picture was good while I looked like a strung-out addict in mine, before reading the listed information.

"Aiden Davey Taylor."

"My friends call me Aiden or Crocket." I tried to give it back to him, but he retreated a step and held up both hands. "I want you to feel safe and comfortable with me, Aspen. Take a picture of it." He hitched his chin toward the license. "Send the photo to a friend and let them know I'm taking you to Dave's bar in Anchor Bay. I'll have Miles do the same when we see him there."

The reservations that rose within me when he mentioned meeting his friend faded. He could be putting on a good-guy routine to get me alone, but it didn't feel that way. Maybe it was the loneliness talking, but he seemed worth the risk. With a slow nod, I stepped off to the side and gestured for him to move off the porch and into the cottage. The moment he was over the threshold, I quickly shut the door behind him to keep the annoying summer bugs outside where they belonged. With my spine pressed against the door, I held his license out between us.

"Can you take a picture and send it to me?" He arched a questioning brow. "My phone is off and buried somewhere in the bottom of my bag."

Gaze locked on me, he nodded and did as I asked, showing me the screen after he sent the photo to the number I rattled off. My shoulders dropped a fraction, and I released a slow breath. While I appreciated his concern, I really didn't want to power up my phone, which I'd turned off the second I sent Barbara my resignation letter.

Cowardly? Maybe. But I would deal with the aftershocks of my actions later.

Much, much later.

"Suggesting that was very considerate and brilliant," I said, shoving my hands into the back pockets of my jeans before propping a foot up against the door.

"That would be because of Caroline."

A flare of jealousy erupted, tightening my stomach. I shoved the emotion down deep with a thick swallow, hoping it didn't show on my face, though the knowing smirk that barely curled the corners of his lips said I did a shit job of hiding how I felt.

"Caroline is a friend and coworker at Uplift. In the past, Miles and I voiced our concerns about her meeting up with men she'd just met, so she started doing the license thing. That way, she was safe, could still live her life, and it put us at ease, knowing exactly who she was with and who to go after if anything happened to her."

My stomach did a flip at the low growl that vibrated his words. What would it be like to have guys like that in my life? Protective and caring yet understanding and not oppressive.

"Plus, she would tell us where they were going." He paused and looked just over my shoulder with a frown. "But for the last month, she's been seeing this one guy, so we haven't had to worry about anyone new."

"And that's a bad thing?" The face he was making made it seem like he wasn't a fan of the new guy at all.

He ran a hand through his styled hair and shook his head. "Not bad, just... It's nothing. How do you like the place?" he asked, gesturing around the small cottage. "Is it what you expected?"

A genuine grin spread across my face as I shifted my attention from the dangerously handsome man to the tight living space. It wasn't fancy or spacious by any means, but it was perfect for one person. The main room was a simple square that worked as the living room, with a love seat against the wall and a single chair beside it. The very basic kitchen had a sink, a small fridge, and a microwave. No surprise that there wasn't a TV, which wasn't that big a deal for me, considering I preferred to read instead of watch anything these days. A door off to the side led to a bedroom with a log frame queen-size bed with the softest duvet on the planet and a cramped attached bathroom.

Everything was practical. Exactly what one would need, since most of a visitor's time was spent outdoors anyway.

"It's perfect. And the view out back is mind-blowing." I gestured to the back door. "I've already lost a few hours just sitting out there, staring at the mountains. I'm excited to see some of the town tonight. It looked picture-perfect on the drive here. I can't wait to snap some shots. Since I'm not here very long, I need to make every opportunity and moment count."

"Then let's get going." Phone still in his hand, he typed out a quick text before sliding it into his back pocket. "Just letting Miles know we're heading to Dave's."

Snagging my thick coat from the hook by the door, I slid it on and flipped up the fur-lined hood. A deep, rumbling chuckle came from Aiden as he held open the door, eyes alight with humor.

"What are you laughing at?" I grumbled as I snatched the satchel with my wallet and camera off another hook and looped the long strap over my head. "It was chilly earlier on the porch, and once the sun finally sets, it'll be downright cold. Don't judge me."

He waited at the base of the front steps, studying my movements as I locked up. "Not judging you, Aspen. I'm laughing because it's practically summer here. Hell, I debated wearing shorts, and you tugged on a winter coat over a sweater. It's adorable and reminds me that we're a bit of a different breed up here in Alaska. Most people wouldn't think this weather is warm, but after the long-as-hell and bitter fucking winter, we do."

The metal key dug into my fingers as I shoved it into a deep pocket, pushing it into the tight corner so it wouldn't accidentally fall out. Instead of moving along the path toward the parking space allotted for my cabin when I stepped beside Aiden, he gave me an uncertain look before leaping up the steps. Fingers around the doorknob, he gave it a few turns and shoves, ensuring it was locked up tight before turning back with a smile.

A swell of emotions had tears burning behind my eyes as my heart melted at the simple gesture by an almost complete stranger. I'd only known the guy a few hours, yet here he was, so concerned about my safety that he double-checked the cottage was secure. I noticed he did it to the back door, too, before we headed out the front.

When was the last time anyone but me cared about my safety?

I swallowed down the unshed tears, not wanting Aiden to see how much that gesture meant to me. Because damnit, I was tired of always having to be on guard, watching over my shoulder, and keeping myself safe.

"I can see that. But even coming from Seattle, this is cold enough to warrant a heavy coat. I hate being cold." Loose rocks and fallen pine needles slid beneath my boots as we walked side by side along the path toward an older-model Toyota 4Runner. "That yours?"

He flung a set of keys up in the air, catching them again with ease. "Yep, that's us. Normally, with the nice weather" —he laughed when I shot him an incredulous look—"I'd drive the bike or four-wheeler around town, but I wasn't sure how you'd feel about riding with me since we just met."

"Do you live close to here?" I smiled when he opened the passenger door for me.

Hand on top of the open door, he waited until I was in

the seat, camera carefully cradled in my lap, before responding. "Yes and no. It's not too far. Miles and I live together in a community our boss built just for Uplift employees. It's cool as hell and nearly self-sustaining at this point. It really is damn impressive what Brandon, our owner, and Carl and Amy, his life partners, created for us. It's a miniature town with a close-knit family-like environment. Sure, we all work together, but we're family now too."

I nodded while biting the tip of my tongue to keep from asking about Brandon and his partners. Because, unless math was different here, he listed three people in their relationship, not the typical two. That seemed to validate the rumor that popped up on social media when conducting my research on Anchor Bay. A few posted about a unique poly community that settled outside town several years back. Uplift was never mentioned or linked in the posts, but the way Aiden spoke about his community, it seemed to be the one they'd mentioned.

As if waiting for my reaction to that revelation, Aiden hesitated a few seconds, watching me before nodding and shutting the door.

I deflated against the seat, blowing a raspberry. That was a lot of information to process, and I now had a shit ton of inappropriate questions I was desperate to ask.

The SUV bounced when he folded into the driver's seat and turned to face me. "Ready?" At my nod, he pushed the key into the ignition and started the engine. After turning the heat on full blast and pointing all the vents my way, he shifted into Reverse and pulled out of the parking spot. "If you want to grab some shots on the way, let me know, and I can slow down or pull over."

My heart gave a heavy thud and, I swear, swelled at his offer.

The seat belt caught, tugging against my chest when I adjusted along the seat to lean on the door and gaze out the side window, my eyes flicking every which way to not miss any of the gorgeous scenery off in the distance. Without me having to ask, Aiden slowed to an almost crawl when we hit the edge of town. Smiling so wide my cheeks burned, I rolled down the window, not caring about the chilly wind filling the SUV, and raised my camera, snapping shots of the colorfully painted buildings and almost-deserted docks and piers. The sun reflected off the choppy water, highlighting the bright colors and unique layout of the town.

"Go ahead." Aiden pulled off to the side and rested a forearm on top of the steering wheel. "We're in no hurry."

The tires continued to roll along the road while cars and other ATVs coasted past us, but not once did he ask me to hurry or complain that I was taking too long. By the time he pulled the SUV into an angled parking space in front of a weathered wooden building, I'd taken hundreds of pictures I couldn't wait to download and sort through.

The hinges groaned when Aiden shoved his door open and stepped out. Busy putting the camera away, I jolted when my door swung open and he leaned against it.

"Get some good shots?" he asked with an expression that told me he was actually interested and not just making small talk.

"Yeah, I think so. I'll know for sure once I get back to the cabin and can look them over on the laptop." He stepped back, allowing me to exit the 4Runner. I eyed the rotting wood façade. "So, this is the place we're meeting your friend?"

"Yep. It's not much to look at, but it's a favorite of us locals. The tourists and visitors stick to the trendier and newer side of town, which is just two blocks that way." He hooked a thumb behind him as we headed for the door. "Ches is a great guy. Pours strong drinks and always has the best beer on tap."

I eyed Aiden, then the sign that had seen better days. The white-painted *Dave's* was barely legible. "So, the guy who owns it is Ches, but the bar is called Dave's?"

Aiden tipped his head back, his long locks of hair swinging with the movement, and laughed. With a wink, he tossed a heavy arm across my shoulders. He paused, still chuckling under his breath. "Dave was Ches's dad. He owned the place before he passed several years back and left it to his son."

The cheerful expression shifted to one of consideration as his honey-brown gaze flicked between my face and where his arm hung on my shoulders. "Is this okay?"

Biting my lip to hide my goofy grin, I nodded.

"Great, because I'm a touchy-feely, invade-your-space kind of guy. If it ever bothers you, let me know. I try to remember that not everyone wants me hanging all over them."

It was crazy that I truly didn't mind. In fact, his touch was almost comforting in a way, despite him being a stranger and sexy as hell.

He reached the door first, grabbing the thick wooden handle and giving it a tug before gesturing for me to go through.

I paused just inside the bar, my eyes taking a second to adjust from the sunlight to the dark atmosphere. Scents of fried food, stale beer, and fish wafted up my nose when I inhaled. Tugging at my coat, I popped the snaps and pulled it off as Aiden stepped up beside me. Every head turned our way, and conversations died as the patrons focused on me.

I swallowed hard, not loving the curious and a few hostile stares.

"You said this was a local favorite. Are there a lot in Anchor Bay? Locals, that is, in the actual town?"

"More than you'd think." A wide hand pressed to my lower back, guiding me forward through the scattering of high-top tables. "The fishing keeps this town going most of the year, but in the summers, we get an influx of visitors who want to explore Alaska. Some locals live in town, but a lot don't. They move here to get away from people, and that's what they do. Build a remote place out in the mountains and only come into town to trade what they've trapped or shot, stock up on supplies, or when they need a tiny dose of socialization, which is what they get here.

"Oh, good, Miles is already here." He pointed toward a table in the corner and then huffed. "Of course he brought her too."

I stumbled, hip bouncing off a chair, when the light shifted, pouring through one of the few windows along the back wall, highlighting a massive man whose intense gaze tracked my every move. Even sitting down, I knew he was well over six feet tall, and with broad shoulders and a thick chest, he radiated power. Short dark hair, barely long enough on top to style, and a thick, almost-black beard that covered but didn't conceal the sharp lines of his square jaw. True hazel eyes never left my face, almost dragging me into his orbit.

Movement to his right drew my attention. I sucked down a shocked gasp, almost choking on a delighted squeal that tried to escape at the same time.

Holy fuck.

Was that really a dog, sitting in a chair like a human, smiling at me?

5

AIDEN

I worked my jaw back and forth, hoping to ease the tension, as we approached the table where a stone-faced Miles and a happy Jubie waited. I loved that animal. She was the best cuddler in Anchor Bay, but I had asked Miles to leave her at home for tonight's meetup. What if Aspen was afraid of dogs or allergic or—

"Oh my goodness," she gasped beside me, cutting off my thoughts. "Shut the front door."

With a quick glance over my shoulder, I double-checked that the door was in fact already closed, but before I could tell her that, Aspen hurried to the table, yanked out the empty wooden chair beside Jubie, and flopped down onto the hard seat.

After haphazardly tossing her coat aside and carefully looping the strap of her satchel around the chair back, she reached out both hands, fingers wiggling, only to pause an inch from the massive Bernese mountain dog's thick fur.

"Is it okay if I pet her?" she asked, wide dark eyes pleading with Miles.

At his clipped nod, her sharp, excited squeal filled the

bar, making a few heads turn our way, and she practically launched herself at the massive animal. After shooting a mind-your-own-business glare to a few of the local guys who were staring a little too hard at Aspen, I turned back, only to find Jubie leveling me with a smug look as she panted over Aspen's shoulder, drool swinging from her loose jowls.

Unfortunately, Jubie seemed to be the more accepting of the two. My best friend, whose expression made me think he was constipated or had accidentally been poured gin instead of vodka, hadn't shifted except for his all-seeing gaze that tracked each of Aspen's movements. When his attention finally swung my way, I smirked, knowing Aspen had caught his eye the moment we walked into the bar. After ensuring she couldn't see the gesture from where she was still wrapped around Jubie, he flipped me the bird and leaned back in his chair, crossing both arms over his wide chest.

I huffed and rolled my eyes. Of course the asshole would pout at getting caught checking her out. Not sure what he was trying to prove with the blank expression and hard looks, but he couldn't fool me. Miles was intrigued whether he liked it or not.

"Tell me everything about her. How old is she? What's her name?" Aspen asked.

"She's five, and her name is Jubie."

I swallowed a laugh at Miles's gruff tone and curt response. Oh, my bestie was fighting his attraction to the energetic, gorgeous brown-eyed woman—and he was failing. Hard.

"That's a unique name and fits her perfectly. Oh my goodness, she's so soft and cuddly." Aspen buried her face in Jubie's soft, furry chest.

"Not as cuddly as me," I responded while folding into

the chair beside her. Under the table, the toe of Miles's boot connected with the middle of my shin. A hiss whistled through my clenched teeth to keep from cursing up a storm. I reached down and rubbed at the spot to ease the pain. "Fucking hell, man, don't break my damn leg."

Aspen stilled and eyed us both before her gaze settled on Miles. A determined expression overtook her face. Sitting back, she used her jeans to swipe away the loose fur that clung to her palms and was stuck between her fingers, then extended a hand across the table toward him.

"Sorry, I basically attacked your dog and didn't even acknowledge you. Hi, you must be Aiden's friend. I'm Aspen, and I am now obsessed with your dog."

The corner of Miles's lips twitched upward as he fought a grin, and he took Aspen's much smaller hand in his and gave it a quick shake.

"Miles or Moose—I answer to both. Jubie here thinks she's part human, which is why she's sitting in the chair instead of lying on the floor beside me as I instructed." He gave Jubie a stern look that I knew didn't mean shit. That dog could lie on the table, and Miles wouldn't care. He and Jubie had a special bond, one we didn't even have. She accepted him, all of him, with zero judgment or concern.

Neither did I, but there was something about the unconditional love of a dog that pulled him to Jubie that I'd never be able to compete with. Not that I wanted to. I was thankful as fuck that he had her, that she could fill the void I couldn't with his PTSD and self-consciousness about his scars.

Aspen's gaze kept darting between Jubie and Miles as she continued to stroke a hand over the dog's wide chest. "Your tattoos are amazing," she blurted out before biting her lip.

The air froze in my lungs, and I waited to see how Miles

would react to her pointing out the ink decorating the exposed skin of his forearms, where he had pushed up the sleeves of his long-sleeved black T-shirt. While the designs were badass, Miles rarely liked people looking too closely, since he got the tattoos to cover up the scars left behind from his last mission as a SEAL.

But instead of shutting down and closing himself off, the six-foot-four badass smirked and laid both forearms on top of the table for her to get a better look. I gaped as he told her about each design and how far up both arms the tattoos went. She didn't reach out, which I was thankful for, as it no doubt would've had him pulling away and hurting her feelings.

I couldn't stop staring at the cocky smile on Miles's face. After everything he had been through in life, every genuine, lighthearted grin was gold. She didn't know the significance of the moment her easy conversation and warm personality created.

If she could make my best friend smile like that more, I'd give her anything to stay longer than the week she planned to be here. The more I was around her, the more I wanted that for myself too. Aspen was like a breath of fresh air after being cooped up for too long. You didn't realize how stale your life was until something new and invigorating came into it. And maybe that was exactly what Miles and I needed.

"I've always wanted full sleeves," Aspen said, absentmindedly stroking Jubie's floppy ears. "But there's never been a good time, you know?"

"What do you mean?" Miles leaned forward, bracing both forearms on the edge of the table, leveling all his attention her way. Though I knew that, even with his focus on Aspen, he still monitored the movements and conversations of everyone in the bar. After being trained by the best of the best, that was his thing, always on alert.

"Because of the somewhat intense aftercare required to keep it clean and heal correctly, it wasn't really doable in my last job. I'm an adventure-slash-nature photographer." Miles just nodded like he wasn't fucking fangirling, considering he had some of her photographs hidden somewhere in our cabin. "I never knew when I'd be sent out on longer assignments. Keeping the fresh ink clean and infection-free while hiking and camping out in the middle of nowhere didn't seem feasible. Hell, on most assignments, I'd go days without showering just to get to the perfect spot for an amazing photo." She looked at us with a grimace. "Not sure why I said that out loud. I'm sure that sounds disgusting. I swear I bathe regularly when I'm home."

Miles arched a thick brow. "Doesn't bother me or Aiden, I'm sure. That's a fairly normal occurrence for us, considering what we do for Uplift. Did he explain what we do for work?" Aspen's head angled one way, then the other in a *kind of* gesture. "The company we work for handles all the excursions and adventure treks for the resort and other visitors that come to Anchor Bay, along with the various rescue missions that come up throughout the year." He pointed at me, then to himself. "Aiden and I handle all the land motor vehicle assignments, such as ATVs, motorbikes, snowmobiles, and four-wheelers. Some outings are day trips, while others last several days, where we carry all our gear with us for however long we're out. So, no, you stating you're okay with all that comes along with long hiking and camping trips isn't 'disgusting,' as you put it, to us."

"That's amazing." The smiles and attention she gave Miles should stir up some jealousy, but only relief and flickering hope swirled in my chest. "You get to be outdoors all the time, and it's your job, as in you get paid to do what you love. How cool is that?"

She turned to face me. "You mentioned something on the way to the resort this afternoon that made me think you're not from here."

I sat up straighter now that her dark gaze was on me and nodded.

"So, where are you from?"

There was no concealing my wince at her question. Clearing my throat, I gave myself a second to shove down the resentment and anger that always surfaced when I thought about the place I used to call home.

"Damn, I'm sorry. Was that too personal?" Aspen sat a little closer to Jubie, as if drawing comfort from the massive animal. "I didn't mean to make you feel uncomfortable."

"Not too personal at all." I shifted in the seat. "It's just that thinking about home carries some baggage. For both of us."

"We grew up together and have been friends since we were seven," Miles added, shocking the hell out of me that he'd offered up that sliver of our past. He normally stayed closed off when meeting new people. Keeping things shallow helped protect him from... well, the world, it felt like most days. "We moved out here at the same time to join Uplift after I left the military."

I swallowed hard and turned my gaze to the table, hating the swell of guilt that ballooned in my chest. He made it sound like he left on his own terms, but I knew differently. If Miles had it his way, he'd still be fighting side by side with his SEAL brothers, but he was here, living half a life with the guy who had failed him.

Me.

Aspen's lips curled in a knowing smirk. "I knew it."

"Knew what?" I asked.

She hooked a thumb in Miles's direction. "That he was former military."

Miles stiffened, drawing Jubie's attention. She licked at his hand, offering him comfort the best way she could. "And what made you assume that about me?"

Aspen shrugged and went back to running a hand down Jubie's spine. "You have this commanding presence about you that says 'I see all and can handle anything thrown my way.' It's noticeable to me as a woman because I'm usually the one constantly on high alert." Miles's shoulders rolled back as his chest puffed out at her basically saying that his observance allowed her to relax a fraction. "What I don't know is which branch of the military." She tapped a single finger against her lower lip, drawing my gaze. "For sure, special forces. Army Rangers?" She paused, waiting for Miles's response.

He huffed an incredulous laugh and flicked his eyes to the ceiling as if that were a ridiculous guess. "No."

"Okay, then, how about Green Berets?"

This time he snorted and shook his head, running a hand over his short hair.

As she studied him, her eyes widened. "Holy fuck, you're a Navy SEAL." At his confirming nod, she blew out a controlled breath. "Wow. That is amazing. No wonder you have that aura about you and why I feel safe around you. Though that could be Jubie here; she looks like a killer." With that, she pulled Jubie's face close and gave her a kiss on the nose. "I should've guessed SEALs from the start. You have a similar intensity to someone I met a while back during an assignment for the magazine. I was documenting a weeklong survivalist-type venture with this former SEAL and our guy from the magazine for a multi-page article that was also being filmed for a TV episode."

"No shit?" I tipped the chair on its back legs. "When was that?"

"Last summer." That smile of hers grew, and she leaned in, as if she was about to divulge a big secret. "It was legit the highlight of my year. I didn't stop smiling once I got home for days. So, James had this great idea—"

"James Peoples?" Miles interjected.

"Yep," she said, popping the *P*. "James fucking Peoples was the survivalist I worked with at the magazine. Guessing you know of him, or the version of himself that he wants the world to see?"

Miles grunted. "He seems like a fucking pretender douche canoe who's obsessed with himself."

Aspen stared at him, eyes wide for a second before tipping her face to the ceiling and laughing so loud the sound echoed through the bar. "You're great at reading people because you are so right!" she exclaimed. "I'll cheers to that all day, every day. Douche canoe, I like it. I've just been calling him a soggy sandwich in my head."

When she turned her attention back to Jubie, Miles looked my way and flicked his hazel gaze down to his almost-empty drink, then to Aspen. It took me a second to catch on. When I did, a frustrated groan rattled in my chest, and I fell forward, the chair's front legs slamming to the floor.

Right. I'm an asshole who invited her for drinks but didn't get her anything. I was too wrapped up in studying their interactions, and it slipped my mind. I was a terrible host, but who could blame me when she was so damn distracting?

"You need a drink to cheers. What can I get you, Aspen?"

She chewed on her lower lip and turned in her seat to stare at the bar. "It's not that I don't trust either of you, but can you grab me a bottle of beer with the cap still on?" She grimaced as if worrying I would be offended. Sensing her discomfort, Jubie turned her head and began licking her cheek. "Any light beer is fine," she said with a giggle. "I'm not picky."

"That's smart," Miles said with a proud expression. "Even if you trust us, we're still strangers, and it's a wise move."

I nodded. "Speaking of safety first... Miles, send her a picture of your driver's license. She doesn't have her cell phone, but you can send it to whatever number she gives you. I already sent her mine before we left The Nest."

Aspen gave him the same number she did me earlier, and while he did what I asked, I stood from the chair. I turned toward the bar but paused when Miles asked me a question that had my stomach dropping.

"Have you heard from Caroline?" I slowly shook my head. "It's not like her to go a full twenty-four hours without checking in," he mused, rubbing a hand along his thick dark beard. "If we don't hear from her tomorrow, let's talk to Hudson."

I rapped my knuckles on the back of the chair and nodded in agreement. It was odd that she hadn't reached out to either of us, but Miles especially. He'd taken on the role of her protector in a big brother type of way. "I'll be right back with our drinks. Hold off on that story about the SEAL and James Peoples until I'm back. I can't wait to hear how that turned out."

At my back, Miles's deep voice sounded, asking Aspen about her old job and photography. My nostrils flared with a deep inhale in an attempt to dim the hope swelling in my chest as I moved toward the bar.

No one was perfect, but it sure felt like Aspen was for us. In less than thirty minutes, she'd pulled multiple smiles and laughs from Miles, made Jubie fall in love with her, and distracted me from the constant regret and guilt that weighed me down daily.

I was getting ahead of myself, but fuck, how could I not? It felt like it was meant to be with her here, with the two of us. Sure, this was just drinks, and she didn't know Miles and I were a package deal with relationships, but this felt like the start of something big.

We needed something, a change, after all that shit with Jessica, plus the looming ominous feeling that had settled over our community and Anchor Bay with the missing women cases.

And maybe, just maybe, Aspen was that change we desperately needed.

6

MILES

Here I thought because of my size and training that I was strong. That my normally ironclad willpower allowed me to resist any temptation that went against a resolution I'd made to myself. Hell, most people thought I was a stubborn asshole because I never swayed from my choices, even if sometimes it was me digging my heels in when I was wrong.

Never said I was fucking perfect.

I was the furthest from that, inside and out.

Earlier, I was adamant that I wouldn't allow Aiden's excitement to sway my decision to keep his new infatuation at arm's length. I couldn't get attached to her, considering I already harbored a crush on the woman based on her talent.

But then entered Aspen Carter, and my backbone of steel and rock-solid stubbornness vaporized to fucking dust. The moment she walked through the door, I knew I was in trouble, and fuck if I wasn't right. The woman radiated genuineness, even with the sadness that lingered behind her dark eyes. While I expected her to be attractive after Aiden's description earlier, he failed to tell me all the little things about her that made her stunning.

A scattering of freckles dotted her button nose and across her cheeks, which moved when she smiled. Big brown eyes stared into your soul as if excavating every dark thought and memory to heal with her brightness and joy. There wasn't a speck of makeup on her face, which she obviously didn't need with her smooth, fair skin that stood out against mahogany hair that fell around her shoulders in loose waves.

But what drew me in most was her smile.

It sucked me in, altered my perspective, and shifted something inside me every time it spread across her beautiful face. I wanted to see that happy, carefree expression every damn day and be the reason it was there.

Fingers tightly wrapped around my cocktail glass, I tipped the vodka soda back, downing the remaining contents in one go.

"How long are you here for?" I asked around the ice cube I rolled around with my tongue.

She didn't look up to answer from where she was making funny faces at Jubie. "A week."

My dog, who normally didn't like strangers, was currently soaking up every kiss and pet Aspen gave her.

"That's a good amount of time. Any big plans?"

Peeking around Jubie's massive head, her big brown eyes met mine from beneath dark lashes. "Not exactly. This was a spur-of-the-moment, I-need-to-get-the-hell-out-of-Seattle trip. I'd love to pick your and Aiden's brains about some trails with gorgeous views where I could stay overnight to capture the landscape in all different lights."

"Not alone," I ordered, tone harsher than I wanted. Thankfully, she didn't shy away, just simply arched a single dark brow in question to my abrupt response. "I know you have all kinds of experience and can do it on your own, but this is Alaska." I racked my brain, mentally scanning the week's schedule, then nodded to myself when I found an opening. "Aiden and I would be glad to take you out for an overnight in-and-out hike the day after tomorrow. I know of a spot that could be perfect for the type of pictures you take."

The sounds of the bar filled the silence between us as she thought over my offer while gently stroking a hand over Jubie's head. "If you're sure it wouldn't be too much trouble, yeah, I'd like that. A lot, actually." I caught the pink staining her cheeks before she tucked her head.

While we waited for Aiden to come back, I watched the slow strokes of her fingers through Jubie's fur, growing more and more jealous of my damn dog. I didn't like being touched and preferred to watch Aiden have all the fun and live vicariously through him, knowing the texture of my burned skin made most women uncomfortable, but I was unexpectedly craving hers. To have that soft touch brushing along my bare chest, slipping lower with every stroke—

A glass bottle slammed against the table, shattering my erotic daydream.

"I got you a fresh one too."

Giving my head a shake, I berated myself for not noticing Aiden until he was right beside me. Under normal circumstances, I was aware of everything around me, a natural habit after my time as a SEAL. Seemed the unique woman with us was even more captivating than I realized.

Folding into his seat, Aiden shot me a confused glance, no doubt noticing he'd snuck up on me, and placed the two unopened beers in front of Aspen.

"Choose the one that looks good to you, and I'll take the other," he offered, gesturing between the bottles.

She studied the labels, reading each carefully before choosing one and twisting off the top with her bare hand. With an impressed grunt, Aiden grabbed the other bottle, slid it close, and did the same.

"Just so you know, while you were getting our drinks, Miles offered for you two to take me on an overnight hike."

Aiden choked on his beer, slamming the bottle to the table as he coughed into a tight fist, wide eyes locked on me.

"You okay?" Aspen asked.

"Yeah, perfect. Just surprised is all. Can't wait," Aiden said, still coughing. "Are you thinking true hiking or hitting the trails on bikes or four-wheelers?"

She took a sip of her beer, brows flying up. "Wow, this is fantastic. You weren't kidding about this place having good beer. And I'd prefer to take the hiking trails, if that's okay. That way, if I see anything along the way that I want to capture, I can grab the shot, and hopefully, with less noise, it will mean more wildlife." She swiveled to face me. "Does that work for the trail you were thinking of?"

"Yep, works great. You mentioned this being an impromptu trip. Do you have the gear for a long hike?" I leaned back in the chair to look under the table at her shoes and nodded in approval at her well-worn hiking boots.

"Yes. I packed knowing I'd be going out daily. I just have nothing for the overnight aspect, but I could purchase a sleeping bag and—"

I waved her off. "Uplift has all that you can borrow. Let's meet up after our morning clients tomorrow to sort through the gear and determine if we need to hit the general store in town for anything missing."

She nodded while taking a drink. I couldn't help the way

my gaze slid to the bob of her throat. Without my approval, images of my hand wrapped around it flashed through my mind, making my cock twitch.

Clearing my throat, I redirected the conversation to distract my horny-ass thoughts. "Now that Aiden's back, tell us the story you mentioned earlier. I'm hoping the SEAL, whoever he was, put the douche canoe in his place."

With a wide smile stretched across her face, Aspen excitedly launched into the story, hands waving as she detailed the disastrous assignment that ended abruptly when the former SEAL called James Peoples out on something inaccurate and dumb, which resulted in the idiot storming off like an angry toddler at being told he was doing something wrong. To make it all worse, James then refused to finish filming the clips needed for the episode of his survivalist show or approve any details, pictures, or commentary taken for the multipage article the magazine had planned to publish.

The douche canoe really was pathetic if he couldn't take being corrected. How Aspen dealt with his superiority complex as long as she did spoke to her abundance of patience and calm nature.

That story led into another, then another, with Aiden and me tossing in our own. Before we realized it, hours had passed, with the three of us drinking and laughing while swapping wild, disgusting, and awe-inspiring stories that revolved around our mutual obsession with nature and anything outdoors. With every story she told and every question she asked to gain more detail or insight into one of ours, the miles-thick wall I'd constructed around my heart through the years weakened.

Thankfully, the stories and her questions stayed light-hearted, never once asking about my years in the service, which felt intentional from both her and Aiden. The few times the conversation lulled or when Aiden got up to grab another round of drinks, it felt like she wanted to ask but somehow knew better. As much as I was drawn to the amazing and beautiful woman, there was no way in hell I'd open up about those years of my life, allowing her a glimpse at how truly broken I was. If she asked, I knew the walls around my heart that had weakened tonight would slam back in place, protecting me from the bombarding memories it would bring to the surface.

Surprising the shit out of me, I didn't want to pull away or close myself back off when it came to Aspen Carter. For the last few hours, I felt no phantom pain, didn't lose minutes in a memory, or worried about what nightmares would haunt my dreams the moment I crawled into bed later.

She was more than beautiful. Aspen was special in a way I'd never experienced. So, every time it felt like a personal question was on the tip of her tongue, I abruptly redirected the conversation right back to her. Which worked out, considering I craved to know every detail of her past, present, and future.

Toward the end of the night, when I couldn't stop watching her, studying the way her perfect lips pulled into a smile, or imagining how they would feel against my own or wrapped around my cock, I realized how much I fucking wanted more of Aspen. More as in taking this beyond the easy conversations to a more physical path. It was obvious Aiden wanted to take it further, too, but we still had a major hurdle to jump before we could even hope for more with Aspen. Despite our hinting about our unique relationship style, we hadn't broached the subject outright. Who the fuck knew if she would be open to the idea of both Aiden and me?

I scrubbed at my beard, not liking the thought of her walking away from us, the calluses along my palm catching on the coarse hair.

Fucking hell, why was I even thinking about any of this? Aspen was only in Anchor Bay for a week. It was dumb to get attached, knowing she would leave at the end of her temporary stay and head back to her life in Seattle, even if she seemed unsure that the big-city life was what she wanted in the future. I sure as hell wouldn't use that uncertainty and sudden life shift to sway her into something with Aiden and me because I had a crush on the woman.

Too lost in the dirty and vivid visions of Aspen and us, for the second time tonight, I failed to notice when someone approached our table. Catching Aiden stiffening in his chair plus a waft of a familiar, expensive perfume snapped me back to the present and put me on high alert. Both hands curled into fists beneath the table as I glared at the unwanted woman while Jubie sat up from where she lay at our feet, a soft growl vibrating from her chest while a corner of her muzzle curled into a snarl.

Glancing at Jubie, Aspen's words trailed off midsentence. Her big brown eyes skipped between me and Aiden, sensing our almost palpable tension that only grew worse the closer Jessica came to our table.

"Are you two okay?" Aspen asked, reaching over to run a hand over Jubie's head.

"Well, hello there, boys. Who would've guessed you'd be here tonight?"

Nostrils flaring in annoyance, back molars clenched tight, I fought the urge to tell Jessica to fuck off.

Pausing behind the chair Jubie had vacated earlier, she

wrapped both hands around the back, her long nails clicking on the wood. "Is this seat taken?"

Lips pulled into a snarl, I didn't get the opportunity to tell her "Hell yes" because Jubie took care of it for me. Front paws on the seat, she pushed off the floor and sat her wide backside down in the spot Jessica wanted.

Smirking at Jubie, Aiden shook his head. "Guess that answers that question."

With a scoff, she stepped back and scanned the bar. "I'll just grab another one from—"

"What are you doing here, Jessica?" Aiden pinched the bridge of his nose. "You're aware that we have the restraining order paperwork all filled out and ready to file with the sheriff."

Instead of watching Jessica's reaction to Aiden's words, I studied Aspen, whose eyes grew to the size of saucers. Fuck. Of course the good thing we had going with her would end before it even got started. All because of one of our past mistakes that seemed to be harder to eradicate than bedbugs.

"Oh, no need to bring that up. I'm not here for you two, just here for a date." She paused, watching both of our faces, no doubt hoping to find jealousy. Licking her red-painted lips, she huffed. "Running into you guys was an unexpected coincidence."

A humorless snort escaped into my water glass as I took a sip. Jessica's calculating gaze slid to me before moving toward Aspen, and a malicious smile pulled at her lips, making her look as crazy as we knew she was. Heart slamming in my chest, I shifted in my seat, ready to react to whatever Jessica tried. "And who do we have here? Your next conquest, I'm guessing? Little plain for your tastes, don't you think?"

"Watch it, Jessica," Aiden practically growled, clenching his beer bottle so tight that every knuckle was void of color. Fuck, he better not shatter that bottle. The last thing I wanted to do tonight was haul him up to Doc at The Nest for stitches again. "If you're really not here for us, then move on." He leaned back, folded both arms over his chest, and leveled her with a blank stare.

Jessica simply smiled, as if enjoying his annoyance, and gestured to Aspen. "Oh, I will, but first, it's girl code for me to warn your new little friend here about what exactly she's getting into with you two assholes."

"Leave. Now." I stroked a hand down Jubie's back in repetitive soft strokes to calm my racing pulse and ease my building anger. I'd never hit a woman, but I sure as hell would pick Jessica up and set her outside the bar if she continued with her little warning.

Fuck, this was bad.

"Did you know?" Jessica leaned in closer to Aspen, who inched back until she was on the verge of falling out of her seat. Aiden tipped forward, ready to catch her if she did. "They only share. A two-for-one special, if you will, but"—Jessica's hateful gaze cut my way—"Miles is too damaged in the head to—"

The harsh scrape of chair legs along the beaten and sticky floor cut off whatever she was about to expose. Aiden took a single, menacing step toward Jessica. Anger and violence vibrated off him.

In a blink, the fake confidence was gone. Jessica's eyes went wide with fear as she stumbled back a step, knocking into a table of locals who yelled at her to back the fuck off.

"Get the fuck out of here now, you fucking cunt." Fuck, he was pissed. Crimson highlighted his cheeks, and his chest heaved with every labored breath. I knew it was her remarking on my damage that sent him straight into a rage. She could've said anything about him, and he wouldn't have reacted, but come after me, and you got the side of Aiden hardly anyone knew existed.

Rounding the table, he put himself between the two women. With the threat to Aspen minimized, I turned my attention to her, expecting to find... fuck, I had no clue how she'd react to the shit Jessica just exposed about our type of relationship and my issues. Brows raised in surprise, I nodded in approval at the evident frustration on Aspen's face.

Huh.

Was she mad at us because of Jessica's revelation? Or was it because the obsessed woman interrupted our fun night?

Sliding my phone from my pocket, I shot off a quick text to Oliver and his dad, the sheriff, letting them know Jessica was here and causing a scene. Though I knew the others around us, who were clearly annoyed with the drama, had already contacted them too.

Careful not to touch her, Aiden herded Jessica away from our table and toward the door. Once they were a safe distance away, I slid the last potato skin from our earlier order closer to Aspen.

"You should eat that." As if lost in her own thoughts, she startled at my words. Her head swung around, cutting off her view of Aiden escorting Jessica outside. "You have to be starving. I know I am."

"I already ate my two. Eat it," she said distractedly and chanced another look over her shoulder.

I stiffened when the door swung open, afraid it was Jessica coming back for round two, but it was Oliver. He hitched his chin my way, letting me know he was there, and stepped back outside to hopefully help Aiden.

"So, are we going to talk about that or act like some random woman didn't just interrupt our night and drop some massive information bombs?"

I rubbed at my jaw, not releasing her questioning gaze. "Do you *want* to talk about all that?" With a single knuckle, I inched the plate to the very edge of the table in front of her.

She shot me a grin and rolled her eyes at my insistence.

"Do *you* want to talk about all that?" she countered before taking a bite of the fully loaded potato skin. Her lids closed as she chewed, a soft, happy moan escaping. Watching her lips, combined with the sound, created visions of her doing that around my cock. I cleared my throat and adjusted my stiffening dick to keep it from painfully pressing against the zipper of my jeans. "You were right. I am starving, despite these delicious potato skins." With a single finger, she slid the laminated menu between us. "How about we order some of those elk nachos next? You both mentioned they were good here."

My lips twitched before the smile I failed to contain broke free. "Yeah, we can, though we'll need three orders. Aiden and I can take down a plate each all on our own."

Leaning back in the chair, I folded both arms over my chest, loving the way her dark eyes zeroed in on where the long sleeves were pushed up. I gave my forearms a quick flex, though showing off backfired when she licked her lips like she wanted to taste my inked skin, sending every drop of blood in my body rushing to my cock.

Looking at the ceiling instead of her tempting mouth, I counted to ten, giving myself time to calm down before I lunged across the table and kissed the life out of her. "And no, I don't particularly want to talk about the shit show that just went down, but I feel you have questions and, frankly, deserve an explanation."

Aspen held up a hand. "You don't owe me anything if you're not ready to explain or share." She shoved the last bite of potato skin into her mouth and chewed while studying me, a slew of questions in her eyes. "But..."

"But you have questions about that little relationship statement Jessica dropped."

"Well, yeah. Who wouldn't?" I nodded in agreement and gestured for her to ask whatever she wanted to know. "First, let's start with the obvious and most glaring question. Is that true about you and Aiden sharing?"

I held her stare and nodded, keeping a composed façade, even though I was anything but calm.

She swallowed hard, jerking her attention to Jubie before taking a sip of her beer. "That's... interesting."

I huffed a laugh. "*Interesting?* That's all you have to say when you just found out the two guys you're having drinks with like to share the same woman?" I leaned in close and made sure her attention was fully on me. "In every way, Aspen. There is no choosing between us. It's both of us or nothing."

Her lips parted, and with the tip of her thumb, she swiped at the corners as if checking for drool. "Okay, that revelation is a bit more than interesting, but I will say I'm not really shocked." Both my brows flew up my forehead in surprise. "Aiden mentioned the man who started Uplift had two partners, a man and a woman. It made me think the rumors and whispers about there being an open-minded poly-type community in Anchor Bay were about *your* community."

Condensation slicked my fingertips. The slippery glass spun along the table as I twisted it back and forth. "Now *that* is interesting. I didn't know there were rumors about us floating around. Where did you hear that?"

Both her shoulders rose in a shrug. "Social media."

"Ah." Inhaling deeply through my nose, I worked through how to explain it to her. "Our community, which I now consider family, is unique in a lot of ways—our multi-partner relationship views being just one of them." I finished my water and pushed the glass away. "We prefer that relationship style for various reasons."

I eyed the empty glass, wishing it would magically fill back up. My throat felt like sandpaper from talking so damn much. Fuck, that was a lot of words at one time. I had always been reserved, the observer between me and Aiden. He held up the conversations, made women laugh, and was usually the one to explain our unique lifestyle. Not me. I was the silent protector who faded into the background, which I normally preferred. Where Aiden couldn't stand silence, I savored it and was more than okay with him being the center of the women's attention when we shared.

Unless it came to Aspen.

Suddenly, I liked her eyes on me and wanted her to ask me questions and tell me all about her wants and dreams. I didn't want to fade into the background with her. I wanted her to see me. Well, the parts of me I was comfortable with, not the ugly, scarred, trauma-suffering parts that needed to stay hidden to not scare her off.

"Sorry about that," Aiden announced as he fell into his chair with a grunt. Angrily swiping his half-full beer off the table, he tipped the bottle back and downed a long drink. "Oliver said for us to stop by tomorrow to officially file the restraining order paperwork. There's no way in hell she was here by chance."

"Do you think she followed you here?" Aspen questioned, peeling the label on her bottle.

"I wouldn't put it past her," Aiden grumbled, studying her working fingers.

She nodded and blew a raspberry. "Okay, so what exactly happened with her? What made her so... that?" She waved her hand in the direction where Jessica had stood.

Aiden and I exchanged a knowing look, and I nodded, giving him the go-ahead to tell her.

"She was a guest at The Nest, a frequent one. We saw her around town a few times, took her out on a couple of day ATV treks when she hired Uplift." Aiden ran a hand through his long hair, tugging at the ends. "One thing led to another. The attraction was there, and she understood our unique... needs."

"Needs as in how you and Miles share women," Aspen added with a smirk.

Aiden spit out the sip of beer he'd just taken, shocked at her comment and no doubt at the teasing quality of her tone. He wiped the mess from his lips and gaped at her.

"I had my suspicions after a few things you said, and Miles confirmed them just now when I asked him about it." She shrugged like her accepting this part of us wasn't a big deal. I eyed her suspiciously. No one accepted our relationship style that easily. "Listen, you're both big boys—"

"Oh, Aspen, you have no idea how right you are." Aiden shot her a cocky smirk.

She attempted to hide her smile as she rolled her eyes. "If your partner is into it, then you do you. Though I do have questions." She glanced at Aiden before giving my upper body a deliberate once-over. "A *lot* of questions," she mumbled around a yawn.

I checked my watch, noting the time. "It's getting late,

and I'm sure you're exhausted from traveling. I heard you had to put up with Langston during the trip. Let's order the nachos—"

"Fuck yes," Aiden said, punching his fist in the air. "Love their nachos."

Aspen smirked and shook her head at his antics. "Well, now we *have* to get them with that kind of response."

"I'll go to the bar and order." Palms to the edge of the table, I shoved my chair back and stood. Her eyes traveled down my body in a slow, sensual sweep. Desire slammed into my gut, making me suck in a tight breath. "We need to get you home before it gets too late." Her dark eyes widened, making me realize my wording. "Home as in you to your cottage at The Nest and us to our place."

For tonight, at least.

Forcing myself to walk away from her, I headed toward the bar to place our food order and use the time to get this surge of need under fucking control.

This woman was dangerous in all the ways that mattered, and that scared me.

I thought being a SEAL prepared me for anything and everything.

And I was.

Until Aspen walked through that bar door and I knew...

I was in so much fucking trouble.

7

ASPEN

Metal groaned as I tugged the heavy door; the force of it slamming closed shook the late-model F-150. Though the movement could also be from the massive dog sitting on the bench seat beside me as she panted, tongue hanging out with strings of drool dripping from her loose jowls. As if sensing my attention, that massive head swung my way to steal a sneaky lick up my cheek.

"Jubie," Miles admonished with zero heat in his gruff tone. I shivered, just like I'd done all night when he talked. His voice held a gravelly sound that made my thoughts go straight into the gutter. "You need consent from people before you put your tongue all over them."

Holy hell, did he really just say that? A tight breath caught in my throat, a fresh wave of heat now flowing through my veins. I pitched forward to see around Jubie to where Miles sat behind the steering wheel.

Earlier, when I first met Aiden, I thought he was the most attractive man I'd encountered in person. With his longish floppy hair, easygoing personality, and body of a Greek god, anyone with eyes would be going weak in the knees around him. Then entered the giant of a man, Miles. Holy Hades. The moment I laid eyes on him, I wanted to climb onto his lap, wrap both arms around his neck, and beg him to hold me. There was a presence about him that made me feel utterly safe.

Not only because of his massive size, but there was a steely look in his eyes. The way he constantly scanned the room silently spoke to how alert he was. Every time his thick arms flexed as he lifted his drink, stretching the cotton of his long-sleeved shirt, I wanted to lean over and take a bite.

What the hell was that about? Had traveling to Alaska turned me into some kind of cannibal where I wanted to nibble and taste these two delicious-looking men? Because until now, I never, *ever* had a biting fetish, an urge to get my lips and teeth anywhere on their bodies they'd allow.

Which, apparently, they were more than open to. Maybe not the biting thing, but for sure the not choosing between them part. There were so many questions I needed answers to, though maybe not tonight. Just being around the two of them for so long, I was already hotter and hornier than I'd ever been in my life.

I wondered if they shared women as in both *dated* the same woman or shared them together in *all* the ways. My stomach did a few flips, imagining Miles and Aiden together with their sole attention on me.

Suddenly, my thick coat shifted from warm and cozy to restricting and way stifling. Popping open the few buttons I closed on our way out of the bar to fight the frosty night air, I fanned open the sides to give my overheated body a bit of reprieve. Thankfully, the truck wasn't on, and the cab was still chilly, instantly cooling my rising body temperature.

"You okay?" Miles asked, eyeing me curiously as he cranked the engine.

"Yep, just..." *Got hot thinking about you and your best friend, together, with me.* "Thought it would be colder at night, so I wore my thick coat." I licked my lips. "You sure you don't mind driving me back?"

He nodded and leaned a forearm along the top of the steering wheel, searching, gaze locked on me. "You sure you're okay with me driving you back, just the two of us?"

I blew out a breath and smiled. "Strangely enough, I really am. Normally, I'm suspicious around new people, which is probably why I don't—" I cut myself off and shook my head. It was not a good idea to spill my guts about how I had no friends and was lonely as hell back in Seattle. "I feel safe with you and Aiden. Honestly, it's nice not being here alone." My eyes rolled to the ceiling at myself. "I know I came alone, but—ugh, I'm not making any sense, am I?"

"You are to me." With that, he shifted the truck into Reverse and backed out of the parking spot along the road a few shops down from Dave's. "And I think being cautious around new people is a good thing. Keeps you out of dangerous situations, especially in a big city like Seattle. What were you going to say when you cut yourself off? Which is probably why you don't..." He trailed off and shot me an expectant look.

Yanking out the hair tie, I ran my fingers through my hair, easing the ache that always formed along my scalp after having it up too long.

"It's kind of embarrassing," I muttered. When he said nothing, I slumped back against the seat. "Even after five years in that city, I didn't really have any close friends. Sure, there were people at the magazine I'd say hello to or have drinks with sometimes, but nothing deep. I keep people out because it's easier that way. Then they can't hurt me. Don't take that the wrong way," I blurted out. "Nothing terrible has happened to me or wounded me deeply. I am the way I am. It's just me, I think." My smile slipped. "Maybe that's why I wasn't really upset with the whole James thing. I never really let him in, so when it officially ended, I was okay. More frustrated at myself after realizing he'd basically entangled me with him so I'd do his bidding—"

"Fucking asshole," Miles grumbled. Jubie sensed his frustration and shifted to lean her whole large body against him.

"I allowed it to happen," I whispered, ashamed that I had let it go on as long as it did.

All because I was so fucking lonely that I settled for the messed-up, toxic shit that brewed between us. I wasn't in love with him—never was. Even the infatuation faded quickly after we started working together more. I was more embarrassed than hurt that I'd let him play puppeteer with my life and career for as long as I did.

I was pathetic.

It was dumb to even imagine me with Miles and Aiden. Even though they shared women, it didn't mean they wanted to share me. Why would they?

"But," Miles said, stopping my self-loathing thoughts, "he was the one doing the manipulating. The fucker knew what he was doing. He's at fault, not you." When I didn't answer, he slowed the truck to a stop and reached across Jubie, laying a massive hand on my knee. "Do you hear me, Aspen?"

"I hear you, but believe you?" I shrugged. "That will take time." Clearing my throat, I forced a smirk, hoping to lighten the conversation. That was enough talk about me and my sad, insignificant life. "So, you and Aiden."

Miles's hand slipped away, and I instantly missed the

comforting weight. My fingers itched to snatch it back and place it on my knee. Or higher.

I shook my head. It had been way too long since I'd had sex. My out-of-control libido made that as clear as a blinking neon sign.

"Been best friends since grade school, yes." He shot a knowing smirk my way. "That was what you were talking about, right?"

"Um, not so much. Have you two always... taken part..." I waved a hand in the air. "In sharing?" I winced in embarrassment and pressed myself against the door, wishing like hell it would just open up so I could tumble out onto the snow-covered roadside. "Sorry, forget I said anything."

"Why?" he asked, not looking away from the windshield.

"Because I'm being nosy," I muttered under my breath. I was very interested in learning more about their lifestyle, but talking about it made me flustered as hell. My heart fluttered like a hummingbird's wings, my palms damp with sweat, and every shift along the seat had the seam of my jeans brushing against my damp panties.

It's now clear I should've brought some battery-powered items on this trip, but during my mad dash to pack, I didn't know I would be wet and needy from the moment my boots hit the dock in Anchor Bay.

And unfortunately, I doubted this place had a sex toy shop around for an emergency purchase.

"No, we haven't always shared women." He rubbed at the back of his neck like he was uncomfortable. "After my time in the service, that's when we started. Though we'd always had the same taste in women—what we were attracted to. Once we moved here and started working for Uplift, we realized we could both get what we needed, and our partner, too, if we worked together. That sounds fucked up—"

"It doesn't," I blurted, cutting him off. "What do you mean, what 'we needed'? I would assume men would flip the other way and say they needed *more* women in the relationship rather than two guys sharing one. And how does it work? Are you saying you share her time fifty-fifty, or do you do *everything* together?" That heat from earlier flared back to life, scorching me from the inside out. Thank fuck it was dark inside the cab, or he would see the evidence of what this conversation did to me on my flushed cheeks.

When he didn't immediately respond to my slew of questions, anxiety spiked, making my stomach drop, worried I'd pushed him too far.

I fiddled with the ends of my hair, keeping my eyes lowered. "You don't have to answer any of that. Sorry, I didn't mean to offend you. Sometimes I let my curiosity run my mouth—"

"You didn't offend me, Aspen," he cut in. I snapped my lips shut to keep from rambling. "I just didn't know how to answer right away because I'd say it's a mix. With the way our jobs work, we're gone at different times, so when one is here and the other is off on an outing with a client, then it's more one-on-one time, but when we're both home, we do everything together."

"Everything?" I croaked, my throat suddenly tight and my mouth dry. Why did I keep repeating that word?

Headlights of a passing car illuminated the sultry look he shot my way. "As I said earlier at the bar, we share everything."

"Oh, wow, that's... nice." I cringed. "Sorry, this is not a conversation I ever expected to have, and I'm kind of in shock."

"Shock?" I nodded and licked my lips. "So, you're not interested?"

Blood pounded in my ears, and I couldn't breathe. "Do you want me to be interested?" I whispered, terrified to hear his answer.

Please say yes.

Please say you want me like I want you and Aiden both.

Please don't say what I know to be true, that you two are out of my league.

The truck slowly rolled to a stop at a red light. Shifting in his seat, he leveled that intense focus right on me. Damn, and I thought I couldn't breathe before. Now I really panted like I'd run a marathon.

"We wouldn't be having this conversation right now if we didn't."

I nodded, but my heart sank a little. "Actually, neither you nor Aiden brought it up. We wouldn't be having this conversation if that woman hadn't come up to the table and dropped the bomb about your relationship preferences. I don't need or want your pity interest. It's okay to talk about this without you having to pretend to be into me."

I swallowed down the lump forming in my throat. Damnit, I knew I shouldn't have gotten my hopes up. *Stupid, stupid Aspen.*

But instead of looking relieved that I gave him an out, a slow grin crept over his handsome face, completely changing his normally stern features to genuine happiness mixed with a dash of laughter. I sucked in a breath, fingers curling into fists to keep from reaching across Jubie and climbing onto his lap. This version of Miles was just as sexy as the alert protector side.

"She definitely did, but that doesn't mean we weren't thinking about it or weren't waiting for the right moment. Think about it from our perspective. You're a beautiful, funny, cool-as-hell woman. Why would you be interested instead of turned off and disgusted by our lifestyle? Of course we wanted to talk to you about it. Jessica just sped up the timing of the conversation." The light turned green. He arched a brow as he turned back to the road and pushed on the gas. "You seem calm and understanding about all this."

Leaning back against the seat, I closed both eyes and released a slow breath. "I know. That's strange, right?" The sound of the whirling tires, and the darkness in the cab made it feel like we were in our own little bubble, which gave me the courage to say exactly what was on my mind. "I won't deny that I'm attracted to both of you. A part of me is excited about the possibility of exploring your lifestyle, while the other, my more rational side, tells me I shouldn't trust you two. I think I'm just confused about life right now. Like I've lost my compass and have zero clue which direction I'm headed. That would explain why I'm not freaking out, maybe?"

Or I was turned on by the thought of both of them to the point that all concerns about allowing them to share me while I was here in Anchor Bay weren't there.

The truck rumbled along the road. Both Miles and I were quiet as we crested the hill and The Nest came into view. There was a lot to dissect and sort through after tonight's revelations. I needed to really evaluate how I felt about them and the idea of sharing them both. The last thing I wanted to do was make a rash decision, say yes, and then back out when it became too overwhelming and hurt them. Plus, just because they liked to share and were attracted to me didn't mean I had to be interested in them. Even though I was—and well beyond the physical attraction. I had fun earlier, more fun than I'd had in ages, and all we did was sit around drinking beers, talking.

Was this too big a decision after my drastic life change?

Or was this perfect timing?

Miles slowed the truck and cut the engine, parking in the spot directly in front of the path that led to my tucked-away cottage.

"I'll be perfectly clear about something." The bench seat shifted when he turned to face me and tossed an arm along the back, his fingertips playing in my hair. "If you're not interested in Aiden or me, we will still be here for you. After everything you talked about tonight, it's clear that you came here for a break from your life in Seattle, and we won't fuck that up for you. Our offering to take you on that hike still stands, no matter what you decide." He rubbed his free hand along the thick black beard covering his firm jaw. "Jessica's interference tonight was a blessing and a curse. I'm glad you know so you don't feel pressured to decide, but I also wished you could've gotten to know us a little more before learning that we both find you sexy and would like to see where this goes between the three of us while you're here."

"I think you're confusing me with someone else," I whispered. "I'm not sexy. Did you hear my story about going an entire week without a shower or proper bathroom?"

He scoffed a laugh and tugged on a lock of my hair. "I heard every word you said tonight." Oh, wow, that was unexpected and made me want to cry all the happy tears. "It solidified what I thought about you."

"I'm scared to ask," I rasped.

"You're resilient, bright, fucking talented as hell, resourceful, and you find joy in the outdoors and all it offers, just like us. We're not your average men, Aspen. You loving the outdoors the way they are meant to be experienced makes you more captivating to us than not."

The tears I held back with his first comment once again

welled in my lower lids and burned my throat. Unable to speak without sobbing, I just nodded and reached for the door handle, pausing with my hand wrapped around the cold metal. "Thank you. That's the most insightful thing anyone has ever said to me."

As I shoved open my door, Miles did the same.

"Stay here, girl," he said, his attention over my shoulder as I climbed out. At nearly ten at night, it was finally getting dark. A bark rattled from the cab, making me laugh. "I'll walk you to your door, if that's okay with you."

"I'd like that, a lot. Thank you."

He pressed his wide palm to my lower back as he guided me along the narrow path. Out of the truck, breathing in the crisp, clean air, I wrangled my crazy emotions. Though with him right at my side, every inhale trapped his cedar and spice scent in my lungs, making me desperate to slide even closer.

"Tonight was a lot of fun." He hummed a noncommittal response. "Exactly what I didn't know I needed. I didn't realize how... lonely and empty my life was in Seattle. Who knew coming to a remote Alaskan town would show me just how much I didn't like my life, even though while I was in it, I thought I did?"

"Alaska is a great place to gain perspective." At my door, I dug out the key from my coat pocket and went to slip it into the lock, but Miles's hand wrapped around my own, gently pulling the key from my grasp. "Let me. Would you be okay if I stepped inside first and secured the room?" With the fading sunlight, I caught his wince. "Not that I expect anything bad, I just... I want to make sure you're safe, and if I don't inspect your place before I leave, I'll worry all night."

Aww. My lips curled into a sappy grin, and I nodded, releasing the key.

After opening the door, Miles flicked the porch light on so I wouldn't be standing in the growing darkness while he stepped inside the cottage. I held a breath, turning on the heels of my boots to press my back against the exterior wall, not liking having my back exposed without Miles at my side. Which was dumb. This place was safer than Seattle, yet I couldn't shake the feeling that something dangerous lurked among the trees, waiting for the right moment to strike.

And considering this was Alaska, it was probably true. A wolverine, bear, moose—hell, anything could be out there.

"All clear." I jumped with a high-pitched squeak, not hearing Miles approach until he was right beside me. "Sorry."

"You move like a ninja for someone your size." I pressed a hand over my racing heart.

"Trained by the best to be the best." His wide shoulders rose and fell in a casual shrug. Not for the first time tonight, I caught the tightness around his eyes, as if moving his upper body in certain ways caused him pain. Running a hand through his short dark hair, he scanned the trees. "Aiden and I have a motorbike trail tour tomorrow, but we should be back after lunch. How about you stop by around two for us to gather what all we'll need for that hike we promised?"

I nodded without even realizing it, too lost in the way his voice caressed my skin and too mesmerized by his lips as he spoke.

"I'll text you the address and directions to our community's homestead from here. It's just on the other side of town, so not far. Tomorrow should be nice enough weather for you to borrow one of the resort's bikes, or you could always ask them to drive you."

"Yeah, sounds good," I said with a wide yawn. That

meant I would need to actually turn on my phone to retrieve the directions, which I was not looking forward to. Surely by now, James realized I was gone, and Barbara no doubt had some words to say about my abrupt departure. "Thank you again for tonight." I leaned against the doorframe, exhaustion from the last couple of days slamming into me. "I really needed it." Lip between my teeth, I debated saying what had been on my mind all night. "Like I said in the truck, I am attracted to you and Aiden."

His dark brows rose along his forehead. "I sense a 'but' coming."

My hair shifted with a slight nod. "But you and him, what you're suggesting while I'm here, was unexpected and threw me for a loop. I'm tired and unsure of pretty much everything right now, considering I just quit my job without another one lined up, ended a toxic relationship, and flew here with no real plan besides having a place to stay. All that is making me feel... overwhelmed. Yeah, overwhelmed is a good word for the mess that's going on in here." I tapped my temple with my index finger.

Instead of responding, he stepped close, wrapped his long, muscular arms around my shoulders, and held me tight against his chest. Stunned, I stood stiff, completely frozen, only blinking at the lone picture that hung on the wall above the sofa. The bear hug was completely unexpected, though when he didn't drop his hold or say anything, the tension slowly melted from my taut muscles, and I relaxed in the safety of his hold. I even wrapped my arms around his waist, relishing his radiating body heat, yummy smell, and overwhelming sense of comfort and support.

To my surprise, his hands never wandered. When was the last time I hugged a man, other than my dad, who didn't initiate more than that simple act? Not a single word was spoken between us, the embrace saying it all.

I was safe.

I wasn't alone.

He had my back, no matter what.

In his arms, I felt protected against the world. All my worries and fears couldn't reach me here. Which was dumb. My life was still a complicated shit show, yet for this brief moment, it felt worlds away.

"Like I said earlier, you owe us nothing. If all you need from us this next week are hiking guides and friendship, then that's what you'll get. Don't let your past overwhelm your future. You don't have to figure it all out now."

"I'm twenty-eight years old," I whispered, eyes squeezing shut. "I should have a career, a husband and family—hell, a healthy 401K." But as I said those words, I knew they weren't my own. "Or at least that's what I'm told by my mother."

"But is that what you want?" His chest vibrated with the soft words, making me melt even more against him.

"I don't know what I want anymore."

Pulling back, he held me at arm's length. "Strip away everyone else's expectations, what society tells you a 'good life' comprises, and focus on what makes you happy." After softly squeezing my shoulders, his hands fell away and casually slipped into the front pockets of his jeans. "Good night, Aspen." He backed up a step, his dark gaze never leaving mine. "If you need anything, call or text me. I'll shoot you that address when I get home tonight."

When he turned to leave, I slowly closed the door, still watching his back as he disappeared into the trees. Once the door clicked closed and the locks were secured, I slumped back against the thick wood and slid down until my ass hit the floor.

Forearms on my bent knees, I scanned the small cottage, suddenly feeling more alone than ever. My heart sank, and a heaviness pressed on my chest, tears threatening to spill over. Wiping at my burning eyes, I did a double take at something resting on the small counter in the simple kitchen.

A groan escaped as I pushed off the floor, barely having enough energy to stumble toward the single piece of paper that caught my attention. I read the lines once, twice, a smile creeping up my cheeks until the muscles ached.

Don't forget to lock up after I'm gone.

Sweet dreams, Aspen.

Until tomorrow.

Just like that, his thoughtfulness, those simple lines from a practical stranger...

And I suddenly didn't feel so alone.

8

———————

AIDEN

The steady vibrations radiating from the seat faded when I killed the Honda's engine. Lifting the sweltering helmet off, I raked several fingers through my sweat-damp hair to push it out of my eyes, only for it to flop back in place immediately despite the effort. The rumble of another bike had me hooking the helmet on the handlebars and twisting to check over my shoulder, spotting Miles tearing along the path, speeding my way.

Normally, this would be a solo tour, since the bikers with us—currently off exploring the trails on their own—were experienced riders, and only two were in the group, but with the dangers lurking around Anchor Bay, Miles tagged along like Hudson advised. Leaning forward, I stared off into the distance, the beautiful scenery and snowcapped mountains still just as breathtaking as they were when we first arrived in Alaska five years ago.

Miles skidded to a stop beside me, dirt and rocks shooting out from beneath the tires before he killed his bike. I watched as he removed his helmet just like I did, wiping off the sweat dripping into his beard, and as I expected, that damn smirk was still on his face like it had been all morning.

"Fuck, you've got it bad," I joked, knowing I wasn't any different. Just those few hours yesterday with Aspen and I was borderline obsessed with the woman. Not in a creepy, make-a-skin-suit-out-of-her type of way, but more of a want-to-be-around-her-and-monopolize-all-her-time type of way. I eyed him as he checked his phone. "Did she write back after you sent the address?"

Without verbally responding, he tossed his phone my way before reaching for his water. I caught it mid-air and immediately flipped it around. With the screen already unlocked and on the text thread, I scrolled up to find the time stamp from earlier in the morning.

Me: Good morning. See you this afternoon.

Me: Let me know if you have any trouble with the address I sent.

Aspen: FML. I forgot how early the sun rises here in the summer.

Me: Sorry?

Aspen: Think any of the shops in town sell an eye mask or something? Another night of little sleep and no one will want to be near me. #grumpy

Me: I can ask one of the women at work if they can spare one. I'm sure they won't mind.

Aspen: And I need coffee. Lots of coffee. Where should I go?

Me: The main building at the resort has breakfast and coffee. Or there's a shop in town that roasts its own beans, Sips. At least that's what Aiden says. It's near Dave's.

Aspen: Ohhh. Fellow coffee snob. Nice. I'll stop by there on my way out.

Me: Out? Out where?

Aspen: Outdoors? I want to get some shots before meeting you and Aiden later.

Me: That's not safe.

Aspen: I'll pack my bear spray, Dad.

I chuckled at her response. Of course the bastard was already obsessing over her safety. Though with all the shit going on, I was glad he was thinking about it, since she wasn't aware of the situation. I frowned at the phone as I continued to read Miles's texts detailing all the safety provisions for going out alone, the gear and weapons he wanted her to pack, and the tracking device she thought he suggested as a joke.

It wasn't.

"We need to tell her," I said as I tossed the phone back to him. "I know we have nothing concrete yet, but I don't like the idea of her going out alone unaware. She thinks all she has to worry about is the wildlife. If she knows what we suspect, then she'll be on guard and be suspicious of strangers who approach her when we're not around."

Miles nodded. "Agreed." Holding up his phone, he frowned at the screen. "Caroline hasn't written me back. She knows I worry about her when she goes out alone."

I huffed and shook my head, recalling all the arguments between those two about her feeling untouchable. Though she wasn't technically a native to Alaska, having moved here with her family when she was a baby, she sure as hell knew the land like one. She took risks when they weren't needed, always going out on her own, which drove Miles's protective instincts crazy. He saw her as a sister to protect after her dad passed two years ago, and he took that role to the extreme.

"When we get back, we'll talk to Hudson." Until Brandon came back from Montana, Hudson was our point of contact for anything related to the case and Uplift. You'd think we would push back, considering a new guy was placed as the company's temporary leader, but the guy was rock-solid, trustworthy, and knew what he was doing on the investigation front. "We could be overreacting. It hasn't been that long since she left, and she's just as capable of being out there on her own as we are. Though it is unlike her. Maybe she just isn't reaching out because it's a dangerous area and knew you would disapprove of where she went."

But even as I said the words, I knew that wasn't the case.

Caroline loved and respected both of us. Even though we weren't huge fans of her going out alone, she would've at least shot a text or dropped a pin. Especially to Miles.

The growing roar of two bikes cut off our conversation as the riders came into view. They slowed to a stop beside Miles, shut off their engines, and pulled off their helmets. Forcing a smile, I hitched my chin in greeting.

"You two having fun?" I asked, pushing excitement into my tone. Usually, I loved these excursions, but today, all I wanted was to be back home, waiting for Aspen.

The one with her long blonde hair braided down her back wiped the sweat off her lips and downed half the water in her bottle. "Hell yes. Damn, I forgot how much fun it is to ride like this. The arenas and crowds are great, but this"—she gestured to the tall trees surrounding us—"is what made me fall in love with riding."

"I'm starving," the brunette one complained. "Did today include lunch or—" She looked between me and Miles, wiggling her brows. "—just eye candy?"

"For fuck's sake," the blonde grumbled. "Don't mind her. She's a shameless flirt."

"Tell me I'm wrong. They're hot as fuck and wouldn't be a repeat who would get all clingy like they always do."

I huffed. "Those are some high standards you have there."

The woman shrugged with a smirk on her lips. "You don't need a good guy to get good dick."

"And on that note," the blonde one cut in. "You mentioned there was a risky spot around here. Now that you know we can ride..." She trailed off, hope in her tone.

With a nod, thankful for the interruption from the other awkward and somewhat hilarious conversation, I tugged my helmet on. "If you're up for it." They each gave an excited shout. "Then, follow me."

All four of our bikes started in unison. With a wicked smile pulling at my lips, I pressed the gas and took off down the trail, knowing our two clients for the day and Miles would follow. Even as the trees flew past me, the thrill of speeding down the uneven and dangerous path thrumming through my veins, my thoughts slipped to Aspen.

Imagining all the fun and deliciously dirty possibilities if she said yes to us.

Boot against the edge of the porch, I knocked it twice, dirt and rocks falling off with each thump, before repeating with the other. Beside me, Miles did the same, gaze scanning the narrow road that cut between the cottages. Leaning against a sturdy wooden post, I took in the small homestead-type town Brandon and his partners built for those of us who work for Uplift. Cabins of various sizes lined either side of the road that cut through the center of our village and led toward Anchor Bay.

At the opposite end from where our cabin was situated was the general store that Brandon's wife and their other partner ran together. While Brandon focused on the Uplift business, Amy and Carl kept our community and all aspects of the nearly self-sufficient homestead running smoothly. In their store, they offered premade meals, grocery items, and personal products as needed. The food they sold was cooked with meat they hunted or caught and produce grown in the small greenhouses that dotted along the outer edge of our community.

Somewhere in the distance, a few dogs barked playfully, causing one of the farm animals Baylee raised to bellow their annoyance at the noise. Inhaling deeply, I held the crisp air in my lungs, savoring the scents of home. Our community wasn't much, but what we lacked in material things, we made up for in love and support for one another. Most of us were veterans with many scars, inside and out.

Thinking of that had me turning my focus to Miles, who walked beside me on our way to Hudson and Calista's cabin. The easy, relaxed smile slipped from my lips. He paused in front of their porch to brush off the fur clinging to his pants and arched a brow, questioning my sudden mood shift. He scanned my face, features falling as he stood tall and crossed both arms over his chest.

"Stop whatever you're thinking about."

The struggle was real, to force my lips upward into a somewhat convincing smile, which, of course, he saw right through to the guilt and regrets I wrestled with internally. "Just thinking about Brandon and Uplift, what he's done for so many of us. What do you think we'd be doing, or where would we be if we hadn't heard about Uplift and dropped everything to be a part of this place?"

Miles scratched at his beard and turned to scan the cabins like I just had, taking it all in. "We'd be unhappy and know we were missing something but wouldn't know what."

"Wow," I mouthed.

"Well, I would. You'd be happy somewhere with a wife and two-point-five kids with a white picket fence and a dog that doesn't shed or drool on everything."

My stomach dropped despite his joking tone. He knew that was what I had wanted. What I thought would make me happy and whole until I had it with the wrong person and everything went to shit.

Including Miles's life and future.

"Fuck that shit about a Doodle," I huffed as we stomped up the steps. "You know I love Jubie." I shook my head as I ran my fingers through my freshly showered locks. "And you know how that whole 'dream life' turned out for me when I gave it a go." I raised a fist to bang on the door, freezing before my skin could make contact, suddenly remembering they had a young daughter who could be sleeping. I adjusted to rapping a single knuckle on the wood instead. "The whole wife-and-potential-family dream failed miserably," I muttered, trying my damnedest to forget about those years of my life I'd never get back. Those years when I should've been with my best friend, protecting him, but instead, I had walked away and gained years of misery.

Muffled voices behind the closed door followed by the snap of the lock disengaging had me forcing an easygoing smile, hoping that would cover the turmoil of emotions still warring inside me. The second the door swung open wide, revealing Calista and Sam, Hudson and Calista's adorable-as-hell daughter, who bulldozed her way past her mom, my strained smile morphed into a genuine one, and the lingering feelings from our conversation disappeared.

Stooping low, I scooped Sam up before she collided with my shins and suspended her high above my head. Her innocent and happy giggles filled the porch further, clearing all thoughts of my failures and regrets.

"Samantha," Calista chastised from where she leaned against the doorframe with zero sternness in her tone. "Remember, you need to wait for Mommy before you run out the door." She blew a raspberry, reminding me of Aspen doing the same a few times last night, and smiled at her daughter, who was now tucked safely against my chest. "Hey, Miles. Hey, Aiden. What's going on?"

Turning my full attention back to Sam, I tossed her in the air again, desperate for more of her sweet smiles and laughter, too engrossed in the joy radiating off the tiny human to respond, knowing Miles could handle the adult conversation.

He shifted on his feet, the boards under his boots groaning with the move. "We're looking for Hudson. Is he around? We haven't seen him since yesterday's meeting."

Out of the corner of my eye, I caught Calista shaking her head. "No. He and Oliver left this morning to look into a lead regarding the case. Is there something I can help you with?"

Miles's dark hair glinted in the light with his slow headshake. "No, it's about the case and Caroline. We haven't heard from her."

"Oh." Calista stood straight, worry now lining her face. "I can try to reach Hudson, though he might be out of cell range. You two are welcome to hang around for a bit if he doesn't pick up." She turned her face to me, and a wide grin spread across her lips. "I'm sure Sam would love some time with her big friend."

At that, Sam reached out, her tiny, slightly sticky palms sealing to either cheek. "Big friend. Play."

"Wish we could, little bit," I said, squishing my lips and mimicking a fish, which had her eyes lighting up and pushing my cheeks in even more. "But we have someone coming here in just a few who we need to meet up with. No playing today." Her hands fell away, and she tucked them under her armpits in a cute pouting stance. "Though maybe we could come by later with Jubie?"

Sam's eyes widened, and her thick blonde hair bounced with an enthusiastic nod. "Yes, big friend and Jubie." She looked over to Miles, who gave her a two-finger wave. "Big friends and Jubie."

"Seems like she's warming up to you," Calista said to Miles, who looked shocked by Sam's words. "I knew she would. It just took some time, considering you're fifteen times her size."

"I'm not that big," he grumbled, shoulders rounding as he squatted low, putting him at almost eye level with Sam, where I had set her down on the porch. "I can come too?"

She nodded and whirled around. "Big friends. Tea and cookies. Jubie and my dog Bacon." Her voice trailed off as she hurried deep into their cabin, no doubt to prepare the make-believe tea and cookies for the playdate.

"We'll come back later. Hopefully, we can talk with

Hudson before teatime," I said, running a hand through my hair. "Would it be okay if our friend came too?"

Miles whirled around to face me and mouthed a "What the fuck?"

"Is this friend like the last one, who you two still can't shake?" Calista asked, biting her lower lip to conceal her growing smile.

I scoffed and waved her off. "No, absolutely not. Aspen is different. She's... special," I said with a confirming nod, more to myself than Calista.

"We just met her," Miles griped while running a hand over his short dark hair in exasperation. I knew what that move meant, considering he did it a lot around me. What could I say? Sometimes I was a lot to handle.

"And you, my all-work-and-no-play friend, haven't stopped smiling since you met her last night. Oh, and what about those texts this morning that you practically giggled over, hmm? When have you ever reread a text string over and over and—"

"You're basing the seriousness of this 'friendship'"—she air-quoted the word for emphasis—"on him smiling and a text?"

I hooked a thumb in Miles's direction with a nod. "Have you met the guy? Any type of communication with someone other than me is a signal that all systems are a go."

"What, now I'm a damn rocket launch?" Miles snapped. "We met her yesterday—"

"And fell in love immediately—"

"Sure, she's cool as hell—"

"Plus, hot as hell," I added, which awarded me a side-eye and smirk from Calista.

"But also leaving in a week," he ground out around his clenched jaw.

The dude was tense as fuck. He needed this to work out with Aspen more than me.

"A lot can happen in a week," Calista said behind her fingers, which attempted to hide her wide, knowing smile. "Well, if she's still around later, bring her too. Though I'm not sure how Sam will react to sharing your attention."

"Very true." I chuckled. "Speaking of Aspen, we need to run. She should be here soon."

Miles and I thanked her for her time and promised to return later before turning on our heels and clomping down the few steps to the short walkway that led to the road.

"What the fuck was that all about?" Miles groused beside me. "What were you thinking, inviting Aspen over to their place?"

"I was thinking of shoving you in the direction you're already headed," I stated over my shoulder. "I'm not saying we kidnap Aspen and keep her—"

"That wasn't a consideration, but now I'm concerned that you thought it might be on the list of possibilities. You know kidnapping is a crime, right?"

My lips curled into a smirk, and I shook my head in exasperation. "All I'm saying is to be open to the possibility that this could lead to more than a few fun nights." Pausing, I turned to face my friend, whose brows were pulled in tight as he stared off into the distance. "She's different. You're different with her. That's enough for me to want to push this further than what we've had before."

"She won't want that," Miles said with a hard shake of his head. "Not with me, anyway. I have too many issues for a woman like her to want to be with long-term."

My shoulders slouched and rounded forward, defeat sinking in. "Just give her a chance, please." I'd fall on my knees where we stood in the middle of the damn road if it meant he'd actually open himself up to the idea of a real future with someone. The fucker was so closed off, I worried about him feeling he had to shoulder the weight of his past and residual pain all on his own. If anything, I wanted Aspen and us to work out because she was strong, resilient, and maybe, just fucking maybe, could be the one to help me save my friend from himself.

Miles's lips pressed into a tight line as he rubbed at his jaw. "I won't stop you if she's who you want to pursue something more… permanent with. I'll be okay."

"And what if she wants us both?" I questioned. "For more than a few orgasms and checking a ménage off her bucket list."

"You think it's on her bucket list?" he asked, a slow smile peeking through, making his beard and cheeks bunch. "Or anyone's, for that matter?"

"A wild ménage night is for sure on everyone who needs air to breathe bucket list."

He nodded and wrapped a hand around the back of his neck, massaging away the tension as he stretched side to side. He parted his lips, ready to respond to our strange turn of conversation, but snapped them closed. Taking two steps, he moved to the edge of the road and scanned the area, clearly having heard something out of the ordinary. Before I could ask what was up, a bike with a familiar dark-headed beauty riding it rounded the corner from the road that led to Anchor Bay. Neither of us moved as she slowed to a stop, stepped off the bike, and took in the row of cabins with a look of wonder on her face.

Miles's shoulders dropped, and his normally stiff posture softened. The woman he was denying he wanted for more than a good time was yards away, yet she still had an instant calming effect on him in all the ways that mattered.

"Just keep an open mind," I mumbled, starting in the direction from where Aspen hadn't moved.

With his confirming nod, we strolled down the road, acting like we weren't speed-walking just to get to her as quickly as possible. My heart raced in my chest with excitement and anticipation of finding out her thoughts on her and Miles's conversation the night before about us sharing her.

I had a feeling Aspen would be the one to shake us out of our rut, that she was everything we never knew we needed to not only survive but live. Though it didn't matter what I thought and felt—those two had to jump on board too. And I only had six days to convince her and Miles that this, us, could be the happily ever after we'd all been looking for.

9

MILES

During the short walk to where Aspen stood in the middle of the street, smiling as if in awe of our small community setup, I studied every detail, unable to look away from the woman. Her long dark hair was pulled back in a high ponytail that swished as she spun in a slow circle, taking in every inch of her surroundings. Scanning her face, I couldn't help the burst of worry that had me pressing my lips into a tight line at the visible purple circles under both of her large eyes. Her fair, smooth skin made the dark smudges even more prominent.

Even exhausted from the lack of sleep, she was breathtakingly gorgeous. Her beauty was natural, effortless, and even though she was overwhelmed the night before, she looked at peace, or at least comfortable with herself. Confidence radiated off her.

That alone was captivating to me. I never put emphasis or focus on how someone made themselves appear to the world, but instead, I concentrated on the core of who they really were. It was crazy how the world could claim certain women were beautiful and flawless despite the constant malice that came through in social media or the news.

As we approached, Aspen's lids slowly fluttered closed, her chest rising with a deep inhale that turned into a wide yawn, which she tried to cover with a loose fist. The urge to fix the problem for her, to protect her from the exhaustion clearly weighing on her, made my fingers twitch at my side, eager to do something immediately. Though not even I could control or change the tilt of Earth this time of year.

An idea wormed into my thoughts, refusing to let go of a way to take care of two of the problems that I needed to solve. Almost to where she waited for us, smiling and waving at having noticed our approach, I cleared my throat to get Aiden's attention.

"I bet Caroline has an eye mask in her cabin that she wouldn't mind loaning to Aspen. You know none of the stores in town will have one."

Aiden's brows furrowed, a deep line forming between them before shooting up his head, no doubt reading between the lines on why I suggested Caroline and not the other women in our community. "Oh, yeah. Right, right. No stores will carry what she needs. You're right about that. We should totally go break into her cabin—I mean pop by her place to see if she has one. If the cabin is locked, you can always accidentally run that battering ram you call a shoulder into the door."

A huffed laugh escaped. "Or I could use the key we both know she keeps stashed beneath that ugly-ass stone frog she painted while drunk on cheap wine after book club that one night."

"Or that. But then you wouldn't be able to impress the pretty lady." He gestured toward Aspen, who started to close the distance, walking beside the borrowed bicycle from The Nest.

Barking a laugh that had the corners of Aspen's lips curl upward, I shoved my friend, making him stumble to the side.

"This is really where you call home?" she asked, gesturing around us with one hand.

Starting at her broken-in hiking boots, I trailed my gaze up her cuffed, loose, water-resistant pants to her tight white tank top worn under a thick cotton red-and-black-plaid long-sleeved shirt that she'd left unbuttoned. Fingers wrapped around the edges of the cuffs, she shot us a hesitant smile.

"We do. Amazing, right?" She nodded, her ponytail swinging with the quick movement. "You found us okay?" Aiden asked, shoving both hands into the front pockets of his jeans and rocking back on his heels. His smile was so damn wide I could see every one of his straight teeth.

She looked at me. "The directions were very... detailed. Thank you. I even appreciated the suggestions on what to wear for today's weather."

Aiden laughed at that while I just dipped my chin in acknowledgment. At least she appreciated it and didn't find it too overbearing, considering I hadn't even known her for twenty-four hours but had given her outfit suggestions.

"It was a beautiful ride here." Leaning the bike against her hip, she dug into her satchel, pulling out her massive, expensive-looking camera. Pressing a button, she waited a second before turning the screen our way. "I stopped a few times to grab some amazing shots of the peaks in the distance. The lighting was perfection."

After flicking through several of the thumbnail-size

photos, Aspen lowered the camera and once again turned her attention to our little town.

"There are a lot of houses." She gestured to the rows of cabins set just off the road for a short walkway and mini lawn. "Does everyone who works for Uplift live here?"

"Yes and no. We all live here, but there are a few vacant cabins. Most are one-bedroom, but there are a few two- and three-bedrooms. Brandon built twenty, hoping the company would grow and need more help. It makes things easier if we're all in one place with the machines and gear. Plus, we're all transplants, so it gives us a sense of family, a community." With zero hesitation, Aiden tossed his arm over Aspen's shoulders, turning them and pointing to the building set at the end of the road. "That's our general store. Brandon's partners run that while he manages the company itself. We're almost fully self-sustaining regarding food." She nodded along, following where he pointed, fully engrossed in his explanation. "We like to use our solar-powered generators as much as possible, though that only works during the summer, since our nights are super long in the winter. We switch to the propane-powered one in the winter if needed, though that's only if the lines from town are down. Plus, we have greenhouses for produce and livestock for milk and meat."

"Wow," she breathed. "This is way beyond what I expected."

"What did you expect?" I asked, my voice a low rumble, which drew Aspen's attention over her shoulder to where I stood.

"I think one of you mentioned small cabins, or maybe I just inferred that based on something else you said." She gestured to the cabin to our right, which was Baylee's before she moved in with Liam. "That right there is bigger than my apartment back in Seattle, not that it was anything to brag about. And you both failed to mention that they aren't rustic or tossed-together log homes. These cottages are right out of a *Better Homes and Gardens* magazine and are fucking precious. Add in how this whole place is laid out, giving some privacy, and it's like a perfect small town designed for a TV show."

Turning all the way around, she smacked a hand to my pec with an eye roll. "You really should've prepared me better for all this adorableness."

I didn't process her words, too wrapped up in staring at the place she touched. Most strangers—hell, most *people*—were too scared of my size and stern demeanor to get close to me, let alone hit me. My heart swelled with hope. Aspen wasn't scared of me, which emphasized what she mentioned last night. She felt safe with me, and the way she molded against me when I yanked her into the random hug said those weren't just empty words. She truly felt safe with me.

"It is pretty amazing," Aiden said after a few seconds of studying her, then me with a wide smile. I flipped him the bird at his fucking meddling. "You should see the inside of the cabins. They're set up so each person has their own space, no matter how many rooms. Each has a large living area, a wood-burning fireplace, and basic kitchen. Most of us normally hang out on the porches when we're not working so we can visit with everyone."

"Adorable. So adorable." Just as she started to say something else, a flash of red and brown scurried across the street. It paused and poked its little head up to check us out before darting off up the steps of Baylee's cabin. "What. Was. That?" Her high, excited pitch had me wincing and fighting the urge to rub at my ears.

"BamBam." Aspen turned her big brown eyes my way,

confusion swirling in their depths. "That was BamBam." I pointed in the direction the lithe animal ran. "She's an ermine."

Aspen's jaw dropped, opening her mouth wide. Snapping it shut, she mouthed the word over and over.

"I think you broke her," Aiden whispered loudly behind his hand while poking a single finger against Aspen's cheek.

Snapping out of it, she batted away his touch with both hands. "Forgive me if I'm in a bit of shock. I'm fairly certain somewhere along the bike ride, I fell off, sustained a concussion, and am now seeing things. Or I'm in a coma, dreaming that I'm in a damn Disney movie, because what the hell? Who has cute cottages in a remote village with tiny woodland creatures running amok?"

Aiden and I exchanged a worried and confused look. Fuck, maybe I did break her. Who knew explaining a slightly domesticated color-changing weasel would be the thing to push her over the edge into insanity? For most people, it would've been when we explained we lived with a whole community that enjoyed the poly lifestyle. For Aspen, it seemed the "adorableness factor" here was the breaking point.

She spun in a circle, gaze bouncing. "So, how do I do this? Should I sing to draw in the birds to land on my outstretched arms while I prance down the street with the little woodland creatures following me, ready to do my bidding?"

"If that's what you want to do..." Aiden trailed off, uncertain if that was the right response. "I'm not aware of a bird that will come to you on command without being trained, but you do you."

"Wait, no, I need a picture." She reached into her satchel where she'd stashed her camera but stopped. "This is real, right?" Reaching out, she pinched my forearm. Well, she tried to, but I flexed, making the skin taut. With a frustrated noise, she whirled around to the unsuspecting Aiden and pinched his arm instead. He yelped and jumped away from the attack, rubbing at the spot she barely touched.

"I think you're supposed to pinch yourself to find out if you're dreaming or not." I swallowed down the laughter and rubbed at my lips to shield my smile from the pouting Aiden.

"How dare you laugh at your best friend's injury."

I rolled my eyes. "No more pinching assaults needed, Aspen. This place is real. You are not dreaming or in a coma, nor do you have a concussion. BamBam is a rescue of sorts and runs around like she owns the place, begging for food from anyone she's familiar with. Our resident veterinarian, Baylee, found her injured as a baby and nursed her back to health. Baylee tried to set her free once she was healed, but BamBam kept finding her way back here. She now prefers to eat food given to her rather than hunt and scavenge."

As I spoke, Aspen's smile grew in utter wonder and excitement, causing fine lines to burst around the corners. My breath stalled, my heart thumping hard in my chest as I took in every inch of her beautiful smile. Our gazes locked, making everything around us fall away. For someone who was always acutely aware of his surroundings, even when asleep, it was unnerving and amazing at the same time. It felt like I could finally take a full breath after barely breathing enough to stay alive for far too long.

"Come on." Aiden lightly grasped Aspen's elbow. "We can show you our place before we head over to the gear storage to shuffle through the supplies for the hike and—"

"Don't forget about the eye mask," I muttered, slipping

both hands into the front pockets of my jeans, suddenly self-conscious.

"You remembered?" Aspen turned to walk backward to face where I trailed behind her and Aiden, who pushed the borrowed bike beside him.

"Be careful," I almost snapped, worry making my tone harsher than I wanted. "You could trip." Rolling her eyes, she flipped back around. "And yes, of course I remembered. I plan to stop by a friend's place to see if she has one lying around for you to borrow."

Stop by, break in... all the same thing.

As we slowly meandered toward our place, the two of them, mostly Aiden, talked nonstop. Smiling to myself at their conversation, I took in our town with new appreciation after Aspen's awe and astonishment at the homestead Brandon built for us. I knew it was special, but after a few years, the newness wore off until she reminded me how extraordinary this place really was.

"This is us," Aiden said, pausing in front of our porch steps. At his gesture toward the white-painted cabin, I watched Aspen, studying her face for insight into her thoughts about the place we called home.

It wasn't much in the way of size, a simple two-bedroom cabin that neither Aiden nor I took time to personalize to our tastes, so it looked like all the others lining either side of the road. The composite siding and trim were well maintained. We all pitched in every other year to keep the paint fresh and helped with other maintenance chores. Three sturdy wooden steps led up to the treated wood porch—so the snow and rain didn't rot it year after year—which spanned the entire front of the cabin. To the right was a single three-person swing that swayed slightly in the light breeze while two plastic chairs sat just off to the side with a tiny table between them. That spot was where Aiden and I spent most nights so we could take in the mountains we hiked and rode daily, plus visit with the others in the community as they trickled in from various outings.

Aspen leapt up the steps, heading directly for the swing, where she tentatively sat down. The chains groaned when she relaxed back and pushed off the wooden porch with the heel of her hiking boot. As she rocked back and forth, Aspen's wide smile from earlier softened into one of relaxed contentment, and her lids fluttered shut with a sigh.

"Do you guys have any idea how lucky you are to live here?" Slowly, her lids blinked open. She shifted to stretch both arms along the back of the swing, which only drew our attention to the way her tank top pulled across her chest. "That view every day." She pointed to the mountains. "A community that accepts you, and cute wild animals running around everywhere." I moved up to the porch, needing to be closer to the woman consuming my thoughts. The wood groaned beneath my weight, though she didn't shift her awe-filled gaze from the distant snow-covered peaks. "This place is paradise."

"You say that now." Arms crossed over my chest, I leaned against the side of the cabin. "You might think differently when winter comes around and it's constantly dark and bitter cold, with snow piled higher than the roofs."

"I bet Jubie loves it," she remarked, eyeing the front door, following the sounds of said dog's loud barks. "And you know, I'm almost certain I would, too, despite everything you just mentioned. Growing up, I loved the heavy winter months in Utah. I know it would be a different extreme of cold and volume of snowfall here, but still. There's something about the cold and snow that is utterly peaceful and makes all the stress in life seem to pause while you watch the flakes softly fall. Give me a warm blanket, a good cup of coffee, and this scenery... I'd probably grow roots where I sat, I'd be there so long."

Louder, more pitiful barks plus frantic scratching from inside the cabin had me rolling my eyes. Jubie knew we were out here and was no doubt excited to see her new friend again.

Dipping inside my pocket, I dug out the cabin keys and headed for the front door, where an impatient Jubie waited. I barely had the door open a couple of inches before the big bundle of fur wedged her way into the opening with her thick head and bounded out with happy yips. Hopping and spinning in crazy circles, making all of us laugh at her antics, Jubie rubbed against my thigh before running over to where Aspen waited for her turn with the jolly animal.

"Well, hello there, beautiful girl," Aspen cooed while scratching behind Jubie's floppy ears. "I missed you last night." Peeking up from beneath her lashes, she shot me a hopeful expression. "What are the odds that I could convince you to let me borrow Jubie for a sleepover?"

"Or you could sleep over—"

The back of my hand slammed against the center of Aiden's chest, cutting off his next words. He shot me an annoyed look, sticking out his tongue like the adult child he acted like most days.

"I'm almost positive The Nest frowns on dogs larger than most children, who leave drool marks everywhere—"

Aspen gasped and covered Jubie's ears. "Don't let her hear you. She can't help her extra saliva condition."

Smirking, I shook my head while rubbing at my jaw. "And sheds half her body weight on a daily basis. At least, that's what it feels like, considering how often I have to sweep our place." I nodded to the smiling dog, who currently had shoestring-like drool coming from either side of her mouth. "And don't worry about Jubie. She is aware of her drooling problem and fully accepts it. Even enjoys leaving little drool love puddles everywhere she goes to let us know she was there."

"Want to see the inside?" Aiden asked, already moving to the door.

Aspen nodded just as her stomach released a loud growl.

"Have you eaten?" I asked, my mind already itemizing what we had in the fridge and pantry.

"Yes and no." Aspen slowly stood from the swing and stepped around Jubie. "I had a granola bar when I woke up, but don't worry about me. I'll figure something out after we're done here." I eyed her as she walked past me with a wide, unconvincing smile and slipped into the cabin behind Aiden.

A granola bar? That wouldn't do at all. Aspen was hungry, and I now had an objective I could fix. Needing to resolve the issue before heading to Caroline's for the eye mask, I followed them inside the cabin, steering straight for the kitchen.

Even though Aspen wasn't mine—ours—I couldn't stand back and not take care of her as if she was. And maybe if she saw how good it could be with us, having someone focused on her health and safety, she'd stay.

With us.

And officially be ours.

10

ASPEN

The paper towel scraped across my lips as I wiped at the smear of mayo from the utterly delicious BLT Miles whipped together after storming into the cottage, grumbling about needing to feed me. Apparently, me being hungry wasn't an option when he was around. That was perfectly okay with me. I liked to eat and didn't care what others thought about my healthy appetite. Sure, I was soft in some areas from not watching what I ate, but I never cared.

Until now.

Because was I really okay with these two fit, utterly gorgeous men seeing me, Aspen Carter, who was not gorgeous or fit, naked? Would they care about the love handles or extra padding around my hips and toss me out before we even got to the fun stuff? They didn't seem like the type, but if they did, I was positive my self-esteem would never recover.

"Thank you, Miles. That was seriously delicious." I folded up the used makeshift napkin and tucked it under the empty plastic plate. When I said seriously delicious, I meant the food *and* watching him. He was undeniably sexy, with the sleeves of his long-sleeved T-shirt pushed up on his thick forearms, exposing the ink I so wanted to lick, his full focus on cooking for me.

Face resting in a palm with my elbow on the table, I tracked him as he moved around the kitchen, not once complaining about having to do the work or asking me to help. At one point, the hairs on the back of my neck stood on end from the sense of someone watching me. With a glance over my shoulder into the living room, I found Aiden studying me as I watched Miles, a knowing little smirk on his kissable lips.

And boy, were they kissable. Or so they seemed. Maybe after I decided on their unique proposition, I would get the chance to see if they were as plump and smooth as they looked.

With a clipped nod, Miles slid the empty plate off the table and set it in the sink. While he scrubbed the barely dirty dish as if the plastic offended him, he and Aiden spoke about their morning, which turned into each man calling the other out about one thing or another. Aiden's full laughter and Miles's quiet chuckles filled the small cabin, bringing a smile to my face as I sat back, listening and enjoying the simple moment.

However, I couldn't help the bit of jealousy that bloomed, tightening my chest. They had this every day: laughter, love, companionship. Living and working with their best friend in a community that accepted and loved them. And as a bonus, they had adorable woodland creatures just running around with cute names like BamBam.

It was perfect.

Even their little cabin, which was bigger on the inside than I expected, held the same warmth and peace that they exuded together. Well, Aiden exuded and worked double-time to pull from Miles. They fit together, each different yet a match with the other. Aiden was the outgoing one, always talking and including Miles or me in the conversation. Though there was a heaviness in his honey-brown gaze when he regarded his friend when he thought no one else was looking. It almost seemed like sadness or guilt. I had noticed it the night before at the bar but obviously didn't feel comfortable then or now to ask what it was about.

Then there was Miles. The clear protector and provider of the two. His gaze constantly bounced around the room, sweeping and exploring. Without a doubt, I was utterly safe in his proximity. Miles was quiet, reserved, and sometimes blunt, but it didn't hurt my feelings. It was just him. His reticent nature compared to Aiden's outgoing one made sense, considering his background.

It made me wonder how much he still dealt with from his time in the Navy and what he saw and did. The SEAL I met on that one assignment mentioned that most come back home with more trauma than they realized and didn't know how to ask for help. And based on a few things at the bar, I had to wonder if his trauma was both emotional and physical. At one point, he caught me ogling his thick, corded forearms. He stiffened as if acting on instinct and quickly yanked down his sleeves, fidgeting until the cuffs covered both wrists.

Though it made me curious more than anything, it made me want to wrap both my arms around his waist and hug him until he couldn't breathe, until the pain that I thought I caught behind his hazel gaze bled out from him and into me.

I barely knew the man, yet the idea of him hurting, sustaining that weight alone, made my heart ache.

"Earth to Aspen." A hand waved in front of my face.

Completely caught off guard, I jerked back, elbow slipping off the table as I straightened in the chair. "Fuck, sorry. I didn't mean to startle you."

I blinked several times, clearing my unfocused gaze, and turned a smile up at Aiden, who studied me with an air of concern.

"You're exhausted. The travel day, then us keeping you up late. You need to sleep." I slid a side-eyed glare to Miles. "Since you said you got little last night."

Shoving off the counter, he started for the front door. Without another word or even looking back, Miles stormed out of the cabin, leaving me alone with Aiden and very confused.

"Um, well, that's..." Aiden trailed off and cleared his throat. "You looked like you were about to fall asleep sitting up. Knowing the way his mind works, seeing you that tired reminded him of the eye mask thing." Brows pulled in tight, he shifted to regard the door. "Or he went to go kill the sun since that's what woke you up so early."

Despite fighting a yawn, the corners of my lips tugged upward. "That's ridiculous." Pushing back from the table, I stood and reached both hands high overhead, a low groan slipping free. The stretch had the hem of my shirt rising, exposing a sliver of my stomach. Fingers gripped around the bottom, I yanked it down only to still at finding Aiden's hooded gaze glued to the section of exposed skin. The tip of his tongue swept along his lower lip, making a shiver slide down my spine like a gentle caress.

"I love your place," I blurted in an attempt to distract myself from the fluttering in my stomach and the heat building in my veins from his simple stare.

Floppy locks of hair shifted with his sharp headshake as if trying to break free of a spell, and he ran a hand through the shiny strands, pushing it away from his face, which automatically fell right back into his eyes. "Oh, yeah, thanks. It's been ours since we moved here. That"—he gestured to the stone fireplace—"is my favorite spot in the house during the winter. I love sitting as close to the flames as possible after coming back from a snowmobile outing. The sounds of it crackling and the smell are winter to me. Add in someone to cuddle with and, if it weren't for my job, I'd never leave that six-by-six area in front of the fire."

My throat suddenly dry at imagining that perfect scene with me in Aiden's embrace, I swallowed hard and awkwardly crossed both arms over my chest, immediately unfolded them again, and then shoved both hands into my front pockets to stop my awkward movements. I wasn't necessarily uncomfortable with him, yet I was. Not because I thought he'd try something I didn't want, but with the way I kept squeezing my thighs together to ease the slow throb, I was on the verge of begging Aiden to ease the ache. I didn't care how pathetic that made me, as long as he helped release the buildup of sexual frustration that started the moment I met him.

"Come on." Tugging one of my hands free, he interlaced our fingers to guide me toward the leather couch. "Who knows how long Miles will be. We can hang out while we wait for him, or if you want to take a nap, you can use my bed."

Another rush of nervous anticipation filled my veins, making me burn from the inside out. His low, husky tone mixed with his words made the swell of need grow, settling at the apex of my thighs in a steady throb. My breath hitched, and my lower belly fluttered with desire. Sweat gathered along the back of my neck with the sudden surge of heat.

Damn, this was bad. All Aiden did was mention his bed, not even suggesting him being in it with me, and I was unbearably hot and ready to say screw it to all my concerns. Not once in my life had I had an instant attraction to someone I actually enjoyed spending time with or had the overwhelming desire to latch on to someone—or someones—like a flying squirrel slamming into a limb or a tree.

"Couch is great," I croaked, voice failing. Rolling my eyes at myself, I fell onto the comfortable cushion, and a moan escaped. I skimmed my palms over the buttery soft leather as the cushions continued to shift, molding around my body. "Oh, wow, this is the most comfortable couch I've ever sat on." The entire frame groaned, shifting under the weight of another. I forced a single lid open and found Aiden sitting on the opposite end, back against the arm, facing me with the smirk that never left his face. "Can I ask you something?"

He regarded me before responding. "I'll answer anything you ask about me, but if it's about Miles, then he needs to be the one to answer whatever questions you have."

"Of course," I said in a rush. "I wouldn't ask you to talk about your friend behind his back."

Aiden's shoulders lowered from around his ears. My brows pulled in tight, studying the motion and what that meant. Did many women either intentionally or unintentionally pit the two against each other or ask questions that weren't theirs to answer?

"But..." I paused and licked my lips, darting my gaze to the unlit fireplace to break his focused stare. Studying the soot-covered stone, I forced myself to ask the question that wouldn't allow me to fall asleep quickly last night. "Why me?"

After a few seconds with no response, I forced my attention to Aiden, who stared at me with confusion in his eyes. "Why you what? What are you talking about, Aspen?"

I searched his face, finding only confusion and honesty there. Fuck. He had no idea what I was talking about. Bile moved up my throat with the sudden drop of my stomach. The yummy sandwich from minutes ago churned in my gut. Shoving off the couch, I stumbled around the coffee table and started for the door. Embarrassment heated my cheeks and had tears burning behind my eyes.

Did I misunderstand him? Didn't Miles say that he and Aiden both were interested in me? But if that was true, why did Aiden not understand my question?

I shook my head so fast to get my whirling thoughts together that sections of dark hair slipped free from the loose bun to frame my face. "Oh my goodness. I'm so sorry. It's just that last night Miles said something, but I must have misunderstood. I just thought when he mentioned both of you..." Sealing my lips shut, I inhaled deeply through my nose to keep the tears from falling.

I barely had my trembling fingers wrapped around the door handle when Aiden's larger frame pressed against my back, his hand sealing to the door, trapping me in place.

"Aiden, please. Let me leave." I rolled my hot forehead along the cool wood, attempting to center myself and my thoughts.

A hand on the back of my neck, slightly squeezing, had me chancing a glance over my shoulder. Worry lines marked Aiden's face as he scanned mine.

"You're not leaving until you talk to me. Help me understand what the hell just happened."

"Last night, when Miles took me home after the bar, he mentioned that you two... well, thought I was attractive, and

—fuck, that sounds ridiculous now that I say it out loud. I must have misheard him."

His hard body pressed against my back, crowding me to the door until my chest and hips were sealed to the solid wood. With a slight tug, the hair still piled on top of my head came tumbling down to my shoulders before gentle fingers swept it off my neck.

"You misinterpreted nothing, sweetheart." My breath caught in my throat at his words and the brush of his lips against my ear. "We both find you fucking gorgeous inside and out and would love the chance to explore this—whatever this connection is between the three of us—further. But I'm trying to be a nice guy here and take into consideration that your whole life was just disrupted and not assume everything you ask revolves around me, Miles, and how we want you so fucking bad that you were all we thought about all damn day."

"Oh." I licked my lips, heart racing. "That's... yeah, wow, that is considerate of you. But I *was* asking about you two and me. After thinking about it last night repeatedly—"

"I love the idea of you thinking about us while you were in bed, sweetheart." His voice was a soft purr that had my breaths coming in short pants.

Focus, Aspen.

"And after all that thinking, I'm confused. Add in the fact that I get all—" I blew out a raspberry. "—flustered at the idea of you two and me, and it makes this all feel unreal. Which is why I asked, why me? Why me, Aiden? Why in the hell would you and Miles want someone like me?"

"Why would we *not* want you, Aspen?" His chest pressed harder against my back, but I didn't feel crowded in a bad way. The brush of his lips along the exposed skin of my neck had me shivering.

With a groan, Aiden's searing body heat disappeared, and a gentle tug peeled me off the door. Once again interlocking our fingers, he guided me to the couch, urging me back into the same spot I had sat in seconds ago.

Both of us settled back on the comfortable cushions, him right beside me this time instead of so far away, and I loosed a breath, hoping to calm my erratic pulse. Adjusting along the smooth leather to face him head-on, I studied his handsome face, memorizing every inch.

He had a youthful look about him with his floppy hair and easy smile. Straight nose, high cheekbones with soft cheeks covered in light scruff that wasn't there yesterday. Aiden was handsome yet beautiful. A desperate urge to trace the lines of his face with my finger had me tucking both hands beneath my thighs.

"What?" he asked, leaning back with a worried expression. "Damnit. I'm sorry if I overstepped just now," he said in a rush. "I just didn't want you to leave, not in an 'I'm holding you captive and never letting you go, keeping you in our nonexistent basement' type of way." Both my brows flew up over my forehead. "Shit, that sounded bad. I just meant I didn't want you to leave upset and without me understanding why. You're unique, Aspen. More so than anyone we've ever met." I waited for him to explain, knowing it could go either way, good or bad. "And we, Miles and I both, are different with you." He ran a hand through his hair and blew out a breath. "You want to know why you, but I can't explain the why because I don't even know what it is specifically that draws Miles and me to you like moths to a flame. Last night, I saw my best friend, who I would give my life for, smiling and laughing more in a few hours than in the entire past year. I caught him watching you, forgetting about his past with you in the room. I see him finally having an outlet for that overprotective energy that thrums under his skin and is as much a part of him as anything else."

"And you?" I asked hesitantly.

"And me..." He licked his lips. "How honest do you want me to be here, sweetheart?"

"Brutal," I blurted.

"I see someone I want to laugh with, who I could see in my arms in front of the fire one day but out hiking and not showering for days the next. Someone whose every inch of skin I want to explore, just to turn around and do it all over again. I want to know what you feel like when I'm deep inside you and hear the way you scream while I devour your mouth while my best friend eats your sweet cunt like the starving man I know he is for you."

Sweat beaded along my forehead, and my chest rose and fell with every labored breath.

Holy hotness.

Did he really just say that out loud?

"But I'm getting ahead of myself," he said, shaking his head. With a deep, chest-rattling groan, Aiden lifted off the couch an inch to adjust himself. "Sorry. Ever since I saw you on the docks yesterday, I've... thought about you."

"Yeah?"

"But I will not sit here, focused on what my dick wants, and ignore what you've been through recently. So tell me, Aspen. How are you doing? Forget about the Miles-and-me situation we dumped on you because we're greedy bastards. How are you coping?"

I stared at his face, unblinking so long that his features went blurry.

How could I think about any of that after his hot-as-sin declaration? All my brain cells, every thought was locked on his words. But the longer I took to respond, the more I considered what he was asking, which slowly eased the burning heat that scorched through me just seconds ago. Blowing out a slow breath, I allowed my lids to close as I searched, excavating the feelings buried beneath the simmering desire, wanting to answer his genuine question truthfully.

"I'm..." I licked my lips. "Free. Am I worried about the future and what I'll do after all this? Yes, but also no. I'm distracted here, where the future and what's next aren't hovering over me like a dark cloud. If anything, the last twenty-four hours have proven that back in Seattle I was simply surviving. I didn't have any real friends. I wasn't happy. James constantly led me on because he always needed something from me—"

"I hope I get a chance to kick that fucker's ass someday," Aiden growled.

"Get in line. But here, right now, I'm happy. Maybe a little relieved that everything that has weighed on me the last few years isn't there anymore. I hated my job in the end, but I didn't understand how much until I left. Everything revolved around James, making sure I got the perfect shot of him, not the perfect shot for the actual article or of the land-scape, which is what I love. It wasn't about what I enjoyed, capturing the beauty only nature can offer. Those shots that take your breath away and pull you into the moment even if you weren't there. That was taken from me toward the end, and now that I realize it... I'm pissed. I'm so fucking mad at myself for allowing him to use and manipulate me, and for being so damn lazy that I didn't even fight it." Shaking my head, I looked down at my clasped hands. "I'm not where I expected to be at this stage in my life, and now I'm wondering if what I wanted out of life is something that will ever happen or if I need to adjust my expectations."

Aiden scooted closer until our thighs met. I sighed at the contact. Somehow, the simple touch had my muscles relaxing. "Where did you expect to be in life?"

"Happy," I whispered. "Secure in a relationship I could depend on." Hot tears filled my lower lids. "I'm so tired of doing it all on my own, you know? Of handling everything that comes my way, of it all falling on my shoulders day in and day out. I want to be with someone I can depend on to share that crippling weight of always thinking of finances, my safety, and everything else involved with living." A single tear leaked from the corner of my eye.

A heavy arm draped over my shoulders, urging me closer. I rested my head on his shoulder while his opposite arm wrapped around me, sealing me against his side.

"Are you right now?" he whispered, lips brushing against my hair. "Happy?"

I searched inside myself to find a truthful answer. "The potential is there, yeah. But right now, I'm just..."

"Confused?"

I shook my head. "Living. For the first time, I want to just *be* and not overthink everything." I gestured between us, my fingertips accidentally skimming along his sculpted chest. "You said everyone needs a reset, and that's exactly what I'm doing."

His calloused palm cradled my cheek, holding me in place as he adjusted so our noses almost touched.

"Can I kiss you?" he rasped, caramel eyes searching mine, almost pleading.

"Yes."

I'd barely gotten the word out before his lips sealed to mine in an emotional, soul-consuming kiss. My lids fluttered closed as a soft sigh passed from my lips to his. With a guttural groan, Aiden scooted even closer, hand slipping from my cheek to delve into my loose hair. His grip tightened, and he used the firm hold to adjust the angle, deepening the kiss.

Desire seared in my lower belly, urging me to climb onto his lap and settle my throbbing core over the bulge restricted by his jeans to alleviate the insistent throb between my thighs. His tongue danced with mine, our lips moving together as the searing heat between us burned brighter. Growing brave, I raked both hands through his hair, nails scraping along his scalp.

"Fucking hell," he groaned. Dropping his hold on my hair, a wide palm settled over my hip, fingers flexing and digging into the moldable flesh just below my ass. With a controlled shift and pull, Aiden urged a leg over his lap, moving me until I straddled him. "This okay?"

I nodded before surging forward to press my lips to his again, desperate for more. His hips flexed, applying a teasing hint of pressure right where I needed it. My lips vibrated with his needy moan, which stoked the heat flowing through my veins even hotter. Sweat beaded along my forehead and down my spine, the temperature in the cabin having gone from comfortable to inferno in a matter of minutes.

My eyes fluttered open at a sound that somehow filtered through the pounding in my ears. A sharp inhale brushed past my swollen lips at finding Miles leaning against the solid wood door Aiden had me pinned against minutes earlier.

Miles's heated observation slid from my face, pausing where my core had settled over Aiden's denim-restrained cock. With a raised eyebrow, he smirked and hitched his chin in a silent command for us to keep going.

My hands tightened around Aiden's shoulders, and a

pitiful whimper escaped, drawing Aiden's eyes to what had captured my full attention. Because that was what it felt like. Miles's observing gaze locked me in place, holding me captive while I squirmed against Aiden.

"Don't mind me," Miles said, voice even deeper than normal. "I like to watch."

It was right then that I knew for certain.

Whatever these two wanted from me, I was all in.

Six days with two hot-as-hell men who wanted me and who I craved in return...

This was my life reset, and I would gladly let them help me forget about what I left behind.

11

AIDEN

My fingers flexed around her hips, the tips digging deep enough that I should worry about bruising her fair skin. I forced myself to swallow the groan that wanted to escape at the way her body molded beneath my grip. It was sexy as fuck. She fit perfectly over me, and I knew the kiss we shared would star in many of the wet dreams in my future.

I blinked at Miles, a slow smirk pulling at my lips. Based on the tent pitched in the front of his jeans, I knew he was just as turned on as I was. He wasn't lying just now. He did like to watch. Though I hoped as he built trust and a stronger connection with Aspen, he'd want to take part more than he had in the past.

I knew someone like Aspen wouldn't shy away because of his scars or make him feel anything less than the hero he absolutely fucking was. But he would need to work that out at his own pace. It wouldn't be an overnight fix, but the longer we were together, the more he would see that she was different.

In the best ways possible.

"Hi," Aspen whispered, gaze still locked on Miles.

With a cocky smile, he shoved off the door and strode toward us, never dropping her stare. Miles paused behind her, directly in front of where I sat on the couch with her straddling me, and reached out to grasp her chin, tilting her face up and back to meet his until she was staring at him almost upside down.

"I'm assuming you made your decision," he murmured while rubbing the pad of his thumb along her lower lip in slow, deliberate strokes. Aspen nodded, but Miles clicked his tongue and pressed his thumb between her lips. "I need words, baby girl."

A groan slipped out as her whole body shivered, which had her vibrating on top of me.

"I think she likes that," I rasped, eyelids closed to keep from grinding her down on my throbbing cock. Fuck, when was the last time I was this hard with no actual skin-to-skin contact? I'd probably explode in my jeans the moment I touched her creamy skin.

"Yes," she whispered around his thumb still between her lips.

He nodded. "Good girl."

"Holy fuck," Aspen and I said at the same time. She jerked her gaze to stare at me, and I just shrugged. I liked bossy Miles, though it didn't happen often.

"Now let's discuss consent," he said, pulling his thumb free to slide his hand down to collar her throat. Stepping between my thighs, he urged her so the back of her head pressed to his lower abs. "We can address consent every step of the way or blanket consent now, with you knowing all you have to say is stop or no and we will, immediately. If you want us to ask your permission every time we touch you, then that will happen. If you want us to take control, then that works too. But we just need to know now, before this goes any further, so we all understand your boundaries and wants."

Her dark eyes flicked to me and searched my own. I smiled while rubbing my hands up and down her strong thighs. "You're in charge here, sweetheart. You say what happens from here on out, and we obey. The last thing we want to do is make you feel uncomfortable or pressured. There are two of us and one of you, so communication is key."

The tip of her pink tongue darted out to wet her lips. "I think... I think I want you two to take control. I don't need you to ask me every step, with every touch. If I'm not ready or it's not something I'm comfortable with, I'll tell you."

"And if you say stop or no or hesitate, we stop." I nodded at Miles, appreciating him taking charge of the conversation. "You're safe with us, baby girl, now and always."

The tension in her body drained at his words, making her settle even harder against me, all while leaning back against Miles.

"Now, do you want me to help you finish what you two started?"

I sucked in a deep breath at the same moment she nodded with a pitiful whimper.

A hum of approval rumbled from Miles's chest. With his free hand, he pulled something from his back pocket and dangled it in front of her face.

"Trust me?" he asked.

"Yes," Aspen croaked out with zero hesitation.

The bright blue mask slid in place over her eyes, easily cutting off her vision. A full-body shiver overtook her, making me bite my lip to keep from moaning her name. Bunching her hair in a tight grip, Miles guided her face back down to mine, hovering her lips so close that our breaths mingled.

"Kiss her," he murmured, hooded gaze locked on our faces.

Not needing to be told twice, I captured her lips with mine and cupped her face, shifting the angle to devour her mouth like I wanted. Both of us stilled when Miles pressed her down harder, adjusting her hips so her core ground against me. Using his hold on her hips, he rocked her back and forth, changing the cadence with every moan or breath hitch that I greedily consumed with our frantic kiss.

"Oh, fuck," she rasped against my lips. Pulling back, she ducked her head, sealing her face against the crook of my neck. Grinding my teeth, I squeezed both eyes shut to keep from exploding in my pants like a fucking teenager. Peeking one eye open, I caught Miles's attention and flipped him the bird. The fucker just smirked, knowing full well that he was torturing me while helping her ease the obvious frustration building earlier about the idea of two men touching her at once.

Her gasp filled the living room. Movements fractured, no longer needing Miles's help, Aspen ground against me as she came with a quiet curse and shuddered. When she slumped forward, breaths slowing and every muscle soft and relaxed, Miles gently pulled her off me, laying her along the couch with her head in his lap. Stroking thick fingers through her hair, he hitched his chin toward my room, knowing I needed to take care of myself if I wanted to walk normally tomorrow.

Peeling myself off the couch, I planted a soft kiss against her cheek and strode to my room, quietly closing the door behind me. Inside my bathroom, I quickly stripped off my clothes, ignoring the massive wet spot on my boxer briefs from the amount of precum her body moving against mine pulled out of me, and stepped into the shower.

I spit in my hand and gripped my cock in a tight fist before even thinking about turning on the water, the need to release an insistent, painful pulse that had to be sated before anything else. A single palm sealed to the cold tile along the wall, I thrust my hips in quick succession, my dick sliding in my grip while replaying the last fifteen minutes like a short porno film.

A familiar zing trailed down my spine and settled in my balls, making my grip tighten to the point of pain and shoving me over the edge. Her grunted name rang through the small bathroom as I came hard, back bowing and knees going weak.

Fucking hell. I slumped against the wall, chest heaving and heart racing.

Holy soul-snatching orgasm.

Peeling both eyes open, I blinked, barely seeing the shower floor through the mess of hair hanging in front of my eyes. That was fucking intense and made me almost wary of how it would be when I came balls deep inside her.

Damnit. Just thinking about it had my dick twitching to life, gearing up for round two.

Not today, buddy.

Shaking my head, I reached to turn on the water, quickly rinsing off the thin layer of sweat that now coated my skin.

After drying off, I slipped on a fresh pair of boxer briefs under the same clothes from earlier since I'd only worn them an hour, plus they smelled like her. Whether it was a certain perfume she wore or just her natural scent, I couldn't get enough and loved that every time I moved, a faint waft rose from my shirt.

Pulling the door open, I started to ask Miles if we were

all set to gather the equipment for tomorrow, but the words dried up, and my feet stopped in their tracks. I blinked, squeezing my lids shut before opening them wide several times to see if the image in front of me changed.

Thank fuck it didn't.

Pulling out my phone, I snapped a quick picture of Miles on the couch, his head lying on the back while Aspen's head, still with the eye mask on, rested on his lap, snoring softly. Both seemed to be out cold, which was a fucking miracle when talking about Miles and a blessing for Aspen, since she got little sleep the night before.

Not wanting to wake them, I slowly crept toward the front door, but a worn board groaned beneath my weight, making me freeze. A quick glance over my shoulder and I locked eyes with Miles, who was now wide awake because of the simple noise.

"Hey," I whispered to hopefully not disturb Aspen. "I'm going to check on the gear we'll need for tomorrow."

He nodded. "Make sure I have my own tent," he grumbled, shooting me a steely look that told me he wouldn't budge on that requirement. "And pack a small one for her, too, just in case. We don't want to pressure her into this by only bringing two."

"Pretty sure what just happened suggests she's into this," I said, gesturing between the three of us. "But yeah, good call. Last thing I want to do is make her uncomfortable." I started for the front door again, only to pause. "What did you find at Caroline's?"

His expression shifted, brows tugging in tight. "Nothing out of the ordinary. All her hiking and climbing gear is gone, so maybe she really is just out doing her thing and forgot to call." We both stilled when Aspen made a soft sound, shifting to lie on her side. In a very unlike-Miles move, he smiled softly down at her. "I'll talk with Caroline when she gets back. It's unacceptable, and she knows that."

Caroline did know that, which made the ball of worry reform in my gut. Forcing a confirming smile, I nodded and reached for the door, quickly slipping out into the late-afternoon sun. Once it was closed behind me, I stepped forward and leaned against the porch post, running a hand through my hair.

Something wasn't right, and I couldn't let this thing with Aspen deter us from making sure our friend was okay. With a resigned sigh, I cleared the few steps, my boots slamming onto the gravel front path. First stop, Hudson and Calista's place to keep my promise to Sam, then to storage to sort through everything we would need for the hike and single overnight camp.

Despite the lingering worry, a smile pulled at my lips.

One night out in the middle of nowhere with just us three.

Things were about to get very interesting.

12

MILES

Silky-soft hair glided between my fingers as I absentmindedly stroked them through Aspen's thick strands while texting with the other hand. Hudson and Oliver wouldn't be back until late tomorrow, needing to stay longer than expected with the Kenai Fjords rangers.

That wasn't a good sign.

Sighing, I closed the phone and rested my head against the couch to stare at the ceiling. It was careless of me to fall asleep with her so close. I couldn't risk her like that again. If I accidentally hurt her, or worse, made her afraid of me because I was lost in a nightmare, I would never forgive myself.

Post-traumatic stress disorder came in different forms, no trigger or reaction the same, even if the individuals went through the traumatizing event together. At least, that was what my therapist and Google told me time and time again. Even one's triggers and daily symptoms evolved as you moved through the stages of healing. Which was utter bullshit. How could I know how to fix something or protect others from myself if I didn't know what was coming next?

For me, in this stage and since the incident, vivid, all-too-realistic nightmares were how my fears and trauma manifested. Some were flashbacks, memories of various missions during my time as a SEAL, which normally didn't make me turn violent in my sleep. Those just left me feeling fucking heavy when I woke up and clung to me throughout the day. It was the nightmares that were crafted to pull every fear from my brain, so fucking detailed they felt real, where I was trapped in that bunker room again or in a situation unable to save a fellow SEAL or hostage; those had me thrashing and punching in my sleep as I desperately tried to save, protect, or live.

I never knew which one would haunt my sleep when I closed my eyes at night. Which was why I slept very little anymore in general. Thankfully, I didn't require too much to still operate at a high level of awareness, but with the addition of the beautiful woman sleeping on my lap, I knew I needed to be on top of my game. Which meant sleeping regularly and getting enough rest to handle anything that came at her or us. After last night, I quickly realized I needed to be faster, stronger, and more aware of every fucking thing around us, almost like how I was daily as an active-duty SEAL.

Not that she wasn't capable of taking care of herself, because she clearly could, having lived in a large city alone for many years. I just didn't want her to *have to* do it alone anymore. Shouldering the burden of safety and security of those around me, of my non-blood-related family, was something I was used to. Not that taking care of her would be a burden.

It would be a fucking honor.

It meant the fucking world to know that Aspen trusted me from the moment we met, and while we were together, she relaxed knowing someone had her back. She believed in me, felt safe with me, and knew that no matter what, I would be there for her. It was a high knowing someone put all their trust in you, put their life in your hands.

What did that make me?

Obsessive, sure.

Crazy, maybe.

Happy? Fuck yes.

A soft sound from my lap had me blinking rapidly to clear my dry eyes and turning my gaze down to where Aspen shifted, fingers slowly reaching up to tug off the borrowed eye mask. Long, thick lashes fluttered up and down several times as her eyes flicked around the room before coming to a stop on me.

"You're okay," I whispered.

Her smile was soft and sleepy and adorable as fuck. The cushions dipped around me as she pressed up into a sitting position. "I didn't mean to fall asleep." As if the memories of what happened just before she slept slammed forward, her eyes widened, and a red blush stained her cheeks. "Oh, hell. Did that really happen?"

I nodded, watching her for any signs of regret, but only found... embarrassment?

With both hands, she raked her fingers through her hair and leaned forward, elbows pressing down on top of her knees. "And then I fell asleep. That's... something."

"You were exhausted from traveling and not sleeping," I said, not understanding why she hid behind the thick curtain of her dark hair. "Hey, what's going on? Talk to me."

Leaning to the side, she swiped away the hair covering her face and looked at me like I was dense. Maybe I was, because I didn't have the first fucking clue what was going on in her head. Maybe she always woke up grumpy after a nap. Not that I was going to ask her that. I might not be great with women, but I sure as hell knew not to voice that thought out loud.

"I'm so, so sorry I did that," she muttered into the palms pressed to her face. Reaching over, I wrapped my fingers around her wrists and tugged, pulling one hand away, then the other so I could look into those big dark eyes. "Can't you see I'm mortified? I swear I'm not normally one to just fall asleep without returning the favor and—"

"Return the favor?" I muttered, and the pieces slowly started to come together.

"Well, yeah." She sighed, flopping back against the couch and tossing an arm over her eyes. "Fuck, you two must think I'm so lame. I mean, who does that? All I can say is I must be temporarily broken because—"

With a frustrated snarl, I gripped her hips, easily lifted her off the couch, and placed her on my lap, facing the fireplace. Collaring her throat in a gentle grip, I eased her back until her spine sealed to my chest and her head rested against my shoulder.

"You, Aspen Carter, are not broken," I whispered in her ear. Her throat worked beneath my palm with a thick swallow. The sensation had me stifling a groan, my mind immediately going to how that motion would feel with my cock down her throat. "And you'll have to explain to me why you're embarrassed, because I'm not understanding. Do you regret what happened between you and Aiden?"

Her long pause had me tensing beneath her.

"Not regret per se, more mortified." Hoping to help her open up, I loosened my hold to swipe my fingertips in long, gentle strokes up and down the column of her neck. "I can't believe I did that. How is it even possible for me, an almost-thirty-year-old woman, to get off by doing that?" Slowly, the tension eased from her muscles, and little by little, she sagged against me. "I'm embarrassed because I dry-humped your friend and then fell asleep—and, bonus, didn't even get to return the favor. And now I wake up to you being all sweet and acting like nothing is wrong when it has to be, right?"

It felt like a trick question, but Aspen didn't seem like the type of woman to play games, so I went with my gut. "Why would things need to be wrong if you enjoyed yourself?"

With a huff, she pushed off my chest and turned to face me, still sitting on my lap but both legs dangling off the side. "Because I fell asleep, and that's just pathetic. Fuck, this is uncomfortable. I haven't done this awkward stage in a long time. A *really* long time," she grumbled under her breath. "You must think I'm not worth the trouble after today."

A growl rumbled in my chest, drawing her attention lower. My knuckle under her chin, I tipped her face back up to mine. "If you say one more negative thing about yourself, baby girl, I swear on my dog that I will drop you over my knee and spank your ass so hard there will be no hovering between that line of pleasure and pain."

My chest heaved from the building emotions as I stared into her wide eyes.

"Did you just say that out loud?" she whispered. "I didn't know real people actually talked like that."

I arched a single brow. "Versus someone who is not real?"

"Well, yeah. Fictional men. Book boyfriends, you know..." She trailed off and blew out a slow breath.

"I don't know, but I'll take your word for it and will consider it a compliment and not scary as fuck since you're still sitting here."

"Compliment for sure. But don't use those naughty words on just anyone or you'll have women, maybe some men, flocking from all over the world to Anchor Bay." She cut a strange look I couldn't decipher my way. "And I kind of like being the one holding your attention, even if it isn't for very long. Maybe an even shorter time frame than I expected, since after earlier, I'm sure this will end today."

"Look, I'll be honest." I leaned back and interlaced my fingers behind my head to keep from touching her everywhere I wanted. A forlorn expression came over her face, and she slowly nodded, as if already expecting the worst. "I don't have the first clue, not the slightest idea, of what the fuck you're talking about." That expression turned to confusion as I spoke. "Nothing about this is awkward to me or to Aiden. If you didn't notice, we were right there with you. Hell, I was the one who pulled all the strings. And fucking loved it. As for returning the favor..." I shook my head and looked toward the fireplace. "Who the hell keeps score?"

"Men," she answered quickly. "Men keep score and, from my experience, do nothing out of the sheer enjoyment of making a woman come."

My nostrils flared as I inhaled deeply to keep the rising anger shoved down deep. "I want to fuck up every asshole who made you think that is a true blanket statement for my gender. You didn't force us to take care of you, didn't coerce us into doing something we didn't want to. We did it because we wanted to. *Really* fucking wanted to. We got to touch you, hear those damn edible sounds you make as you chase your orgasm, and see that gorgeous flush all over your fair skin. There is no need to return the favor because there *was* no favor. We all enjoyed it."

"But the falling asleep thing." She rolled her eyes. "What a way to impress someone. 'Thanks for the orgasm. I'm just going to pass out right here, on your couch, while you have to sit there uncomfortably.'" She sat up straight and twisted to look around the room as if it was only then that she realized Aiden wasn't there. "Where is he anyway?"

"You falling asleep afterward did the opposite of what you're thinking." I locked my gaze with hers so she could see the truth in my words. "You sleeping on me, trusting me, was a fucking honor. You felt so safe and comfortable around us that you fell asleep on our couch, in our home. That's a damn power trip, to know you trust the two of us so much that you slept. So don't belittle that, please, because I'm honored you did. And Aiden went out to take care of the supplies for tomorrow. We both wanted you to sleep as long as you could."

"Miles," she whispered, tears filling her lower lids. Panic swirled, making my chest tight. "I've never met anyone like you. Thank you for being honest with me and telling me I'm overreacting without telling me I'm overreacting." Her tongue peeked out to run along her lower lip. "So, now what?" Her gaze shifted around the room as if she was nervous, and she tucked a few strands of hair behind her ear. "How does this"—she gestured between us—"work exactly? Now that I've kissed Aiden, do I need to kiss you too? To keep things even? This is my first—" She angled her head to the side, teeth sinking into her bottom lip. "—throuple? I think that's what the cool kids call it these days. I don't want anyone to feel left out or—"

Her plump lips molded around my two fingers where I pressed against them. Her brows narrowed, making an unexpected chuckle rumble in my chest. "Baby girl, this isn't a competition. No one is keeping score. If you want to kiss me, you kiss me, but that is for you to decide when you're ready, not because you feel forced—"

Before I could even finish, she lunged forward, shoving my fingers away to seal her lips to mine. My lids slid closed, savoring the feel of the kiss. Eager for more, I palmed the back of her head, fingers tightening in her hair to hold her exactly where I wanted her. Everything was perfect and erotic as fuck. The way her lips slid against mine, the tentative way her tongue danced and explored, was everything I never knew I needed. This wasn't desperate or lust-driven; it was deliberate and filled with emotions I couldn't separate and label if I tried.

"How is this possible?" she murmured against my lips. Pulling back, she stared down at me with something like awe in her eyes. "How did yesterday morning feel like my life was crumbling around me, but today it feels like it's actually starting for the first time? How did you do that?"

Cupping her face, I held her steady and pressed a firm kiss to her forehead, unable to respond because I had no fucking clue. I wanted to tell her that she did the same for me. The weight of everything I shouldered felt lighter with her at my side.

"How did I end up catching a ride to The Nest from a random hot guy who is like a two-for-one special?" I barked a laugh at her comparison, making her smile widen. "Where both are not only good-looking but good guys and might like the outdoors more than me?" She tilted her head and studied me. "Well, that has yet to be validated. Our hike will be the ultimate test."

"So, you're telling us to bring our A game to impress you?" I asked, chest shaking with restrained laughter.

"Well, yeah. What if we get out there and you... can't start a fire or get all whiny when you get dirty or are attacked by a plethora of summer bugs? By the way, those insistent bugs and the all-day sunlight need to be listed in bold red letters when entering the state. Like a warning of some kind."

Planting a soft kiss to the corner of her lips, I nodded. "I'll get with the Department of Travel for the State of Alaska and tell them to get on that."

With barely any effort, I shifted to the edge of the couch and stood, taking her with me and carefully setting her down, holding on until she was steady on her feet. My heart leapt in my chest at the squeal of delight followed by her laughter that bounced around the room. Laughter was something this cabin hadn't heard in a long time. Too many nights, Aiden and I sat on the front porch to distract ourselves from how empty the place felt with just the two of us and how quiet it had become in recent years.

I loved the fucker like a brother, and we got along great, but it had started to feel like something was missing between us.

I studied Aspen out of the corner of my eye as she stretched her arms high above her head.

Maybe that missing piece...

Wasn't missing anymore.

13

ASPEN

"Thanks for understanding about Jubie needing to stay with Miles," Aiden said after a minute of silence had passed as we weaved our way out of their community and toward The Nest. "Nighttime is when he needs her the most, and I knew he wouldn't tell you that. So, thank you for pretending like it was your idea for her to stay behind."

I just smiled and nodded, even though his eyes were on the road and not on me. "Even though I'd love a cuddle partner, she is his dog. I didn't realize she was a service animal." Shifting in the seat, I studied Aiden's profile. "I'm guessing he needs her because of his time in the service?"

His features tightened, as did his grip on the wheel. My lips parted, and I sucked in a breath, ready to retract the question, only his response cut me off.

"Jubie isn't technically a service dog—she wasn't specifically trained for that—but yeah, she helps him when things get to be too much. Not sure how she knows, but she does. Jubie gives him the comfort and support that neither I nor anyone else has been able to up to this point." He shot me a knowing look out of the corner of his eye. "Though he is quite chatty with you, so maybe that will change."

I held up both hands. "Just because I'm easy to talk to means nothing."

"But it does. I've never seen him talk to a stranger as much as he has you, nor give two shits about their feelings. He's kind of an asshole," he said with a smirk.

"I think..." I let out a slow breath. "Anyone who's been through what he has—and I don't even know the specifics—probably keeps everything close to the chest. It's easier to act like an asshole toward people you don't see sticking around instead of letting them in, giving a piece of yourself, and then them walking away. Was there a specific incident that made him need Jubie that much more or just his overall time as a SEAL?"

"Yes."

I smiled. "That's not an answer."

"True, but it's the best I'll give you. It's not my story to tell." The way his tone dropped told me there was a lot more to all this than Aiden let on. "You ready for our hike tomorrow?"

I knew what he was doing, using that question to change the subject, but who was I to stop him? I'd known him and his best friend for a little over twenty-four hours. Trust took way longer to build. My heart sank. Did we have that kind of time to get to the point where they would trust me with their pasts and regrets?

"Not sure if we talked about this earlier, but I set out three tents. If you want to share"—he waggled his brows suggestively—"then we'll only need to bring two."

"Okay, but why not one? I mean, aren't you and Miles kind of a package deal? Why bring a second tent at all?"

Aiden huffed a laugh. "Yeah, we are, but what we enjoy

doing together has nothing to do with actual sleeping." He shifted along the seat and switched hands on the wheel. "Miles requires his own tent. Always. Sleeping is... one of his challenges. That's all I'll say about that, and I would appreciate it if you don't make a big deal out of it tomorrow. He might be a big fucker and could kill almost anyone with his bare hands, but he's sensitive about his trauma and how it manifests. I just don't want to see him pull back from this, you know?" Reaching over, he placed a palm on my knee and squeezed. "Because I sure as hell don't want this to end before it really gets started."

"Of course," I whispered, my breath catching as his hand slid higher up my thigh. "So, if I say yes to the two tents, then I'd be sharing with you." I tapped a finger against my lips like it was an actual tough call to make. "Decisions, decisions."

"I'll make sure you stay nice and warm all night, sweetheart. And very, very relaxed." He shot me a wink before turning back to the road. It wasn't dark out yet, and the roads were nearly deserted, but when we passed a car or truck, Aiden always waved as if he knew everyone in town. Who knew? He probably did, with his outgoing personality. "And don't worry, we're only talking about where we'll be sleeping. Not... other fun things."

"Like photography?" I offered tongue in cheek.

"Well, yeah, of course. And just a heads-up—I photograph best in the nude."

My loud laugh rumbled around the truck. Wiping at my eyes, I nodded, cheeks burning from my wide smile. "Noted. Though, after everything with the douche canoe who I won't bring up right now, I think I'm done with any pictures with humans in them. Nature, animals, that's what I want to get back to."

He nodded. "Well, if you ever change your mind, just say the word and all my clothes will disappear."

"So generous." I giggled.

"Only with you."

The lights around the resort came into view, telling me the ride was almost over. I checked over my shoulder to make sure the borrowed bike was still in the truck's bed and hadn't somehow escaped during the short drive.

As I stared out the side window, gazing at the beautiful scenery, I thought about this view being something I saw every day, not just for six more.

"Did you picture yourself being here, in Alaska, in a very open-minded community with your best friend?"

The truck slowed at a stop sign. "No. Not at all," he huffed.

"So, what *did* you picture if these idyllic scenarios you've found yourself in weren't your goal?"

He paused, his thumb thumping on top of the steering wheel. "I was married once. To a woman who I thought was my goal, my future. Turned out I was wrong, and then my goals shifted after Miles officially came home. We both needed to get out of the town we'd grown up in, both of us running from the demons and failures chasing us. He knew about Brandon's company through a friend of a friend, and the rest is history."

"Married, huh?" He nodded. "I haven't found anyone I would consider spending even a weekend with, much less the potential of forever. Think you'll do it again?"

He shook his head and shrugged. "I don't know. That marriage didn't go the way I planned, you know?"

"What happened?"

He sighed and swiped a hand across his mouth. "I was in the Navy with Miles. Did I mention that?" I shook my head and leaned toward the middle of the truck, not wanting to miss a word of his story. "We planned to go into the SEALs together, but my on-again, off-again girlfriend from back home convinced me we could make us a real thing if I let my contract run out. I believed her. Miles didn't. Of course, he saw right through her trap, and once I was back home for good, things got bad quickly. There were a few times I had to call the cops just to get her to stop coming at me."

"She hit you?" I gasped.

He nodded solemnly. "And I knew I'd never lay a finger on her, even if the cops who showed up at the door those few times had some choice words to call me because I wouldn't. So, I drank a shit ton more than was healthy and lost job after job because I was just so fucking miserable that I didn't have the energy to even try to keep one. My parents tried to help, but when you're in that dark space, it's easier to stay there than take the helping hand someone is offering."

"Yeah, and sometimes the last person's help you want is your parents', because they'll never let you live it down." There was no hiding the bitterness in my tone. The way Aiden shot me a raised brow told me he heard it too.

"Exactly."

"So, what happened for you to end that horrible chapter of your life and move here?"

"Miles," he said, voice hoarse with an emotion I couldn't read. "He..." Aiden cleared his throat. "Again, not my story to tell, but he came home, and I knew my best friend needed me. And honestly, I needed him. I filed for divorce and gave her everything she asked for just to be done with it all, but with the clause that she could never reach out to me again, and it was final. But even with all that shit, there is still one future goal I haven't totally given up hope on." His caramel eyes cut my way. "A family, kids. Even if they aren't my own. It was the one thing my ex knew I wanted badly and made sure never happened, though now I'm grateful for that. I have nothing tying me to her."

"You really want a family, kids, as in multiple?"

"Why do you sound surprised?" he asked, tone a little defensive.

I licked my lips to give myself a second to get my mind working straight. "It's just that most of the men I've met really only want to participate in the family's making, not the actual parenting part."

"You've really met the worst of our gender, haven't you?" he said, tone stiff.

It was my turn to shrug. "I guess, yeah. Plus, growing up on a ranch, my dad worked from sunup to sundown, so my mom was the only one who did the parenting. Once I was old enough, he taught me what to do to help around the ranch and not really much else. So, I guess I grew up with a bit of gender-biased roles. Then, at the magazine, I watched guys talk about their children with the same enthusiasm they had when discussing red-line edits for their articles."

"What about you?"

"What about me?"

"Do you want a family? Kids? The whole thing with a white picket fence?"

"White picket fence, no. That feels... confining, limiting even. I don't want to be held back from going and doing and exploring. If I were to have a family, then the person I was with would know that about me and allow me to keep this part of myself that wants to be free by doing it all together, with or without kids. So family, kids... yeah, but it would have to be with the right person who understood me. I'm tired of putting what I want as a side note."

The truck slowed as we eased to a stop outside my little cabin. Aiden turned the key, killing the engine, and reached for the door.

"Hope you don't mind, but Miles demanded I walk you to your door and make sure all is safe inside the cabin before I let you go in. Oh, and he also mentioned that today might have overwhelmed you a bit, so I'm to ensure you're safe, then get my ass back home." His cheeks bunched with a wide smile. "Such a bossy fucker, that bestie of mine."

"Well, I don't mind at all."

Shoving the door open, I stepped out into the crisp evening air, tugging my coat tighter around me as I used a hip to shut the heavy metal. The silence was comfortable as we walked side by side toward my door, Aiden wheeling the bike even after I offered. Once he leaned the borrowed bike against the side of the cabin, I handed over the key just like I'd done with Miles and gestured toward the door in an open invitation.

Back against the side of the cabin, I stared into the grouping of trees that surrounded the area. Though there was sunlight, it was still hard to see in the thick underbrush. Somewhere close, a bird sang, followed by a heavy gust of wind that whistled through the trees. The crack of a limb or a stick and the rustling of leaves to the right had me standing straight and scanning the area for whatever caused the sound.

Pulse racing, I forced myself to slow my breathing, in through the nose and out through the mouth, knowing it was more than likely a squirrel or from the gust of wind. But it wasn't just the sound that set me on edge. There was something out there that made me feel like I was being watched.

"All clear."

A scream raced up my throat as I leapt a foot off the ground, whirling around with a fist raised. Aiden's eyes went wide as he stepped back and held up both hands.

"Everything okay out here?" he asked, stepping farther out onto the porch and scanning the area in front of the cabin, brows pulled in tight.

Palm pressed over my hammering heart, I nodded. "Yeah, just woodland creatures making me think the boogeyman is out there."

His hand hovered over the sidearm resting on his hip. "What did you see? Was someone out there? A man?" A large palm cupped my shoulder and pulled me behind him.

All I could do was nod at his back, even though he couldn't see. His response was a bit over the top at me being jumpy and joking about the boogeyman.

"Aiden, is there something going on that you should warn me about?" I hedged. "I figured you'd brush me off and say it was a deer or something."

Spinning around, he squished me against his hard chest, and both arms wrapped around my back to squeeze me tight.

"We're really not supposed to talk about it since we know very little, and the sheriff doesn't want to scare tourists and visitors away from Anchor Bay." Pulling back, Aiden scanned my face, the fading light just enough for me to see the worry clouding his features. Anxious nerves had me trembling as I waited for him to explain what that meant, because it didn't sound good. "But you need to know. You *deserve* to know. Tomorrow, on the hike, Miles and I will explain everything. Okay?"

"Why not now?" I asked, voice shaking from the rising fear. My gaze darted around the darkening area as if some unknown threat might jump out and attack.

Some of the tension eased from his features. "Because my bossy-ass bestie also told me to get you inside quickly so you could get a proper night's sleep." Attempting to lighten the conversation, he winked. "Something about not sleeping much once we're all together."

My own worries faded with a soft laugh, though a sliver of fear of something out there that I wasn't aware of still lingered in the back of my mind. "Are you sure Miles was the one who said that? That doesn't sound like him."

Aiden's smile grew wider, faint dimples popping on both cheeks. "Look at you, already knowing us so well you can tell our comments apart. Okay, fine, that last part was all me, though Miles does want you to get some sleep. Overprotective mother bear, that one."

"I like it," I admitted. "It's nice not needing to be the only one looking out for my safety. Being in Seattle alone was exhausting. So, you call it bossy, but I call it comforting."

"Tomato, potato."

"That's not how that goes." I giggled.

"But it got you to laugh, so it worked."

As if things shifted into slow motion, he leaned down and sealed his lips to mine. It was soft, almost like a promise of something more to come before he pulled back. Tugging me into his arms, he hugged me tight once again.

"Tell me to go," he whispered into my hair. "Tell me to walk back to the truck, drive home, and fall asleep to dreams of you." My heart raced, but a shy smile crept up my lips. "I don't want to go."

"I don't want you to go either," I murmured. It was nice not being alone, having someone there who wasn't just a physical body close by but someone who was attuned to you. I'd gotten used to being ignored by others in favor of their phones or computers, and I didn't realize how hurtful it was. "But if we're doing the hike you two described earlier, then I do need to get some sleep. I'm going to make the best out of the time we have out there."

Aiden's lips brushed along my ear. "Me too, sweetheart."

Cheeks hot, I just nodded and stepped back, reaching for the door handle. Once safely inside, I gave Aiden an awkward two-finger wave and a whispered "Good night" before closing the door and flipping the lock. A dreamy sigh escaped as I fell back against the door with a wide, goofy grin on my face that reflected on the glass door that led to the back porch area.

Gritting my teeth, I shook off the urge to rip the door back open and chase Aiden down to beg him to stay. Needing more distance to stay strong, with palms to the door, I pushed off and headed toward the bathroom to get ready for bed.

The moment I stepped onto the tile and saw the toiletry bag and scattered products on the counter, it hit me. When packing for the trip, I forgot one big item I wasn't aware I'd need.

A damn razor.

Because one, my legs hadn't seen a razor in over a week already.

Because two, neither had my armpits.

Because three, it had been way, way longer since the more intimate parts of my body had seen any type of trimming or landscaping. Fuck, I might need to hunt down a hedge trimmer to tackle that job.

Head tipped back, I groaned at the ceiling. "Fuck my life. Fuck body hair. Fuck me hesitating on that damn laser hair removal Groupon."

Returning to the door, thankful I hadn't even taken off my coat yet, I flicked the lock and pulled the door open.

Back outside, without Aiden's comforting and protective presence, the stillness in the air, along with the shadows passing through the trees, had an ominous feeling sweeping over me. I paused, one foot hanging over the single step, as a chill crept down my spine and the hairs on the back of my neck stood on end.

Swallowing hard for courage, I shrugged off the strange feeling making me all kinds of paranoid and continued down the steps to the path that led toward the main area of The Nest. Surely the front desk—or sometimes, in small places like this, the bar area—had backup supplies offered for little things their guests might have forgotten.

Fingers crossed, because if they didn't, then I'd have to ride the bike into town with a bit of hope and a prayer that a general-type store was open.

The thin layer of gravel that made up the trail ground beneath my boots with every step, the sound somewhat cathartic, easing the worry from Aiden's odd warning. Tucked off the path were the other cabins. Sounds of laughter and voices carried through the trees. Every few steps, I couldn't stop myself from glancing over my shoulder, the feeling of being followed nagging at me. For the billionth time, I slowed to scan the area but didn't see anyone. Breathing through the rising fear, I picked up the pace to a fast walk. It wasn't long before my breaths sawed in and out in heavy pants from the nerves and quick gait.

The rustle of leaves and a sharp gust of chilled wind sent my hair flying into my face, blinding me for a few seconds and pushing me into a slow jog. Heart pounding, whole body trembling, which made me stumble on the uneven surface, I dared another look behind me. A hysterical laugh bubbled up, escaping in a loud hacking from being out of breath at finding two wild ferrets rolling and running just off the path, chittering back and forth to each other.

Slowing my pace and clasping both hands behind my head to calm my heaving breaths, I cursed at myself and rolled my eyes to the darkening sky. I was being paranoid and working myself into a damn heart attack. Nostrils flaring, I continued toward the main building, relief flowing through me when I rounded a sharp curve on the path and bright lights came into view.

The curve had the way I'd just come from appearing in my peripheral. Movement, almost nothing more than shadows shifting, had me pausing and turning fully, squinting into the trees to see what caught my eye. My stomach dropped. A dark figure that didn't belong to a woodland creature, big or small, made me freeze.

A booming voice coming from the direction of the main building had me whipping around toward the noise. Two people walked out the glass front doors, arm in arm.

Shaking my head, I turned back, only to find nothing unusual there.

Squinting both eyes, I scanned back along the path but couldn't find the person I swore I saw hiding in the trees.

Maybe it was just my imagination.

Or maybe...

It wasn't.

14

AIDEN

The last pack slammed into the bed of Miles's truck. I leaned against the faded blue paint, wiping the dribble of sweat that slid down the side of my jaw as I watched Miles and Jubie lumbering my way. Jubie trotted beside Miles, trying to keep up with his long strides and occasionally jumping to snag the stick my best friend taunted his dog with, just high enough to where she couldn't get it.

A small smile pulled at his lips, and I knew I wore a similar one. We were both excited for the next twenty-four hours. Yes, there was that potential of taking things further with Aspen, but it was also about the time we would get to spend with her in the great outdoors, where all three of us loved to be. It was special when we could take true outdoor lovers out on hikes, knowing they would appreciate all that Alaska offered. Seeing the awe on someone's face, some even shedding grateful tears, was fucking special as hell.

What were the odds that Aspen would be open to hiking naked?

"What are you smirking at?" Miles muttered as he

leaned against the truck beside me. "Whatever it is, that look always spells trouble for both of us."

I shook my head and ran a few fingers through my hair. "Just excited, I guess. It's been a while since I've felt this." I tapped at my chest where the excitement felt almost physical, bubbling inside me. "This buzzing anticipation of a hike I've done hundreds of times."

Miles nodded while throwing the slobber-coated stick as far as he could. We both watched Jubie prance off. "I know what you mean. We've done this trail so many times it's lost its shine, but this time with Aspen..." He trailed off, allowing me to fill in the words he clearly couldn't voice.

"It feels fucking sparkly?"

Miles barked a laugh and shoved at my shoulder. That sound rumbled in my ears and went straight to my heart, making it feel even fuller. Fuck, I loved seeing this side of him again. If this was what Aspen did for him, eased that burden he carried around, then I'd do anything to make her stay.

"What are your thoughts about kidnapping?" I mused as I rubbed at my clean-shaven jaw, a basic, sketchy-as-hell plan forming.

"That it's a felony? What the fuck kind of question is that?"

Both shoulders rose and lowered in an exaggerated shrug. "Just thinking out loud here. Don't get all high-and-mighty over something like legalities on me. Come on, let's go." As I reached for the door handle, I paused. "Oh, I might have let the creepy shit going on around here slip last night to Aspen, and I also might have promised her we'd explain everything." I shot him my best puppy dog eyes, hoping it would keep him from punching me. "For her safety, you know."

"Fucking hell, Aiden. You know what Hudson and Oliver—"

I jumped into the truck and slammed the door shut, cutting off his boisterous response. Not that it did any good, considering he was driving the truck I just sealed myself into. Not my brightest moment.

The whole frame shifted as Miles slid behind the wheel after loading Jubie into the bed, face tight with frustration.

"You looked better with that smile from earlier. Let's go back to happy Miles, eh?"

"Then don't go pissing me off." He slammed the key into the ignition and started the engine. "You know the sheriff doesn't want us talking about it with anyone outside the community."

"That's a load of bullshit, and you know it. How many people have gone out on that trail alone or unprepared for what could happen because they've kept quiet about it all or refused to listen to our theories?"

Really just *a* theory, as in a single very strong one.

The one that revolved around some sick bastard snagging unsuspecting women off the challenging trail that went from Anchor Bay to Kenai Fjords National Park, sometimes killing the male partner who traveled with them. We couldn't figure out why or even what he was doing with them. My gut churned, and the light breakfast I ate rose in my throat just thinking about what he could be doing with them if the missing women were still alive.

"It's the best way to keep her safe," I added, knowing that would woo him over to my side. "She deserves to know."

With a heavy, resigned sigh, he finally nodded in agreement. Behind us, Jubie barked from the truck bed, head hanging over the side, allowing her fur and tongue to flap in the wind as we drove toward The Nest to pick up Aspen.

"But not all the details. We can't jeopardize their investigation like that, not when there are families who deserve answers and victims who need justice."

He had a point.

I didn't have to like it, though.

Restless energy buzzed beneath my skin, the anticipation of seeing Aspen again making me vibrate from the inside out. I couldn't sit still, much to Miles's frustration. The entire drive, I fidgeted in the seat, unable to get comfortable for long, played with the radio dial a few hundred times, and rapped my fingers on both knees to where I was even annoying myself. But I couldn't settle down. There was a lot of pressure around this hike, yet not really. I knew without a doubt she'd have a good time, would get some amazing shots, and have that peace only nature could offer to settle her swirling thoughts. All that was a guarantee, but I wanted her to fucking love it.

Love our time together.

Love us three together.

Love us.

Groaning, I tapped the back of my head against the headrest. "I hate feelings. They fucking suck trying to unweave it all."

"You're too far gone on her, aren't you?"

I scoffed and pointed an accusing finger at him. "And you're not, Mr. Smiley Pants?" He smirked as if to prove my point. "See, there it is again. You can't say you don't feel it. She's different in all the ways that matter."

He ran a hand over his short hair before wrapping it around the back of his neck. "There is something between us, but I'm not sure it's what you're feeling. You think with your dick more times than not."

"It's more than that this time," I protested, crossing both arms over my chest. "And don't do that. Not to this."

"Do what?"

"Deflect. You're just saying that to make me doubt what I'm feeling, what you're feeling, too, because you're scared."

He shot me an *I'll murder you right here while driving if you say that shit again* look that had me sealing my spine to the door. I swallowed so hard it made an audible sound.

"I'm not fucking scared. But you're forgetting a bunch of shit, overlooking things I know will push her away. You have that ability to forget how women react to me. I fucking don't. So don't say I'm scared when you know—when you pull your head out of your ass—why I'm guarded."

The guilt that had seemed to abate for the last twenty-four hours roared back to life, putting so much fucking pressure on my chest that I couldn't breathe. I stared at Miles, desperately sucking down slivers of air.

When he glanced my way at a stop sign, his eyes widened. In a flash, he leaned over, unclipped my seat belt, and shoved my head between my knees.

"Fuck, I'm sorry, brother. I didn't mean for it to sound like an accusation." More guilt swirled, knowing he was beating himself up for stirring the guilt I constantly drowned in. "I'm just trying to be levelheaded and not let myself get too close for a shit ton of reasons. I shouldn't use my scars as an excuse, but I do because I'd rather think it has something to do with my body than her finding out about the other broken parts of me and walking away. I don't want that for you."

"And I'm tired of seeing you just existing," I said, finally able to breathe. Slumping against the window, I sealed both eyes shut, relishing the coolness seeping from the glass to my forehead. "There is so much more out there than what you're allowing yourself."

"Yeah, well, not all of us rebound as easily as you. Just give me time. Let me go at my pace. Things have been getting better, even before Aspen arrived."

Even if I didn't sleep with a single wall dividing our rooms, able to hear him crying out in his sleep or thrashing around in his bed, I would've known the lie in his words.

"Keep an open mind, okay? She's special, even if you won't admit it to yourself yet." Pulling up to her cabin, I reached for the door handle but didn't shove the door open. "And I know you know that. I see it in the way you actually talk to her instead of communicating via caveman grunts and scowls." The corner of his lips twitched upward. "Come on, let's go get our girl and get this hike started. I, for one, can't wait to see where the next twenty-four hours take us."

Outside the truck, Miles rounded the hood and fell into step beside me. "Which head is thinking that?"

My laugh rumbled through the trees. I opened my mouth to respond when Miles went completely still. I paused, too, staring at my friend, wondering if he was having some kind of medical emergency or just needed to fart.

It could go either way.

But the second I noted the way his features pinched in concentration, gaze flicking from side to side, taking in every detail, stance wide and ready for an attack—oh, and the gun in his hand—I, too, went on high alert.

"What is it?" I asked, my hand sliding back toward my belt holster. The moment my palm touched the rough grip of my Glock, a fraction of my nerves eased.

"I don't know," he murmured. "It just feels off."

"If you're saying it's off, something is fucking off." I

trusted his gut instinct implicitly. If there was a threat close, he knew about it. Part of it was trained into him as a SEAL; the other part was all him. He'd always had that gut instinct. Which was why he initially told me to stay away from my ex-wife and Jessica.

At some point, I'd listen to him.

Maybe.

Probably not.

"Go to the cabin. Protect Aspen."

I widened my eyes at him. "And what the fuck are you going to do?"

The motherfucker rolled his eyes at my concern. "Snuff out the threat."

"And then what?"

An intense look overtook his face. "Whatever needs to be done to protect what's mine."

I started toward the cabin but paused. "You just referred to me and Aspen as yours. You realize that, right? No take backs."

"Shut the fuck up," he grumbled and stalked out into trees.

"Just know I won't let you forget that subconscious slip," I shouted over my shoulder.

Jogging along the path, I leapt up the few steps, fist already raised to pound on the door. Only it swung open before I could make contact. Which really sucked because my momentum kept me moving forward, stumbling inside.

"What the hell?" she shouted as I skidded to a stop.

Whirling around like nothing happened, like I didn't just trip and barge into her cabin, I pointed to the door. "Shut it." Eyes wide, she slammed it shut. "Lock it." Without looking away, she reached out and flipped the deadbolt.

Once that little safety measure was in place, I stomped to the back door to ensure those were locked up tight.

"What the hell?" she repeated, hands going to her hips.

"Sorry, we were on our way to collect you—"

"I'm not a garbage can on the curb."

I snorted a half laugh. "Fine, we were on our way to get you." I arched a brow to make sure that wording suited her. With a smirk, she nodded and gestured for me to continue. "When Miles sensed something off around your cabin."

She stilled and quickly jerked her gaze away. "Oh, really-ly?" she mused while playing with the ends of her hair. "That's strange."

Her tone, posture, fucking everything was off. Stalking toward her, I moved into her line of vision. "What aren't you telling me?"

She waved me off but chewed on her lower lip, an anxious tic. "It's probably nothing," she said with a forced laugh that wouldn't fool anyone.

With a low growl, I crowded her back until her spine flattened against the wall, forearms pressed on either side of her head, caging her in with no escape. Holding her unbelieving gaze, I leaned in close. "Tell me."

"And here I thought Miles was the bossy one," she snarked, chewing on her lip again.

"Aspen," I demanded, my tone sharp.

She blew out a raspberry and rolled her eyes. "It's really nothing."

"I'll be the judge of that."

Eyes narrowed, she huffed. "Fine. Last night, I was headed to the main building—"

"Aspen." I pressed my forehead to hers. For a moment, I stood there savoring the simple contact. "Why did you leave the cabin after I dropped you off?"

Pushing me back, she crossed both arms in front of her chest, and a stubborn glint flickered in her eyes. "Why shouldn't I have walked around the area when it was still fucking light outside, Aiden? Remember, I am an adult, fully capable of taking care of myself."

"You are, but still, what was so important that you left the safety of your cabin to walk around alone?"

With her lips pursed and a death glare leveled right at me, I almost retreated a step at the steam practically coming out of her ears. "I needed something personal, okay? And had a wonderful glass of wine at the bar while I was there. It was fine. I was fine, but..."

"But what?"

Both hands tossed in the air, she finally relented. "But when I was walking along the path toward the main building, at one point or another, it felt like I was being followed or watched, maybe. It was probably my imagination, though."

She mentioned the feeling of being in possible danger so nonchalantly that frustration boiled in my veins. Gazes locked in an unspoken standoff, neither of us looked away until the front door vibrated—fuck, the entire cabin shook at the pounding on the other side. Knowing full well who it was, I sidestepped around Aspen to release the deadbolt. The edge clipped my forearm before I could yank my arm back when the door burst open with enough force that it dented the opposite wall.

Miles's large frame filled the doorway, sweeping an assessing look around the cabin. Aspen's gaze turned glassy, her breathing picking up as she gave him a slow perusal from the tip of his boots to the beard he trimmed earlier just for the trip while I studied her reaction. Seemed someone liked intense Miles a whole lot.

A quick glance at me, then her, taking in our stiff posture and tension between us, and he arched a single dark brow in silent question.

"Find anything?" I asked, shifting out of his way for when he marched to where Aspen stood, which would certainly happen after I dropped the information bomb she shared with me before he arrived. Miles shook his head, his only movement as he waited for me to explain what he just walked into. "Oh, and interestingly enough, after I dropped Aspen off last night, she went out on a little adventure to the main building. She said she felt like she was being watched or followed at one point. Not sure if I mentioned this or not... she went alone."

Aspen tossed up both hands and grumbled under her breath. Miles's eyes narrowed to thin slits and locked on her, which had Aspen's widening to the size of dinner plates. He cleared the distance between them in two quick strides and crowded her against the wall like I had seconds earlier.

With a pleased smile, I settled on the couch and stretched out both arms wide along the back to watch the show, wishing I had some popcorn to go with the inevitable entertainment.

Things were about to get spicy.

"You. Did. What?" Miles clipped, voice deceptively soft.

"You're both acting like I tried to pet a mama moose, cuddle a damn bear, or accepted candy from a guy in a white panel van. It was a short walk to the main building to get what I needed. Nothing scary or dangerous happened." Though the way her voice dropped with each word signaled that wasn't exactly true. "I'm here, unharmed, after walking there and back—"

"Did you feel eyes on you on the way back too?" Miles cut in.

"Just on the walk there," she whispered, chin tipped up so she could meet his hard stare. "And I don't appreciate you two making me feel like I did something wrong when I didn't."

Miles blinked in utter astonishment at her single finger pressed to the center of his chest.

"It wasn't safe to go out alone at night like that," he borderline growled. "I don't want you taking your safety so lightly. What if there was a bear—"

"Obviously, I'd do what you should do in that situation. Offer it honey and make it my best friend," she sassed with an eye roll, hands going to her hips.

"Oh shit," I snickered. "You've done it now, sweetheart. Hope you like hiking with a sore bottom, because that's his favorite way to punish naughty girls like you."

"What?" she squeaked, frantic gaze bouncing between me and Miles. "You cannot be serious right now. I did nothing wrong."

"But you put yourself in danger, so..." I gestured to the fuming Miles. "You made the decision, and now you have to reap the consequences."

My friend leaned in until his lips pressed to her ear, whispering something I couldn't hear despite leaning forward and angling my good ear in their direction to catch his words. Whatever was said had her cheeks flaring bright red and lips parting on a soft gasp.

A hand flew up to cover her open mouth. "You wouldn't dare."

Miles's responding smirk was sharp. "Fucking watch me. Now turn that ass around and place both palms on the wall for me." His deep tone rumbled around the room, leaving no room for argument.

A needy groan rattled up my throat. I shifted along the

stiff couch, gripping my throbbing cock to adjust where it pressed against the fly of my pants. How in the fuck was I hard as stone and everyone's clothes were still on?

"You're p-playing with me," Aspen stuttered in utter shock—and maybe a healthy surge of arousal based on the way she clenched her thighs together.

"Nope. Do as I said, baby girl, or you'll earn additional licks to that perfect backside."

Wide dark eyes shifted my way, drifting to my lap, where my hand was wrapped around my cock still tucked away inside my jeans. I studied her reaction to ensure there wasn't a hint of hesitation or fear lingering there. Yesterday, she gave carte blanche consent and promised to let us know when we took it too far, so we had to trust her to know her own limits and say something if she wasn't on board.

Having waited long enough for her to comply of her own free will, Miles wrapped both hands around her waist and whirled her around with ease. Both of her palms slapped to the wall, preventing her from falling over when he jerked her hips back. A hand tangled in her long hair, he forced her chin to tip up and back into an arch, shoving her perfect peach-shaped ass higher in the air.

"You say stop, and we stop. Understood?" Miles grated out through clenched teeth. At her whispered yes, he hitched his chin my way. "Want to help me serve out her punishment for taking unnecessary risks?"

"It was necessary—" The loud smack to her right cheek cut off her words, followed by a high-pitched squeal. "I needed a razor, you assholes."

Miles smacked her other cheek with just as much force as the first. "All you had to do was call us, and we would've gone to fucking Seattle to get you one. When you committed to giving this a try, you signed up for us taking care of you—in every way."

Not needing to be asked twice, I leapt off the couch, pausing next to Miles to wait for directions. This side of Miles was a fucking blast, and I couldn't wait to find out what he had planned for both me and Aspen. What Aspen probably didn't realize was that she scared Miles, and this was how he responded. He needed to remind her that she was important and regain some semblance of control over the whole situation.

Maybe this was his version of therapy.

"Since you weren't aware that you should call or text us, that we'd do anything for you if you asked, today's punishment will lean more toward the pleasure side than pain." Aspen whispered a curse and dropped her head as far forward as Miles's grip on her hair would allow. "But don't get me wrong, baby girl. You're still getting this ass spanked. We'll just have Aiden sweeten the deal."

"I like the sound of that," I said, stroking a single finger along Aspen's cheek. "What do you have in mind?"

His free hand moved around her waist, slipped under her long-sleeved shirt, and pressed to her bare skin. Aspen's gasp turned into a needy whine as his fingers danced along her stomach, playing with the waistband of her pants.

A wide grin spread across Miles's face. "How about you eat her tasty cunt while I spank her ass until she remembers that we're always here for her and her safety should always take priority, no matter the situation?"

"Yes," Aspen rasped between heavy breaths. "Solid plan. Ten out of ten, five stars, and a stamp of approval on this plan."

With an arched brow directed my way, Miles landed a third hard open-palm smack to her ass. The sound echoed around the room, almost covering Aspen's string of muttered curses. Almost.

"I don't need your sass." He leaned in close until his hard dick tenting his jeans rubbed against her sore backside. "And it's 'Yes, sir' during punishments or when I'm inside you. Understood?"

Hand shoved down the front of my pants, I squeezed my dick hard at the familiar sensation of an oncoming orgasm. "Fucking hell, man, watch your words. You're going to make me come in my damn pants."

Miles's hazel eyes rolled to the ceiling at my dramatics. "You took care of yourself fine with nothing but your hand yesterday after she rode your lap, and for the last thirty damn years. I'm sure you can do the same thing again while you kneel to eat her pussy."

I could only blink at him.

Holy fuck.

Did I just die and end up in threesome heaven?

"If you're done whining, get on your knees and help me bare her to us so we can get started."

Dipping beneath her arm, I stood so Aspen was between us and pressed my lips to hers in a searing kiss. "You ready for this?"

Pupils blown wide, lips parted and swollen, she nodded.

"Good, because I dreamed of how you would taste all night. Let's find out if I was right."

I dropped to the hardwood floor in front of her, never looking away from those dark eyes of hers. Cupping the back of her thighs, I slowly slid both hands up until they reached her waistband, fingers toying with the top button.

Time to find out if my dream was right.

15

MILES

Heart slamming in my chest, I watched with rapt attention as Aiden's fingers popped the top button of her pants loose and slowly worked the zipper down, exposing a peek of teal lace panties. Lungs tight, as if I'd run a marathon with zero training, I couldn't take a full breath. Every concern vanished. My only thought was seeing what hid beneath that lace.

My fingers flexed, tightening around Aspen's thick hair as Aiden worked the dark gray quick-dry hiking pants over her ass, exposing smooth skin. I swallowed a groan and reached down to shift my hard dick to relieve some of the near-painful pressure. A sweet scent wafted through the room when Aiden shoved the material down her thighs until it bunched above her knees. I greedily inhaled, savoring the scent of her arousal, needing it imprinted on my lungs and stored in every damn cell so it would be a part of me forever.

"Holy fuck," Aiden rasped, staring at the apex of her thighs.

Adjusting my stance, I leaned to the side, a guttural

groan rumbling in my chest at finally laying eyes on her gorgeous, shaved pussy. Her mentioning needing a razor now made sense.

"Look at your pretty little pussy." He trailed a knuckle along her shaved mound. "Did you shave this for us?" She barely nodded because of my firm grip. "You're so fucking perfect for us, sweetheart." Leaning forward, he pressed a reverent kiss to the top of her glistening slit, already wet with arousal, while peering up through his lashes to watch her reaction. "I'm looking forward to licking all this up with my face buried between your thighs."

In an erotic-as-hell demonstration, he swiped a thick finger through her arousal and held the slick digit up for me to see it glisten in the bright cabin lighting. Without second-guessing myself, I snapped out a hand, fingers wrapping around his wrist, and jerked it higher toward my face. Aspen's hooded gaze followed the movement, lips parting in a desperate moan as she watched me slip Aiden's finger between my lips, sucking her essence off him.

My chest rumbled in pleasure, lids fluttering closed as her sweet and salty taste invaded my mouth.

Heaven.

Pure fucking heaven.

No. It was better than that. She tasted like...

Home.

Releasing my hold on Aiden's wrist, I shifted back behind her, attention zeroing in on where my palm caressed her round ass. Grabbing a handful, I watched, mesmerized, as her flesh spilled between my fingers.

"Fucking gorgeous," I murmured, more to myself than for anyone else to hear.

"My thoughts exactly," Aiden muttered. Looking down, I found him spreading her wide with both his thumbs, a dreamy, heated expression on his face. "I think we both need a grip, don't you?"

I hummed my approval, knowing exactly what he suggested, and hell yes, I was down. With a not-so-gentle tug on her hair, smirking at her soft gasp, I leaned forward to whisper in her ear. "What do you think about that, baby girl? Want both our fingers in that tight cunt to keep you steady while I spank this ass?"

"Yes," she basically whimpered. I tightened my hold on her hair, pulling it even harder in warning. She hissed. "Yes, sir."

"Good girl." She relaxed a fraction, telling me she loved the tiny praise. I filed that bit of knowledge away for later. "Now, spread those knees as wide as you can for us." A satisfied smile tugged at my lips when she instantly complied, all the sass from earlier gone.

Aiden slid the tip of a single digit into her opening, teasing her with the minimal penetration. Her soul-vibrating moaned curses had me chuckling. His mop of hair shifted as he pitched forward on his knees and sealed his mouth over her pretty pink pussy, no doubt sucking that swollen clit based on her stiffening muscles. The clink of metal had me huffing a laugh, knowing exactly what Aiden's other hand would do while he played with her.

Again, I skimmed a hand along her ass, though this time right between both cheeks, then used my thick fingers to spread them apart. My dick twitched in my pants, desperate to be free at the sight of her tight back hole. *Soon*, I told myself, if she was open to it. Damn, I hoped she was. I continued toward her core until my fingers bumped against Aiden's as they pushed into her. Careful not to hurt her with too much at once, I eased a single finger inside her tight cunt, right alongside my best friend's. My lids slammed shut, and my hips flexed forward, dry humping the fucking air at the feel of her snug, slick walls.

"Just imagine what she'll feel like around our cocks," Aiden said, words muffled with his face still pressed between her thighs.

In and out, we worked our fingers in tandem until her knees shook and soft, begging moans filled the cabin. Releasing her hair, I moved to the side just enough to take a half swing and smacked my hand on top of her right ass cheek.

Her sharp cry and the tightening of her pussy around our fingers as she came spurred me on, fueling the demanding need flowing through my veins.

Again and again, I spanked her pink ass, alternating quick smacks to each cheek until both were cherry red. Knowing she was close to a third or fourth orgasm, I slid a finger down between her cheeks and lightly pressed against her back hole.

That did it.

Her screaming my name and the walls of her cunt tightening around my finger as she convulsed nearly had me coming in my pants like Aiden almost did earlier. A pleased sound hummed in my throat as I squatted until my face was in line with her ass. Pressing a gentle kiss to each cheek, I stood and gripped her hair again, this time right at the base of her neck so I could angle her head to the side.

I only gave myself a second to take in her flushed face, glassy eyes, and drooped lids before I slammed my lips onto hers for a brutal kiss. I poured all the need and want for her out of myself and into her, letting her feel exactly what she did to me.

What only she alone had invoked in too long.

Lightheaded, breathing ragged, I forced myself to pull away before I devoured her whole.

"I...," she panted with a lost look on her face. "Have never done that before."

I smirked and curled the finger still inside her, making her gasp. Pulling it free, I lifted the drenched digit to my lips and sucked it between them, swirling my tongue to clean off every delicious drop.

"Holy fuck," she breathed.

I nodded in agreement but didn't say a word.

Her lids slammed shut, and a moan escaped, her whole body shuddering followed by Aiden's grunt, telling me he'd had his own fun too. Though who wouldn't with that taste on your tongue and her pussy between your lips? A thump sounded when Aiden sat back, spine slamming to the wall with a dazed, almost blitzed-out goofy grin on his shiny mouth. Dick still in his hand, eyes closed, and a satisfied look on his face, I knew he was good.

With careful movements, I slowly slid her pants back up her thighs and secured the zipper and button despite my reluctance to cover her up.

Now that I'd had a taste of her and felt her slick, tight walls, all kinds of images of what we three could do together invaded my every thought. There was no going back now. I wanted it all with her and Aiden. I hated to admit I was wrong or that Aiden was right about me being scared to open up to Aspen. If having this all the time meant exposing the ugly side of myself to her, I knew it would be worth it. Though if that backfired, then I'd probably never crawl out of the dark hole I occasionally found myself trapped inside.

Lifting Aspen into my arms, I carefully carried her to the couch and sat, securing her on my lap. Her head fell to my shoulder, and a satisfied sigh pushed past her parted lips.

For several seconds, we all sat in peaceful, content silence until she shifted to get more comfortable, adjusting her backside against my painfully stiff cock.

I knew the moment she felt me, as she instantly stilled. Her small palm on my sternum, she pushed herself back as her dark eyes scanned my face with an adorable little frown curving the corners of her lips.

A shuffling sound across the room had her gaze sliding to Aiden, his dick thankfully tucked away once again, who had squatted low to clean up his mess with the white bath towel he found somewhere in the cabin. When she swung her attention back my way, questions swirled in her worried gaze.

"Don't," I murmured and ran a hand over her head. "I'm all good, baby girl."

The way her lips pressed into a firm line told me she didn't agree. Without uttering a word, she moved her ass against my leaking cock again while watching for my reaction. I ground my teeth, a sharp hiss escaping as I fought the urge to explode in my pants.

Taking pity on me—thank fuck, because I couldn't hold off the certain orgasm much longer with her doing that—Aspen moved off my lap. Squeezing both lids shut, I mentally walked through the steps of disassembling an assault rifle to help calm my cock down enough to where I could walk normally.

The brush of pressure along my belt had my eyes snapping open.

I nearly swallowed my tongue at the sight of Aspen kneeling between my spread thighs, fingers hesitantly working at the belt's clasp. I opened my mouth to tell her to stop, that I hated being touched, but the words wouldn't come. In fact, my dick hardened even more, the painful throb increasing at the closeness of her hands and mouth.

"Please," she whispered while holding my intense stare. "Let me..." She paused and licked her lips like she was unsure of her next words. "Please let me be your good girl now, sir."

My cock twitched, and I tightened both hands into fists where they rested on the couch to keep from reaching out to her. Done cleaning, Aiden watched from by the door, eyes wide, almost frozen in place, probably afraid that if he moved, it would break whatever spell she'd weaved over me. It had to be some kind of magic, because there was no other reason why I would now help her unfasten the final two buttons on my pants and willingly lift my hips off the couch for her to tug the thin fabric over my hips, freeing my rock-hard cock. Knowing any farther would expose the burn scars that marred my thighs, I sat hard, keeping the pants where they were.

"Wow," Aspen whispered, gazing wide-eyed at my dick. The awe in her voice prompted me to fist the steel-hard length and give it a harsh tug, just the way I liked it. "I don't think that will fit... anywhere."

My laugh was deep and dark, rumbling around the room. "Oh, baby girl, there are at least three places on you that I know it will." Long dark lashes fanned down her face as she gaped at me. "You have me where you want me. Now, what are you going to do?"

Palms on my thighs for support, she pitched forward, swiping her devilish tongue across the head to greedily lap up the dripping precum. Her hum of approval nearly did me in, forcing me to grit my teeth to keep from ending it all too soon. Peeling my fingers away, she removed my hand to replace it with her own, gripping the base in a firm hold while she sucked me past those lush lips.

A hissed string of curses exploded out of me, my hips flexing off the couch to shove more of my length deeper into her mouth. A tap against my hand had me looking away from where her lips wrapped around me. Gripping two fingers, she guided me to palm the back of her head.

My fingers flexed in her hair, delving into the silky strands. "You are my good girl, aren't you?" I praised. "Let's see how much of me can fit in that mouth of yours." Her hum of approval had me clenching my jaw. "This won't take long," I huffed.

Holding her in place by her hair, I tilted my hips up while urging her down to take more of my cock. I cursed when she gagged, throat constricting tightly around me when I hit the back of her throat. Easing back, I repeated the motion each time, working a little more of my cock into her mouth and down her throat.

"Fucking hell, I can feel you swallowing," I grunted. Reaching my free hand down, I collared her throat and squeezed lightly the next time I went deep. The added pressure, along with her hot, slick mouth engulfing me, had a zap of tingling pleasure shooting down my spine and hitting me right in the balls. "Fuck, I'm going to come, baby girl. Pull back if you don't want to swallow." Staring down at her, I licked my lips and waited for her gaze to lock on me. "Because if I come in your mouth, I want you to swallow every drop."

Her lids fluttered closed, and she responded by taking me deeper than ever without my help.

I was done for.

Utterly fucking done for when it came to this amazing woman.

With a guttural groan, I came hard, holding her while I fucked her mouth until the very last tremble faded. Energy spent, I slumped back against the couch. Chest heaving with every labored breath, I stared wide-eyed at Aspen as she wiped the corners of her smiling lips.

Yep, I was 100 percent lost on her now.

And I knew without a doubt that the more I got to know her, feel her, have her, the deeper I'd fall.

Somehow, my soul was at peace with this strange and crazy turn of events.

I just needed my brain to catch up and jump on board too.

Then form a plan with Aiden to keep her here in Anchor Bay.

With us.

For good.

16

ASPEN

My wide, full-face smile didn't drop even as I huffed along the steep trail. At this point, my cheeks ached, considering the dopey grin started after the unexpected activities in the cabin. It wasn't because of the very fun time we had—well, that put the grin there, but the breathtaking scenery all around me had locked it firmly in place.

Then there was Jubie happily trotting beside us as we moved along the trail, rotating between who she would walk with. There was no contest that she was the best dog I'd ever been around. I would for sure miss her companionship when I left in less than a week.

Well, fuck, that thought dulled my radiating joy. Remembering that all this was temporary and would end sooner than I'd like had the wide smile fading as a melancholy feeling settled over me for the rest of the hike. Even as I snapped photos that I knew would turn out great, capturing the surrounding beauty, I couldn't bring myself to appreciate it the way I had earlier.

With a resigned exhale, I took a sip from my water bottle and leaned against a nearby tree, the thick bark digging into my skin despite the long-sleeved shirt. It hurt as a dull ache filled my chest just thinking about leaving the beautiful state and all its magnificent views behind for a pollution-riddled, lonely big city. I glanced over my shoulder at the two men who had started to set up our camp for the night.

Indeed, too beautiful and perfect to leave behind.

I turned back to view the valley below us, the wide, roaring river snaking through it. Unfocused stare locked on the moving water, my thoughts wandered to all my options, good and bad, for when my trip was over. It was too crazy to even consider staying, right? Wasn't that exactly what happened with that Jessica woman who became too obsessed with them and didn't leave?

I swallowed hard and took another drink to clear the lump in my throat. Just the thought of Aiden and Miles moving on, doing what we've done, sharing in the same heartfelt conversations, and laughing with someone other than me had my chest tightening with an unsettled feeling. It wasn't jealousy but worry that maybe I was putting too much of myself into all this, feeling more than what they were.

That would really suck hairy bear balls. To feel this deeply about them and share what we'd shared, just for it to mean little to them. It had only been three days, but it felt like we were all on the same page, or maybe I misread the whole situation and this was what they did all the time, no matter the woman. There was the chance that, in their minds, I was simply a convenient hole to fill. A willing woman who enjoyed the same things they did and was open to being shared.

"Gorgeous, isn't it?"

I startled, too lost in thought to notice Aiden's approach. "What?" I refused to look his away. "Oh, the view, yeah. Gorgeous," I mumbled.

He studied me out of the corner of his eye. "Did you get some good photos today?"

I just nodded, still too lost in the idea of me being in way deeper than them to really voice a response.

"All right," he said, stepping in front of me to block my view—not that I was actually seeing any of it, too wrapped up in my awful thoughts. Though, with his handsome face hovering over mine and those honey-brown eyes gazing down at me, my focus had shifted to him. "Out with it, Aspen. What's going round and round in that mind of yours?" He tapped my temple before tucking a loose lock of hair behind my ear.

"What makes you say there's something on my mind that I need to get out?" He wasn't wrong, but it was a shock that he noticed.

"Because all day today, you've been on cloud nine—"

"Life-altering orgasms by two hot guys will do that to a girl," I muttered under my breath, making him chuckle.

"Well, yes, there was that, but it was more too. You couldn't stop smiling during the hike. I swear, a few times I caught tears in your eyes as we passed some of the more breathtaking views of the mountains." He wasn't wrong, and I wouldn't apologize for getting emotional about nature's beauty. "But now there's this"—he slid a finger along my cheek and jaw—"pensive look. So, tell me what's wrong."

I chewed on my lower lip until he tugged it free with his thumb.

"Aiden," I rasped, my nerves making my throat thick and

mouth dry. I didn't want to ask, not when it could ruin what we had going on. I was having fun and wanted that to continue, but I also needed to know where they stood in all this before I sank any more into their orbit. "Am I just another hookup, a fun time, to you and Miles?" He scanned my face, brows pulled in tight. "If I am, that's okay. I just need to know, you know?" I cringed, knowing I sounded like a whiny idiot who had gotten addicted to them. From their touch to their company, everything about them drew me in deeper.

"You think with all the stories we've shared, the time we've spent with you, and what happened this morning between the three of us that this is a normal hookup for us?"

I shot him an incredulous look and rolled my eyes. "Well, yeah. You and Miles do this kind of thing all the time. I just need to know so I can protect myself and—"

A shocked gasp escaped my parted lips when Aiden stepped closer, crowding me toward the tree until my spine pressed against the rough bark.

"Sweetheart, this is different. What we have with you is nowhere close to what we've done in the past."

"You don't have to lie to me," I whispered, searching his face for any hint of deception. "I'm a big girl. I can take the truth."

"Then listen to it when I give it to you," he gritted out. "What we've done with other women was nothing, and I mean fucking *nothing*, close to what we've shared with you. The others were just..." He tipped his face to the sky with a controlled breath. "I don't want to say they were just convenient, because that's disrespectful to those women, but that's exactly what it was. We discussed up front that there was no relationship potential. They were no-strings-attached hookups, and they were on board with that."

"But you didn't have that conversation with me," I stated. "You only talked about wanting to spend time with me and the sharing part."

He nodded, focused over my shoulder, where I heard Miles still setting up the campsite. "We didn't because, for me and Miles, we both knew this and you were different. We didn't want to think about only having you once and then walking away. This is so much more than that. Don't you feel it?"

The imploring expression lining his face had me forgetting my earlier reservation and nodding. "I do feel it, so much that it scares me."

"What are you scared of?"

"Of this being more to me than to you two. Of getting my heart broken. Of considering a life change because of a few great days with two guys who might up and leave me the second someone better comes along or they get tired of me."

"First, we won't leave or get tired of you. If anything, it might be the other way around. And second, yes. Hell fucking yes, keep thinking about that life change, of not leaving."

I froze. Not even my lungs worked as I stared up at him in disbelief. "What are you saying?"

"I'm saying we want you, Aspen, all of you, for more than just this week. If that means figuring out a long-distance situation, then we'll do it. Just, at the end of your time here in Anchor Bay, don't say goodbye for good."

"We just met," I countered, not really sure why. Did I really want to talk him out of wanting me, of figuring things out after my vacation was over?

"It doesn't feel that way, though, does it?" The tip of my ponytail swished along the back of my neck with a slow headshake. "It feels right. Fuck, everything feels right when you're around. And..." He considered me for a few seconds before continuing. "I love my best friend." The conviction and emotion that thickened his voice had tears burning behind my eyes. "When he's with you—hell, even when you're just on his mind—he's different. Happy even. I want that for him. He deserves it more than any man I know."

"What about you?" I asked, reaching up to cradle his jaw in a single palm.

Light lashes fluttered closed while his chest rose with a deep inhale.

"I don't want you to leave because you make the silence quiet." I blinked, not sure what he meant by that. "When I'm alone or even with others around, the lulls or quiet stir up every regret and all the guilt I've compiled through my life, terrible memories, everything I try to lock away. I couldn't even appreciate this amazing state most of the time because of the silence that came with it. Until you." A single tear leaked out of the corner of my eye. "From that first drive to the resort, you quieted my demons with just your presence. You soothe the broken and jagged parts of me that are left." Reaching out, he grabbed my hand and brought it to his chest. "I can finally fucking breathe without nearly drowning in my guilt."

I slid my hand up his chest, around his neck, and cupped the back of his head to urge his mouth down to my own. He came willingly, soft lips pressing against mine in an emotional kiss that I felt deep in my soul.

And the apex of my thighs.

After earlier, it seemed the floodgates on my hormones had burst open, and even this simple, beautiful kiss had heat racing through my veins and my core pulsing.

As if sensing the shift, Aiden grabbed my ass and lifted until my legs wrapped around his waist. A quick gasp escaped, swallowed quickly by his urgent kisses, when my back once again pressed to the rough tree bark.

I pulled away to catch my breath, allowing Aiden access to kiss along my throat. My gaze slid toward the makeshift campsite where I zeroed in on Miles, who was now just a few steps away, perched on a massive rock with his intense stare locked on us and a daring smirk on his lips.

My heart racing a thousand beats a second, I held his hooded gaze. Despite the chill in the air from our high elevation, sweat slicked my skin from the radiating heat pouring off Aiden, adding to the inferno scorching my veins.

"No one out here but us, baby girl." Miles's deep, rumbling voice sent a bolt of desire racing down my spine. "Well, us and that moose down there."

My head snapped around so fast it hit the tree while trying to see past Aiden to the valley. His humor-filled chuckle vibrated against my skin as he placed a soft kiss beneath my ear.

"Never thought my best friend, with the assist of a damn moose, would be the ultimate cockblock." With one more soft kiss to my lips, he eased his firm hold on my ass, slowly lowering my feet back to the ground. "Yet here we are."

"Damnit," I grumbled. "My camera is—"

Miles stood and held out my camera case. "Right here. With the sun setting and the angle, I assumed you'd want to grab some shots."

"Thank you." Carefully taking the most expensive item I owned from his hands, I quickly worked it free from the protective case and powered it on. Standing on the edge of a cliff that offered the best overlook of the valley below, I raised the camera and snapped a test picture before checking the viewing screen to see what I needed to adjust.

Needing a better angle, I moved, the loose dirt beneath

my boots shifting, throwing me slightly unbalanced. My heart dropped, breath caught in that half a second as I tilted forward. Before a terrified sound could escape, two large hands gripped my waist and tightened, pulling me against a firm chest.

Looking up and over my shoulder, I smiled at Aiden. "Thanks for the save." But when I pulled out of his arms, he only allowed a single step. I shot him a look, to which he responded with an exaggerated shrug.

"You do your thing. Focus on the pictures you want. I'll be here to make sure you don't fall to your untimely death."

"I thought you guys were a part of an adventure *and* rescue company. Are you saying you wouldn't rescue me if I took a little tumble?"

"I'm saying I'd rather keep you close so I don't have to feel that minor heart attack again like I just did when you slipped. Let me have some peace of mind, yeah? I won't bother you or get in your way. I just want to be here close, just in case."

My teeth sank deep into my lower lip, and I fought my wide grin as I turned back around. "Okay."

"Plus, I'll take every opportunity to have my hands on you."

"And there it is." I laughed. With a slight headshake, I raised the camera to my face. "Ready to potentially save me from myself?"

"Always, sweetheart. Always."

"THAT ONE," Miles said, pointing at the viewing screen, his arm brushing along mine. "That's the one where you somehow captured the majesty of this place."

I clicked to the next picture, which was a snapshot of a particular bird Aiden had excitedly pointed out on the hike earlier. I had no idea how the man could get any more adorable, but he constantly surprised me by upping his cuteness factor, like being an avid birdwatcher.

Going to the next picture, I tensed, knowing Miles didn't know I had taken one of him and Aiden earlier. Aiden's arm was draped over Miles's wide shoulders as they hiked ahead of me. With the light shining around them, it was a beautiful picture of two best friends. You could practically feel the love and trust they had for each other in the photo itself.

Biting my lip to hide the growing smile, I turned to look over my shoulder at Miles. His attention was still on the camera when I leaned in and placed a quick kiss to his cheek before turning back around and settling back against him once more.

Did they pack me a camping chair? Yes.

Was it set up and just on the other side of the small firepit? Yes.

Was I using it? No.

Before I could sit in my seat, Miles pulled me onto his lap and wrapped an arm around my waist, preventing me from getting up. Not that I tried. No, being in his arms, relaxed against his solid chest, was way too comfortable to fight.

"This is a keeper for sure," I murmured. "You two look happy and at peace out here."

"Looks can be deceiving," he whispered. "Though with you here, maybe that picture rings a little more true than before."

"You weren't happy?" I asked. Shifting on his lap, I angled myself to face Miles.

Lips in a tight line, he stared into the billowing smoke

coming off the fire. Apparently, there was an herb that you could add to a fire so the smoke would keep the summer bugs and mosquitoes away.

"I would say *surviving* or *existing* is the right word for what we were doing before you arrived in Anchor Bay."

"And now?" I asked, voice tight with emotion as I studied his face.

He reached up and brushed a few strands of dark hair off my face that the wind had jostled free. Gazing into my soul, he held that intense stare for a few seconds before responding. "Now, I have hope for more. But..."

Cupping his strong jaw, I brushed a thumb over his beard, loving the way it felt on my skin. "But what?"

"I know it won't last."

"Because I'm leaving?"

He shook his head, lids falling closed as if he couldn't bear to look at me while he said his next words. "Because when you see just how shattered I am inside and out, you'll walk away. And I can't risk that, can't risk you taking those last slivers of hope I have when you leave. I'll be beyond saving at that point."

Tears flooded my lower lids, but I refused to let them fall. Leaning in close, I brushed my lips against his in a barely there, supportive kiss.

"I can't promise I won't leave, because no one knows what tomorrow will bring. But I will promise you I won't walk away from you because of who you think you are. I might not have known you for long, but I see you, Miles Jackson. And the person you are in here"—I pressed a hand over his heart—"is someone worth fighting for."

His lips quirked upward. "And who are you planning to fight for me?"

"You. I'm going to fight you for the real man I know is inside you, the one beneath whatever you're afraid of."

"I'm not afraid," he rasped.

"Okay, big guy, you're not afraid." Patting his chest, I turned back around. "But don't hold back. Show me everything you are. Because I'm not afraid either, and I think you'll be surprised at how amazing it will be when you let go of whatever is holding you back."

"What if you're wrong?" he whispered in my ear, causing a shiver to race down my spine.

"What if I'm right? Isn't that enough to try?"

"How?" The word was more of a hiss that escaped through his clenched teeth.

"Start small. Tell me something small that maybe you haven't told anyone other than your best friend. We could start like that, every day sharing something about each other that we've kept buried or hidden from everyone else."

The wood in the fire crackled, the only sound besides the buzzing bugs all around the campsite. We sat in silence for so long that I wondered if I'd pushed him too far, asked too much.

"I'm not sure anything about what I've been through is small."

"How about you tell me why Aiden always looks shell-shocked when you touch me or when I touch you?" It was something I'd noticed several times, even tonight when Miles had pulled me down onto his lap. Aiden had frozen where he was lowering into his own chair, eyes wide and fixed on where we touched.

Once again, silence settled between us, but this time, I didn't allow worry to worm its way in. It seemed Miles needed a few seconds to gather his thoughts, and I needed to be patient, allowing him that time since this was clearly a sensitive topic, and exposing the deeper sides of him was a new challenge.

"Because when we've shared in the past—hell, since I got out of the hospital and left the Navy—I haven't allowed anyone to touch me. A handshake or something small isn't a big deal, but skin to skin, or something more intimate, has been a solid no for years."

Brows furrowed, I studied him over my shoulder. "Then how did you share?"

Something like worry flickered behind his eyes. "I just watched."

"Watched," I repeated like an idiot. "So, how did you... enjoy it?" I cringed, making laughter rumble in his chest. He lifted a single hand and wiggled his fingers, giving me a pointed look. "Oh. Oh," I whispered. My mind immediately went to earlier, my face heating. "So, today when I... you know. You didn't want that—"

He cuffed the back of my neck and pulled me close until our noses brushed. "It was fucking amazing. Don't you dare question that. I could've said no, but I didn't. You on your knees for me, feeling your hot, wet mouth around my cock, knowing the remarkable woman who touched me made it everything to me. Not *okay* but fucking *everything*. Aiden is shocked by how I go out of my way to touch you because I can't stop. I crave the feel of your skin, your lips on mine, and ever since this morning, I can't stop fantasizing about fucking that perfect mouth again and dreaming about filling your tight cunt that squeezed the fuck out of my fingers with my cock, over and over and over again." My breaths came in quick, shallow pants. "I want to feel you beneath me, feel you all around me, touch you everywhere you'll let me, and press the boundaries of what you're embarrassed to crave."

"Holy fuck," I rasped, sweat now beading along my forehead and causing my shirt to stick to my back.

"I want it all, with you and Aiden. And that's all because of you, Aspen. No one else has ever tempted me, pushed me, made me fucking *want* it like you do. I'm not ready to tell you everything, but that... that is my one share for the day."

I nodded and glanced toward the other occupied chair, where Aiden sat on the opposite side of the flickering flames, his gaze fixed on the small fire. Almost as if he felt my stare, his honey-colored eyes shifted and met mine, a small, forced smile pulling at his lips. Worry churned in my gut, wondering what had happened to the happy, laughing man from earlier.

Miles's arm tightened around my waist as his lips brushed along my ear. "Don't worry about him. He gets lost in his head sometimes."

I nodded. He'd alluded to that earlier, but I was confused about why. What caused him to get lost in that guilt and regret he said drowned him daily? "He mentioned something about that but not why."

"Because he thinks it's his fault that I am the way I am." My lips parted, ready to ask why Aiden would feel that way, but Miles wrapped his fingers around my throat and tightened. Urging me to lie back against his chest, my head resting against his shoulder, Miles's other hand slipped beneath my shirt, settling a rough palm over my stomach. "I have an idea of how to pull him out of his head." I stilled as Miles's fingers dipped beneath the waistband of my pants. "You want to play, baby girl?"

"Yes, sir," I barely pushed out with my erratic breaths and his hold around my throat.

"That's my good girl."

Holy fuck.

It was official.

I was the luckiest woman on the planet.

And I intended to savor every second I had with these two men.

For now. But hopefully for longer than the three of us ever imagined.

17

AIDEN

All the memories, plus the sadness and regret that came along with them, vanished like they weren't just holding me hostage. Through the billowing smoke keeping our campsite bug-free and bursts of sparks, I watched as Miles did something that continued to take me by surprise despite him doing it multiple times in the last two days.

He touched her.

Willingly held her tight against him with a hand wrapped around her throat, lips against her ear, with his dark eyes locked on me, watching and gauging my reaction. Then his other hand dipped beneath her shirt and then her pants, and all thoughts focused on imagining what he planned to do next.

The chair creaked under my shifting weight when I adjusted my rock-hard dick to keep it from pushing against the zipper of my tech pants, tenting the front. Not that I cared if either of them saw how their connection and touch affected me. It was only us and the animals out here. If there was anyone close who shouldn't be, Jubie wouldn't be sleeping soundly next to Miles and Aspen.

"See that, baby girl," Miles said, loud enough for me to hear. He pressed a kiss against her temple. "Our distraction worked. You're all that's on his mind now."

That clever, meddling motherfucker.

I had the best friend on the damn planet.

"She wants to play," Miles said with a wink. "What do you say, brother?"

My heart clenched at the term that fit so well with how we felt about each other.

Standing, I adjusted myself. Not that it mattered. The thin material didn't hide just how turned on I was at watching Miles touch her. Moving in front of where Aspen sat on his lap, I squatted low, putting my face almost level with hers. I searched her glassy gaze and studied her flushed cheeks and parted lips.

"You like that idea, don't you?" I whispered while reaching out to dip a single finger beneath the collar of her shirt to trace along the base of her throat beneath Miles's hold. She nodded, licking her lips without looking away. "I think it's time we got to see all of this tempting body of yours, don't you?"

My knees cracked as I pushed to stand. I held out a hand to help her off Miles's lap, which she instantly took. She swayed on her feet for a second, and I grabbed her waist to keep her steady.

A sharp crack echoed through the air, loud enough that Jubie raised her head before lying back down with a huff.

Aspen's eyes widened, and her breath hitched when Miles spanked her ass again.

"If you can't tell, he's an ass man," I chuckled. Gripping the hem of her long-sleeved T-shirt, I waited a beat, giving her time to protest before lifting it up and over her head. Both arms went up willingly, allowing the thin material to slip off with ease, followed quickly by the tight black sports bra she wore underneath.

Without looking away from the most delicious-looking tits I'd ever seen, I tossed both articles of clothing to the chair she never occupied, not caring if they made it or not.

"I need a taste before I go any further," I murmured, more to myself than to her. Cupping her full breast, I pinched the already-pebbled tip, and she rewarded me with a sharp gasp. The rustle of clothing told me Miles took over undressing our girl from the waist down.

I paused where my lips hovered just over her nipple, which was begging me to pull it into my watering mouth, and looked up through my lashes, finding her gazing down at me.

Our girl.

That was exactly what she was—and hopefully would be for a hell of a lot longer than a few days. Just thinking about her leaving had me slipping out of the lust fog.

As if sensing me pulling away, a massive hand palmed the back of my head, taking me by surprise. Applying pressure, Miles guided me closer until my lips brushed against her soft skin, once again distracting me from my thoughts.

"Suck her into your mouth," he rumbled on the other side of Aspen. "You want that, don't you, baby girl? Want Aiden to suck on those needy tits of yours, biting and marking you as ours?"

Her guttural groan in response had my lips pulling up in a smile before I flicked out my tongue, teasing her hardened nipple with the tip. Squeezing her breast a little harder, I sucked her past my lips. My groan vibrated against her skin, making her gasp. Lost in the need for her,

I nipped and sucked before switching sides to do it all over again.

Aspen shifted, both her palms coming up to slap the top of my shoulders as if she needed me to stay upright. Pulling back just enough to look down her stomach, I muttered a curse at the sight of Miles's thick fingers moving in and out of her tight cunt.

"The animals are getting a show tonight," I chuckled. Reaching down, I gripped my hard cock over my pants and squeezed, hoping it would take the edge off a little.

"Come here," Miles demanded, pulling Aspen back down to his lap. "Take off her boots and finish with her pants."

I knew he said something. Words of some kind spilled from his mouth, but nothing made sense at seeing her thighs spread with Miles's hand between them while the other pinched and tugged at her nipples, still glistening from my spit.

"Aiden," he snapped. My gaze slowly lifted to his. "Boots, pants. Now."

Squatting once again, I untied one boot, then the other, pulling both off before reaching for her pants to toss them aside like the rest of her clothes.

"I think he needs to feel what your hot, dirty mouth can do to a cock," Miles murmured while kissing her neck. Just him saying it had my dick twitching from the zap of desire that raced down my spine, straight to my balls. "What do you think, baby girl? Want to show Aiden just how good a girl you are?"

A cry erupted as her muscles went stiff before slumping against Miles, chest flushed and heaving with every ragged breath.

"And what about you?" I asked, already working the button of my pants.

"I'm good right where I am," Miles rumbled against her skin.

Aspen's long dark lashes fluttered open, and a small frown pulled at her lips. Shifting to the side, she stared up at Miles. "What about what I want?"

He must have done something with the two fingers still buried deep inside her, because she gasped before narrowing her eyes.

"And what do you want, sweetheart?" I said, shoving my pants down to my thighs and gripping my dripping cock in a tight fist. She stared at where my hand moved up and down my shaft, making me grunt. "If you keep looking at me like that, I won't last long."

"I want..." She nervously cleared her throat. "I want both of you."

I arched a brow while dragging a thumb over the slick head, making me shiver. "Is that so?" She nodded. "How do you want us, then, sweetheart? We're at your command."

It was true. Whatever she wanted, it was hers. Hell, she could ask for my balls on a plate with a side of fucking rice and I'd gladly serve both up to her.

Instead of answering, she turned back to Miles, chewing on the corner of her lip as if she was afraid to ask for what she really wanted.

"Tell us what you want, baby girl." He leaned in and captured her lips, nipping at the same spot she was chewing. "You want both of us?" She nodded. "Like earlier?" Her head shook back and forth.

"I want you," she whispered, almost too quiet for me to hear.

"How do you want me?" Miles practically growled. He

dropped his hold on her breast to encircle her throat. "Tell me."

"I want you inside me while Aiden is in my mouth."

And like the cool guy I was at hearing those words in her soft voice, I choked on my own fucking spit. Coughing, I slammed a fist to my chest over and over. Not that Aspen noticed, Miles keeping her full focus on him by the hold on her throat.

"To be clear, you want me fucking your sweet cunt while Aiden fills your mouth with his cock, fucking your throat the same way I did earlier."

"Yes."

Miles's fingers shifted as he tightened his hold and arched a brow.

"Yes, sir," she rasped, barely able to get the words out.

His grip loosened and slid down to her chest to play with her tits again. "Such a good girl you are, Aspen. *Our* good girl."

"Yesss," she moaned, eyes squeezing shut as Miles pinched her tight nipple hard.

"You heard her." I reached out the hand not holding my dick and gripped her hand to lift her off Miles's lap. When she slammed into me, I cursed my shirt, the fucking material keeping me from feeling her bare skin pressed against mine. "Condom?" I asked over her shoulder to Miles, who was busy unbuckling his belt.

He grunted in acknowledgment, lifting his hips to dig one out of his back pocket while simultaneously jerking his pants down to his thighs. With a smirk, I whirled Aspen around so her back pressed to my chest. One hand cupped a full tit while the other snaked down her stomach to grab her pussy in a possessive hold.

"Tell me this is ours and ours only," I panted against her

ear while slipping a finger inside her drenched core. Miles, finally situated, watched my finger move in and out of her, licking his lips while he jerked at his massive cock. "Look at what you're about to have deep inside you." Aspen whimpered and trembled against me. "He'll touch places inside you no one has ever been."

"Fuck," Miles grunted while rolling the condom down his cock. The second it was on, he shifted forward to grab her from me. Instead of spinning her around and sinking deep inside her, he pulled her just close enough for her tit to swing in front of his face. A savage sound rumbled from his throat as he latched on to her, sucking hard. Aspen's back bowed, shoving her creamy ass higher in the air.

I grabbed both ass cheeks, spreading them apart. Staring at her tight hole, I squeezed her even tighter.

"Have you ever taken someone back here, sweetheart?"

Please say no. Please say one of us would be the first.

"No, just toys."

Miles and I groaned, the combined sound filtering through the peaceful evening.

Miles released her tit. "Fuck, baby girl. You like toys?" She nodded as he switched sides, this time nipping at the side of her breast hard enough to leave a small mark. "You were made for us, Aspen. Everything about you was crafted perfectly for us. Now turn around and sink down onto my cock." Cupping her face, he held her steady, staring up into her hooded gaze. "I'll try to be as gentle as I can be, baby, but I'm no gentleman, and I'm fucking aching to be inside you."

When she turned, I took her face between my hands and sealed my lips to hers, following her down as Miles slowly lowered her back to his lap. I knew the moment he pushed inside her pussy because they both moaned, Aspen's mouth opening, allowing me the chance to slip my tongue in to tangle with hers.

Miles's rasped curses filled the area. Standing tall, I looked down at where they were connected, almost coming right then at the way her perfect pussy was stuffed full of his cock.

"How does she feel?" I grunted while tugging at my dick.

"Tight," he said through clenched teeth. "She's fucking strangling me in the best way possible."

Gripping Aspen's chin, I tipped her flushed face up to mine. "How does he feel, sweetheart?"

"I can't... it's too much," she gasped.

"But you're taking him so well," I praised, which had her preening. Our girl had a praise kink—noted. That was more of Miles's area, but I'd do anything if she liked it. "You ready for one more cock to fill you up?"

Instead of answering, her jaw went slack and her lips popped open.

"Fucking hell," I muttered. "I might not last long," I said, more to Miles than her.

"Even with this damn thing on, I'm already close. She's heaven." His hands came up and grasped both breasts, pinching her already-abused nipples between two fingers. "Ah, shit. Do that again, baby girl. Squeeze me."

Gaze locked on her parted lips, I stepped closer, guiding my dick into her waiting mouth. The first feel of her hot breath had a shiver racing down my spine. I slipped in farther and her lips closed around me, tongue lightly tracing the underside of my shaft.

Inhaling deeply to keep from exploding, I tipped my head back to stare up at the faintly lit sky. In and out, I fucked her hot mouth, pushing deeper with every thrust until she gagged around me. But it was when she started to move, bouncing up and down on Miles's cock, that her groans and pleas vibrated along my shaft and did me in.

Biting my lower lip, I gazed down at her as I threaded both hands into her hair, holding her steady.

"Swallow for me, sweetheart. I want to feel that throat working around my cock while I come down it."

Sinking all the way until her nose brushed my taut abs, I cursed loud enough to be heard back in Anchor Bay as she did just as I asked. The feel of her throat constricting around me, tightening around my sensitive head, had me bursting. In and out in quick thrusts, I fucked her mouth through my orgasm.

Completely spent, I stumbled back, my still-semihard cock slipping from her lips. With me out of her mouth, Miles kicked it up a notch, lifting her higher than before only to slam her down on his dick while he lifted his hips. Up and down he fucked her rough, Aspen's cries of pleasure enough to stir my dick despite having just come harder than ever.

With a harsh curse, he slammed her down, his fingers slipping between her folds to pinch her clit. She came with a scream that slowly faded into a silent one, her mouth still hanging open as she collapsed back against Miles.

The two shifted in the chair with their combined labored breathing.

I stared at them, committing the moment to memory because I knew it was when our lives officially changed.

And we would never, ever be the same.

18

MILES

S omething had changed deep inside me.

It was as if the dam broke, split wide open, and all the pent-up anger, pain, and fear were now freely flowing through my veins, infecting me yet not. I'd kept so much held back for so long, not wanting those dark, twisted feelings to affect my daily life. Even if that life was spent barely surviving.

Then the cure I never expected, the demolisher of my well-constructed barrier to those locked-up feelings, appeared in a perfect little package.

Aspen Carter.

Fist to my chest, I rubbed at the building ache at being away from her, even if it was only a few feet. I stared at the small tent she and Aiden had disappeared into just minutes earlier. The desperate need to be in there with them was a band around my chest, making it harder and harder to take a full breath.

For the first time in forever, I didn't want to be alone, didn't want to fight all the shit in my mind without someone there holding me, comforting me through it. It was fucking embarrassing how deeply I needed something as small as a hug, a simple touch, anything from her to remind me she was there.

And maybe to remind me that so was I. What was left of me after the explosion nearly killed me, at least.

A soft whine came from beside the chair, and I reached down to run my fingers through Jubie's fur, letting her know I was okay. Normally, the fact that I had my four-legged best friend at my side no matter what was enough. Pitching forward, I stared down into her dark eyes, so full of love and acceptance.

Before Aspen, just looking into Jubie's loving eyes, knowing she was there for me, was all I needed.

Not now.

Maybe never again, which was more fucking terrifying than the memory-inspired nightmares that invaded my sleep.

A pop of the dying fire pulled my stare to the glowing embers and fading flickering flames. Sweat beaded along my forehead, and my breaths drew short.

I knew what that kind of heat would do to the skin. What it felt like consuming you from shoulders to heels. The pain and agony that wouldn't ever stop, even in the hospital and years later. The scarred skin on my back tugged uncomfortably, and phantom flames burned as my gaze went unfocused.

Jubie's sharp bark had me shaking my head and jerking out of the chair. I stormed away from the fire to gulp down heaping lungful of cool air while reminding myself I wasn't back in the Middle East or burning alive.

Again.

Unwanted tears stung my eyes as I gazed into the darkness that had finally fallen but wouldn't last long. It was insane to want and need Aspen like I did, not when she didn't know all of me. When she heard what I'd done in the past, saw the evidence on my body and truly understood how fractured my mind was, she, like so many others, would either pity me or be disgusted.

Thankfully, most of the people in our small community were fellow veterans from various branches of the military and didn't gawk or comment when my scars were exposed. Which was probably why I felt more at home here than I did in the town where Aiden and I grew up. No one there understood that I didn't want them to feel sorry for me or get all teary-eyed with guilt-laced gratitude.

I was a warrior. I understood the high stakes when I enlisted and even more so when becoming a SEAL. The missions we went on, the things we did and saw, were forever engraved inside me, but I did it all with a heart bursting with love for my country and brothers in arms, knowing we were protecting so many innocent people from seeing those horrors or being in danger they never knew existed.

Turning, I stared through my watery vision at their tent, listening to their soft whispers and Aspen's occasional giggle. A single tear slipped from the corner of my eye while my lips tugged upward.

They were here, happy and safe.

And to keep them that way, I'd shove down the now pulsing need to be with them, to hold Aspen tight in my arms and beg her to never let me go. What I wanted didn't matter. Staying away and sleeping on my own like I did every night was the best way to keep both of them safe from me when I wasn't in complete control.

My glassy-eyed gaze slid to my tent, utterly dark and cold, lacking the light that Aspen and Aiden brought to my life. I sucked down a deep, steadying breath and wiped the rogue tear away. Feeling sorry for myself would accomplish nothing; I needed to suck it up and do what I had to do. At my tent, I forced my fingers to grip the tiny metal zipper and unzipped the door to step inside, Jubie hot on my heels like she always was.

Because no matter how much I wanted Aspen snuggled against my side tonight, reminding me that I didn't have to fight this battle alone, she was safer with Aiden.

And I'd bear that familiar heavy weight of loneliness that always filled my chest at night if it meant both of them were safe.

19

ASPEN

"I don't think I've stayed up this late without alcohol somehow being involved in a very long time," I mused as I slipped into the lightweight sleeping bag. A full-body shiver shook my shoulders as the cold, slick material caressed the exposed skin of my legs and stomach. "Dang, it's cold away from the fire."

"Says the woman sleeping in her underwear." Aiden chuckled as his pants dropped. Thanks to the headlamp he wore, I was gifted with a full, unobstructed view of his muscular legs as he stepped out of the puddled material. Damn, there was something about thick, manly thighs that did it for me.

Who was I kidding? All parts of Aiden and Miles did it for me.

"Says the guy sleeping in *his* underwear," I sassed back.

"Not quite." With a wink, he hooked both thumbs into the waistband of his gray boxer briefs and tugged them down. My jaw went slack, eyes basically popping out of my head with my gaze locked on his long, thick cock.

How the hell did I fit that thing in my mouth earlier?

"Gotta stop looking at me like that, sweetheart. It's past your bedtime, and I need my beauty sleep." I snapped my jaw closed, teeth clattering with the sharp movement. "Good girl."

My groan echoed through the tent. Falling back to my pillow, I tossed an arm over my eyes and hot cheeks. "How can I not stare when you're standing there naked, looking all hot and perfect?"

He lay on top of his sleeping bag and tucked both hands behind his head. Without my permission, my eyes slid down his chiseled chest, rippled stomach, and paused on his dick that twitched against his thigh.

There wasn't a penis in the world that I would ever consider pretty, but fuck if Aiden's wasn't a work of art. Penis art. Maybe I could make a living by taking pictures of his perfect cock if the whole wildlife and scenery photography thing didn't work out as I hoped.

Or was that considered porn?

Either way, it was a terrible idea. If I captured his penis in all its glory, then other women would see how magical it was, plus the man attached to the art-like penis, and come to Anchor Bay in droves.

"I'm not perfect," Aiden said after a minute of me gazing longingly at his dick.

"Hmm," I finally responded, forcing my gaze up to his face, only to pause. There were none of the laugh lines that always marked his smiling face, no twinkle in his eyes that told me something mischievous was playing out in his mind. All lingering thoughts of how to get him over into my sleeping bag to use his perfect cock evaporated. "Aiden?"

"You said I was hot—which, thank you—but I'm not perfect. Far from it, actually." His brows dipped, and that far-off look overtook his stare. "Someone perfect wouldn't have made all the mistakes I made or almost gotten his best friend killed because of them."

I sucked in a sharp breath that whistled between my teeth. "Tell me what happened." He rolled his head to face me. "None of us are perfect, Aiden. I didn't mean it like that."

"I know you didn't," he whispered. "Sorry, I'm being so fucking dramatic, distracting you from my dick. Fuck," he groaned. "I cockblocked myself."

A giggle escaped, and I rolled over, laying a cheek on my tucked hands. "We have time for me to stare at your dick and continue to dream about my penis art photography business."

His brows flew up over his forehead. "Penis. Art."

"It's a new trend." I bit my lower lip to keep the smile from growing wider.

"Fairly certain porn has been around for a while, plus I'm not sure I like this idea of penis pornography. I'll end up in jail for murdering the unlucky models you hire."

I rolled my eyes. "Just your penis because it's pretty." His mouth opened and closed a few times. "Want to talk about it?"

"My cock? Always." His smile was just as forced as the lightness in his tone.

"Aiden," I rasped.

"Aspen," he said, copying my exasperated tone.

"You want me to stay?"

"Of course," he said in a rush.

"Then give me more of you." His brows waggled as he flicked his gaze down at his dick. "You know what I mean. Show me this is real by telling me something real."

"Pretty sure my dick is real." He grinned. Slipping a

hand free, I shoved at his bare shoulder. "Fine. But quid pro quo, sweetheart."

"Agreed." I held out my hand, which he slipped into his. Instead of shaking it, he drew it close to his lips and planted a soft kiss on my knuckles. "What do you want to know about me?"

He studied me, gaze scanning my face for a few seconds. "When we first met, you mentioned that your mom said photography was a waste of time."

"You remember that?" I whispered in sheer awe. "Why?"

"I remember all the things about the important people in my life."

"But I'm not, or I wasn't then. I was just a stranger." And now I was just a...

Fuck, I could not go there right now.

"I had a hunch of what was to come. The way you talked about your mom made me think things weren't that great between you two. Tell me."

"Wow, going deep here, Dr. Phil." I rolled onto my back and stared at the top of the tent. "She's old-school, I guess you could say. I loved playing outdoors and helping my dad on the ranch, but she thought I should be inside, learning to cook and clean and be a proper wife one day. I've never seen my dad make a single meal for himself, and I'm pretty sure he thinks the fact that his clothes reappear in his closet daily is magic and not my mom's doing. When I showed interest in photography, she dismissed it, said it wasn't necessary or even a viable career until I got married, and then it could be a hobby while the kids were in school."

"Until you got married and had the 2.5 kids," Aiden mused. "So, she had grand aspirations for your life."

"A husband and three kids," I corrected as her disappointed voice rang in my ears as if she were right beside me.

"Never achieving my own dreams or wants. Those were her aspirations. When I pushed back, which was often, she would tell me I'd never make it. That it wasn't right for me to want more than a family and a husband telling me what to do."

"Aspen." His hand breached the small gap between our two sleeping bags and grasped mine, interlacing our fingers in a tight hold.

"So, when I left to pursue my career in something that gave me joy and hope, she basically told me I'd be back, and when I failed and came running back home, I needed to be ready to finally fall in line with what was expected of me." My breath was shaky as I blew it out in a slow stream through pursed lips. "It's why I came here when everything happened with James. I can't go home to that. I haven't failed," I whispered. "I just got... sidetracked, and I'm trying to find my way back to me. The life I want to live that makes me happy and fulfilled."

"Do you think you could find that here?" Aiden asked.

My hair slid along my sleeping bag as I turned to face him once again. "I don't know. I want to think so. I feel like I could, but I lost my way once because of someone else distracting me from my dreams. What if it happens again?"

There. That was it. The fear that had wormed its way into my heart and mind, but I hadn't been able to pinpoint it until just now.

"I get that, I do, but what if you had two people wanting to help you stay on the path to your dreams? There to help you and support you no matter where that leads. A community that wants you to succeed in whatever makes you happy because this life is too fucking short, filled with too much shit, for any of us to do anything but what keeps that light flickering inside us."

"How did you get so wise?"

His features shuttered. "By making a lot of mistakes I regret daily."

"Your turn to spill your innermost thoughts and secrets." I gave his hand a squeeze in encouragement. "You might feel better once you tell someone, if you haven't already."

"I haven't." His soft exhale brushed along my exposed arm. "I'm the reason Miles got injured, and was forced to leave the one thing he loved."

My eyes flicked between his. "I don't understand."

"There was an attack, the last mission he went on, and I wasn't there to stop it."

My mind reeled, trying to connect the pieces, but what he said made little sense. "How could you have been there?"

His throat bobbed, the movement barely noticeable with the faint light from the headlamp he'd laid on the floor between us.

"I told you before that we both intended to become SEALs one day. When our first couple years in the Navy were up, he signed a new contract, and I didn't." My heart ached hearing the tremble in his voice. "I let my ex convince me to stay home, find a regular nine-to-five job, and get married instead of fulfilling the dream I had with my best friend. What we had planned since we were kids."

"I don't understand how that means you're the one who got him injured—"

"I wasn't there for him," he rasped. "If I would've followed through with what we promised each other, I would've been there with him..."

"Then maybe you both would've been hurt, or worse." My heart leapt into my throat at even thinking that. What if things had turned out differently and these two amazing men weren't here now, with me, giving me the best slice of life I'd ever experienced?

And it was because of more than the soul-shattering orgasms.

They were showing me how to truly experience life with someone—or someones, in this case—who truly supported you.

Aiden shook his head. "No, if I would've been there, I could've stopped it. Don't you see, Aspen? My best friend almost died and has lingering pain and so much trauma all because I chose someone else over him. Someone who turned out to be so fucking awful, who made me so damn miserable every damn day. I almost lost Miles, and I will never, ever forgive myself for not being there when he needed me most."

I let that last statement hang in the air for a moment before responding.

"But you're here now," I whispered. Reaching over, I ran my fingers through his soft, silky hair. "And I see the way you watch him, making sure he's happy and taken care of." As those words left my lips, it was like a light bulb went off in my mind. "He's why you started sharing." Aiden nodded. "Because he wouldn't touch anyone, could only watch."

Everything was making sense, and it was really fucking beautiful how strong and tight these two men were. They wanted the best for each other and constantly gave of themselves to ensure the other was happy.

"It was terrible when he first came home. It's still not great. His nightmares keep him from sleeping at night and sometimes follow him into the day. He also has..." Aiden looked at me. "The scars sometimes hurt, which pulls him back into that last mission that almost killed him. He didn't want anyone touching him, it was too much, but then it turned into more of him being used to being standoffish. So, yeah, the sharing, him watching, helped him get through those first few years. Until you."

"I don't know why," I whispered. That was the truth.

"Whatever it is..." Aiden sat up and shifted to lean over me, his face hovering just over mine. "Please, Aspen, please don't stop." His soft lips brushed mine in a barely-there kiss before he fell back onto his sleeping bag. "I think that's enough trauma bonding for the night, don't you? I need my beauty sleep, remember?"

At my distracted nod, he clicked off the light, dousing us in darkness.

"Good night, Aiden," I whispered.

"Good night, sweetheart."

For several minutes, I stared into the darkness, mind still whirling with his revelations. This thing between the three of us was intense, yet I wasn't overwhelmed like I was when I first arrived here. I felt more settled and at peace than I had in years. Even though I had no clue where all this would lead, I was happy, right here, right now.

And that was everything.

I JERKED AWAKE.

Heart racing, eyes wide open, I stayed completely still while trying to figure out what woke me. Soft snores came from my right, telling me Aiden was still asleep. Straining my ears, I listened for any sounds outside the tent. Thankfully, a bit of too-early sunlight offered enough visibility for me to see that no one else was in the tent besides us.

No axe murderer in here. That was a win.

When no suspicious noises came, my lids slowly fluttered closed, too heavy to keep open without the earlier surge of adrenaline pumping through my veins. Only for them to snap open again at a pained, wounded sound from somewhere outside the tent. My breathing shallow, I slowly unzipped my sleeping bag just enough to quietly wiggle out without waking Aiden. Before opening the door, I grabbed the shirt on top of his pack, the one he set aside to wear on our trek back to Anchor Bay today. After slipping it over my head, I unzipped the door enough to slip through.

Inhaling the crisp, chilly morning air, I kept my senses on high alert while taking a second to appreciate the surrounding beauty.

Until the wounded animal cried out again, this time mixed with a thrashing sound.

My head whipped one way, then the other, gaze searching the small clearing. A tendril of smoke trailed into the air from the few embers left glowing in the center of the ring of rocks we used to contain the fire and smoldering remnants, but other than that, I found nothing.

I wasn't scared or worried that whatever was out there would hurt me. My heart ached at the sound, knowing something was in pain, and I desperately wanted to help, do anything to stop its agony.

A soft whimper, one I'd heard before, had me narrowing my gaze on the single-person tent several feet from where I stood. Soft dirt coated the bottoms of my feet, and loose pebbles poked into the soft skin with every hesitant step I took toward Miles's tent.

Pausing just outside the thin, domed canvas, I leaned closer, putting my ear as close as I could without actually touching it. A pained moan, clearly human now that I was close, made my breath catch and heart cramp.

Miles.

My fingers hovered over the door's zipper, fingertips brushing the tiny metal. Another of Jubie's soft whines floated in the air from inside the tent, the scrape of nails against the waterproof bottom. Breath burning in my lungs, I waited, pleading with anyone or anything that would listen that whatever Miles was dealing with, alone, was finally over.

Nightmares.

That was what Aiden said plagued Miles from his time as a SEAL and whatever happened during that last assignment. I didn't need to know the details to understand it was bad, horrible enough that it still haunted him now, years later.

Swallowing down the building tears, I retreated a single step, then another until the back of my legs hit the edge of a camping chair. The same chair Miles had held me in last night, taunting and teasing his best friend to pull him out of his head. Lowering into the canvas seat, I stared at Miles's tent as if just monitoring him would somehow offer the comfort I knew wouldn't be welcomed if I ripped open that door and attempted to smother him with it.

But I couldn't just leave. Not when I knew he was in there fighting a battle alone.

Reaching over, I tossed a few leftover dead branches onto the glowing embers, hoping the fire would catch just enough to chase the too-early morning chill from the air. After dusting off my hands, I tucked both knees to my chest, using Aiden's large T-shirt as a makeshift blanket, pulling the soft material up and over my bent legs.

There was no way I could go back to sleep now.

Might as well stay up and keep watch over Miles.

Whether he wanted me to or not.

20

AIDEN

I wasn't sure what woke me, but I instantly knew something was wrong.

Bolting upright, I immediately looked to my left, where I last saw the woman who was becoming as important as air to both me and Miles. Panic surged at finding her sleeping bag tossed open, empty. With a curse, I pushed to my feet and lunged for the already-open door.

I couldn't breathe. Terrible scenarios ran on a loop in my mind over and over, each time getting worse and more vivid. The second my bare feet hit the soft dirt just outside the tent and I took in the campsite, my world stilled.

What. The. Actual. Fuck.

"Miles?" I hedged, taking a tentative step toward my utterly still friend.

He didn't respond, gaze fixed on the slight frame folded into the chair from last night that I just might have bronzed to commemorate one of the best nights of my life. Pausing at his side, I fought the urge to reach out to him, to do fucking anything to get him to snap out of whatever memory he was trapped inside.

"Why the fuck is your dick out?"

I blinked at Miles before slapping a palm over my mouth to quiet the bark of laughter that would've surely woken up the sleeping beauty in front of us.

"I woke up, and she was gone. Pants didn't seem like a priority."

His dark eyes cut my way. "Pretty sure pants should always be a priority, but I get it." His gaze slid back to her. "When she's involved, everything else ceases to exist but her and her safety."

I waited for him to explain what the hell I'd walked in on, but he stopped talking and went back to just staring at Aspen.

"Miles," I whispered.

"Aiden."

"What the fuck is going on?"

He looked at me again. "I was hoping you knew. I woke up to Jubie scratching at the door, begging to go out like something was wrong. When I did, I noticed Aspen asleep in the chair."

"And you've been standing here, watching her sleep since?" He nodded. "And I thought I was the one she'd think was a serial killer after my captive-in-the-basement slip yesterday."

"What?"

"Nothing," I grumbled. "We should just go back into the tents and let her sleep. We can find out why later."

"What if something happens to her?" he asked, slight panic raising his voice.

"We can leave Jubie—"

The words dried up, and we both froze at a soft sound coming from Aspen's parted lips. Her long dark lashes fluttered open. The chair shifted beneath her as she jerked, eyes wide, flicking between us.

"Um, hi," she rasped, voice thick with sleep. She shifted and winced, hand coming up to press against her neck. "Shit, I slept funny."

"Why did you sleep out here, in a chair?" Miles demanded, arms now crossed over his chest and feet spread in a defensive position.

"Um." Her gaze slid to me before dipping down. "Really? Still no pants?"

Tossing both hands up in the air, I strode for the tent. Pulling the boxer briefs off my pack that I had set out, I yanked them on before going back out to join them.

"What?" I asked, catching them both smirking at me.

"Nothing," Miles replied, though it seemed he hid a laugh.

"I said you had a cute ass." She made a pinching gesture. "I just want to pinch it."

"That is oddly..."

"Adorable?" she added.

"Erotic."

"Can we all please get back to why I found Aspen out here sleeping? Alone?" His dark brows furrowed. "What did you do?"

"Um, it wasn't because of him," Aspen cut in before I could. Miles and I both shifted our full attention to her. Playing with a few strands of hair, she kept her gaze anywhere other than on us. "It was you."

Miles frowned and tapped his chest. "Me?" She nodded. "What did I do?"

"Nothing," she said in a rush. "But I heard something and came out here to investigate."

"Alone?" I growled. "Don't you know the dangers out here?"

"Not really," she snapped back. "Because neither of you have told me about whatever danger is lurking out there besides being mauled by a bear."

"Which is a valid concern out here," Miles stated with a firm nod. "And you're right, we didn't talk about that yesterday on the hike up, but we will after you tell us how I'm the reason you're out here alone, sleeping in a fucking chair."

Oh, bestie was pissed. If Aspen didn't have a solid reason for being out here, he was going to wear her ass out.

Hope I got to watch when he did.

"You really want to know?" she hedged, shooting me a worried glance.

Oh fuck.

"Yes," Miles demanded.

"The noise," she whispered. "I thought it was an animal or something, so I stepped out of the tent, and that's when I realized the sound I heard was coming from your tent."

Miles was now frozen, staring at her with a blank expression on his face.

"You clearly didn't wake him up or go into his tent, so why didn't you come back in with me?" I asked frantically, glancing between them.

"He sounded"—she shrugged—"upset or hurt or, I don't know—"

"Answer the question, Aspen. Why didn't you go back to bed once you realized it was me?"

Aspen lifted her chin, meeting his cold dark eyes. "Because I didn't want to leave you to fight whatever it was you were dealing with alone."

And there went the rest of my heart. What was left of the shredded organ now belonged wholly to the fierce, adorable, sexy-as-fuck woman in front of me.

"So, you stayed," Miles stated. Aspen nodded, refusing to drop his stare. "So that even if you weren't in the tent with me, I wouldn't be alone."

"Well, yeah. I mean, I'm kind of tired of doing all this on my own, so I figured you were too. Even if you didn't know I was out here, it still felt better than just leaving."

Miles's nostrils flared, chest ballooning out with a heavy inhale. Before I could get a word out, he scooped Aspen out of the chair and smashed her against his chest in a hold so tight I wondered if she could breathe. Face buried against her neck, he said nothing, letting the emotional hug say it all for him.

One arm wrapped around her waist, Miles pulled back and ran a hand over her wild hair.

"Thank you," he rasped.

Jubie leaned against his leg, nose tipped up, sniffing Aspen's side. With a little maneuvering, she finagled an arm free, dropped her hand, and rested it on Jubie's head.

Knowing the moment was more special than any of us could put into words, I hurried back to the tent, snagged my phone, and snapped a few shots with the early-morning sun rising behind them.

Perfect.

The moment.

Them.

Us.

All of it was almost too perfect to be true.

I just hoped it actually was.

"AND ALL THE MALE VICTIMS..." Aspen trailed off as she stepped out of the truck.

"There are six that we know of in the last year or so that we believe should've been labeled as suspicious deaths instead of accidents," Miles explained.

"Because the female hikers they traveled with were missing instead of being found with the men's bodies," she said, pausing at the pathway that led toward her cabin to face us.

"Exactly." He opened the tailgate to make it easier for Jubie to jump down. The dog's massive paws barely made a sound when she landed and trotted over to where Aspen and I stood.

"And how many female hikers are you saying have gone missing off the trail in the last year?"

"Thirteen, though two of the victims' bodies were found months later, badly decomposed."

"Yet you still think it's tied to the other missing women's cases," she hedged with a frown. "Seems suspicious, sure, but I don't know if they're all connected."

"We don't either, which is why the guy who owns Uplift asked a SEAL buddy, Hudson, a detective down in LA, to come help run the investigation." I tossed an arm over her shoulders and turned us both, starting the short walk to her cabin. "The sheriff doesn't think there's a case. He thinks the women just got lost or were victims of unfortunate accidents. Which could've happened. Sure, the trail is difficult, but we believe there is enough suspicion to warrant an investigation. Hence why we want you to be extra cautious when you're alone."

She angled her head from side to side. "People get hurt or go missing all the time in parks and nature preserves. I can only imagine how much more dangerous a trail is here than anywhere else. Maybe it's more about people coming here unprepared, expecting it to be all about the magnificent views and not the crazy-hard terrain and climate. Because I'll be honest, I've hiked and explored a lot of different locations, and this place... the beauty is deceiving. You don't realize how remote and treacherous it can be out there."

"But you had fun?" I asked, leaning down to plant a kiss on her forehead.

"I had... there isn't a word that describes the last twenty-four hours with you guys and being out there," she said, angling a wide smile up at me.

"I'm sure you captured it in your pictures," Miles offered behind us.

"Hopefully." The excitement and energy in her tone was palpable. Digging the cabin key out of her front pocket, she reached for the door handle with the other hand. "I just need to..." Stopping, she frowned. "That's odd."

A massive body wedged itself between Aspen and me at her comment. I rolled my eyes at Miles's back.

"What is it?" he demanded.

Not verbally responding, she pushed the door, which opened with ease. I narrowed my eyes at the key still in her other hand. "I'm positive I locked it," she stated.

"It *was* locked. I double-checked it before we left," Miles said, sidearm already in his hand, stepping over the threshold. "Aiden, on my six."

I pulled my own weapon, a shiver rolling down my spine, making the hairs on my arms and the back of my neck stand on end, the moment I entered the cabin. I adjusted my hold on the Glock, the rough grip caressing my palm, offering some comfort that I was armed if anyone was inside. After clearing each room twice, we met Aspen where she stood just inside the cabin by the open door.

I gave her a quick once-over, cataloging her pale face, arms crossed around her waist, and the way her nervous gaze jumped from side to side as if expecting someone to jump out of thin air.

Damnit, she looked absolutely terrified.

Holstering my gun, I pulled her into my arms and rubbed a hand along her spine in reassuring strokes. "You're all right. No one is in here but us. We're positive."

"But someone was." I shot my best friend a pointed "shut the fuck up, dude" look. He just shrugged in return. "What? She needs to know that someone has been here. The door was locked when we left, and the cabin just feels off."

Well, he had me there.

"Was anything stolen?"

Slowly releasing my tight hold, I took her hand in mine and guided her to the single bedroom. "I don't think so, but why don't you go through your things to double-check? I'll be right here with you."

Teeth gnawing on her lower lip, she nodded and hesitantly slipped our joined hands apart. I stuck closer than her fucking shadow as she moved around the room, searching the bags I remembered helping with that first day, inspecting the contents of a few small ones in the bathroom, and rummaging through a computer bag next to a tiny desk.

Blowing out a slow breath, she looked up from where she knelt on the floor. "Everything is here. Could we be imagining this?"

I shook my head as I scanned the room. It didn't make sense why someone would break in and not steal anything.

The computer sitting on top of the desk would've been easy to grab, but they didn't.

What the fuck was going on in Anchor Bay?

"I called the sheriff," Miles said when he stormed back into the cabin from the back door, gun still clutched tightly in his grip. "Said he'd swing by when he could. I'll stay and wait for that lazy fucker to show up. Aiden, you take Aspen to our place. There is no way in hell you're staying here tonight, baby girl. Please don't fight me on—"

"I agree," Aspen cut in. "No pushback from me. I don't *want* to stay here alone tonight."

"Thank fuck for that," I grumbled to myself. "Come on. I'll help you pack everything up." I interlaced our fingers and raised her hand to my lips to kiss the back. "Though if you want to leave the underwear..." I waggled my brows, hoping to ease the tense moment. The slight curve of her lips was all I got, but it had to be enough for now. Later, I'd help her forget all about the break-in and her fear.

It took her less than ten minutes to get everything packed up and loaded in the back of the truck. Sliding behind the wheel, I gave Jubie's head a soft pat while shooting Aspen a reassuring smile, then cranked the engine to head home. Shuffling had me glancing over around Jubie's large body, finding Aspen digging around in the bottom of the satchel that had her laptop and camera. Before I turned back to the road, I caught her pulling out a cell phone, only to stare at the blank screen.

"If your phone is dead, we can plug it in when we get to the cabin," I offered.

"Oh, I'm sure it still has a charge."

I shot her an arched brow in question. "So, then, why aren't you using it?"

"I turned it off when I left Seattle, only turning it back

on for a few minutes to get the address Miles texted me and write him back. There were a lot of missed texts and phone calls that I actively avoided before powering it back off." She blew a raspberry, which drew Jubie's attention, who took that as an open invitation to lick her face. "I haven't turned it back on since, and I'm not sure I want to now."

"Why?"

"It feels like combining two different lives." She shrugged and draped an arm around Jubie's massive body in a side hug. "The messages and voicemails that are waiting for me revolve around my life in Seattle. I feel like they might interrupt or burst this happy bubble that I've found myself blissfully stuck inside."

"Then keep it turned off." I flicked the blinker and slowed to make the turn. "Right?"

She nodded, then shook her head. "This might sound childish or dumb, but after what happened back at the cabin, I want to check in with my parents. I didn't even call to tell them I quit my job and was headed to Alaska for a week. I don't know. I just want to talk to them both."

"Then turn it on and call them?" Confusion had the statement almost coming out like a question. Sure, her mom sounded difficult and unsupportive, but if Aspen wanted to talk to them, then she should, even if she had to ignore the messages from her old life in Seattle.

"It's just all so damn complicated, and I have no one to blame but myself since I all but sprinted out of Seattle." With a sharp headshake, she shoved the phone back into her bag and gently set it between her feet. After a few seconds of silence, she poked a single finger at my shoulder. "Distract me from the inevitable. Tell me a funny story about you and Miles growing up."

A slow, mischievous grin pulled at my lips. If she wanted

a distraction, I knew a mutually embarrassing story that would do the trick.

"Okay, so this one time in high school, I convinced Miles that we should go streaking in the dead of winter…"

21

MILES

Muscles bunched, strung tight with the tension pulsing through me, I marched up the steps and paused on the front porch to say hello to the best dog ever. I crouched in front of the sprawled-out mass of fur and drool to give her exposed belly a few rubs, but seeing Jubie and running my fingers through her thick fur did nothing to calm the anger and fear burning in my chest.

We found absolutely nothing in Aspen's cabin at The Nest to point to who had been inside. Though if you asked the sheriff, he'd tell you we found nothing because nothing had happened. The old fool kept grumbling under his breath that we were paranoid and overly protective of our newest girl.

It had taken everything in me not to snap the bastard's neck after the first comment. By the time he left to find the idiot general manager, I had plotted multiple scenarios regarding his untimely death, each more creative than the last. Only knowing I couldn't be with Aspen if I went to prison for murder kept me from following through with the pulsing urge to end the asshole's life.

However, when the sheriff made the offhanded comment about trouble seeming to find me, all the fight dissolved, leaving me confused and worried that maybe he was right. Which meant whatever was after Aspen could be because of her association with us.

The notion that *we* put this amazing woman in danger made panic like I'd never known swell in my chest. But there was no way I would walk away from this, from her. I would just need to set more safety precautions for when she wasn't with me or Aiden. We could and would handle anything or anyone who tried to harm our girl. It was when she wasn't with us that had me terrified, which, starting tomorrow, would be most of the day because of clients we already had booked.

Maybe a tracker would ease my mind enough not to be distracted when she wasn't at my side.

Jubie's muzzle opened, releasing a disapproving grunt as she lifted her gigantic head off the fake wooden planks when I stood, dusting off the fur now coating my palms. Shooting my special girl a small grin, I headed for the door and slowly pushed it open. After shutting the door behind me, I paused, immediately sensing something different— not off or wrong, just different from the normally empty cabin feel we'd grown used to.

Taking in the room, my gaze paused on the source.

Aspen. A freshly showered Aspen, if her wet hair was any sign.

Perched on the edge of the couch, phone clutched tight in her hand while holding her bent head with the other, her voice traveled through the room as she spoke to the person on the other end of the line. My pulse picked up at the slump of her shoulders. I started toward her, only to pause upon catching sight of a woman on the screen.

"I know what I'm doing, Mom," Aspen said, her smile tight as she gazed at the phone. She didn't glance up as I slowly backed away so as not to interrupt the conversation with her mother.

"See, Aspen, I don't think you do. You actually had a decent job back in Seattle that you just up and left. We didn't raise you to just walk out on your employer like that. I'm starting to wonder if us giving you the freedom to put the photography dream behind you was best for your future. Look at you—no job, no husband, no prospects. Alone and in Alaska, doing what?"

"Taking pictures, Mom," Aspen replied, sounding so defeated I almost didn't recognize her voice.

My fingers curled into tight fists, and a low, frustrated grunt vibrated in my chest. She deserved to be happy, always supported, and loved, no matter what. I didn't give a fuck if the person on the other end of the line was her mother. I was seconds from ripping the phone out of Aspen's hand and telling that woman just what I thought about her.

"I don't understand you, Aspen. I really don't. And what makes this whole situation worse is you walked away from someone who could've supported you, who could've given you a family. But you ran away from him and all your responsibilities. What you did was incredibly selfish. I hope you realize that now."

That fake smile from Aspen shifted to a shocked expression as she gaped at the phone.

"Wait a second, Mom. How do you know all this? I called to say hey and let you know where I was. I haven't mentioned anything about me leaving the magazine." Her voice trembled with restrained emotion. "And who the hell are you saying I left behind?"

"Since you didn't feel the need to call and inform us of your little breakdown..." I stifled a curse and dared a step toward Aspen. Her gaze jerked my way, dark eyes widening. "I was concerned about you when you didn't return my messages, which is very rude, Aspen. When you get home, we will have a long discussion about respecting your parents."

"How did you know, Mom?" Aspen gritted out, jaw clenched so tight I worried about her teeth.

"Well, this James fellow, very kind and utterly concerned about you, called and told me everything."

"I highly doubt that," Aspen muttered under her breath. "And what did *James* have to tell you, Mom?"

"That you two were a couple, that he really saw a future with you, even though you were the independent type. A family, Aspen. He talked about wanting a family with *you*." It was my turn to gape at the device in Aspen's hand, at her mother's incredulous tone. Was she really shocked that someone would want to marry and have a family with Aspen? Because that's exactly what it sounded like. "He was worried about you and called to see if I knew where you were and if you were okay."

"And what did you tell him?"

"That I hadn't spoken to you, but I was certain you were fine and that I'd let him know once I heard from you. But I think it would be best coming from you, dear. Rebuild that bridge before he walks away, realizing you're too much trouble."

"What the fuck?" I murmured before I could restrain myself.

"Is someone there?" her mom said, and Aspen winced.

"Please don't let him know you talked to me, Mom. He's not who you think he is. Did you not question his claims about us being a 'couple' when I never once talked to you about him over the years?"

A long sigh came from the phone, amping up the anger burning in my veins.

"Fine, fine, if you want to throw away a perfectly wonderful future, that is on you. I was just thinking if you wanted to stay in Seattle, he was a good option. Though it sounds like you just need to come home."

"I am not coming home." Aspen laughed with zero humor.

"How are you going to live, support yourself, have a roof over your head with no job or husband to keep you?"

Keep her? What the fuck? Was this woman pulled from the Dark Ages?

"Just because I left the magazine doesn't mean I can't make a living selling my pictures online or—"

Her mother's snort cut her off, and a broken expression flitted over Aspen's face.

Having heard enough, I started toward the couch, ready to crush the damn phone to keep her mom from spewing her messed-up lies, but Aspen raised a palm my way, stopping me.

"It's time you give up on this crazy dream, Aspen, and figure out your life. You're getting older, and there comes a point when you'll be beyond the age of what any man would want for a wife. But don't worry, it's not too late. When you get home, I'll introduce you to a few of the men from church who are—"

"Are old enough to be my dad," Aspen shrieked while leaping from the couch.

"Aspen Bee Carter, do not raise your voice at me. They are good men who will provide for you, take care of you, and give you the family you need to feel fulfilled in life."

"I don't need children to feel fulfilled, Mother," Aspen snapped. "I'm doing just fine and have no plans to alter course."

"You're a foolish child, Aspen. This photography thing is a hobby, a fool's dream. Get your head out of the clouds and realize your purpose in life, the one you were created for."

"And what is that?" Aspen said, sounding resigned while rubbing at her temple.

I really didn't want to hear the answer to her question, knowing it would piss me off, but I couldn't force my feet to move.

"To be a wife, a mother. Aspen, this is who we are. Jobs and careers just distract women from their true purpose, the only fulfilling one that we have."

Grinding my back molars to keep from shouting at the phone, I spun on my heels and quietly marched to my bedroom. Stripping off my sweat-soaked shirt first, I tossed it onto the bathroom floor. Mind still on their conversation, I toed off both boots, stepped out of my pants, and kicked everything to the side, taking my anger out on the clothing instead. Behind the glass shower door, I turned the handle all the way to the left. Goose bumps rippled along my skin at the freezing-cold water that sputtered from the showerhead and cascaded along my skin.

Palms sealed to the smooth gray tile wall, I dropped my head forward, allowing the now-lukewarm water to flow over my shoulders and down the ruined skin on my back. Streams poured along my face, falling to the river-stone floor, and swirled down the drain, taking layers of dust and sweat from the hike down with it.

Lost in thought, a mix of overthinking about what happened at Aspen's cabin and processing the conversation between Aspen and her mom, I failed to hear soft, tentative footsteps.

"Miles?" I jerked up straight. A bolt of panic sent my heart racing. "Sorry, I'm interrupting, but... um..." The uncertainty in her voice had me stilling to catch every soft-spoken word. "I just wanted to apologize for what you heard out there. I don't want you to think I believe all the crap she spewed during the call. Because I don't."

I let that statement sink in for a few seconds before responding. "What do you believe, Aspen?" Fuck, her sweet voice and knowing she was just on the other side of the shower door had my cock twitching between my thighs. Reaching down, I gave it a firm squeeze to calm it the fuck down. Now was not the time.

"What do I believe?" she repeated. "Honestly, I don't know anymore." I barely heard her answer over the water beating against my skin. "But I just wanted you to know... fuck, I don't know... that I'm not like her, I guess. I didn't want you to get the wrong idea that I'm doing this with you and Aiden because I need someone to take care of me."

"You mean the life you were created for?" I scoffed. "That's some bullshit thinking. You know that, right?"

"I do. But she's my mom. I can't cut her out of my life for her backward thinking, even if she drives me insane and pisses me off. She loves me. She just goes about showing it in strange, controlling ways."

"If she doesn't support you when you're pursuing your dreams, then I'm not sure why you don't stop answering her calls and cut ties with her." I ran a thumb over the crown of my cock, my shoulders trembling with a bolt of desire.

"Because sometimes I wonder if she's right. Not about everything but about some of it. What am I even doing with my life?" Through the frosted glass, I watched her lean against the wall and slide down until her ass hit the tile floor. "I don't want to move home. That's not the answer. But how am I going to support myself? Maybe this is a pipe dream, one that won't get me anywhere."

"But you're happy."

"It just feels like what I do doesn't matter. I'm not out saving lives or curing cancer. I take pictures of animals and landscapes—so what? I'm not doing anything important or life-changing—"

"Stop," I commanded, tone sharp. Shutting off the water, I pulled open the shower door and shot her a stern look. "Stop talking about your career like it isn't special."

"They're just pictures," she whispered, eyes glued to my semihard cock.

"Aspen," I practically growled, my restrain waning as she licked her lips.

Slowly, her gaze slid up my naked body, and it was only then that I realized what I had done without even thinking twice.

I stepped out of the shower naked, knowing she was there.

Everything was out on display for Aspen to see.

Tattoos.

Muscles.

Dick.

Scars.

My heart raced, pulse pounding in my ears. Yet it wasn't out of fear of her rejection or disgust, but more at the huge fucking milestone I'd just achieved. This moment was fucking epic, and she had no idea. Aspen was the first woman in years who I'd bared myself to, and by the hooded look directed my way, she liked what she saw.

Shaking my head to redirect my thoughts from fucking

her against the wall and back to the previous important conversation, I grabbed a towel off a wall hook and quickly secured it around my waist. And fuck if her little pout when I covered my cock from her view wasn't tempting and adorable all in the same breath.

I stepped toward her only to freeze. It was one thing for her to see my front. There was minor damage from the explosion there. My back was a different situation completely. Ninety percent was covered in second- and third-degree burn scars. Even though nearly every inch was full of ink, the raised skin was still noticeable.

"Damn, you're way too good-looking for someone like me," Aspen said with awe in her tone. Her tongue slipped out to wet her lower lip as if imagining lapping up the streams of water trickling down my chest.

Her words snapped me out of my frozen state. One foot in front of the other, I marched up to where she sat. If my one-track mind wasn't narrowed in on proving to her they weren't "just pictures," I would turn her over my knee and spank her ass for putting herself down. It was Aiden and me who didn't deserve someone like her.

So full of light and life.

Beautiful and tough.

And all ours.

"Come on, I have something to show you." I extended a hand down. The second her fingers slid into mine, I eased her off the floor and tugged her against me. "What you do is important. They aren't just pictures to some people, baby girl. To someone, whether or not you realize it, those pictures are *everything*."

"I don't understand," she whispered, dark eyes flicking between mine. "What do you mean?"

I dipped my chin. "It's easier if I show you."

Palm pressed to her lower back, I guided her in front of me so she wouldn't see my back—baby steps and all that shit. In the bedroom, I motioned toward the bed. Keeping the towel wrapped around my waist, I snatched a lightweight button-up shirt off a hanger in the closet and threaded both arms through the short sleeves. Leaving it open, I stepped back toward the bed, feeling her questioning stare following me as I knelt near the nightstand.

Fingers blindly searching beneath the frame, I paused when they brushed against a small metal storage box. Tugging it closer, I clutched it between both hands and rose, perching on the edge of the mattress beside Aspen.

The tiny metal hinges creaked, bits of rust falling off the sides as I raised the lid and peered inside. The sweet woman beside me inched closer, peering around my arm to look inside the mysterious box on my lap.

"They aren't just pictures," I rasped while flipping through the various photos and keepsakes for the evidence of my words. A small smile tugged at the corner of my lips as I pulled a wrinkled magazine page free, the paper soft from the number of times I'd smoothed it out over the years. Without another word, I unfolded the paper and held it out to her.

Trembling fingers gently grasped the edge. Holding it out in front of her, Aspen stared, eyes wide and lips parted, at the proof of my awe and appreciation for her talent, which started years before I even laid eyes on her beautiful face. I had no idea then that the woman who inspired me to keep fighting would someday be the one sitting beside me while I shared this secret that only Aiden knew about.

"I don't understand," she said after a few seconds of silently staring at the wrinkled picture of a peaceful landscape blooming with pinks and reds from the setting sun. It felt so real, like you could just step into the page and be right fucking there with the photographer. It was as if you could feel her own love for nature in the single picture printed all those years ago. "Why do you have this?"

Careful to not rip the delicate paper, I plucked it from her fingers and laid it on top of the towel covering my thigh. With the side of my hand, I carefully smoothed out the thicker wrinkles.

"My mom would send me all kinds of things during long deployments despite not knowing where I was or what I was doing. She made sure I knew that there was someone back home thinking about me." My hand shook as it took another gentle swipe along the paper. "This picture was in one magazine she sent, and it spoke to me the moment I saw it. It felt like I was right there, back home, enjoying the country I fought for. It gave me hope of being home one day soon and getting to see that view with my own eyes, reminding me that while I was in a living hell, someone out there was safe and free to take a picture like this. It reminded me what I was fighting for."

A soft hand draped over mine, stilling the repetitive movement.

"And then when I was in the hospital," I choked out, "I kept this taped where I could always see it. Every day, pushing through the pain and devastation of knowing the only thing I was good at—fighting alongside my brothers— was done, I'd look at this picture, and it gave me the will to keep working to get the fuck out."

"I had no idea," she whispered. Turning, I startled at the silent tears leaking down her cheeks. "I loved this shot. The landscape felt alive with this energy that I had to capture."

"You did, that time and so many others." Pulling out a few others I kept, I handed them over to her but continued to stare at the original photo. "You're talented, Aspen. You're not just taking pictures that people flip through for a few seconds, then forget about the next. Your shots, what you capture, speak to so many people who need reassurance that there is still peace out there. For me, it was a reminder of what I fought for, that you could be out there doing what you loved because I was out there protecting your freedom to do so."

"I'm speechless," she murmured, and I gently wrapped my hand around her throat. "I had no idea that something as simple as a picture in a magazine could do that."

"There is nothing simple about your photos, Aspen," I rasped.

Wide dark eyes leaking tears stared up at me. "Thank you. Thank you for sharing this with me. It's..." She lifted the ripped magazine pages and pressed them to her chest, right over her heart. "Everything. And I'm beyond honored to know that something I did helped you, a genuine hero, get through the hard times."

Dark times would be a more accurate description.

Words bubbled in my throat, desperate to escape for the first time. Instead of someone sitting there, trying to pull the story from me, I found myself eager to tell her everything.

Hoping that telling her about that last mission would heal the still raw and jagged scars buried deep within me.

Nothing else had worked, but maybe I was simply waiting for her.

For the one who inspired so much hope and determination to push through the pain.

It was time. I needed to tell her my story.

22

ASPEN

With a sigh, Miles rested back on the bed, one arm tucked beneath his head as he stared up at the ceiling. I couldn't stop my gaze from dipping to take in his defined bare chest because holy fuck, he was chiseled perfection. Who the fuck knew a chest could actually look like that in real life? And then there was the massive cock now hidden beneath the thin white towel. My fingers twitched to skate along his skin, to dip beneath the soft cotton and wrap around his dick.

But his solemn tone brought all those erotic thoughts to a screeching halt.

"It was supposed to be a simple mission." Even my lungs failed to work as I sat perfectly still, desperate not to interrupt the moment. Somehow, I knew this was a big deal; him sharing any sliver of his past was monumental and not something I should take lightly. "Sixteen children and three teachers were taken from a school and held hostage. Within moments of the incident, my SEAL team was called into action and debriefed on the situation. We were the closest team and the most qualified, since the Delta Force team we were paired with was out on a separate mission. With our military's vast resources, it only took a few hours to get the information we needed to form a solid plan and move out."

Needing to be closer, I laid my head on his shoulder and wrapped an arm around his waist, squeezing him tight.

"We cleared the location of all hostiles before heading down to the lowest room where the heat signatures indicated the hostages were being held." His chest rose and fell with a heavy sigh. "The kids were okay. The teachers..." My fingers curled around the worn fabric of his shirt, worry and unease building in my stomach. "They'd taken the brunt of it all to keep the kids safe. Despite their protests, we got the adults out first to get them the medical attention they needed. One by one, we carried the kids out, not seeing a single hostile. Two others and I carried them to the next set of team members, who ran them out to choppers. The hallways in the basic structure were narrow, only big enough for one of us to walk through at a time. With the last kid in my arms and the other two SEALs already gone with their kids, I rounded a corner and froze."

My breaths came in short, quick pants as I waited, knowing whatever came next would probably haunt me forever.

"Somehow, we missed one hostile during our sweep. He blocked my only exit, and as I worked through how to shoot the bastard with the kid in my arms, he held up a lit Molotov cocktail. I couldn't lift my gun fast enough with the kid screaming in my ear and thrashing around. I yelled for help when he threw it. A few seconds was all I had to act, though it was instinct."

"You turned," I whispered, voice cracking with the unshed tears clogging my throat.

"I turned." His hand wrapped around mine and pulled it

around his waist beneath the shirt. Grabbing a single finger, he brushed the tip along his side, allowing me to feel the rippled skin. "The explosion shot me forward down the stairs. Somehow, I caught myself before I crushed the little girl still clinging to me and sobbing for her mom. I found out later she was only ten years old."

I slapped a hand over my mouth to quiet a sob.

"I took the brunt of the explosion, so she was okay but terrified. I just remember being unable to move, the flames roaring around me, the thick black smoke, and whispering in her ear over and over to not be scared. That help was coming. I knew my brothers had heard the explosion and would come, which they did, but it was too late for me. After pulling the kid to safety, they used anything they could to put out the flames." His chest rose and fell with deep, labored breaths. "I have nightmares, memories of the pain. Feeling my skin on fire and there being nothing anyone could do about it. I passed out before they even carried me out of that shithole. When I woke up next, the pain was so intense I threw up. I was lying face down with doctors shouting around me, but thankfully, they knocked me out. Then I was on a flight to Germany, where I spent two months in the ICU before being transferred stateside to a specialized burn unit. The doctors did their best, but there wasn't much they could do but keep me comfortable while I healed."

"Miles," I whispered. Palm to the mattress, I pushed off the bed to stare down at the amazing man, but he refused to meet my searching gaze. "Look at me."

A lone tear leaked from the corner of his eye. "I'm afraid of what I'll see," he rasped, still staring at the ceiling, unblinking.

My heart shattered into a million pieces at his pleading

tone. This amazing hero, strong, honorable, and selfless, was afraid.

My still-damp hair shifted along my shoulders with a small headshake. Reaching up, I cradled his beard-covered jaw and forced his face toward mine.

"Please," I urged.

"It's not just my skin that's wrecked, Aspen. It's all of me. From the inside out, I'm ruined." More tears leaked down his cheeks. "I don't deserve you, and you sure as hell don't deserve to put up with all my bullshit—"

"You shut the fuck up right the fuck now," I snapped. That got his attention. Wide hazel eyes blinked at me in shock. "Do you think this changes anything? That I'll look at you differently?"

"It has with others."

And now I wanted to murder people.

Not sure what that said about me, that with those four words, I was suddenly okay with the possibility of becoming a serial killer. But I would. For him. To end the lives of any asshole who made this remarkable man beside me feel anything less than the true badass hero he was.

"Do you think so little of me?" I whispered.

"I'm just going off people's reactions in the past."

"But I'm not them. I see you, Miles. I see all of you and am so fucking honored that you'd share this piece of yourself with me. You're a hero."

"I'm not—"

"Let me finish," I begged. Grabbing his hand, I slid a leg over his torso and shifted to straddle his hips. "You're an amazing warrior who has somehow kept a beautiful piece of yourself hidden deep in here." I pressed our combined hands to his chest. "The way you treat me with such reverence and respect, more than I've ever had in my life, is everything. I'm safe with you, Miles. You make me feel like I can take on the world with you at my side. When my mom said all that shit, you being in the room gave me strength and confidence, which allowed her words to just slide off me instead of burying deep like they have in the past. Yes, earlier, I barged into your bathroom to make sure you didn't think her beliefs were my own, but it was more than that too. It's why I came to you, not Aiden. I needed this impervious strength that only you can give." My hands trembled, and my bit of truth fought its way past my lips. "I need you both more than I've ever needed anyone or anything, ever. And I'm terrified of what it means and what will happen to me when it all ends."

"It means we were meant for each other," he said. Reaching up, he cupped my cheek and swiped at the rivers of tears streaking down my face.

"Then believe me when I say this. Those aren't scars to be ashamed of." His grip tightened but was still soft enough not to hurt me. "They're a fucking badge of honor. You saved that little girl's life and took the brunt of the explosion for her. You didn't even think twice about sacrificing yourself, your body, and possibly your life for some stranger. And if I'm right, it wasn't the first time you'd saved someone by putting your own life in danger, whether they were in your arms or at home snug in their beds with zero clue about the danger that lurked in the shadows that you and others handled so they could live and sleep in peace.

"So, no, Miles, these aren't just scars. They're a road map of the warrior that lives inside you. Yes, you're insanely attractive, but that's not what draws me closer every time we're together. It's you. All of you. And I'm sure as we go through this, getting to know the good and bad and worse, you'll find I have scars too."

He huffed. "Don't think so. You're perfect, Aspen."

"I'm not. I'm so far from it that it's scary you think so."

"I have to agree with my bestie on that one, Aspen." I jerked and looked over my shoulder. Aiden leaned against the doorframe, watching us with a soft expression. "You've never given yourself the credit you deserve, Miles. You're a hero to so many, yet you don't see it. Ever."

"You two are ganging up on me," Miles grumbled. Gripping my hips, he shifted me lower.

"Only because we see you, Miles," I whispered, "and are so fucking proud of you."

"Fuck," the two men rasped.

"You know how to cut straight to the heart, don't you, sweetheart?" Aiden appeared beside me, his palm sealing to the back of my neck. "How about you show him just how much you appreciate him?"

My pulse raced and heart skipped a beat. Sliding my gaze from Aiden's blazing stare over to Miles, I sucked in a breath at the intensity there. Gone was the sadness and worry; only desperate need and want flickered in his hazel eyes as he studied the way my peaked nipples poked through the thin cotton of my shirt.

"Have you felt her perfect cunt yet?"

I checked over my shoulder at Miles's words to Aiden.

"Not yet, but if it's anywhere close to heaven like her mouth, I have no hope of lasting."

A delicious shiver raced down my spine at being talked about like I wasn't here, yet everything they said stroked the broken pieces of my self-esteem that I had wondered would ever be put back together again.

"Oh, you'll last," Miles grunted, shifting his hips to press his hardening cock between my thighs. With only the thin towel and the soft material of my joggers between us, I felt every inch, which made my core tighten, desperate to be filled and stretched like the night before. "I won't allow anything else."

I sucked in a sharp breath, stomach flipping at his commanding and dark tone.

Hands gripped the hem of my T-shirt and pulled it over my head. Both men cursed at finding me bare beneath. After taking a shower, I had zero desire to put a bra back on, so here I was, nude from the waist up and very okay with being exposed to their heated gazes.

Arms wrapped around me from behind, palms engulfing both breasts and pinching the pebbled tips between two fingers.

"You ready for us, baby girl?" Miles asked while gently brushing some damp hair off my face.

I knew if I said no, both would back away and give me the space I requested. But I didn't want fucking space. I'd had space. So much damn space that I felt alone in a crowded room before them. I was tired of space, tired of being so damn alone all the time.

"Yes." My moaned answer vibrated around the room.

Hell fucking yes, I was game.

Today. Tomorrow. Every day we were together, yes.

23

AIDEN

The metal chain creaked as the wooden swing moved back and forth. Arm tossed around the back with Aspen's head against my chest and a wide smile on her face as she watched Miles and Jubie playing off in the distance, I wondered if life could ever get better. Fingers stroking down her side, I smirked when she twitched and smacked my hand away.

"Ticklish, are we?" I asked, tone husky. Fuck, how could I want her again so soon after we just had her? But I did. Maybe I'd always have a semihard cock with Aspen in our lives.

"Maybe," she huffed and shifted to smile up at me. "I can't believe this is your life. You get to do this every day." With a sigh, she went back to watching Miles and Jubie. "It's amazing how this place makes all the stressors that weighed me down in Seattle vanish. I don't care about social media, world news, or even next week. All that matters is soaking up the moment, right here, right now."

"I know exactly what you mean." Using two fingers, I brushed a few stray locks of hair away from her face.

"Starting tomorrow, it's back to work for us, though. We have two clients in the morning and one in the afternoon." I bit my lip to keep the next words from tumbling out, but they still came despite me knowing deep down I might not like her answer. "Will you still be here when we get back?"

Aspen stilled beneath me. I held a tight breath as she swung her legs around and sat up straight, turning to face me.

"What do you mean?"

"Here at the house." I stared into her dark eyes, getting lost in the depths. "I like you, Aspen. *We* like you." I angled my head in Miles's direction. "I guess I'm a little afraid of what will happen if or when you walk away."

She scanned my face, brows pulling in tight. "What are you asking me?"

I licked my lips. "For you to stay," I rasped. "To give this a chance to be more than a fun week."

Her lips parted, then closed.

Fuck, what was I doing? It was too soon to bring this up, even if she hinted at it on the hike, but we were running out of time. She would have to leave in only a few days, and that scared me shitless. How could I live without Aspen after knowing her?

"Just think about it. You don't have to answer right now, but I wanted you to know."

"Know what?"

"That this isn't a fling for me or Miles. I knew it before, but after today..." I cleared my throat to ease the sudden tightness. "He opened up to you, Aspen. I'm not saying that you have to stay because my best friend is finally becoming more like the man I remember, but it is a big deal. It means you're special to him."

"And you?" she asked. "What about you, Aiden? Do you want me to stay?"

"More than my next breath." Threading my fingers through her hair, I tugged her closer and pressed our foreheads together. "I didn't realize that Miles wasn't the only one not living, just going through the motions. You've changed that, changed me, and I never want to live in black-and-white now that you've introduced the color that I thought was gone forever."

"Aiden," she rasped and held my face between her soft palms. "This is so much, and I feel like at any moment, reality is going to come crashing in and pop this perfect bubble I've lived in the past few days."

"But what if it doesn't? What if there isn't a bubble, and we three together really are that perfect? What if all we were missing in life was each other?"

"This is crazy. I don't even know you. You don't know me, and—"

"You know both me and Miles better than any person here, who we have spent years living alongside. And I do know you—the important things, at least. I might not know all the details of your past or even your birthday, but I know who you are. I see you, Aspen Carter, and you are just as beautiful inside as you are out."

Tears leaked down her face, and I pulled back, horrified that I said something wrong.

"Fuck, I'm moving too fast, and now you're scared I'm going to lock you in the nonexistent basement if you don't agree to stay, and—"

A finger pressed to my mouth, cutting me off. "Um, that was not the direction of my thoughts, but now that you mention it, maybe it should have been?" A smirk tugged at her lips. "These are happy tears, Aiden."

I slumped backward, pulling her with me. "Thank fuck I didn't just ruin the best thing that's ever happened to us."

"You really think that?"

"I do. Just give it some thought, yeah? Every day could be like this. It doesn't have to end."

Her hair slid along my cotton T-shirt with her slow nod. I released a relieved breath at the slight movement. Heels pressed to the porch, I shifted the swing back to restart the slow, rocking cadence.

After a few minutes, voices interrupted the comfortable quiet as two people strolled down the street, heading our way. I lifted the hand not wrapped around Aspen in greeting.

"Who is that?" Aspen sat up straight and smoothed out the sides of her T-shirt.

"Finley and Dax, our pilots for the helicopter and seaplane tours. They also make emergency supply runs when needed, which they don't mind since both would prefer to be up in the air than anywhere else." Standing, I stretched both arms high overhead before moving toward the steps and leaning against a post, watching as the two drew closer. "They're best friends, have been since serving in the Air Force together."

"And now they're here working together." Aspen stopped beside me and wrapped an arm around my waist. "Are they... do they have a third?" The grimace that scrunched her face was adorable.

"No, and they aren't even together that way." Not yet anyway. They were blind idiots. Neither realized the other was head over heels in love with them. "But that doesn't mean they'll even think twice about us."

"Hey, Aiden," Finley called out with a wide smile on her face. Dax pushed at her shoulder, making her stumble to the side, and she retaliated by shoving Dax across the street. "You're such a pest," Finley said with a laugh. "I'm dumping you out of the plane tomorrow without a parachute."

Dax draped an arm around her shoulders and gave her a friendly shake. "Don't tease me with a good time, love."

"Um, are you sure they're just friends?" Aspen asked under her breath.

"They seem to think so."

"Besides, I might jump out on my own," Dax said, voice having lost all humor. "I'm not looking forward to a few hours stuck with that rich asshole fucker."

When they paused in front of the porch, I said, "Aspen, these two are the best pilots ever to step foot in Anchor Bay. Finley and Dax." I pointed to each before gesturing to Aspen. "And this is Aspen. She's staying here for..." I looked down and laughed at her panicked expression. "A bit."

"It's nice to meet you both," Aspen said, reaching out to shake their hands.

"Hi. Do you like books and wine by chance?" Finley blurted, cheeks going pink.

"Do not try to wrangle her into your book club," Dax joked before turning to Aspen. "They don't discuss books, just drink wine and talk about..." He raised a brow at Finley. "What do you guys talk about?"

"Oh, I know that answer. The first rule of book club," Aspen said with a shy smile to Finley.

"You don't talk about book club," Finley finished. They broke out into a fit of giggles while Dax and I just stared at them, confused as hell.

"It just so happens that I love wine and reading books we might never talk about," Aspen said, smiling so wide her eyes crinkled at the edges. And fuck if that didn't make my heart swell in my chest. She looked so damn happy, and instead of being jealous that it wasn't me or Miles putting that smile on her face, all I felt was ecstatic.

"Awesome," Finley exclaimed with a loud clap. "Our next meeting is Friday. Will you still be here?"

My held breath burned in my lungs as I waited, gazing down at Aspen, who peeked up through her long dark lashes.

"Yeah, I think I will be."

Without thinking, I pulled her flush against me and sealed my lips over hers in an all-consuming kiss. Somewhere behind me, one of the pilots whistled, but I didn't give two shits. After a minute, Aspen pushed back with a palm on my chest, out of breath and lips slightly swollen.

"Aiden." I glanced over my shoulder at Miles's voice. He angled his head toward the two men I hadn't heard approach. For half a second, I worried he was pissed at me for making out with Aspen in front of everyone, but the slow smile and heated expression he shot the woman wrapped in my arms told me otherwise.

Tucking Aspen against my side, I shifted my full focus to Hudson and Oliver. My earlier joy and excitement faded as I took in the stony look on both men's faces.

Fuck, this couldn't be good.

My hold on Aspen tightened. "How did it go with the rangers?"

Hudson's gaze flicked to Aspen before coming back to me. "It's worse than we thought. We'll get our notes together and debrief everyone soon. We just wanted to stop by and see if either of you had heard from Caroline."

I shook my head and ran a hand through my hair, tugging at the ends. Fuck, I was a shit friend. I hadn't thought about her possibly being missing, too wrapped up in everything about Aspen. Guilt swelled in my gut, making me nauseous.

"Us either." Oliver shifted on his worn boots. "We've tried to locate her boyfriend—"

"Jasper," Hudson practically growled, hands curling into fists at his side. "I never liked that fucker."

"But she did, based on the sounds that came from her cabin at night," I said under my breath, making my friend snort.

"We haven't gotten to talk to him yet. Now that we're back, we'll both head out to his place to see what he knows."

"I'm sure Brandon wouldn't mind you using the four-wheelers to make that trek easier on you both. Jasper's place is way out there." I looked down at Aspen to fill her in a little. "You think this is remote? His place is fully off-grid, just the way he likes it."

"Something isn't right, Hudson." Miles turned his full focus to Oliver. "That father of yours needs to stop denying something is going on here and get some fucking answers. Someone broke into Aspen's cottage while we were on an overnight hike, and your asshole father tried to convince me that nothing had happened. I don't understand why he's pushing back so hard when there is ample evidence to warrant a deeper investigation."

Oliver ripped the ball cap off his head and rubbed at his temples. "I don't know either. All I can figure is he feels he's worked too hard to keep this place safe all these years, and the idea of someone out there hurting people on his watch is easier to deny than accept. Fuck if I know, though. I'll talk to him. After this trip and talking to the rangers, there's no putting off opening an official investigation."

My muscles bunched. *Fuck, what did they find out?*

"I went into Caroline's cabin," Miles said with a shrug,

like it wasn't a big deal. "Nothing was out of place. All her hiking and climbing gear was gone as if she were going out, like she told me she was a few days ago."

Aspen's bony elbow dug into my side, making me hiss. "Ouch, angry little—"

"Can you introduce me?" she asked, brows raised.

And I was a fucking rude-ass moron. "Shit, sorry, sweetheart." Clearing my throat to stop the three men's whispered conversation, I waited until I had their attention. "Guys, this is Aspen Carter. Her cabin was the one broken into at The Nest. Aspen, this is Hudson, a friend of our company's owner and a detective from LA, and Oliver, Anchor Bay's deputy sheriff."

Aspen waved at them. "Nice to meet you both." Before she could say another word, her stomach growled loud enough that all of us hid smiles or stifled chuckles. "Shit, that's embarrassing."

"More for these two idiots here," Oliver said, slapping Miles on the back of the head. "Your girl is hungry. Fix that."

A wide smile stretched across my face.

Fuck yes, she was our girl.

I locked eyes with Miles. "Dave's?"

He nodded and jogged up the steps. "I'll just grab her coat, and we can go." He let out a sharp whistle, and Jubie appeared from around the cabin and happily trotted behind Miles, disappearing inside.

"Now for the big decision," I muttered to Aspen.

"Um, yes, we are getting nachos."

I barked a laugh and kissed her forehead. "Are we walking, biking, or driving to town?"

She shifted to stare up at the still brightly lit sky before smiling up at me.

"Walking. We're totally walking, and I'm bringing my camera."

***

THE COUCH GROANED beneath Miles's weight as he sat on the opposite end, careful not to disturb Aspen. The movie we turned on after getting home from dinner played on the screen, though neither Miles nor I paid it any attention.

Stroking a single finger along her cheek, I studied her face.

"Something felt off tonight at Dave's," Miles whispered. "Did you notice?"

I nodded. At first, I thought it was because the last time we were there, we ran into Jessica, but that wasn't it.

"I didn't see anyone in there I didn't recognize, all locals."

"Doesn't mean that there wasn't a threat, though, if we both felt it."

We stayed silent for a few seconds, not wanting to voice our mutual fear that the person hurting women and other tourists was part of our tight-knit community.

"Did you find out what Hudson and Oliver uncovered in the national park?" I asked, swallowing down my apprehension. "It didn't sound positive."

"I talked with them briefly and got an overview but no details. The basics are that we now know for certain there are more missing female hikers based on what the rangers were able to pull together, and the number of mauled male hikers has spiked too. Exactly what we've seen on this side of the trail."

I blew out a slow breath. "You think Caroline is okay?"

Miles sighed and rubbed a hand over his head. "Fuck, I

don't know. I'm trying to stay positive, but..." He shook his head. "She would've reached out. Even if Caroline was out of cell range, we all have sat phones that would've worked." I opened my mouth, but he cut me off before I could even get a word out. "They're turned off, both her cell and the sat phone, so we can't trace either."

"Damn," I muttered. "Did the sheriff really suggest that we made up the break-in at Aspen's place?" He nodded, hands tightening into fists on the couch. "That's fucked up."

"He also said trouble followed us." I snorted, and Miles shook his head. "He's not wrong, Aiden."

"What the fuck does that even mean? It's not our fault that Jessica turned out to be some obsessive stalker who wanted to chain us to beds and ride our dicks like her own personal pogo sticks."

He blinked at me, mouth opening and closing.

"What?"

"That's... dark." Miles smirked. "The shit you watch, man, it's getting to your head. Stick with your damn birds. They're less..."

"Murdery?"

"Likely to add to your violent imagination."

I arched a brow his way. "Pretty sure you like my imaginative ideas occasionally, though last night around the campfire was certainly the best you've ever had. Fuck, that was hot. And then getting to sleep beside her all night... It feels right, all of this. You, me, her, out there doing what we all love."

Miles's smirk fell. "I heard her on the phone with her mom earlier."

The leather groaned as I shifted, careful not to wake Aspen. "And?"

"And she's old-school, thinks it's a woman's key role in

life to get married and have a family." I nodded along with his words. It aligned with what Aspen shared with me. "I'm just saying that if this between the three of us works out, it will be difficult to get her mom on board with accepting our relationship. I don't think she'd ever approve of her daughter being with two men."

I winced. "Do you think that would make Aspen change her mind about us?"

Miles shrugged. "I fucking hope not."

"You know how bad I want that, though," I rasped. "A family. Kids."

His features softened. "I know. You could always borrow Hudson's kid when you're feeling all 'family man.'"

I barked a laugh. "Yeah, because that doesn't sound creepy as fuck. 'Hey, can I borrow Sam for a while to play daddy? But don't worry, it's not what you think. I really want a kid of my own, but I won't steal yours. Pinkie promise.' Pretty sure Hudson, or hell, even Calista, would have me skinned and my heart ripped out before I even finished the question or got to explain."

As if the idea entertained him, Miles grinned. "Yeah, you're probably right. Don't listen to me."

"The thing is, now that I've met Aspen, I don't want a family with just anyone, Miles. I want it with her. Only her."

His lips pursed, and a concerned expression flashed over his features. "We need to take it slow, not scare her off. There are two of us and only one of her." He glanced out the window. "I'm glad Finley invited her to their wine club—"

"Book club," I corrected with a chuckle. "And why?"

His gaze shifted back to Aspen and lightened. "I think she's been alone for a long time, and I like the idea of her having people other than us to lean on. Even though I want to be her everything, I know she'll need more than us."

A soft sound came from Aspen, freezing both me and Miles. Long dark lashes fluttered as she slowly woke up. Pushing off the couch, she looked from me to Miles with a dreamy smile on her face.

"Sorry I fell asleep," she said around a yawn.

"You had a long day, sweetheart," I offered.

"I'm exhausted in the best way possible." She shot us both a sly smile. "Wonder why?"

"We aim to please around here, sweetheart. As much as you'll allow us to."

Miles stood and held out a hand to help her off the couch. Once she was in his arms, he lowered his lips down to hers in a gentle kiss. My cock stirred, watching them as the kiss deepened into something more. With a frustrated groan, he pulled back and pressed a firm kiss to her forehead.

"Good night, baby girl."

"Wait," she called out. "Are we not all sleeping together?"

He shook his head. "Someday maybe, but not tonight."

I nodded, totally understanding. Despite him sharing his past, he still worried he'd hurt her. I didn't think he would, but I also didn't want to push my friend faster than he was ready.

Interlocking our fingers, I led Aspen, who still looked over her shoulder with a sad little frown on her lips, to my room and quietly closed the door, cutting off her line of sight to Miles's room.

"You're positive he'll be okay?" she asked, shifting from foot to foot. "I don't like him being alone."

"Yes, he'll be okay tonight, but I'm sure he won't turn down snuggles in the morning."

She arched a questioning brow. "Just snuggles?"

"Or more, of course. Though right now, that's exactly

what I want. It killed me last night, not getting to hold you." I pointed toward the bathroom. "All your stuff is still in there from earlier. Once you're done, come crawl into bed with me so I can spoon the shit out of you all night long."

"Spoon the shit out of me, huh? Such a romantic." Soft giggles echoed through the room as she disappeared behind the bathroom door.

And after she was done and in bed with me, despite my dick attempting to stab her in the back, that was exactly what I did—and I loved every second of holding her through the night.

24

MILES

"Fuck, you're a grumpy asshole this morning," Aiden groused as he poured coffee into a travel mug, lip curling in disgust at the black liquid. He wasn't a fan of how I made coffee but he didn't wake up early enough to run to Sips for his fancy-ass shit like normal.

No need to wonder why. If I had Aspen in my bed, I wouldn't have woken up early for something as simple as coffee either.

"Fuck off," I snapped, proving his point, if his arched brow was any indication. Scrubbing a hand over my face, I groaned, hating that he was right. "I don't like leaving her unprotected."

With a slow nod of agreement, he leaned a hip against the kitchen counter. "I get it, but like we discussed five times already this morning, we don't have a choice. Plus, we can't keep her locked up in our cabin, Miles, or expect her to stay here all day, every day of her own free will."

"Why not?" I griped and took a sip of my coffee, savoring the bitter flavor.

"Now who sounds like a serial killer?" Aiden joked while

pointing my way. "She'll be fine. Aspen is a capable woman who understands the dangers out there and is prepared now."

"I should get her a gun." Or a knife. Or both.

And a Taser.

"Yes, we should, but that can't happen right this second, Mr. Anxious Pants. We don't know if she's had any gun safety instruction or even feels comfortable firing one."

He had a point.

I fucking hated it, but he had a point.

"I'll put in an order for a Taser from Brad at the gun store," I grumbled.

"You do that, you overbearing mother bear." I shoved Aiden's shoulder as he walked past, headed for the front door. "We need to leave in ten minutes to get the bikes ready and not be late."

I nodded, too focused on texting Brad about the Taser. Putting the phone into a side pocket of my black cargo pants, I swiped my mug off the counter and headed toward the front door. A soft laugh filled the chilled morning air the moment I opened it, which brought a smile to my face and eased some of the anxiety that had built the second Aspen was out of our line of sight.

She was simply on the front porch reading, and I'd gotten all worked up. Fuck, how would I make it through the day, miles away from her and hours without communicating?

"You guys are killing me," she huffed, though the smile on her lips said she wasn't really frustrated. "Go do your jobs. I'll be fine."

I leaned a shoulder against a post and took a sip of coffee. "What are your plans for the day?"

Aspen peeked up through her lashes while taking a

small drink from the mug in her hand. She grimaced. "First order of business, go into town and get a decent cup of coffee. You guys are great at a lot of things." Pink stained her cheeks, making me smirk. Damn right, we were. "But making coffee isn't one of them."

"He made it special for you."

I shot Aiden the bird, making him laugh.

"So, the tar-like texture is special?" She eyed the steaming liquid with disdain.

I did the same. Damn, if she didn't like my coffee, then we could get one of those fancy machines that had been on Aiden's Christmas list for the past two years. Maybe that would make her stay inside. All day long, with the door locked.

Her next words pulled me out of my head. "After I grab drinkable coffee, I might go hiking to get more pictures."

"No," I growled, standing up straight and widening my stance.

"Um…" Aspen looked at Aiden while chewing on the corner of her lip. "That's actually not your call, Miles. There's a lake at the end of Wolf Run Trail I researched before coming here. It's said to have amazing views and is a quick in-and-out, nothing that will require me to stay overnight."

"And I said no," I gritted out. I sounded like a stubborn asshole, but for her safety, I'd be anything I needed to be to protect her. Even if that meant protecting her from herself. "It's not safe. You know why we feel that way. It has nothing to do with your capability."

Her look of annoyed determination softened as she stared up at me. "I get it, Miles. I do, and if I go up there, I'll be careful. I haven't decided yet anyway. I might just hang around town and snap some pictures there."

I didn't like that either.

Fuck, why couldn't we just lock her up in our cabin until we came home?

"I think you might have broken him." Aiden stood from the swing and poked a single finger into the center of my chest. I swatted his hand away with an annoyed snarl. "Nope, still alive and grumpy as hell."

My nostrils flared with the deep, calming inhale to keep from knocking out my best friend. "I just want you safe, Aspen, which means staying here."

"And I won't sit around your cabin waiting for you two to come home while you have all the fun," she snapped back.

"It's our job," I clarified. "We have to do it or we wouldn't be leaving you. It's not like we're going out on a hike for the hell of it and leaving you behind."

"I get that, but your job is fun, being out in nature where you get to ride bikes and snowmobiles." The swing rocked side to side when she stood, holding up the hand that didn't have a death grip around the coffee mug. "Trust me, Miles. I can take care of myself. Promise. I've been doing it on my own for a while now."

Wrapping an arm around her shoulders, I pulled her close until both of her arms went around my waist.

"Nothing can happen to you, baby girl. I know you've taken care of yourself, and you've done a hell of a job on your own. I just don't like it. Hell, thinking about you living in Seattle alone makes me see red, and I didn't even know you then." Her dark hair ruffled with my slow exhale to calm my racing pulse. "And I do trust you—it's every other fucker out there that I don't."

"Not trying to ruin the sweet yet controlling-as-fuck moment, but we gotta go." Aiden slapped a hand on my shoulder and squeezed. "I don't like it either, but there's nothing we can do about it. We have a job to do, and you said no to locking her in the basement."

Aspen's head whipped around to Aiden, and her eyes narrowed into thin slits. "You don't have a basement."

He shot her a wink as he walked off. "Don't give him any ideas. He'll probably start the plans for one today while we're gone. Enjoy your day, sweetheart, and please stay out of trouble."

After pressing a hard kiss to the top of Aspen's head, I reluctantly retreated a step, hating to put distance between us.

"Be good," I ordered with a stern look, which had her rolling those dark eyes to the top of the porch.

"Or what, Mr. Bossy Pants?"

At her sassy tone and mischievous smirk, I closed the distance between us once again and bent low until my lips brushed the shell of her ear.

"Or I'll turn that fine ass of yours so red you won't sit for days without thinking about me. Don't test me on this, Aspen. The other day's punishment was gentle compared to what I'll do if you put yourself in danger."

Her throat worked with a hard swallow. "Just so I understand. If that was gentle the other day, then what's your idea of not gentle?" she asked with parted lips and crimson cheeks, glassy eyes blinking up at me.

A dark chuckle rumbled in my chest while my cock twitched just imagining the future punishment. "Not gentle would be Aiden's cock balls deep in your cunt with me taking your ass while I spank you raw."

With one slow blink, then another, she gaped up at me. "Oh."

Huffing a laugh, I stepped back, taking in her flushed cheeks and quick breaths. "Fuck, baby girl. Based on how turned on you look, maybe that's more incentive to be a naughty girl than not."

A single slender shoulder rose as she shot me a sassy wink. Damn, this woman would be the death of me.

"Fine, if taking us both at the same time isn't a deterrent to be good, I could always threaten to hide your camera or have us hold out on you as punishment."

Dark eyes widened before narrowing. "You wouldn't dare."

"Which one?"

"Either." Rolling her eyes, she tossed up her free hand. "I'll be safe and aware of my surroundings, stranger danger, and all that if I go into town. Promise. Now go." She shoved my shoulder, though I barely even shifted with the push. "Before you're late for work."

With a clipped nod, I forced myself to turn. Boots slamming to the steps, I picked up the pace to a quick jog to catch up with Aiden, who was already halfway down the street. As we rounded a corner to take the path to the equipment shed, I chanced one last look over my shoulder. Aspen still stood on the porch, both forearms resting on the railing, coffee cup in hand, the wind whipping at her loose hair. Noticing me, she smiled and made a shooing motion with her hand.

My heart lurched, thumping almost painfully in my chest at the picturesque scene.

Aspen Carter was absolutely everything we wanted and never knew we needed.

And I'd do anything to keep her safe.

No matter the cost.

25

ASPEN

An appreciative hum vibrated in my throat as I took another sip of the impeccable blend of milk and coffee from the oversized bear-shaped mug. This was absolute heaven. Delicious coffee, beautiful scenery outside the large window beside my table, and nothing to do.

Well, that last part wasn't exactly true.

Glancing away from the window, I eyed the trail map resting on the wooden table in front of me and debated for the thousandth time since I sat down if I should do what I wanted or obey Miles's order. I fully understood his reasons for being insanely cautious—though overbearing was a better word—but I was an independent woman who hadn't been told what she could or couldn't do in a very long time.

Part of me wanted to go on the hike just because he told me I couldn't.

I huffed into the cup. Who did he think he was telling me, a fully grown adult, where I could or couldn't go because *he* deemed it unsafe?

However, another part wanted to listen to him because

he had a point, and if I listened, I'd more than likely be rewarded in all the best ways.

A soft, lovesick sigh blew past my lips as I turned my gaze back out the coffee shop's large window. Light gray clouds blocked the sun, making it feel later in the day than midmorning. I checked my watch and glanced at the map again. If I left before noon, then I would be back before the guys were done with work, which meant I wouldn't lose any of the precious time we had left together.

Thinking that shifted my thoughts from the hike to what Aiden brought up on the porch yesterday. They wanted me to stay. As in not leaving when my reservations at The Nest were over. Which was great since I wanted to stay.

I *wanted* to stay, right?

What if this was some vacation high where anything goes and reality didn't matter? That could be the case, but what we had, what I felt for them, seemed deeper than that. Almost like this place was meant to be my forever. Just the thought of going back to Seattle or even just leaving Anchor Bay made my stomach sour, so why would I when I was utterly happy here?

The tiny bell above Sips's door rang when the glass door swung open, allowing a man I hadn't seen before to rush through. The older man behind the counter paused what he was doing to frown at the new person as he beelined to a door labeled Employees Only. Taking another sip, I turned back to study the brightly colored buildings on the other side of the street, but the newcomer reappeared, hastily tying a wrinkled apron around his waist.

"You're late," the older gentleman complained in a huff. "That's twice in the last week, Jasper."

My ears perked up at the name. Wasn't that the name of

the missing woman's boyfriend, the one Hudson and the deputy sheriff mentioned they wanted to talk to?

"Damnit, I know. Sorry, Paul. It won't happen again. Things have been..." His words trailed off when his swinging gaze landed on me. "Unusual."

I sat frozen in my seat, unable to move, as Jasper stared me down with a harsh expression from across the café.

"Oliver came in asking about you." Jasper's assessing stare snapped when his head whipped toward Paul, eyes wide. "I told them you'd be working today."

A muttered curse barely reached my ears. Shaking his head, Jasper grabbed a wet rag and shoved away from the counter.

"They won't leave me the hell alone. I'm going to clean the tables." But instead of stepping toward the ones with empty mugs and plates on top, he walked straight over to me. Pausing at my table, standing so close that I scooted toward the window or my shoulder would've brushed against his thigh, he said, "I don't know you, but I've seen you around town."

My throat closed up.

What the fuck kind of opening line was that?

A suspicious one, that was for damn sure.

"Taking the trail to Kenai Fjords or just visiting?" he asked, eyeing my half-empty mug. "Want another latte?"

"Visiting," I rasped as I drew the mug close to my chest, afraid he'd take it no matter what I wanted. "And no, thank you. I'm good."

"Which trail are you heading to?"

It suddenly felt like I couldn't catch my breath. "How—" My voice broke. "How did you know I planned to go hiking later?"

Light, almost white brows pulled in tight, forming a line

between them. "Well, you just confirmed it, but I asked based on the trail map you've got." He tilted his shaved head toward the map unfolded on the table. "Want a local's advice on which ones are the easiest?"

Heart hammering in my chest, every internal alarm bell rang in my head at the eerie way he studied me, waiting for my answer. Jasper was as much a stranger as Aiden that first day, but Aiden put me at ease instantly. This guy was the complete opposite. I wanted to run from him while checking over my shoulder to make sure he didn't follow.

"No, thank you. I can manage on my own." Hoping he'd get the hint that I was done with the conversation, I shifted in the seat to stare out the window. His looming presence remained there, making the hairs on the back of my neck stand on end for several long seconds before grumbling under his breath about rude tourists and walking away.

Once he was behind the counter, I slumped in the chair, breathing deeply to slow my racing pulse. The mug trembled as I raised it to my lips and took a sip of the now-cool coffee.

Movement outside the window drew my attention to a tall man wearing a cowboy hat and the smaller woman who walked hand in hand with him as they strolled down the street. I couldn't see their faces, but their body language spoke to the strong romantic connection between them. I swallowed down a squeal of delight when something moved on the woman's shoulder and I instantly recognized the little fur ball.

BamBam.

The awkwardness from earlier was now a distant memory as I slouched back in the seat with a wide smile on my face.

Yes. Yes, I wanted to stay.

Not only because of Anchor Bay and the adorable woodland creatures I could potentially befriend but them.

I wanted to stay here with Miles and Aiden in the perfect tiny community that had lovable dogs, ermines running about, and who knew what other animals I had yet to discover. I was safe here, desperately wanted. So, why in the hell would I consider leaving when everything I was missing in my life was here?

With my mind made up on that drastic life change, I finished the last bit of coffee, folded up the trail map, and pushed away from the table. Now, to grab the gear from my cabin at The Nest that I left behind yesterday before heading out to the trail. My decision to stay only solidified the necessity of going on the hike. I would need a decent income from my photos to not drain my savings, which meant I needed more pictures.

I might stay here for Aiden and Miles, but I sure as hell wouldn't lose myself in the process.

Been there. Done that.

Never again.

WITH A DETERMINED EXHALE, I forcefully shoved the cabin door open. The heavy wood bounced against the opposite wall and closed again. I pressed a palm to the center, keeping it wide open. Feet still firmly planted on the porch, I leaned inside, frantic gaze jerking around the open-concept cabin for any signs of danger. When nothing jumped out to kill me, I dared a hesitant step over the threshold.

The door slammed shut at my back, making me jump despite expecting the sound.

Ears straining to hear over the blood pounding in my ears, I inched my way deeper into the living room. As the seconds ticked by with nothing happening, my shoulders dropped, and each breath came easier.

Chafing both hands along my biceps, I gnawed on my lower lip, still not 100 percent convinced I was truly safe. It didn't feel as off as yesterday when we walked in, but it certainly didn't feel as welcoming as the cute cottage did the first day.

In fact, it felt hollow.

Cold.

Lonely.

Shaking off the unease, I grabbed my pack from the hike with Aiden and Miles and began unpacking the things I wouldn't need for a quick in-and-out hike. All I needed was different lenses for my camera, snacks, water, and maybe more snacks, just in case. I really should've eaten that delicious-looking muffin at Sips.

Studying the sad pile of munchies, I groaned and looked to the ceiling in exasperation. If I wanted more than a single granola bar and beef jerky stick, I'd have to visit the resort's outfitting store before heading out. After double-checking that I had everything, I scanned the cabin one more time before reaching for the door handle.

Except it twisted beneath my hovering palm before I could grip it.

Stupid. Stupid Aspen.

I forgot to lock it behind me.

A rush of adrenaline had me gripping the metal and yanking the door open. The man standing on the other side of the door gasped and stumbled backward like I was the one who surprised him.

"Who are you, and what do you want?" I said breathlessly, my pulse racing like I'd sprinted a mile.

Long, thin fingers gripped at the material of his pressed button-down shirt right over his heart. Lips parted, he gasped for air while swaying on his feet.

"Oh, I did not expect you to be here," the stranger wheezed.

Setting down my pack, I crossed both arms over my chest and waited for him to continue, taking the moment to memorize everything about him. Middle-aged, dark hair graying at the temples, and a somewhat familiar face now that I could look while not freaking the fuck out. My eyes narrowed on his face like that would help me place where I'd seen him before. Strangely enough, despite his attempt to enter my cabin, I didn't feel threatened by the stranger—more annoyed than anything.

"I am so sorry," he said in a rush, now that he had his breath back. "I stopped by to make sure everything was secure after the incident yesterday." I raised both brows, not commenting. "Forgive me, Aspen." A repulsive shiver raced down my spine at my name coming from his lips. "I'm Charles Parks." Still, I waited. "General manager of The Nest."

I relaxed a fraction. That was why I recognized him—I'd probably seen him around the property since I arrived.

"So, is everything okay inside?" He shifted, attempting to see around me, but I jerked the edge of the door closer to block his view. A flash of annoyance crossed his face before settling back into a fake smile.

"Yes." I cleared my throat. "Miles and Aiden made sure of it."

I had no clue why I threw their names out there, but it felt like a life raft, something to hold on to while standing in front of the stranger as my suspicions grew. How convenient that he came to check on my cabin in the fifteen minutes I'd been back since I left yesterday.

"Right," he grumbled. He slowly took me in, pausing on the pack on the ground by my boots. "Going for a hike?"

I nodded.

"Take one of the four-wheelers or bikes if the trailhead you're wanting is quite a distance away." He waited as if hoping I would volunteer which trail I planned to take. *Fuck. No.* "Well, if everything is good here, then my work is done."

He didn't do any work, but okay.

I slumped against the doorframe when he turned to leave, only to stiffen when he whirled back around.

"I know this isn't my place, but I feel the need to warn you." My stomach flipped as fear flooded my system. Rocking back on the heels of his shiny black dress shoes, Charles slid his hands into the side pockets of his slacks. "They're dangerous."

"The trails?" I asked slowly.

He scoffed. "No, those men and women who work for Uplift." I felt my brows furrow, which was apparently all he needed to continue. "The owner of the place loves them and refers only their tours and excursions to our resort guests. I can only assume the owner doesn't know what I know."

I stifled a sigh, very over the conversation already. "And what do you know?"

"Those people are not who you think they are. Their owner focuses on mostly employing veterans. You know what that means?"

I blinked down at him. "That they're badass and already come with some serious training?"

"Loose cannons, unpredictable," he said like I was the dumb one. "They're dangerous because you never know when one might snap. Another female guest recently talked to me about two of the men in the group and confirmed my suspicions."

"Right," I drawled. Grabbing my pack off the ground, I tossed it over my shoulder, flicked the lock on the inside of the door, and stepped out onto the small porch, closing the door behind me. I jiggled the handle to ensure it locked. "I'm guessing this female guest is the same one the two men have talked to the sheriff about?"

The same one who tried to embarrass them at the bar that first night.

I should've punched her in the boob when I had the chance.

"Well, that's because she just wants them to apologize for leading her on—"

I held up a hand, cutting him off. "Thanks for the warning, but I'm going to stick with my first impression of those two men and everyone else who works at Uplift. They've been nothing but helpful and kind."

A flash of annoyance came and went before he pursed his lips and nodded. "Well, don't say I didn't warn you about the danger. Things shift quickly here in Alaska. Anything could happen when you least expect it."

I gaped at his retreating back.

Why the fuck did that sound like a threat?

And why the hell didn't I listen?

26

AIDEN

Whistling a cheerful tune, I leapt up the few steps, riding boots slamming to the porch with a thud. My stomach growled, reminding me it was lunchtime, but I didn't care about food. Unless the food was Aspen's pussy—then I'd be all about eating until I had my fill. Hopefully, she was back from town and happy to see us.

Our afternoon client called to say they'd changed their minds and wanted to book a horseback trail ride with our resident cowboy, Liam, later in the week instead. When we found out that we'd get to head home to see our girl sooner than expected, both of our moods instantly perked right the fuck up.

Ready to call out her name, I swung the door open with a flourish, but my wide smile slipped immediately, sensing she wasn't there. Stomach sinking with every quick step, I strode to the kitchen to check for a note on where she might have gone. Finding the counter bare, I swept an assessing gaze around the cabin, snagging on the coffee cup she used earlier sitting in the sink, still full of the oil-like substance.

Like me, she wasn't a fan of Miles's ultra-dark coffee and

mentioned needing a decent cup, which meant the only coffee shop in town.

Sips.

I shifted to eye the clock on the stove. It was almost two in the afternoon, though it felt much later because of the darkening skies that prevented the sun's bright afternoon rays from pouring through the windows.

"Good thing that client canceled. I just got a fucking weather alert," Miles muttered, the door slamming shut behind him. "We're under a snowstorm warning."

I huffed and shook my head. "Of course we are. Alaskan weather likes to keep us on our toes. When do they expect it to hit us?"

Miles stared at his phone as he made his way through the living room. "In a few hours for Anchor Bay. We shouldn't get too much snow, maybe a few inches. The worst will hit the mountains." For the first time since he entered the cabin, Miles looked up from his phone and glanced around the room, lips dipping into a frown. "Where is Aspen?"

Knowing shit was about to hit the fan, I lifted my shoulders in a shrug as I raised both hands. "Not here, obviously."

His frown morphed into a scowl as he tapped the phone screen before holding it up to his ear. My gut churned with worry when he yanked it away with a barked curse.

"No answer?"

"Went straight to voicemail," Miles bit out. "I bet she turned it off after that call with her mom yesterday."

"Yeah, she seemed hesitant to even turn it on when we were in the car." I pointed to the cup. "She mentioned wanting decent coffee." Like a bull in a china shop, my best friend just grunted his acceptance and stormed toward the front door. I sighed. "Guess that means we're going to Sips."

Before I could close the door, Jubie dashed out, racing after Miles with happy yips.

His truck turned over, the engine roaring to life just as my fingers wrapped around the door handle. With a curse, I flung the door open and jumped inside the cab after Jubie before Miles could shift into Drive and leave us both behind.

"Fucking hell, man," I snapped as I leaned against Jubie, who sat in the middle smiling like this was the best day of her life, so I could slam the door shut. "Please don't kill me on your frantic mission to find her."

"She better be there," he hissed. Both hands tightened on the wheel, knuckles going white with the fierce grip.

A frustrated groan escaped as I tapped the back of my head against the headrest. "Aspen is a grown woman, Miles. She can do whatever the hell she wants to do. We have no say in where she goes or what she does." The words were true but still tasted bitter. I wanted to have a say, more to keep her safe than to control her, but it was a fine line between the two.

"Fuck."

His outburst snapped my attention out the window, making me curse under my breath. At first, it was just a few thick flakes, but it quickly turned into a heavy flurry of snow pouring from the gray skies. This wasn't a big deal for us. This was Alaska. It snowed here, and we were prepared for it.

But Aspen wasn't.

And she wasn't with us where we could keep her warm and safe.

Instead of slowing for the weather, Miles pressed harder on the gas, shooting down the winding road that led to town. Faster than we'd ever clocked before, he jerked the truck into an open parking spot down the street from Sips and cut the engine.

I was out before the tires had stopped, striding to the only coffee shop in town worth a damn. Behind me, stomping boots and soft panting told me Miles and Jubie were hot on my heels.

The bell overhead rang as I jerked the glass door open and stormed inside.

Paul, the owner, stood tall, arms crossed over his chest as he stared me down, gaze shifting to just over my shoulder when Miles stepped into the shop. The man Paul had been talking to turned. I didn't even try to hold back my annoyed grumbling.

Charles Parks, The Nest's newest GM, who hated me, Miles, and every other employee of Uplift for some unknown reason. He held my glare as I approached the counter.

"You know she can't be in here," Paul said, hitching his chin at Jubie, who answered by standing on her back paws and putting the front ones on the counter. Drool dripped from her jowls to the clean surface, making me chuckle.

"Worthless animal," Charles grumbled.

"The fuck did you say about my dog?" Miles responded, his tone deadly.

Charles jumped and swallowed hard before retreating a step, then another, headed toward the front of the café. "We can finish that conversation later, Paul. I'm not comfortable being here with them." With that snide remark, he dashed out the door, speed-walking past the wide window until he disappeared down the sidewalk.

"Where is she?" Miles demanded, glaring at Paul.

My eyes went wide as I stared at Miles. Okay, so apparently my bestie devolved into a rude brute when his girl was missing. Not that I was much better, but I had to be if we wanted this conversation to result in us finding Aspen, since she was clearly not here.

Before Paul could respond, I held up my hand, drawing his attention.

"He's referring to Aspen Carter. New to town, long dark hair, brown eyes, adorable nose?"

Paul rolled his eyes and tossed the rag he used to clean up Jubie's constant drool over his shoulder. "She was in here earlier." He eyed me, then Miles. "She was a nice girl, polite, and actually appreciated my coffee."

"Where. Is. She?"

I winced at Miles, noting the way his face had fallen into the impassive mask I knew spelled trouble for anyone who stood in his way of getting what he wanted.

Which, in this case, was finding Aspen.

"Calm down, big fella," I whispered to him, then turned back to Paul. "We're looking for her since she wasn't where we thought she would be. With the storm rolling in"—I gestured to the window and the snow pouring down, already accumulating in a few areas—"we want to make sure she's safe."

Paul studied Miles before sighing. "She only stayed for one cup of coffee." He stiffened, which made both Miles and me stand tall. Gaze locked on the Employees Only door, Paul's bushy brows furrowed. "And had a conversation with Jasper when he came in for his shift—late again. After that, she left." He shrugged and wiped down the top of the pastry display case. "I never should've hired him. He left his shift early, about the time she did, saying he didn't feel well and needed to head out. Damn kid. No wonder he can't hold down a job."

I stood frozen, barely breathing.

"Jasper Cain?" I rasped.

Paul hummed and nodded while scrubbing at a dried spill.

Barely able to move, I chanced a look at Miles, who had gone utterly still and cursed.

Fuck.

Fuck.

Fuck.

Caroline's boyfriend, whom Hudson and Oliver couldn't pin down to discuss our concerns about her being missing, not only talked to Aspen but left when she did.

This was not good.

My stomach rolled with dread, and bile crept up my throat while my chest tightened painfully, making it hard to breathe.

"Aiden." Miles's bark jerked me out of my spiraling dark thoughts, each worse than the last. "Let's move."

I could only nod in response, too wrapped up in my head. This was all my fault. I shouldn't have sided with her, should've made her take Miles's concern more seriously. If I had stood with him and told her she was under house arrest, unable to leave unless one of us was with her, then she would be in my arms and not missing.

If she was hurt...

A hard shove sent me stumbling to the side, my shoulder bouncing off the brick of a building. I shook my head to clear my thoughts and glared at Miles.

"Stop it," he snarled. Firm grip around the back of my neck, he guided-slash-forced me along the sidewalk toward the truck, where Jubie already waited. "Get out of your head and stop whatever you're thinking. Let's check her cabin. She could be there."

"Or she could be dead because I wasn't there. Because I didn't warn her or—"

"It's not your fault, Aiden," Miles said the second we were all in the truck cab. He started the engine and reversed out of the parking spot before turning toward The Nest. "Everything bad that happens around you isn't your fault." I hated the softness of his tone, like he was talking to an upset child. "I know that damn ex of yours made you believe you were ground zero for all that's wrong in the world, but you're not."

"She has to be okay." I was barely able to get a word out around my tight and dry throat. "She has to be, Miles." I winced at my pathetic, pleading tone.

Adjusting his grip around the steering wheel, Miles shot a worried look my way before nodding. The rest of the drive to The Nest was quiet, only the sound of windshield wipers squeaking with every pass to clear the thick snowflakes. Even Jubie, probably sensing the tension, was quiet and hyper-focused.

After what felt like hours of driving, we topped the hill, and The Nest appeared. Almost hitting a few guests wandering around and snapping pictures of the falling snow, Miles tore through the resort, tires squealing to turn toward Aspen's cottage.

Like earlier in town, I was out of the truck, door left wide open for Jubie to follow, before Miles had even put the truck into Park. A deep, booming bark followed me as I raced down the path, heavy boots punching through the thin layer of snow that accumulated on the ground. Leaping onto her porch, my boots slid along the slick wooden planks, sending me skidding into the door.

Ignoring the aching places that had slammed into the thick wood, I gripped the door handle and gave it a hard turn, praying that it was unlocked so I could barge inside and not have to wait for her to answer.

But it wasn't.

Locked.

Pounding one fist on the door while running the other hand through my damp hair, I yanked hard on the ends, breathing deep to keep from sinking into all the dark and violent thoughts that swirled and threatened to swallow me whole.

Fuck my ex for turning me into this mass of guilt and fear when anything wrong happened. After being blamed and accused of anything that wasn't perfect, I believed in preparing for the worst when something happened.

"Not here?" Miles called behind my back.

I dropped my fist and sealed my forehead to the cold wood. "Or she's just not answering."

"Locked?"

"Yep."

A wide palm wrapped around my shoulder and forcefully shoved me away from the door. Taking my spot, Miles knelt and pulled his lock-picking kit out of his cargo pants' side pocket.

I blinked, wiping away the mix of sweat and snow off my temples. "We're breaking in?"

He grunted as he worked the two picks into the lock. "It's either this or we round up that Charles fucker and ask him to let us in. We both know he'll tell us to fuck off, and then we'd be right back here, with me doing this."

Hands on my hips, I watched as he worked the lock. "Then I change what I said to a statement, not a question. We're breaking in."

"Hell yes we are, and when I get my hands on our girl," Miles said with a slight growl, jamming the picks into the metal as his frustration rose, "I'm going to enjoy every second of punishing her for making us worry."

Impatiently waiting, eyes flicking between his tools and the door handle, I begged the door to swing open on its own and for Aspen to come out confused. But it didn't. After a resounding click, Miles palmed the doorknob and gave it a hard twist, swinging the thick wood door into the cabin.

With a nerve-steadying inhale, I followed him into Aspen's cottage, so terrified of what we would find that my whole body trembled.

But after scouring the cottage, it was what we *didn't* find that tipped me over the edge into full panic.

Aspen was gone.

27

MILES

It helped to focus on all the pleasurable options to punish Aspen for making me worry; then I wouldn't notice the fear-induced pressure swelling in my chest. As I stayed frozen in the doorway, Aiden shoved past me, yelling her name, desperation in his tone. Barely breathing, I scanned the room for any signs of where she might be.

Moving to the middle of the living room, I turned in a full circle, scrubbing a hand over my face in a lame-ass attempt to calm the fuck down. I was no good to anyone if I allowed the panic and worry to overtake rational thought. Blowing out a steadying breath, I rolled both shoulders back and scanned the room a second time, slower than before, to not miss a single clue.

That was when my gaze snagged on something by the door.

No, not something tangible, more of a tickle in the back of my brain that something was missing. My eyes narrowed into thin slits while I racked my sluggish thoughts to understand why the blank space by the door felt important. Aiden stopped at my side, words flowing out of his mouth faster than ever, but I blocked him out, continuing to stare at the empty area, excavating my memories for why the fuck it was significant as to where Aspen might be.

It hit me like a punch to the gut.

"Her pack from yesterday," I muttered, more to myself. "Didn't she leave it by the door?" I could've sworn I remembered it being there while Deputy Dipshit shuffled around the room, grumbling about Aiden and me causing all the trouble in Anchor Bay.

Aiden stepped closer, hands on his hips, before turning with raised brows. "I don't remember her carrying it out yesterday when we left. I had her bags, and she had her camera bag. So yeah, maybe it was there."

"But it's not now."

"I'll check her room. Maybe she came here and moved it."

I slowly nodded when Aiden stormed off but continued to focus on that space.

A second later, he called out from the bedroom. "Not here. Neither are her hiking boots, but I think she wore those yesterday at our place. Wait a second..."

I spun on my heels and marched into the bedroom.

Aiden pointed to a small pile on the floor. "Aren't those her dirty clothes from the hike and overnight gear?"

"So, either someone was here, went through her pack, and then took it, or..." I jerked my wide eyes to Aiden, who had the same horrified expression on his face. "She came by here and dumped the things she didn't need for an in-and-out hike."

"Like she mentioned wanting to do earlier this morning," Aiden finished, face going pale as he stared at the snow pouring down outside the window.

We both started toward the door before we even

discussed our next steps. Double-checking that it locked behind me, I sprinted down the path to catch up with Aiden and Jubie.

"Wolf Run, that was the trail she mentioned this morning," I shouted as I rounded the truck hood. I glared up at the gray sky. In the few minutes we were in the cabin, the wind had picked up, and the snow fell in heavier sheets. "We'll need to talk to Hudson about borrowing the four-wheelers and let him know where we're headed."

"She could already be on her way down, and we're overreacting," Aiden suggested after slamming the truck door shut behind him.

The engine roared as I reversed out of the parking spot. "And what if she isn't? I'm not risking her life and safety on an assumption." I gestured out the windshield to the falling snow. "This storm is way damn worse than they predicted. I can't imagine what it's like on that trail, considering the higher elevation at the peak." Both hands tightened on the wheel as my fear and worry grew. "I doubt she knew about the incoming storm since we didn't even know. It was supposed to stay north, but obviously that didn't happen. Fuck!" I exclaimed, slamming the heel of my hand to the dash. "I knew we should've locked her in the cabin."

Aiden huffed an incredulous laugh while he rubbed at his temples. "That would make her resent us and leave. We've been over this. We're lovers, not kidnappers."

"Speak for yourself," I grumbled, jerking the wheel to take a tight turn. The back tires spun on the slippery road.

"About the lovers or kidnappers part?"

I shot him a knowing look before focusing back on the road. Aiden's defense mechanism to not drown in an ocean of guilt during high stress was making jokes, diverting his thoughts from the situation to protect himself. If my friend needed to distract himself, then I could play along. I was trained for this type of high-stress moment; it was what I excelled in in my past life.

"The kidnapping part, obviously. You've witnessed first-hand the lovers part."

"Touché," he said with a forced smirk.

"After we talk to Hudson about this potential rescue mission, we'll grab the gear we might need and head out. The trailhead for Wolf Run isn't too far from us, so we can take the four-wheelers. We should bring extra supplies for her on the off chance we need to hole up in one of the emergency shelters until the storm passes."

We could do this.

Find Aspen.

Kiss the hell out of her.

Then spank her ass for putting herself in danger.

We just needed to find her first.

28

The life-threatening situation I found myself in wasn't my fault.

Well, maybe partially mine, since I ignored Miles's warning about the dangers on the trail. I thought it would be an easy in-and-out, something I'd done hundreds of times before on my own, so why would this hike be any different from the others? That was my first mistake of the day, with many more to follow.

It started out great. The hike up was absolutely gorgeous and easy, though steep and not well marked. When I reached a crystal-clear mountaintop lake, I knew I had to stop. Within the first hour, I'd taken hundreds of pictures of various animals that came to the water for a drink. With the sun covered by the growing gray clouds, it added a soft, suspenseful feel to the pictures that I knew would turn out amazing after editing them on my laptop.

I was on a nature high, if that was a thing. For hours, I sat on top of a rock along the shoreline, staying perfectly still despite the quickly dropping temperature and whipping wind to snap shots I knew had the potential to bring in the money I'd need to stay in Anchor Bay without requiring the guys' financial help.

I really didn't want to depend on them for everything. Which pushed me to sit, ignoring my chattering teeth and numb fingers, staying way longer than I should have with the inclement weather.

But when the first few flecks of snow started to fall, the cold settling into my bones was forgotten as I gazed in wonder at the silent beauty. After a few minutes, I quickly realized that though the snow was beautiful, it was also thick, falling in heavy sheets and accumulating on the already-cold ground faster than I expected.

Knowing it could get dangerous with the narrow trail and steep inclines on the way down, I hurried to pack up my gear, cursing at myself for sitting for so long when my muscles and joints protested with the movement.

As I bent over my pack, shoving the last bit of trash into a side pocket, the somewhat dangerous scenario turned into a life-threatening, pee-your-pants-in-fear situation. A medium-sized light brown bear lumbered around a large boulder, freezing me on the spot. Heart racing a thousand beats a second, I sealed a hand over my lips to muffle my ragged breaths, hoping to stay quiet enough to not draw its attention.

No such luck. It swung its massive head in my direction, billowing clouds pouring from its snout stuck high in the air as if sniffing something, and started moseying my way.

Which meant its gigantic body was now positioned between me and the only feasible way out of the lake area, unless I wanted to scale the jagged cliff that wrapped around the back half of the water.

Not excited about becoming bear food, I slowly slid down the rock, boots barely making a sound when they hit the sand and mud along the shore. Keeping my eyes locked on the animal, I crouched low to crawl behind another scattering of rocks for cover, purposefully leaving my pack with food behind as a sacrificial lamb of sorts. Careful not to drag my camera across the rocky and damp ground, I eased around the massive rock until the bear disappeared from view. Brilliant plan, except I wasn't aware that where I sought shelter, small waves of water had soaked the ground from the wind whipping over the top of the lake.

I swallowed a pitiful and frustrated whimper, not wanting to draw the bear's attention. Things couldn't get worse unless I actually dove into the lake, fully submerging myself in the freezing water.

As if sensing my growing frustration with the unexpected events, the clouds seemed to open up, dumping more and more snow, covering everything around me in a thick layer of white.

Fuck.

In below-freezing temperatures, which my light coat was useless to ward against, plus wet boots, socks, and now pants, I was royally screwed with zero clue about what to do next to save myself from being eaten or dying of hypothermia.

The ripping of material and loud huffs of heavy breathing had my stomach sinking. I was trapped where I was, freezing mist coating my face and body, going numb until Mr. Bear was done. Time slowed as I sat, muscles tense and tight from the cold, listening to the bear shred through my pack's contents, no doubt eating all the yummy snacks I purchased from The Nest while the snow continued to fall, sealing my fate.

By the time the munching stopped, the snorting and stomping of heavy steps long faded, and I dared to peek around the boulder, everything was covered in a pristine blanket of white, minus the terrifying paw prints that led back toward the way the bear came.

I slumped back against the rock, hand to my chest as I gulped down lungfuls of air. Fuck, that was close. Never once in all the times I'd hiked in my life had I encountered a bear this close. In the past, we'd kept a significant distance between us and them when out on location for the magazine which was why I didn't even think to bring bear spray.

Idiot. I was a damn idiot.

Knowing I needed to get myself out of the shallow, icy water immediately, I slowly stood, muscles and joints protesting, and eased from my hiding place. A frustrated grumble escaped that sounded way louder with the silent snow pouring from the sky and surrounding quiet. That jackass bear shredded everything. There wasn't a single thing to salvage. Even the pack itself was ruined.

After scooping up the remains, my body now trembling and fingers numb, I tied the thick, ripped ribbons of canvas together into a makeshift sack to keep the trash from spilling out and started toward the trail.

Only to quickly realize it was gone.

Well, not literally gone, but hidden somewhere under the inches of snow that had accumulated and added to the thick patches of icy, dirty snow that had yet to melt from previous storms that dotted the area. It hit me like a punch to the gut as I frantically scanned the area for any hint of where the trail had started. I was truly, thoroughly fucked. The already poorly marked and hard-to-navigate trail was daunting before the snow; now it would be dangerous as hell to even attempt to start the hike down.

Could I attempt it and pray to the Alaskan gods that I was on the right path? Sure, but that was an amateur mistake. Seasoned hikers knew to stay put so they didn't potentially wander off the trail, becoming lost and far from the path where rescuers would look first.

I was stuck. Dropping the useless pack, I stomped to a set of rocks away from the water and sat on the opposite side to use it as a shield from the whipping wind.

"Damnit, Aspen." My fogged breath pushed back into my face where it was tucked against my chest. I tightened both arms around my shins, curling into an even tighter ball to preserve what little body heat remained. A thicker coat, gloves, and a hat would've been great, but unfortunately, I'd left it all in the cabin, not thinking the weather would turn as quickly as it did.

It was fine.

I would survive this and laugh about it later.

Hopefully.

Maybe.

Rocking back and forth to keep the blood flowing to my extremities, I berated myself over and over. All I had to do was wait for the guys to be free, and they would've come with me. But no, Mrs. I'm a Capable Adult had to prove my competency and independence by coming here all alone and, bonus, unprepared for snowmageddon. Okay, this was probably not snowmageddon to Alaskans, but it felt like it to me.

Sharp, jagged edges of the rock I leaned back against pierced through my light jacket and sweater, poking at my spine as I shifted along the damp ground. I glared at the asshole snow. Once beautiful and calming, now all I wanted to do was flip it the bird.

For the hundredth time, I debated saying fuck it and trying to make my way down the mountain. Shaking my head, melted droplets of snow flicking onto my already-wet jacket, I forced myself to stay put. Staying where I was until someone came for me was my best option, even if that meant ever so slowly turning into a human popsicle.

Lungs tight, I worked to huff warm breaths into my frozen hands before tucking them back under my armpits. Someone—or two someones—would come looking for me. That, I was certain of.

Hopefully before I turned into the crazy guy at the end of *The Shining*.

Fuck, Miles was going to be furious. That thought had renewed heat thawing me from the inside out. But my heart sank thinking about Aiden. He probably blamed himself for this, even though I was the dumbass who didn't listen to their warnings.

Minutes turned into what felt like hours of waiting, fighting to stay awake as my heart rate slowed. I eyed the sky, wishing I could see the sun to attempt to guess at the time. Surely by now the guys had realized I was gone, right? But that didn't mean they knew where to look.

Damnit, why didn't I leave a note for them?

Oh, that's right. Fucking creepy Charles.

My brows pulled in tight as I stared at the snow around me as if it had all the answers. What the hell was he doing at my cabin anyway? It felt fishy that he stopped by to check on the place when I was there and alone. But how would he have known I was there unless he had cameras or something?

Blowing out a breath, I tucked my chin in close. None of that mattered now. Nothing mattered but getting the hell off this trail and back with my guys.

In front of a fire.

Beneath a thick blanket.

Naked.

My numb lips twitched upward at that thought. Even with Miles's punishment warning, I still couldn't wait to be with them. With them, I was and would always be safe.

And cherished.

And well fucked.

Which kind of went along with the whole *cherished* part. What better way to let your girl know you loved and adored her in every way than to worship her body with mind-blowing orgasms?

With the back of my head pressed to the rock, I angled my face up to the sky, studying what little of the sun peeked through the rolling clouds. Best guess, it was about midafternoon, or hell, maybe early evening. With only being here a few days, I hadn't become proficient in understanding the sun's position in regard to time for this area, so who knew what time it really was.

I could check the time on my phone, but the bear crunched it beneath its killer paws when digging around for his stolen treats. Hopefully, Miles and Aiden were on their way and would save me from a very slow and terrible death.

A pitiful whimper escaped, the cold in my toes and fingers almost painful now.

All I had to do was hold on. Miles and Aiden would find me.

I just hoped it wasn't too late when they did.

AIDEN

The wind and pelting snow sliced across my cheeks, burning the exposed skin as we carefully made our way along the trail. The tightness in my chest had nothing to do with the below-freezing temperature. We didn't expect the storm to shift south, so I doubted she packed anything warm enough for the sudden wintry weather. Though this was Alaska, and the weather was fickle. We could even experience all four seasons in a single day. It was that crazy.

Again and again, I called out her name, my desperate voice disappearing into the whipping wind. With every step, fear grew, making my stomach sink. Jubie trotted beside Miles, leaping and diving into the snow mounds, happy as a dog with that much fur could be in the snow. Which was why I snapped my attention her way, heart leaping with hope, when Jubie's loud, alerting bark rumbled through the area and she darted past me. Miles and I exchanged a quick glance before taking off after her.

The air bit in my lungs with every breath, but I didn't give a fuck about the discomfort as I followed Jubie's tracks toward the small mountain lake at the trail's end. Barely seeing the tip of her tail wagging above a large rock, I raced that way. Slapping a hot palm to the snow-covered stone to stop the momentum that would send me tumbling over the rock, I peered over to the opposite side.

"She's here," I bellowed over my shoulder, though I knew Miles was only a few feet behind me. Snow crunched under my boots as I rounded the boulder, allowing myself a second to check her for any obvious injuries. Aspen's movements were sluggish as she batted Jubie's swiping tongue away from her face.

Squatting low, I brushed wild, wind-tossed hair off her forehead and cursed at the icy feel of her skin. "Aspen, sweetheart, we're here. We've got you."

Cracked lips pulled up into a trembling smile as her dark eyes met mine. "Fucking finally."

I huffed a laugh at her words and reached out to give Jubie a thankful head pat. "Ready to get out of here?"

"I'm not sure I can," she said, voice trembling with the chatter of her teeth. "I've been sitting like this, turning into a human popsicle, for a while. I think my muscles are frozen this way."

"I found her pack. Looks like a bear went through it." I swiveled on the balls of my feet to inspect the bag Miles held up. "How did she not get mauled in the process?"

"Sacrificial lamb," she muttered, snow-covered lashes fluttering closed.

"We need to get her warm now," I barked, looping my arms behind her back and legs and hauling her against my chest as I stood. "Take her camera." I inclined my head to the piece of equipment still cradled to her chest.

Carefully pulling her stiff fingers away, he tucked it into what was left of her pack, securing it all together before looping the still-functioning strap over his shoulder.

I eyed the way back down the mountain. "She won't make it with as slow as we'll need to go with the snow and one of us carrying her."

Miles nodded in agreement, hazel eyes scanning our surroundings. "I studied the map while you were packing up the last of the supplies. We're about a mile from an emergency shelter that Brandon built last year. That will get us out of the elements, and it has a wood-burning furnace for situations like this one. It's closer than making our way down to the trailhead."

I followed him with Aspen in my arms, Jubie trotting beside me, knowing he had the details covered. All I needed to do was stick close and step where he stepped.

I studied the shredded and tied pack swinging along Miles' back. "Fuck, how did the bear not get her too?"

"Because she's smart and probably left it out in the open while she hid." Miles's barked laugh echoed through the area. "That's what she meant by sacrificial lamb. Funny girl. Though if she would've listened to me—"

"We can discuss that later," I yelled for him to hear me over the wind. "She's fucking freezing to death in my arms, Miles. Get us to the shelter before we lose her for good."

With a confirming grunt, he picked up his pace, every so often pulling out his compass and slightly adjusting course. "We'll take turns carrying her while the other leads to ensure the path we're walking is stable and not an ice shelf or something worse."

"I've got her a little longer. You just get us there quick, brother."

Despite our urgency and desperation to get Aspen somewhere warm, our pace was slow to make sure we all made it to the emergency shelter in one piece. Ice shelves up this high were a genuine concern and had injured or killed many hikers in the past.

When Miles estimated we were halfway, we switched responsibilities. He carefully seized Aspen from my arms, and I took the lead. When the small shed-type shelter came into view, my footsteps stumbled at the tsunami of relief that flooded through me. I wasn't nearly as frozen as Aspen, but carrying her with her wet clothes seeping into my dry ones had dropped my body temperature, and I knew Miles was in the same boat.

Fingers wrapped around the thick wooden latch, I lifted the makeshift lock and jerked the door open. The inside was as basic as the outside. Rough wooden planks for a floor, unfinished walls exposing the insulation, an old-school furnace in the corner, and a few sealed tubs tucked in the back corner that I knew held several blankets.

Miles stepped in after me and squeezed around to the side, the shelter not giving us much room to move around. After making sure Jubie was okay—she was smiling while rolling around in the snow, so I took that as a yes—I closed the door to keep out the wind and swirling snow. When I turned, Miles placed a firm kiss to Aspen's damp forehead and laid her trembling in my outstretched arms, then kneeled in front of the furnace.

After pulling open the small iron door, he peered inside. "There are a few scraps of wood in here." Unbuckling his pack straps, he pulled it around and unzipped a side pocket, taking out a fire starter bundle and lighter. "I'll get what's inside started, then head out for more wood. Hopefully, I can find something not too wet."

It only took a minute for him to get a flame going, the fire starter and old wood catching quickly. With a satisfied nod, Miles stood, dusting both hands on his waterproof trail pants, and turned, quickly surveying the shaking woman in my arms.

"We need to get her wet clothes off and her wrapped up in the dry blankets. It won't take long for the fire to warm this small space." Without a second look back, he pulled open the door and stepped out into the snowstorm. Jubie's joyous barks sounded from the other side, followed by Miles's voice calling her name.

"Is he mad?" Aspen asked, her teeth chattering, words slightly slurred. "At me?"

I shook my head and carefully lowered her to the worn floor. "He's not mad, just very focused on that fire to get you warm. Let's get these wet clothes off you." Knowing her muscles were stiff from the cold, I carefully maneuvered the sweater and T-shirt over her head, leaving the dry sports bra on for now. My own fingers slightly numb, it took several tries to untie her hiking boots, but when I did, I cursed under my breath. "Fuck, Aspen, your socks are soaked through. I thought your boots were waterproof."

Yanking both off, I tossed them aside and held up a single foot to assess the damage. A relieved breath brushed past my lips at finding her toes bright red and cold but no signs of frostbite. I made quick work of undoing her pants and tugging the damp material down her very pale legs.

"Let's find those blankets and get you wrapped up. Can you scoot a little closer to the fire for me?" Without waiting for her response, I turned to the stack of tubs and ripped off the lid of the one on top. Coarse material bunched beneath my firm grasp as I hauled one blanket out, then another. "These aren't soft but are no doubt effective." Flapping one open, I wrapped it around her shoulders and helped her sit up to tuck the ends under her ass. I put the other one around her legs, securing the opening around her feet to keep out the chilly air.

The whole time, Aspen stayed quiet, watching me move about the space. Ripping off my coat, I hung it up on a loose nail and started draping her clothes over any available surface to help them dry.

"Aiden."

Spinning on the balls of my feet, I faced the little Aspen burrito, fighting a grin at how cute she looked. "Yeah? You okay? Warming up?"

The blanket bobbed with her slight nod. "I'm sorry." Tears welled in her lower lids. "I'm really, really sorry. I should've listened, but I thought..."

Forgetting the clothes, I moved to sit behind her, tugging her swaddled form between my legs and helping her lean back against my chest. Both arms wrapped tight around her, I rested my chin on her shoulder.

"You thought you could do the hike because you can, sweetheart." Her body shook with a silent sob. "I'm not mad or frustrated or disappointed in you. Neither is Miles. But do you want to know what we are?" She shifted just enough to face me. "Fucking relieved. We didn't know where you were or if you were hurt, and we freaked the hell out."

She snorted. "Even Miles?"

I huffed and nodded. "Especially Miles. He almost killed us and a few unsuspecting pedestrians, driving like a maniac while we searched for you."

Her bottom lip quivered, but this time, I knew it wasn't because of the cold. "I should've left a note at your place or mine, but I really thought I'd be home before you were back." A sliver of the earlier worry dissipated at her normal speech pattern, no more slurring from her numb lips.

"What happened? We found your pack ripped to shreds and everything in it."

Panic filled her face, and she struggled against me. "My camera! I had it with me—"

"It's fine, sweetheart. We peeled it from your death grip and wrapped it up tight in your pack to keep it from getting damaged. You can check to make sure it's all good once you've warmed up."

With a reluctant nod, she relaxed against me and began explaining everything, from the time she left our place to when we showed up. My hold tightened, making her shift in discomfort, at the mention of Jasper. And to top it off, fucking Charles, and then the worst threat of them all: the bear.

"Pretty sure you described a teenage brown bear, Aspen."

The door swung open, letting in a burst of icy wind and showering of snow before Miles kicked it shut behind him. He eyed us before stomping over to the stove and dropping the armful of wood onto the floor.

"You really think it was a brown bear?" she whispered, gaze locked on Miles, who stiffened at her words.

After shoving several thick limbs and branches into the fire, he shut the metal door and spun around to face us. "What did you just say?"

It wasn't a question but more of a *Did I hear you correctly?* based on his stern tone.

"Um, that's what Aiden thinks ripped into my pack. I only got a few glimpses of it before I hid." A muscle along Miles's jaw pulsed with how tight he clenched his teeth. "I was about to head back down because of the snow when he came around a boulder and blocked the trail. Instead of scaling the cliffs, which I knew I couldn't do, I left my pack with the snacks and hid around another set of rocks." Her lips tugged down. "What I didn't expect was for part of the lake's edge to be there, so my pants and boots got soaked while I waited for the bear to finish going through my stuff."

"It could've been you," Miles hissed. "That could've been you, Aspen." He stood and paced from one side of the shelter to the other, which was about two of his long strides, before turning around and doing it again. "It's why I wanted you to wait for us. Alaska differs from anywhere else. It's wild and dangerous. Look at the weather today. No one expected this, and it almost killed you."

I shot Miles a glare when Aspen shrank back against me.

He sighed and hung his head, looking utterly defeated. "Don't you get it, baby girl?" He looked up through his lashes, allowing Aspen to see how absolutely wrecked he was. "You're too precious to risk yourself like this. If anything happened to you—" His deep voice cracked. "I said what I said not to control you but because nothing would matter in life if something happened to you, if you were taken from us after we just found you." He dropped to his knees, the shelter shaking with the impact, and cupped her cheeks between his large hands. "Living wouldn't exist if you weren't here with me, with us."

Leaning forward, he sealed his lips to hers. A soft laugh escaped me when he pulled back and Aspen leaned forward, not wanting to break the connection.

"I'm relieved that you're okay." He arched a single dark brow. "But you'll still get that punishment I promised." At his dark chuckle, I tilted Aspen's face my way to see what was so funny. A crimson blush stained her cheeks, which were deathly pale minutes earlier. He hummed and rubbed a hand over his thick dark beard. "I'm wondering if you came up here just so I would follow through."

"And what was that?" I asked, brushing my thumb along her lower lip. "The punishment you promised."

When no one responded, Miles hitched his chin at her. "Tell him, Aspen."

"Taking both of you at the same time while he spanked me," she whispered, breaths growing shallow and fast.

A slow smile pulled at the corners of my lips as I searched her face. "Is that so?" She nodded. "And would that be my cock fucking your perfect mouth and Miles stretching your tight cunt with his dick?"

Wet hair swung from side to side with her quick head-shake, her cheeks darkening even more. Those wide brown eyes flicked to Miles, who waited like he had all the time in the world to allow her to explain.

"Or one of us in your pussy and the other filling your ass?" I mused, loving the way she squirmed against me. Aspen released a faint whimper and nodded. "Hmm, that sounds like a perfect punishment for you putting your life in danger. Though I'm disappointed to say, when we gathered all the supplies, I didn't pack the lube."

A frustrated groan escaped as her lids squeezed shut.

"I think she's disappointed," Miles said with a chuckle, the emotionless mask from earlier gone with his faint smirk.

"I know *I* fucking am," I grumbled. "Just something to look forward to when we get home. Plus, we have to prep you to take us like that." I leaned close and brushed my lips against her cheek. "Don't worry, sweetheart. Prepping your ass is half the fun."

Soft, most importantly, warm breaths brushed across my face. "I think I'm good now," she said. "I'm kind of sweating after all this talk."

"Not even close." I shifted to face Miles as he stood and

started for the door. "I'll get more firewood just in case. Keep her warm any way you need to, Aiden."

A barked laugh escaped at the smirk he shot over his shoulder before leaving the shelter. Pretty sure that was his way of telling me to get creative with warming our girl up.

Hell fucking yes.

Her ass brushed against my cock when she turned to look up at me through wet lashes. Keeping our gazes locked, I worked a hand beneath the blanket wrapped around her until my hot palm rested against the cool skin of her lower stomach, pausing just above her mound. Her lips parted with a gasp as my fingers splayed wide.

"Aspen, are you on birth control?" I whispered while tracing around her belly button.

"Yes, I use the shot kind. Why are you asking me? If it's about condoms, I don't mind—"

"Do you want to be?" I watched her expression shift to confusion. "On birth control."

She frowned. "What are you talking about, Aiden?"

"I'm talking about..." I swallowed to steady my shaking voice. This was the worst damn time to bring it up, but I had to know where she stood on the subject. After the family conversation with Miles in the truck, the fear of losing her pushed the urgency to know her thoughts about a family and kids to the forefront. "Do you want to be on birth control, or would you be open to letting it wear off someday in the future to see what happens?"

Her stomach tensed under my fingers, and I froze.

Damnit, me and my big-ass mouth. In my need for answers, for the hope of a family with this amazing woman, I'd pressed too hard and faced making her uncomfortable.

Before I could divert the conversation to a safer subject, she answered.

"I'm not sure what you're asking me, Aiden."

My gaze flicked between her dark eyes, finding open curiosity, not caution. I licked my lips and cleared my throat. "I'm asking if, in the future—not now, but someday—you would want a family. Do you see yourself having kids with someone like me? You mentioned wanting someone who wouldn't hold you back and would let you live your life, and I—we—could be that for you." Her jaw went slack as she stared up at me. "I've mentioned that I want a family, and I was wondering if you did, too, with the right people."

Tense silence stretched between us. Worry swelled in my chest, making it hard to breathe under the pressure, until she spoke, silencing my anxious thoughts.

"Not right now while I'm figuring out life, but I want a family with someone who wouldn't try to cage me into the mother role and nothing else. I know you and Miles wouldn't do that to me. You've proven that over and over in just the past few days. I've never been against having kids, just the idea of that being my entire identity, giving up everything else to only be a mother." She rolled her eyes. "You can guess why that's a fear of mine after everything I've shared about my own mother."

My smile grew wide, and a dull ache bloomed in my cheeks. "Really? You're open to kids one day?"

She nodded, her own lips splitting into a grin.

"When I have my life more figured out, yeah. Like I said, it's never been about not wanting a family. I've just never met someone, or two someones, who I could see myself doing it with. But then you and Miles barreled into my life, and..." Her smile turned soft. "The idea of making a family with you two sounds just about perfect, now that I think about it."

A cheerful hum vibrated in my throat. Heart racing with

the flood of excitement and desire her words created, I dipped my hand lower, fingers slipping beneath the top of her panties. "Hearing you say that is such a damn turn-on. The idea of you pregnant with my kid, or Miles's." My cock twitched against her backside. "I'm hard as fuck imagining your round belly and knowing we did that." Lifting my hips, I ground against her. Her startled gasp turned into a guttural moan, making me harden even more. "How about we practice now?"

Aspen tracked my every move as I shifted to kneel in front of her. Hands on top of her bent knees, I gazed down at her flushed face, waiting for her answer.

"Practice," she said breathlessly. "Practice to get me pregnant?"

"Fuck," I groaned. "Yes. Letting me sink between your creamy thighs, fucking you so hard and coming inside you, then staying there, my dick stuffing you full, not allowing a single drop to escape." With my free hand, I adjusted my dick so hopefully it wouldn't have a zipper impression later. "And then do it again and again, pumping your pussy full of our cum."

Brushing a single finger along her inner thigh, I pushed her panties aside to cup her shaved mound and slid a finger between her drenched slit. "Fuck, sweetheart. You're soaked." I held up the single glistening digit for her to see before slipping it between my lips. Her delicious flavor exploded on my tongue, making me groan as I sucked off every drop. "It seems like the thought turns you on too."

"Of you and Miles," she breathed. "Always. Of the pregnancy thing..." Her shoulders shook with a shiver that I knew had nothing to do with the temperature. "Never thought it would turn me on, but I want that, yes." Keeping her gaze locked on me, she dropped her knees to the sides, pulling open the blanket and giving me an amazing view of the apex of her thighs.

My lips curled at the sliver of cloth keeping me from seeing all of her. Reaching out with both hands, I gripped the sides of the flimsy material and yanked. It stretched out, digging into her skin, her soft hiss barely reaching my ears, before the fabric snapped and fell to either side of her hips.

Eyes locked on her perfect pink pussy, I licked my lips, ready to devour her whole. The tiny taste from earlier only fanned the need burning inside me to have her flavor imprinted on my tongue. My gaze traveled up her stomach to her heaving chest.

"Take it off," I growled, hitching my chin at the damn sports bra that kept me from seeing all of her beautiful body. Reaching down to the knife secured to my belt, I pulled it free and aimed the sharp tip between her heaving breasts. "Or I'll cut it off."

Her brows flicked up her forehead, a wild look flashing in her dark gaze. "Do it."

"With pleasure," I hummed. Careful not to nick her creamy skin, I ran the sharp edge along the tight fabric until the last few threads snapped free. The material slid along her tits and dropped to the side. "Much better," I praised while pinching a peaked nipple between two fingers and giving it a hard tug.

Her lips parted, the gasp music to my ears.

"Now, back to the meal I was looking forward to."

After securing the knife back in the leather sheath, I dropped to my stomach between her thighs. Using both thumbs, I spread her apart and leaned forward to lick her from hole to clit, sucking on the swollen bundle of nerves until her hips lifted off the ground.

"Stay still, sweetheart. The bit of pain I have in store for you is punishment for making us worry today." I glanced up at her flushed face. "Don't ever do that again, you hear me? I know you're capable, and I love that you're independent, but you're not alone in this anymore, Aspen. I don't think I could go through another day like today, worrying if my life was over just when the best chapter so far started."

She opened her mouth, but I didn't wait to hear her response. Instead, I sucked her between my lips once again, though this time, I grazed my teeth along the swollen flesh. Aspen cursed and shifted, attempting to wiggle away from the too-intense feeling. Gripping her hips, I held her down, keeping her in place as I sucked and nipped at her clit while licking up the sweet liquid from her entrance. Within minutes, her cries turned hysterical, switching between begging me to stop and pleading for more.

Right where I wanted her.

Absolutely desperate for me.

Without stopping the torture, I worked the buckle of my belt open and then quickly undid my pants, shoving one side down my hips before doing the same with the other. A cry of protest made me smirk as I sat back on the heels of my boots.

Aspen's wide eyes followed my movements as I ripped the sweatshirt over my head, the small shed too fucking hot now to keep it on while I fucked her full of my cum. My fingers wrapped around my cock, tightening until the knuckles went white.

"You ready for me to fill you up, sweetheart? For me to fuck you so deep that you'll feel every pulse of me exploding in your tight little cunt?"

She whimpered and nodded.

I hummed my approval while scanning down her flushed body, beyond happy that our time together not only made her so fucking desperate for me but warmed her up in the process. I crooked a finger, beckoning her to me.

A dark chuckle that would rival Miles's vibrated in my chest as she scrambled to sit up and then kneeled in front of me. Her gaze was locked on my leaking cock, but I shook my head, gripping her chin when she attempted to lick off the stream of precum.

"That's not for your mouth." Taking handfuls of her round ass, I lifted her with ease and positioned her dripping core over my dick. Spreading her wide, I slipped my throbbing head into her pussy. Locking my gaze on her glassy one, I smirked. "Hold on to me, sweetheart. This will get rough."

Then I brought her down hard while thrusting up into her. Her scream echoed in the tiny shelter, her pussy quivering around me as the orgasm I kept from her earlier shattered her. Rocking her back and forth with me balls deep, she whimpered, forehead on my shoulder as I drew out the aftershocks of the soul-altering orgasm I knew she just had.

Behind me, the door flew open. A glorious burst of cold air caressed my sweat-slicked back and fanned strands of Aspen's hair around my face. Miles didn't say a word as he moved about the small space, adding more wood to the fire and setting the rest aside for later. Outside, I heard Jubie's playful barks and yips followed by the crunch of snow.

"Punishment?" Miles asked, stopping behind Aspen, gazing at her exposed ass.

A smile crept up my cheeks. "A little bit—"

"He tortured me," Aspen mumbled against my neck.

With a huff, I released my hold on one cheek and swatted it hard enough to sting. My lids slammed shut, and I groaned at the way her cunt tightened around my cock.

"Maybe we start the warm-up to the punishment she really deserves for today," Miles mused.

"I think," I rasped, the restraint to keep from pounding into her to find my own release making my voice tight, "that's a great plan. But make sure you save everything for her hot pussy, brother. She wants us to fill her up. Both of us."

He hummed his approval as he kneeled behind us. "Does she now?" He kissed along her spine, making Aspen wiggle and tighten around me. "Lift her up."

With slow and controlled movements, I eased Aspen off my steel-hard cock until she hovered just over me, the heat from her pussy tempting me to push her down again. Miles's fingers slipped between her thighs, dipping inside her. Aspen peeled her face off my shoulder and straightened enough to look down at where Miles's two fingers filled her up.

"What are you doing?" she breathed.

"Getting you ready for a glimpse at your future punishment, baby girl." He kissed her shoulder as he pulled his fingers free and slid them back out of our view. Aspen's hooded lids flew open, her eyes wide. "Relax for me, baby girl, and I promise we'll both make you feel so fucking good." He glanced down to where I knew his fingers were working into her tight hole. "And fill you up so much that we'll both be dripping out of you for days."

Miles grunted a curse. "Fuck, you like the idea of that." His gaze lifted to mine. "Your turn."

With a shaky breath, I slowly lowered her back down, her hot pussy even tighter with Miles's thick fingers firmly stuffing her other hole.

"Holy fuck," I grunted, thrusting up into her. "Fuck, that's tight."

"Imagine how tight she'll be when it's my cock inside her and not just my fingers."

I grunted in agreement, which was swallowed up by Aspen's pleas for more. Sweat slicked my forehead and dripped down my temples as I pounded into her while simultaneously slamming her down onto my cock. Our harsh breaths mingled, desperate kisses sloppy as I spiraled higher and higher, totally consumed by the feeling of her, the moment, and the absolute fucking need to fill her.

My lids snapped open at the feel of skin against my lower stomach. Miles had snaked a hand around to settle between us. His eyes met mine, and a sinister smirk pulled at his lips. Whatever he did to Aspen had her screaming loud in my ear as her cunt strangled my cock. With a string of grunted curses, I thrust into her hard as my own orgasm ripped through me.

Thank fuck for teamwork, because Miles held on to Aspen as my muscles trembled from the mind-shattering orgasm and I almost dropped her. Soft murmurs sounded in my ears as he kissed and whispered along her shoulder, sweeping her hair away to press soft kisses on the back of her neck.

"Such a good girl," he murmured into her ear.

She muttered something unintelligible before slumping forward and pressing her forehead to my shoulder. Miles shifted back and stood to rummage through his pack, pulling out a sanitizing wipe to clean his hands.

With careful movements to keep her safe and my cock from slipping free, I leaned forward until her back pressed to the life-saving blankets that were wrapped around her earlier. Palms pressed to the rough, wooden floor on either side of her head, I gazed down into her dark eyes.

And I knew.

Without a doubt, I was 100 percent in love with Aspen Carter.

"Despite the whole almost-freezing-to-death part—"

"And almost getting eaten by a bear."

Aspen stuck out her tongue at Aiden with an adorable nose scrunch for cutting her off.

"And the somewhat treacherous hike down the snow-covered trail—"

I scoffed and shot her a dull expression. "*That* was not treacherous."

Aspen's focus shifted from the small screen on her camera to level a glare my way. "It turned out to be a successful hike." I held her glare with one of my own. "Don't be so grumpy, Miles. These pictures from yesterday are some of my best, and that's before editing. These will bring in some money for sure. Once I figure out how and where to sell them." That last part was muttered under her breath.

I dipped my chin in agreement, having already seen a few of the shots, and shifted my attention back to the plowed road. Despite all the dangers and scares from the last twenty-four hours, I couldn't stop the slight smile that pulled at my lips. Last night was monumental. It deserved to have its own holiday dedicated to it, and it had nothing to do with what the three of us did together.

For the first time since leaving the hospital, I slept with someone—two someones—in the same room. Not that long of a time frame, considering we passed out late and Jubie woke us up at first light, begging to go out and play in the snow, but it was still a significant milestone.

It sparked a tiny flame of hope that it could be the first of many future nights not sleeping alone. I had zero doubts that Jubie would readily pass the torch of being my lone bed buddy, though she would always be welcome in my bed no matter who else was in it. Hell, after everything she'd done for me, Jubie deserved her own king bed.

The radio was playing some old country song as we cruised along. The early-morning sun streaked through the few clouds remaining from the dissipating storm, high-lighting the beautiful landscape surrounding Anchor Bay. That flicker of hope burned brighter. This overall lightness could be how I felt every day from now on. This emotional freedom had been missing for too long. There was an eager-ness for a new day and excitement for what it would bring instead of dragging myself through the same emotionless routine, barely surviving one day to the next.

Looking back, I'd starved myself. Not in the food sense but from the joys of life. Now I knew what Aiden meant about us barely surviving instead of living before Aspen burst into our lives, shocking our systems back to life.

A giggle had me glancing from the road, finding Aiden whispering something in Aspen's ear, her smile just as wide as his. The two burst out laughing, filling the truck's cab with so much fucking joy it was almost tangible. My grin grew as I absorbed every bit of happy energy pouring from the two.

Realization hit me in the heart so hard it skipped a beat. This was it. Everything had finally come together, our missing piece slotted into place, making both Aiden and me happier than we'd ever been. Making us whole.

As soon as I had that thought, a wave of fierce protectiveness followed, and both hands tightened on the wheel. Now that we'd found this, her, it was my responsibility to protect it and prepare for a future together.

Mentally creating a checklist of all the things we needed to move Aspen in with us, I steered toward The Nest so she could grab a few things before coming back to our place. With the road plowed and the streets fairly empty, it was a simple drive, but as we headed through the town, worry sat in my gut like a hundred-pound weight.

Nothing good lasted long for me.

"What's wrong with you?" Aiden asked. Of course he'd picked up on the apprehension slowly overtaking the earlier carefree feeling.

"Nothing," I muttered while pressing my sternum to ease the building pressure in my chest.

Arm snaking behind Aspen, he shoved at my shoulder, making me curse and adjust my hold on the wheel to keep us from veering off the road. I shot him a stern look before turning my focus back out the windshield.

"Everything is all good, Miles. Enjoy it instead of preparing for when it will end."

Damn, he doesn't miss a thing, does he?

As the truck crested a hill and The Nest came into view, a viselike grip encircled my chest and tightened, making it difficult to take a full breath. Something wasn't right, but I didn't know what.

Good thing I didn't have to wait long to find out.

ASPEN

It was the stiff silence, the almost palpable tension suddenly filling the truck that jerked my focus from the camera to glance between the two men. The question asking what was wrong never left my parted lips when I tracked their pointed stares to the decked-out Escalade parked in front of the path that led to my cabin.

The single parking spot was reserved for my cabin. The only time it was occupied since checking in was when the guys came to pick me up or drop me off.

Odd.

My stomach rolled with the rush of nervousness flooding through my veins.

I carefully set the camera on my lap. "Wonder who's SUV that is?" I asked, my voice shaking from my heart slamming into my chest. Something was wrong, very wrong, but I didn't have the faintest clue what. That was almost more nerve-racking.

"No idea. Looks like a rental," Aiden murmured, leaning forward and squinting like that would help us identify the owner. His sharp whistle pierced through the truck. "A fancy rental. Who knew something like that even existed in Anchor Bay."

Miles parked the truck directly behind the SUV, blocking it in. I shot him a confused look when he turned off the engine.

"If it's the same person who broke into your cabin, I don't want them to leave until I talk to him or her first."

"And by talk, you mean..." I arched a questioning brow, though I had a feeling I knew exactly what he meant based on his fierce tone.

Miles's lips curled upward in a knowing smirk. "That depends on them."

"Miles," I protested, but that was all I got out before he shoved open the door and stepped onto the plowed asphalt. His command for Jubie to stay in the truck's bed rang out before the door shut.

Shaking my head in exasperation, feeling this was getting blown out of proportion all because of someone parking in my spot, I swiveled to face Aiden, hoping he'd be the reasonable one. "Please don't make a big deal out of someone taking my spot."

His honey-brown eyes cut my way before focusing on the SUV once again. "What if it's more than that, Aspen? What if the person in that Escalade is here for you, knew this was your cabin?"

I blinked at Aiden, my mind suddenly going blank. "Why would someone be here for me?"

"Let's find out before we all get worked up over this." Interlacing our fingers, he lifted my hand to press a kiss to the back and shoved the door open with the other, guiding me out of the truck after him.

Miles stood at the driver's side door, hands cupped

around his eyes to peer into the SUV. Stepping back, he shook his head to let us know no one was waiting inside.

Aiden's hand tightened around mine, squeezing until I let out a hiss of pain and attempted to yank free. He flashed me an apologetic expression before tugging me down the path, following Miles.

Pulse racing, blood pounding in my ears, I kept my head on a swivel, glancing every which way for the owner of the SUV. The memory of the night I felt followed on the way to the main building had the hairs on the back of my neck standing on end.

At the base of the stairs that led to the closed front door, we stopped at Miles's back when he held up a hand. Holding my breath, I waited, listening for whatever froze him in his tracks. From the other side of the cabin door came a muffled male chuckle followed by a loud voice, though the words were too distorted to make out.

Before I could even come to terms with the idea that someone was in my cabin, both men had their sidearms drawn and pointed at the closed door.

"I'll lead. You cover." Miles glanced down at me over his shoulder. "Aspen, stay between us until we know who we're dealing with and what they want."

Eyes wide, I turned to Aiden but couldn't get a word out. Features firm and emotionless, the happy and mischievous man I had hopelessly fallen for was nowhere to be found.

Despite Miles's size, his boots didn't make a single sound as he moved up the steps and reached for the door, testing the handle. Lips pursed tight, he sent a clipped nod back to Aiden, who shifted behind me, placing a hand on my shoulder. Holding up three fingers, Miles slowly ticked them down.

Shoving the door open, he stormed into the cabin, gun

raised immediately, causing surprised shouts to cut through the tense silence. My ears perked up, the tone and cadence of a voice catching my attention.

I knew that pompous and arrogant voice. All too well, considering I'd heard it almost every day for the last few years. Anger quickly replaced the bubbling fear, sending raging heat burning through my veins.

"You've got to be kidding me right now." Shrugging off Aiden's hold, ignoring his barked demands for me to wait, I barreled into the cabin, knowing exactly who I would find inside.

Weaving around Miles, who stood blocking my view, I stopped beside him, crossing both arms over my heaving chest, and glared at James fucking Peoples, who stood in the middle of the room with both hands in the air.

The happy bubble keeping reality at bay the last few days popped, my past and present colliding in the tiny cabin.

"What the hell are you doing here, James?" Movement from the other side of the room snapped my gaze toward the couch. I scoffed with an eye roll at the creepy asshole Charles sitting with his hands raised. "Now we know how you got into my cabin when I know for certain I locked it yesterday."

Charles's gaze narrowed as he slowly lowered a hand to gesture toward James. "Mr. Peoples said you were expecting him, and he would be more comfortable waiting for you in the cabin. A celebrity like him, of course, I accommodated his request, and him being your fiancé, I allowed him access to your cabin."

My arms dropped to my sides like deadweight while my jaw hung open.

"Her *what*?" Aiden practically growled at my back.

With one more scathing glare at Miles, who had yet to lower his gun, James shifted his attention my way. In a flash, the annoyance and anger were gone, and his famous fake mask that had fooled the world was in place. His bright blue eyes, which had drawn me in at one time, softened as a wide smile spread across his face.

"I've been worried sick about you, Aspen. Where have you been? I've been waiting for you to return here at the resort since yesterday." His mask slipped a fraction, some of his arrogance showing through, as he eyed Miles and Aiden. "Who are these two men with guns? Come over here where it's safe, sweetie. I'll protect you."

A humorous laugh escaped as I shook my head in disbelief. "What the hell are you doing here, James?" I repeated.

His features hardened. I knew it was because I didn't immediately follow his orders. "What do you mean, what am I doing here? I came to retrieve you and take you home." Pressing his lips into a tight line, he looked over his shoulder at Charles. "You were a big help, and I thank you for being so very accommodating, but I need to talk to my fiancée alone. This is a private conversation." His blue eyes flicked to the two men at my side, a minuscule sneer curling his lip. "That goes for you two as well."

"Not going to happen," Aiden responded at the same time Miles snapped, "Fuck off."

James's nostrils flared with annoyance, clearly not liking their responses. "This is between me and Aspen. As a known name, I don't want anyone else hearing about my private life only for you to run off and sell the story or post it on social media." When I didn't say anything, his narrowed gaze landed on me. "Sweetie, this is insane. It's time to stop all this."

Hands back on my hips, holding on tight to keep from

wrapping them around his throat, I met his glare and arched a challenging brow. "Stop what, exactly?"

Back pressed to the wall, Charles inched his way around the room. Miles's alert gaze tracked his every move until he turned and bolted out the door. A fraction of the tension in my shoulders eased when he disappeared from view. The man made me uncomfortable in a way I couldn't describe, and I hoped it was the last time I saw him—which was probably wishful thinking, considering how small Anchor Bay was.

"Aspen," James snapped, grabbing my attention away from the open doorway.

"Don't you fucking raise your voice at her," Miles barked, taking a challenging step toward James. My heart squeezed at the steel in Miles's tone.

"Why don't you leave like I told you to," James retorted, crossing his arms defensively over his chest.

Like a thousand-pound weighted blanket wrapped around me, exhaustion from the last twenty-four hours had me stumbling to the couch on trembling legs. Falling onto the stiff cushions, I leaned forward, elbows pressed to the top of my thighs, resting my face in both palms.

"Stop acting like you have any authority here. Just say what you came to say, James." My weary voice carried through the silent cabin.

When no one responded, I peered through my fingers. Across the room, Aiden leaned against the front door, concern lining his features as he studied me. Miles still stood across from James, but his gun was now lowered, though not holstered, and James had covered his earlier anger and annoyance with the fake mask he wore so well.

"Sweetie—"

I tossed up a hand, slicing it through the air. "Don't call me that. *Ever* again."

With a quick, assessing glance at the tense Miles, James took a hesitant step toward the couch, hands raised as if approaching an upset animal. "I came here for you, sweet—" I leveled him with a scathing, narrowed-eyed glare, stopping him before he could finish. He nervously cleared his throat. "I came here for you, Aspen."

"Why would you do that?" I groused.

His perfectly shaped brows rose a fraction, as much as all that Botox would allow. "I know why you left." Gaze flicking between me and the guys, James inched around the narrow coffee table to sit on the couch next to me. I immediately leaned the opposite way to put distance between us. "I came to tell you in person that I understand what you're doing and to bring you back to Seattle, where you belong."

I gaped at him. "What exactly do you understand I'm doing?"

His gentle laugh and pat on my knee were all kinds of patronizing. "Leaving without notice, flying to Alaska—it was all to regain my attention." Somehow, my jaw dropped even lower in utter disgusted astonishment. *What the what?* "Listen, I know I've been hyper-focused on my career as of late, but I did that for you, for us. Don't you see? I was building a life where you didn't have to work or go out on-site with me and the others. Everything I've done was for you. I never lost sight of what was really important, but after this disappearing stunt of yours, I realized you did."

"What you never lost sight of was how my pictures and research elevated your career to what it is today. I wasn't important to you. You needed me. There is a huge fucking difference."

"You, Aspen," he emphasized. I snorted and rolled my

eyes. "I never lost sight of you, though it would appear I didn't make that clear. Which is why I'm willing to overlook all this when we get back home, and I've talked with HR—"

"What will you overlook?"

Aiden winced, rubbing a shoulder at his ear to ease the pain from my high-pitched shriek.

James sighed and pinched the bridge of his nose in obvious exasperation. "You leaving with no warning or note. You could've talked to me and told me you felt ignored. I would've corrected your assumption that I was focused on us and redirected your frustrations to the actual cause."

"Which is?"

"You're jealous, and that's okay. But I don't care about my fans. I only have eyes for you."

"I was jealous," I repeated, voice flat.

"But you left with no notice, leaving me fucking worried out of my mind and without a photographer this past week." Ding, ding, ding. There it was. The real reason for his frustration and coming here. "This irresponsible and drama-type behavior isn't like you, Aspen. Don't let your emotions ruin the great thing we have going."

My mouth opened and closed like a fish, unable to speak, my mind having gone blank.

"I'm willing to move past all this," he continued. "Forget the last few days ever happened because I love you that much. And I have something that will help you feel more secure in our relationship. Help settle your neediness a little."

What's the prison time for murder these days?

At my nonresponse, James's worried features shifted into a wide smile. Tilting to the side, he dug something out of the back pocket of his too-tight jeans. My stomach dropped when his fingers unfolded, exposing the small velvet bag resting in the center of his palm. I wrapped both hands around the tops of my knees to hide how badly my entire body shook. "I know you've wanted this commitment for a while, and I think it's time to make us official." Pulling the ties he tipped the bag depositing an enormous diamond ring into his hand. "We make a great team, you and me, and now the world will know you're mine. I've already scheduled a press release to announce—"

That was it. Finally, my frozen brain fired back to life. "What the fuck did you just call me?" I shoved up from the couch, backing away from the ring like it held a venomous snake instead of a huge fucking diamond ring.

James's smug expression shifted to confusion. "Mine? Why are you shocked? You are mine, always have been."

Overwhelmed, I shook my head, trying to make my thoughts make sense. Ripping out the band around my thick hair, I ran my fingers through the long strands, gripping it into a makeshift ponytail at the base of my neck. Gaze lowered, I inhaled deeply to center myself enough to respond to the delusional man I was once infatuated with.

"I can state with a hundred percent certainty that I am not yours, James. All I have ever been is a convenience, someone you only paid attention to when you needed me for something. You're kidding yourself, seeing what you wanted to see."

"Are you drunk?" He shoved off the couch, fake concern back on his face. "You're not acting like yourself, Aspen."

Nostrils flaring with a deep inhale, I released it slowly through pursed lips in an effort to calm the rage bubbling inside me.

"This, you and me, whatever toxic mess we were, is over." His eyes went wide in surprise. "I didn't leave to get your attention. I left because I walked into the conference room and found your head between Barbara's thighs." A shocked expression flashed across his face before it morphed into one of disappointment. "And you know what? I'm glad I did. It proved to me that I didn't matter, showed me what a damn idiot I had been for years. *Years*, James." I took a menacing step toward him. "I did your bidding, waited for the tiny crumbs of affection you gave me, all because I thought I loved you."

"Aspen." James sighed dramatically. "I'm sorry you had to witness that with Barbara. It's not what you think." I waved a hand, giving him the floor to explain. "You're perfect for me, Aspen. We love all the same things, and your talent with mine makes us perfect. But don't take this the wrong way—"

"I'd be careful how you finish that sentence," Aiden cut in. "Let me know if you want my gun, sweetheart." His care-free wink my way was forced, but I appreciated it all the same.

"It's just that... look at you." I held out a hand, palm up in Aiden's direction, and waggled my fingers for his firearm. "I love you, but I'm just not that attracted to you anymore." A hundred-pound weight dropped in my stomach. His words didn't matter, but they still hurt. "Maybe if you wore makeup more or fixed your hair some other way than that plain ponytail thing you do. You could try going blonde like I suggested last year—"

Miles moved faster than I could track. One second, he was feet away from James; the next, a loud crack rang through the cabin, followed by James's pain-filled scream. I gaped at Miles's muscular back as it shifted with his labored breaths. On autopilot, I walked to his side, pressing a gentle palm to his lower back so I didn't startle him. A barked surprised laugh escaped at seeing James on the floor, holding his jaw, blood dripping from the corner of a split lip.

Miles's furious expression shifted to me, immediately softening. Wide palm cupping my jaw, he brushed a thumb along my cheekbone. "No one talks about you that way. No one."

I nodded slowly, letting him know I heard him.

Scanning my face one more time, he shifted his attention back to James. "Aspen is perfect in every way, and it speaks to how fucking shallow and self-absorbed you are that you would even suggest she change anything about herself. And she was right. She's never been yours and never will be."

"And what?" James scoffed, pressing against the floor to sit up. "You think she's yours?"

Aiden's heavy arm draped over my shoulders and tugged, sealing me against his side. "Ours, actually."

James's blue eyes widened in shock. "You're fucking kidding me. Aspen, you cannot be serious."

I leaned more weight into Aiden, loving his support. "I'm not going with you back to Seattle, James. I've decided I'm staying here in Anchor Bay."

"With us." Aiden planted a kiss on the top of my head. "Miles and I will take good care of her."

James shoved off the floor to stand and dusted off his designer jeans. "So what, you're going to stay here because you're getting gangbanged—"

Miles gently caught me before I could fall when I stumbled to the side because Aiden's body was no longer there to support me. The cabin vibrated, wood groaning when James's spine slammed against the wall, held there by Aiden's hand around his throat.

"What she does, what we do, is none of your concern.

She's happy, you fucking idiot. Can't you see that? If you really loved her, then you would've seen how miserable she was back in the city."

I released a slow breath to calm my racing heart and stepped out of Miles's comforting hold. Hand on Aiden's shoulder, I gave it a squeeze.

"It's time for you to leave, James. Alone. I'm not going back with you—"

"Why don't you call your mother before you make any rash decision you can't take back, Aspen?"

I pursed my lips and shook my head. Damn, he wanted to fight dirty. Should've expected this as a last-ditch effort to keep me doing his bidding.

"Did she tell you she called me to let me know where you were?" *Of course she did.* "She wanted me to come here to talk some sense into you. This isn't just about you, Aspen. You're being selfish. We could make this work. You just need to listen to us."

Oh, they were a team now. How cute.

James's wild blue eyes flicked to Miles, then Aiden before swinging back to me. "Do you think your mother will approve of this? Of her daughter getting railed by two fucking meatheads and staying in this Podunk, ass-backward—"

Nope. He did not get to talk about them or Anchor Bay that way.

Pulling my arm back, I tightened my fingers into a fist and swung it at James's face. Instantly, sharp pain radiated up from my hand, vibrating along my arm all the way to my shoulder. My sharp hiss whistled through my clenched teeth as I rapidly shook out my hand to ease the pulsing throb. It was Aiden's laughter that had me stilling and finally taking in the aftermath of punching the bastard.

"Good girl," Miles praised, running a hand down my spine in gentle strokes.

I shot him a dramatic pout. "Why didn't you warn me that punching someone hurt so bad?"

Aiden's arms wrapped me up from behind, squeezing me tight.

"That was sexy as hell, sweetheart," he whispered in my ear.

"Pretty sure you think everything I do is sexy," I said with a fake exasperated sigh.

Turning me around, he smiled. "Guilty as charged."

Feeling an angry glare burning the back of my head, I turned to James, leaning against Aiden for support.

"I am staying here with them, and there is nothing you can do or say that will change my mind. I'm happy here. Really, really happy. I found my passion again, and these people, this town, are everything I never knew I needed. There is nothing waiting for me back in Seattle."

James's face dropped, as if only now it was sinking in that his plan to take me back home wouldn't work.

"This is not how I saw this conversation going," he muttered while tenderly prodding at his swelling lip.

"I don't doubt that. You didn't see me, haven't really seen me in a long time, James. In this new chapter in my life, I'm putting myself and what I want first, and you're not in it. I hope you have a safe trip home, and I really wish you well, James. Good luck with everything."

Not having anything else to say, I turned and shuffled to the bedroom, softly closing the door behind me. With zero energy left in my exhausted body to shower, I stripped off my stiff and dirty clothes before pulling on a pair of comfortable shorts and a matching sweatshirt. The bed frame creaked when I collapsed face-first onto the mattress with a groan. The thick duvet molded around me. My sigh brushed across the soft material, relishing the comfort after sleeping on the hard floor the night before.

Raised voices sounded from the other room, followed by the front door slamming shut. Seconds later, the bedroom door creaked as it slowly swung open, and quiet footsteps shuffled toward me. Gentle fingers brushed a few rogue strands of hair off my face.

Aiden searched my face. "You okay, sweetheart?"

I nodded, hair rasping along the cotton material. "Is he gone?"

"Yep. Miles wanted to escort him back to the seaplane to tell Finley and Dax to get him back to Seattle before nightfall."

I snorted. "Should've known he was the rich asshole they talked about picking up yesterday."

"He's not the only one in the world." A soft sigh escaped me as his fingertips brushed up and down my back. "Naptime?"

"Yeah. I need a shower, but I can't muster up the energy for that just yet."

His lips pressed to my shoulder. "There's time for that later. Sleep, sweetheart. I won't let anything happen to you, and I'll be right here when you wake up. You're safe."

As I drifted off to sleep, brain fuzzy and lips loose, I let three little words slip out.

"Love you, Aiden."

His lips softly brushed over mine. "And I'm obsessively in love with you, Aspen Carter. You're mine, and I'm—we're —never letting you go."

Sounded like perfection to me.

32

ASPEN

My muscles strained as I pulled open the weathered wooden door. Instantly, laughter and the delicious scent of food greeted me as I stepped over the threshold into Dave's. Taking a second, I scanned the high-top tables, only to have movement in the back draw my attention. The amazing group of women I was there to meet waved at me from a table in the corner, which I returned while heading to the long bar to place my drink order. Elbows on the rounded edge, I grinned at the familiar face on the other side, currently wiping away a few water droplets glistening on the polished wood left by someone else's drink.

"Hey, Kale, what are you doing here? I thought you worked at The Nest?"

Palms pressed to the edge of the bar, he leaned forward, slightly curly hair falling along his forehead as he shot me a warm smile and nodded. "I pick up shifts here, too, when I can." He flicked his wild dirty-blond hair out of his eyes. "I work all kinds of odd jobs around here. What can I get you? A glass of chardonnay like you had the other night?"

My cheeks heated, and I pressed a hand to my chest.

"I'm flattered you remembered." Kale was no Miles or Aiden, but the man was very attractive. He was no doubt a hot commodity in Anchor Bay.

His wide shoulders rose and fell in a casual shrug before he shoved off the bar. "I'm a bartender. It's kind of my job to remember things like that. Plus, I had fun talking with you that night. You're a cool chick, Aspen."

I resisted the urge to hide my face in my coat's collar. "Thanks. Did you hear I'll be hanging around Anchor Bay?" I couldn't help the wide smile that crept over my face, the joy swelling in my chest becoming too much to hide.

He paused and turned, brows raised in interest. "Really? Decided to stick around to conquer that crazy hike to the Fjords?"

I shook my head. "Nope. I'm, uh, staying with the Uplift group. Aiden and Miles particularly." More heat flooded my cheeks, warming to the point that my coat turned constricting. Pulling it off, I tossed it over the back of a bar chair. "And to answer your question, yes, please, to a glass of chardonnay. I'm meeting the girls." I hooked my thumb toward their table.

He nodded and turned to grab a wine bottle from the fridge, snagging a glass in the same movement. "I had heard about you and those two." He glanced at the door and frowned. "Are they coming in too?"

"No." I leaned against the bar, watching as the delicious liquid flowed from the bottle into the glass. "They're out again, like the last couple of days, to help search for Caroline."

My stomach dropped just saying her name out loud. Miles and Aiden were beyond worried about their friend, and I was too. Eleven days had passed since anyone had last heard from her, and everyone assumed the worst.

His features turned solemn as he nodded in understanding. The liquid in my very full wineglass sloshed when he slid it across the bar to me. "It's terrible, all of it." Someone I didn't recognize—which wasn't surprising since I was still learning the faces of all the locals—called out for another round, drawing Kale's attention. "That drink is on me. Consider it a 'Welcome to Anchor Bay' gift."

Smiling to myself, I picked up the glass, careful not to spill a single drop as I wove between the high-top tables toward the ladies waiting for me. Taking the empty chair beside Finley, I tossed my coat over the back and sat down, placing the wine gently on the table.

"I'm so glad you could make it," Baylee called out from the other side of the round wooden tabletop. "I wanted to apologize for running off the other day when we met. Betsy needed me, so I couldn't stick around to chat."

Smooth glass rim pressed to my lower lip, I took a long sip of the crisp liquid. "Totally understand. But who is Betsy? I don't think I've met her yet."

"Betsy would be our resident asshole goat," Finley said beside me with a teasing grin. "Who Baylee treats like a child—well, all our animals, actually, not just Betsy."

"*One* of our goats. Betsy and her new kid are doing fantastic." Baylee looked down at the table and spun an empty water glass between her hands. Sadness seemed to waft off her, unlike the other day when I spied her and her boyfriend, Liam, walking along the sidewalk in downtown Anchor Bay.

My lips tugged down slightly as I studied her. It wasn't my place to ask her what was upsetting her, but I felt like I needed to. I started to ask when someone stormed up to the table, slammed a heavy purse down on the floor, and slumped into the last empty chair.

"I will end up murdering him. I just know it." The beautiful petite woman tipped her face to the ceiling and groaned. "With my bare hands, if I can manage it."

"Aspen, meet Juno, Uplift's newest scheduling coordinator and social media guru," Finley said. Juno smiled at me across the table, which I returned. "Juno and Langston have this 'I hate you, but I want to fuck you' relationship going on. The rest of us have bets on if it'll end in murder or babies."

"Shut the hell up, Finley. There will be no talk of babies with that bastard. Ugh, he is such an asshole."

The name tickled at a memory. It took me a second to place it. "Oh." I sat up straight and leaned forward. "Is Langston the guy who drives the boat from the airport?" I wrinkled my nose, remembering the rude asshole.

"I see you've met the bastard and are an excellent judge of character, based on that look," Juno grumbled. Then she smirked. "I knew I liked you."

"I say you just fuck it out," Finley stated after finishing her beer and slamming the empty glass to the table. "Or..." Her smile grew, and she shot me a wicked look. "You don't have to take part, but you could always try voyeurism to deal with your sexual frustration and just watch him and West together." The sip of wine caught in my throat, making me cough. "Actually, maybe I should give voyeurism a go, now that I'm thinking about it."

"Right, let's ask Dax what he thinks about that." Juno narrowed her eyes at the woman beside me, whose smile had frozen at the mention of her best friend, Dax. "Like you're one to throw stones, Miss 'I'm in love with my best friend, but I won't tell him because—'"

Finley stretched over the table and shoved Juno's shoulder, cutting her off. "I'm not in love with Dax." She pursed her lips. "Well, not in the way you're talking about."

"Right," Baylee muttered under her breath. "Can we please stop talking about all the dicks around us and get to why we're all here?" I nodded, relieved that the relationship venting never made its way to me. "What book are we pretending to read for our next book club meeting, and who is bringing the wine?" She shot a look at Finley. "If it's you, then I need to preapprove what you're planning to bring, because that crap you had last time was barely drinkable."

"But we still drank it," Finley grumbled.

"Well, yeah, it was a version of wine, so..." Juno shrugged and stood. "I'm going to get a drink. Anyone need anything?"

After she grabbed Finley's beer request, I leaned back in the chair, slowly sipping on the decent wine, listening to Finley and Baylee discuss what book they wanted to pretend to read next month. I couldn't stop the slow smile that crept up my lips, loving every second of the moment.

Two hotter-than-hell boyfriends who treated me well and loved to worship my body every chance they got, plus new girlfriends who liked wine and books...

Anchor Bay was truly a dream come true.

AFTER AN HOUR AT DAVE'S, the only thing we accomplished was running up a bar tab and laughing until our cheeks hurt. Smiling to myself, a little tipsy from the three glasses I downed in that short time frame, I slowly made my way back to Aiden and Miles's cabin. They'd asked me to call it ours since I'd officially moved out of The Nest, but it was too soon, and it felt strange since it was theirs before I arrived.

With the warmer temperatures and crystal-clear sky, I took the long way back, knowing the guys wouldn't return for a while. At least I had Jubie to look forward to greeting me and not an empty cabin. Excited about the certain nap and exceptional cuddles in my future, I picked up my pace, very ready to snooze with Jubie's massive body next to me to sleep off the fuzziness coating my thoughts.

Leaping up the porch steps, keys in hand, I quickly unlocked the door and swung it open, humming a pop song as I stepped over the threshold.

"Jubie," I sang over my shoulder as I tugged off my coat and hung it on a hook by the door.

Whirling around to search for my snuggle buddy, my wide smile that had been firmly in place since Dave's vanished. I blinked, unable to understand what I was witnessing with the wine clouding my thoughts.

Frozen in place, I stared at the strange woman hovering over Jubie's limp body by the open back door. She said nothing, only stared back, as if she was just as shocked to see me, Jubie's back legs clutched in her tight grip.

Nothing made sense. Why was she here, and why did it look like she was attempting to drag the ninety-five-pound dog out the back door?

"Um..." I licked my lips, still studying the woman's face when recognition hit me. "It's you, the woman from the bar that first night. It's Jessica, right?"

Jubie's legs slapped to the floor when Jessica released her hold to stand tall. She was beautiful, that was for sure, but in a cruel way. Anger and malicious intent wafted off her, warning me away even from across the living room. I dared a single step closer, holding both hands out in surrender. My gaze kept flicking to Jubie, who had yet to stir, and the woman tracked my every move.

"You know me?" I nodded in response. "They talked about me, then." Jessica huffed a humorless laugh. A cruel smirk pulled at her lips. "That figures. Men always realize they used and abused the good ones when it's too late to come crawling back."

"Yeah," I drawled, not really agreeing with her but knowing it was best to play along with her delusions in this situation. I'd seen enough crime shows to know you didn't disagree with the crazy person in the room. "What's wrong with Jubie?"

And what the fuck did you do to her? I wanted to scream.

Jessica shrugged like the unconscious dog wasn't a big deal. "Just sleeping. I think." She nudged the unmoving Jubie with the toe of her tennis shoe. "Pretty sure. I wasn't certain about her weight for the drugs, so maybe not."

I swallowed hard to silence my pitiful whimper that was desperate to escape at her words and nonchalant tone.

"Let's go with just sleeping." *Please let Jubie just be sleeping.* "What are you doing here, Jessica?" I dared another step, keeping my movements slow and controlled to not startle her. I didn't know if she was armed, which had me proceeding with caution. When I reached the other side of the couch, I wrapped both hands around the back in a death grip.

"What am *I* doing here? What are *you* doing here?"

"Checking on Jubie," I blurted. Pretty sure telling her this was my cabin now, too, would not go over well with Miss Crazy Eyes.

She narrowed her eyes like she didn't believe me. "I've decided it's time to finally leave this shitty little town, but first, I wanted to give those two assholes a little payback. So they would fully understand what they did and pay the consequences." Her voice rose with every word until she was almost shouting. "They can't keep doing this to women like us." I nodded, even though I didn't understand the craziness she spewed, which had nothing to do with the wine fogging my brain. "When I watched you, I knew—"

"You knew what?" I gaped.

Jessica rolled her eyes and slipped both hands into the back pockets of her jeans. "Don't look so surprised and outraged. I did it for you. Maybe you should be a little more grateful rather than all judgy." All I could do was nod back. She continued. "I needed to see if you were like me, falling for two men who would shred your heart into tiny little bits that would never be put back together again."

"Oh, yeah, of course. And yes, thank you for checking in on me. That was very... thoughtful." Fucking hell, I was terrible at this appeasing-a-crazy thing. The TV shows made it seem much easier. It would be nice if I could call for help, but my new cell phone was in my coat pocket by the front door. Jubie's best bet was for me to keep Jessica talking until the guys arrived, whenever that would be, and maybe we would both make it out of this unscathed. "Wait, were you the one who followed me that night?"

She tilted her head to the side. "You need to be more specific."

Right. "The night I walked alone to the main building at The Nest taking the path that wove through the cottages."

"Alone? No, why would I do that?"

"Um, because you said you watched me?"

"Only when you were with them." She rolled her eyes like her answer made all the sense in the world. Maybe it did, to her. "Well, there was the whole cabin thing. We're about the same size. Did you know that?" I looked at her, then down my frame. "I really liked that green sweater. It fit perfectly, and the material was super soft. I ordered one once I left."

My sluggish thoughts grasped on to that creepy-as-hell comment. I tightened my hold on the couch to keep from bolting out the front door.

"Yeah, that's a good sweater." One I would never wear again. I inched along the couch, hoping to get close enough to see if Jubie was breathing. "And what did you find out after watching me with them?"

"That they were doing the same thing to you that they did to me. We are the innocent victims in their fucked-up mind game, and you'd end up just like me. Broken and angry. They have to learn that they can't keep doing this to us. Which is why I'm here and why you're going to stop coming closer and turn around and walk out the front door like you saw nothing out of the ordinary going on."

Her matter-of-fact tone made it sound like she expected me to immediately obey her ludicrous command.

"Or," I responded, "we could talk this out. You tell me all the things that are making you angry while I make sure Jubie is okay."

The corner of her lips curled in a sneer. "The dumb animal is fine. Why do you care what happens to her? It's just a dog."

My hands tightened into fists behind my back. "What did she ever do to you?" I snapped, anger getting the better of me.

"Well, for one," Jessica held up a single finger as if to tick off the reasons. "She never liked me, and I'm almost positive that's why those assholes dumped me. Two, she means a lot to them, and if I hurt her, then I hurt them. And three..." She dropped her hand and shrugged. "That about sums it up. If I want to teach them a lesson to never hurt women like us again—and I'm not sure why you're not thanking me right now—then they need something that will hurt them to the core, like they did me when they strung me along."

Oh. Fuck.

Damn that third glass of wine. If I hadn't chugged the last few gulps, then maybe I could've formed a decent plan. Scratch that, a plan in general, because as I stood there, heart hammering and sweat dripping down my spine, I had nothing. Zilch. Zero ideas on how to get me and Jubie out of this mess.

"Jessica," I pleaded, "you don't want to do this. You don't want to hurt an innocent dog." I shifted around the couch, putting myself only a couple of feet away from her and Jubie. "She didn't hurt you. They did."

"But hurting her will cause them pain and delightful suffering, so that makes things even. Then maybe I'll feel better, get over all this anger and hurt festering inside me." She jabbed a finger at her chest, tears filling her lower lids. "I'm just so angry with them, and they deserve what's coming to them for making me feel this way."

"Hurting Jubie won't make you less angry with them and their actions. I think you know that."

With an exaggerated, frustrated groan, she narrowed her eyes at me and reached behind her. I blinked in surprise at the large Buck knife, shiny steel blade already out, that was now in her tight grip. She flipped it around, rotating the handle without nicking her fingers with the sharp blade, proving she knew her way around a knife.

Great.

Because I for sure did not know my way around any type of weapon, nor was I armed with one, not even my fucking phone.

Damnit.

A low buzz sounded in my ears as I weighed my options, heart racing so fast my breaths came in quick, short pants like I'd just run a mile instead of standing still, watching some crazy lady validate her plan to hurt Jubie.

No.

I couldn't let her cause Jubie any more harm than she'd already inflicted. Jubie was... innocent, perfect, slobbery happiness wrapped in a whole lot of fur, and absolutely everything to Miles. Miles was everything to Aiden, and those two had, in just over a week, become everything to me. I wouldn't let this loon cause them more pain, not when they'd both been through enough trauma in the past. And the fact that they had done nothing wrong. She might feel like they lied and used her, but I knew Miles and Aiden wouldn't do that. It wasn't who they were.

Jessica was angry and volatile because they didn't want something long term. But that was life; that was dating and putting yourself out there.

Maybe it was the third glass of wine talking, but... no matter what happened next, I knew I would do anything to keep Jubie safe. That made more sense than doing nothing and allowing Jessica to cause Jubie or the guys pain. Plus, if Jubie was injured or worse while I stood and did nothing to stop it, that just might destroy me anyway.

So, I made a plan... ish.

How that would play out, only time would tell.

And I had a feeling I wouldn't have to wait long.

33

ASPEN

With a dramatic sigh, Jessica tapped the side of the blade against her jean-covered thigh. "Fine, if you're not leaving, you can help me. Doing it here works better, actually. Letting them find her." She slid her crazy eyes to Jubie, her brows furrowed. "Not really sure how to do this, so I guess I just..." Raising the knife, she made a stabbing motion and nodded. "Seems simple enough."

Barely breathing through the fear squeezing my lungs, I stepped closer, both hands raised, palms out. "Please don't do this," I pleaded. Hot, unshed tears burned behind my eyes.

"I have to. This is how men like them learn. I've taught others in the past, though this might be my best lesson yet." *Oh wow.* Squatting beside Jubie, she balanced on the balls of her feet. "If you won't help, then don't get in the way. I don't want to hurt you while I do what has to be done, but I will."

And there it was.

The line in the sand.

"No," I rasped, voice barely more than a whisper. "I won't

let you do this, Jessica. Jubie didn't hurt you. I'm begging you, don't do this. Walk away."

She tossed her long hair over one shoulder to look up at me with a malicious grin. "I don't think so, Aspen. It's too late for her and them."

But it wasn't.

Because I was here to stop it, no matter what.

Time shifted into slow motion as she raised the hand gripping the knife, sharp point aimed right at Jubie's chest. With no weapon in sight, not even a damn lamp to swing at her head, I was out of options. Well, good options, which meant I needed to move forward with terrible option number one.

I didn't hesitate; the adrenaline pumping in my veins amped me up more than a thousand cups of coffee. With as much force as I could muster to clear the small distance, I launched myself at the terrible woman, hands outstretched to tackle her, and then...

Well, I hadn't gotten that far.

The glinting knife was just above Jubie's side when she noticed me and raised both hands, but nothing would stop my momentum. I smashed into Jessica with a grunt, something slicing through my skin, leaving fire in its wake. Together, we flew backward, the world around me spinning during the short free fall. Her back slammed to the floor, and her pained cry rattled around the cabin a second before I dropped on top of her with a grunt that cut off when my forehead bounced off the unforgiving wood.

My teeth rattled with the impact. The taste of copper filled my mouth where I bit my tongue or cheek, but that didn't matter with the raging inferno of agony pulsing from the wound on my arm. I'd barely taken a single breath before it exploded from my lungs with the hard shove that threw my limp body off Jessica. Crying out in a mix of pain and anger, I rolled to my back. Gasping, attempting to breathe through the agony, I blindingly felt for the wound. Hot, sticky blood coated my skin, pumping freely and dripping to the floor.

A muffled curse had me rolling the back of my head along the floor toward the sound. Jessica struggled to stand. Stumbling, she caught herself on the wall with the hand not pressed against the growing crimson stain on the thigh of her light jeans.

"You fucking bitch," she screamed, tears leaking down her face. When she looked at me, her eyes went wide, focused on my arm. One step, then another. She slowly backed away, shaking her head. "No, no, no. I'm not going down for this."

Well, that was not the reassurance that I needed.

Panic filled my veins. Crying out, I lifted my arm, gasping through the pain, barely glimpsing the long, wide gash that ran from my wrist to elbow. I let it drop back to the floor, but I didn't feel the impact.

"What's going on?" My thoughts swam. "What happened? Jubie," I called out. "Jubie!"

"Damnit."

I looked at Jessica, her form blurrier than a few seconds ago, and why did it sound like she was talking underwater?

Eyes wide, she stumbled out the open back door, gaze locked on me until she turned and fled. All I could hear was my own rasped breaths sawing in and out of my tight lungs. My tongue felt too large for my mouth, thick and dry, as I tried to call for her to come back. She couldn't get away with this.

She didn't come back.

With the palm of my uninjured arm pressed to the hardwood, I pushed myself up to a sitting position, sliding a few times with the slick blood—my blood—coating the floor beneath me, and leaned against the couch. With some help, I gently lay my injured forearm on my lap. Bright red liquid pumped from the wound, soaking my jeans instantly. The room spun and my stomach rolled at my first up-close look at it.

A whimper had me slowly looking at Jubie.

Jubie.

I had to help her, and get help for myself before...

Knowing I had little time before I blacked out from blood loss, I gritted my teeth and used the couch as leverage to help me stand. After a few tries, I was up, though I wavered, body swaying with the way the room rotated.

Arm cradled to my chest, I started for the door, bouncing against the furniture and wall to keep me upright. A pitiful cry scraped up my throat when I finally made it to the door. Shoulder to the wood for support, I considered grabbing my phone. Even with the blood loss and wine-saturated brain, I knew that would be a waste of precious time.

The only local numbers I had were the guys', and who knew where they were. I needed help *now*. Not only for myself and Jubie but to chase after Jessica. She couldn't get away, not when I knew without a doubt she would try again or even move on to something worse, like harming the guys directly.

The tacky blood coating my palm had it slipping around the smooth metal door handle before I could get a grip and twist it open. The bright sun pierced my eyes as I stumbled out onto the porch, my shoulder slamming into a post, which saved me from tumbling over the railing.

Lips parted, breaths frantic and way too shallow, I

blinked to clear my vision, scanning the empty street for anyone around who could help me. Voices and movement had my gaze sliding to where two forms rounded one cabin, their backs to me as they walked in the opposite direction. From where I was, plus the tears and hair clouding my vision, I couldn't tell who it was, but it didn't matter.

Anyone here would help me. I knew that as firmly as I knew I loved Miles and Aiden.

Careful not to face-plant, I stumbled down the porch steps and began shuffling my way toward the two men.

"Help," I rasped, licking my dry lips. "Please," I begged, forcing more strength into my voice, hoping they'd hear me.

They paused and turned, giving me a burst of energy to keep moving toward them.

As soon as they started racing my way, as if knowing help was imminent, my legs gave out, sending me crumpling to the road. The ground vibrated beneath me, and then a familiar face loomed over me, blocking out the too-bright sun. Langston's dark gaze scanned my face, brows pulling in tight like he was actually concerned.

"Holy shit. Look at her arm, Lang. Fuck, Aspen, what happened?" I slid my gaze to the person who spoke. Liam, Baylee's boyfriend.

"Help Jubie," I rasped.

Langston and Liam shared a look I couldn't read before Liam disappeared. With gentle care, Langston stepped back and ripped the black T-shirt he wore over his head. If my thoughts hadn't been stilted from the wine, concussion, and now blood loss, I would've appreciated his defined chest and attempted to make out the design inked there.

A loud tearing sound rang in my ears, drawing my attention away from his tattoo and to the shirt he'd ripped in two.

"This is going to hurt, but I need to bind the wound to

slow the bleeding until I can get the emergency supplies from my gear bag." His hands hovered over my arm, fingers tightening around the black cotton. "I'm going to touch you, okay?"

I guess I nodded, because he went to work wrapping the wide strip of cloth around my forearm. I bit back a scream, teeth almost cracking, as pain shot up my arm. Fresh tears leaked from my eyes as I squeezed them shut.

"The dog is out cold, drugged maybe." Liam's voice went in one ear and out the other. "There are signs of a struggle in their cabin, too, Lang. The back door is wide open with a fresh blood trail that leads out, which obviously isn't Aspen's." He squatted beside me and pushed the hair off my sweaty forehead. "You're going to be okay."

"Jubie," I whispered despite my raw throat.

"Hey, it's okay." Liam's wide palm brushed along the top of my head in a comforting gesture. "I texted Baylee a 9-1-1 message. She's on her way to focus on Jubie."

Something tightening around my bicep had me biting my lip hard, my teeth puncturing the soft flesh. Blinking through my glassy vision, I barely made out the makeshift tourniquet Langston's thick fingers were finishing tying off.

"Call her guys," Langston barked. "Tell them to get their asses back here now, and call The Nest's doctor while you run to my place for my medic kit."

"You have a horrible disposition for a doctor," I mumbled, thoughts growing even fuzzier from the pain and blood loss slowly shutting down my body.

Instead of being pissed, a small smile tugged at the corner of Langston's lips. Shaking his head, he slid both arms beneath me and hauled me into the air, securing me against his bare chest.

"Put your arm on your stomach while I carry you back to

the cabin." When I did as requested, Langston started toward Miles and Aiden's place. "And I agree with you, I would've been a shit doctor. But in a combat zone, my shitty attitude and demeanor didn't matter as long as I kept soldiers alive."

I filed away that bit of information for later.

"Miles and Aiden are on their way," Liam said from somewhere behind us as Langston hauled me like a bride into the cabin. "Calling the doc now. Be right back with your stuff."

The leather groaned as Langston laid me on the couch, quickly finding a pillow to prop up my head.

"This will not feel good." I blinked at him. "Fine, it's going to hurt like hell at first, but it'll get better, promise." Features set into a firm line, he wrapped his fingers around my wrist and lifted my injured arm. "Keeping it above your heart will help with the blood loss. That, plus the tourniquet. You'll be okay, Aspen." With gentle fingers, he brushed a few damp strands of hair off my face. "Can you tell me what happened?"

"She was going to hurt Jubie," I slurred. My lids grew heavy, slowly shutting and refusing to reopen.

A hard shake to my shoulder jostled me along the couch. "Hey, none of that. You want to see your guys when they get here, right? Keep them from killing me."

With determined effort, I forced my lids back open, fighting to keep them that way. "Why would they do that?"

Langston shifted on the balls of his feet where he crouched beside me. "Men like them, like us, have shit reasoning when finding their girl injured and some big asshole looming over her."

"You're not a big asshole." Not sure when I changed my opinion of the guy, but here we were.

He scoffed. "Right. Now, back to what happened. Who wanted to hurt Jubie?"

"You have to stop her." A bolt of urgency had me pushing off the couch like I was in any condition to chase after Jessica. "She wants to hurt them. Please," I begged, "don't let her hurt them."

With a soft grip on my shoulder, Langston gently guided me back down to the couch. "Don't worry, I won't let anyone hurt my friends." He gave me a half smile. "Based on the huge egg-shaped bump on your head and gash on your forearm, it seems you fight for your friends and family too. Maybe I misjudged you, Aspen Carter."

"Or Alaska changed me," I murmured, lips numb.

"Ah, Alaska only brings out the core of who we are. It doesn't change us."

"You're a military medic *and* a philosopher?" That made me think of when I met Aiden and said something similar. "Where are they?" I cried, voice shaking.

"They're almost here, but first, I need to know one thing. Can you focus for me?" I nodded, locking eyes with him. "Who are we hunting, sweet girl? Who will I make pay for hurting you and trying to hurt my friends?"

"Jessica," I said automatically, like I'd been given truth serum and couldn't stop the name from leaving my lips.

A dark expression overtook his face. "Hmm, good to know."

My eyes widened when he shifted. Panic had me reaching out, wrapping a hand around his wrist. "Don't leave me," I pleaded. "Not until they're here. I don't want to be alone."

His lips parted but snapped shut, his words cut off by someone bellowing somewhere outside the cabin. The stomp of boots pounding against the porch followed more shouted demands of "Where the fuck is she?" and my name being called repeatedly.

The moment they entered the cabin, relief swamped me like a comforting blanket. They were here, which meant I didn't have to be strong anymore. Miles's face appeared over mine, and the tears that had only dripped from my eyes now erupted into massive waterfalls.

"Who hurt you, Aspen?" More tears flowed down my cheeks that he swiped away with gentle strokes. "Who am I hunting for this?"

I was still unable to get words out around the silent sobs. He scanned my face before sliding an angry look to Langston.

"What. The. Fuck. Happened? And why the hell is your shirt off?"

As if he knew it was coming, Langston gently set my arm on my chest right before Miles lunged for him, sending them both crashing to the floor. I twisted my head, too shocked to do or say anything as they rolled around, sending the coffee table flying against the stone fireplace. In a practiced move, Miles flipped around, pinning Langston to the floor with a hand wrapped around his throat.

For as much of an asshole as Langston was, he was apparently well versed in how to not agitate a man on the verge of snapping. Not once did he attempt to break Miles's choking hold; instead, Langston lay beneath him with both hands up, looking calm and patient.

"Sweetheart." The utter distress in Aiden's trembling voice made more tears cascade down my cheeks, dripping onto the couch. "My sweet, sweet Aspen, who hurt you?" His voice cracked as he cradled my cheek, gaze searching my face. "Who do we need to kill for laying hands on our special girl?"

Noise at the front door had every head swiveling in that direction. Miles jumped up, drawing his sidearm in the same movement, only to immediately lower the barrel and holster the gun.

Liam crept into view, his hands up, though one held a red canvas-type bag with a white cross on the side. "Easy there, boys. Just bringing Lang his medic kit to help your girl while we wait for the doc." Liam eyed Langston, who was still laid out on the floor, before looking at Miles with an arched brow. "You know he didn't do this, right, Miles?"

Miles gave a confirming grunt before he begrudgingly held out a hand to help Langston off the floor. He started to say something else, but his attention snapped to the across the room. "Jubie." My heart shattered at the despair in Miles's voice. I couldn't see them where I lay, but I heard a noise that sounded like he slumped to the hardwood floor. "Who hurt them in our own home?"

"Liam called Baylee," Langston said. "She'll be here to handle Jubie's medical needs." Storming over, he took the offered medical bag and leaned in to whisper to Liam, who nodded and took off through the back door. "And call Oliver," Langston shouted after him. "We need everyone out there looking for her."

"Her?" Aiden and Miles exclaimed at the same time.

"Yes, her," Langston snarled while unzipping the bag. "That Jessica woman did this to your dog and girl. Though what I'm gathering is she actually went after Jubie, but Aspen stepped in and got herself knifed."

Okay, maybe he was back to being an asshole.

"Your girl here saved her life." He opened his bag and rummaged through it, pulling out a wrap of some kind. "This is special gauze that will help slow the bleeding, but I'll have to unwrap what I did earlier to get it on." He waited until I nodded. "As soon as the doc gets here, he can get you some pain meds before taking you to the clinic, where you'll need a shit ton of stitches to close up the gash." He looked to Aiden, then Miles. "I'll make sure they're with you the entire time. You won't be alone."

"Okay." My hand snapped out and wrapped around his forearm. "Thank you."

His features softened for a second before he cleared his throat with a clipped nod.

With his full focus on the task at hand, I turned wide eyes to Aiden, who still hovered close. "Please don't leave me."

His expression turned fierce. Kneeling beside me, he wiped at my damp cheeks. "Never, sweetheart. We're here, no matter what."

Almost completely numb, I didn't really feel Langston removing the old bandage and wrapping it with the new one. With the guys there, knowing they were safe and someone was on their way to help Jubie, all the fight drained out of me. Body molding against the cushions, I let my heavy lids fall despite the frantic shouts around me.

Quickly, the voices faded into a dull hum. My sluggish heartbeat pounded in my ears.

But I wasn't scared, not really.

Aiden said they wouldn't leave me, no matter what.

And if they were here, then everything would be okay.

For me anyway. For Jessica...

I really, really, *really* hoped not.

34

AIDEN

Miles's harsh whispers sounded from the corner of the exam room, his knuckles now white where he gripped the phone as he ran the other hand over his beard in agitated swipes. Keeping one eye on him to ensure he didn't punch another hole through the wall, I studied Aspen's beautiful face, relaxed in sleep. Whatever pain meds Dr. Richards gave her knocked her out cold, which was good and bad.

Good, because the doctor sewed up the massive laceration—forty-two stitches—without her feeling a thing. The bad, her sleeping soundly indicated a possible concussion Dr. Richards diagnosed based on the goose egg on her forehead. He wanted her awake, but that wouldn't happen until the meds wore off, though she would need more to manage her pain level.

Grabbing a sterile wet rag, I swiped it across her pinkish skin slowly, cleaning the dried blood coating her fingers. I glanced at the clock over the door that led out to the small clinic. It had only been two hours since we stormed into our cabin after getting Liam's urgent call that Aspen was hurt and needed us. Thankfully, Langston was not only a medic in the Army but also trained as an EMT, providing the emergency trauma support we needed during rescue missions or just around Anchor Bay.

A soft sound snapped my attention from watching Miles pace to Aspen just as her dark lashes fluttered open. After several blinks, her gaze locked on me. I slumped against the table at the swell of relief that flowed through me. Not saying a word, I ran a single finger over her cheek, down her jaw.

A pain-filled expression flashed across her face when she shifted along the crappy clinic bed.

"Try not to move, sweetheart," I rasped. "You're at Dr. Richards's clinic. Miles and I are both here." She licked her lips and glanced around, brows furrowing. I hitched my chin at Miles to get his attention. "End that call. She needs to see you."

Without a goodbye, he tapped the screen and strode to stand beside me. Her body instantly relaxed, and her lips curled into a soft smile.

"You're here. You're both here," she whispered, voice cracking.

Reaching over, I grabbed the cup of water the nurse left and nudged the straw between her lips. After a few drinks, I pulled it back and set it on the table.

Beside me, Miles vibrated with the need for answers. I was proud of him for not immediately demanding—

"What happened?" he barely got out around his locked jaw.

I rolled my eyes and jabbed an elbow into his stomach, making him grunt. "We talked about this, you overbearing, grumpy asshole." I looked to Aspen, shooting her a goofy grin. "This guy can't read a room, am I right?"

Her smile widened. "But he's *my* overbearing, grumpy asshole," she rasped. "And you're my mischievous mediator."

"I'm not grumpy," Miles muttered.

Aspen and I exchanged a humor-filled look before laughing in unison. Shaking her head, she glanced down at her bandaged arm, all humor fading.

"How bad was it?" she asked, not looking away from the white gauze.

"Forty-two stitches, and the doc thinks you have a concussion." Miles planted a hand on either side of her head and leaned in close. "You scared the shit out of me, baby girl. I've never felt more all-consuming fear and help-lessness than when I walked in to find you on that couch, bleeding out."

"I'm sorry," she said, eyes going watery. She looked past him to me. "I'm so sorry."

"Hey." I shoved Miles out of the way. "You have nothing to be sorry for. This wasn't your fault. But please, never put yourself in a situation like that again. I died a thousand deaths between the time we got the call that you were hurt until your big, beautiful brown eyes blinked open just now."

"But she was going to hurt Jubie." Grimacing, she lifted her injured arm and rested it over her stomach. "I got back from the book club meeting, where I drank one too many glasses of wine." Miles grumbled something under his breath, and I elbowed him in the ribs to shut him up. "When I got to the cabin, she was there, dragging Jubie toward the back door. I didn't know if she was alive or not, but I still had to do something." Tears broke free and dripped out of the corners of her eyes. "She wanted to hurt Jubie to hurt you two, and I knew it would." Her gaze went to Miles. "I know how much Jubie means to you and how much you need her."

Miles's features softened. Cupping her cheek, he brushed away the trickling tears with each swipe of his thumb. "I cannot tell you how much I appreciate you protecting Jubie, but don't you see you mean more to me? That I need you more?" Her head tilted side to side. "I love my dog, baby girl. She's been with me every step of the way, but you and Aiden are my life, my world. I would be devastated if something happened to Jubie, but I'd lose everything worth living for if something happened to either of you."

My throat closed up with unshed tears.

"I love you, Aspen Carter." Her eyes widened at his admission. "I'm in love with everything about you. Your independence, which drives me fucking insane." Her wide smile trembled as more tears poured down. "Your soul-healing dark eyes, adorable freckles, and open heart. You accept me, all of me, and from now on, I never want to know what it's like not to have you in our lives."

"I love you, too, Miles," she cried, trembling on the bed with her happy sobs. "You deserve to be loved. You deserve everything because of what you've done and who you are. I'm amazed by you."

There was a sharp knock at the door before it swung open. Dr. Richards walked in, attention on the chart in his hand.

"Give us a second, Doc," I asked, making him look up from the papers.

"I need to check—"

"Out," Miles demanded, pointing toward the door. "Now."

With an annoyed huff, he turned and walked back out, slamming the door shut behind him.

"You two are insufferable," Aspen said, smile so wide that the corners of her eyes crinkled. "You should go apologize, Miles. He is the one who stitched me up, right? And we need him to not be pissed so we can get out of here and go home."

At the mention of the word *home*, Miles and I exchanged a worried look.

"What? What aren't you two telling me?"

"I'll go talk to the doc," Miles said, storming out of the room, leaving me to explain to Aspen what we'd decided while she was unconscious.

I glared at his back until he closed the door, shutting off the sounds from the clinic. Shaking my head, I perched on the edge of the bed and studied my hands.

"We can't go back there. Not after finding you like that and knowing Jessica was there. It doesn't feel like home anymore." I dared a look over my shoulder, surprised at finding relief on Aspen's face. "You're okay with us making that decision without you?"

She nodded. "I didn't want to go back there either. Not after..." Her whole body shivered along the thin mattress.

Pushing off, I grabbed another blanket the nurse left and draped it over Aspen's legs.

"I was afraid you'd be angry that we decided without you."

"I'm glad you did so I didn't have to bring it up, thinking I was asking you two to leave your home for me."

Her soft skin slid beneath my knuckle as I stroked it along her jaw. "Don't you know we'd do anything for you, Aspen? Anything?" Inhaling deeply for courage, I repeated the words

I wasn't sure she heard the other day. "I love you, Aspen. Anything you need or want, I'll do. I don't just want a life with you. I want everything. The good, the bad, and all that in between. I never realized that this soul-consuming feeling was love. I thought I loved before, but now I realize it wasn't even fucking close to how consumed I am with how I feel for you. Twice in the last week, I thought I'd lost you, and each time, it only solidified that you're a part of me now. You're in my heart so deep that it wouldn't keep beating if you weren't here."

"Oh, Aiden," she whispered. "You have so much love and happiness to give, and I want you. I want everything that you have to give all for myself. I love you too, so much that it feels like my heart may burst in my chest because of how full it feels. You two have shown me what true love is, and I will never let either of you go."

Supporting myself with a hand on either side of her head, I leaned in close and pressed a soft kiss to her forehead.

"Never letting us go, sweetheart. I will hold you to that."

Her grin was all happiness and love. "I hope you do."

Hours ago, I thought my life was over, and now...

Now I realized it was only really beginning.

35

MILES

Sitting on the top porch step of our temporary cabin, our home until the three-bedroom one we wanted was cleaned out and move-in ready, I ran my fingers through Jubie's thick fur, watching Aiden and Aspen rock back and forth in the porch swing. My smile dropped, catching the white gauze wrapped around Aspen's forearm.

Two days ago, the best thing that ever happened to us was almost taken away.

Jubie grunted and nudged my shoulder with her wet nose, telling me she sensed the anxiety spike. Thankfully, the drugs wore off quickly, and after twenty-four hours under Baylee's care, Jubie was back to her old self. So far, we hadn't noticed any side effects, but Baylee demanded she stop by daily for the next couple of weeks to check in.

We almost lost her and Aspen all because of someone we'd introduced into their lives. My heart gave a painful thud just thinking about how devastated Aiden and I would be if we had lost our future with Aspen. The only bright side out of the whole shit show was that the threat to her, Jubie, Aiden, and me was gone.

Liam tracked the blood trail Jessica left when she fell out the back door and found her body almost half a mile away in a remote area. The way he explained it, she was already dead when he found her from the gash on the inside of her thigh that severed an artery. Though I wasn't sure if that was exactly true. Something about the way his lips curved up in a knowing grin spoke to there being more to that story.

I would hopefully find out one day soon so I could thank the bastard for ensuring the threat to our family was finished. We would have more challenges, but hopefully none as violent as this one.

Movement down the road had me leaning forward. Knowing the trio was headed this way, I pushed off the rough boards to stand. A groan slipped out as I stretched both arms high in the air, fingertips brushing the porch overhang.

"We leave, and this place goes to hell," Brandon said, his arm draped over his partner's shoulders. Their size difference was comical, his six-foot-five frame towering over her barely five-foot stature.

"Welcome back," I said, taking his outstretched hand, then turning to Amy and Carl. "We missed you guys."

Breaking out of Brandon's hold, Amy leapt up the stairs and wrapped her arms around my waist, squeezing me so tight I couldn't take a full breath.

"Come on, baby, let the man breathe." Carl carefully extracted Amy and pulled her back against his chest. "We just landed and heard about..." His gaze slid to Aspen, who had left the swing to stand beside me. "Everything. Hi, you must be Aspen Carter." He shook her hand. "I'm Carl Taylor, and these are my partners, Amy and Brandon."

"I cannot believe this happened here," Amy exclaimed, tossing her hands in the air. "This place is normally so safe that we leave our doors unlocked." She stepped closer to Aspen and pulled her into a much gentler hug than she gave me. "I'm so sorry this was your introduction to our community, to Anchor Bay."

"It hasn't been all bad," Aspen said, shooting a smile up at me. "And there are bad people everywhere. At least this place comes with great scenery."

"You mean me and Miles, right, sweetheart?" Aiden draped an arm over Aspen's shoulders.

Amy's eyes went wide, flicking between the three of us before squealing so loud that Jubie whined and lay down, paws lifting to cover her ears.

"You're kidding me right now, right?" I shook my head, chuckling at her palpable excitement. "I am so happy for you three. We have to go on a triple date."

"Did you just make that up, baby?" Brandon asked, covering his growing grin.

She huffed and flipped him the bird. "Maybe, maybe not. Either way, it's now a thing, and we're doing it." Amy leaned in close to Aspen, lifting her hand to whisper behind it, though she spoke loud enough for us all to hear. "We can talk about all the things, living with two overbearing, protective, grumpy—"

"That's enough out of you." Amy squealed in delight when Carl wrapped an arm around her waist and hauled her backward. Lifting her slight frame with ease, he tossed Amy over his shoulder and slapped her ass hard. "Get the business talk done, then come find us. We can catch up on everything not Uplift around a few beers at Dave's."

Brandon watched them go with a gentle look on his face that vanished when he turned to me. Crossing both thick tatted arms over his barrel chest, he hitched his chin toward the cabin.

"Let's go inside to talk about Caroline and—" He stopped mid-sentence to look at his phone screen. A frown tugged his lips down, and he lifted the device to his ear. "Hey, Oliver. What—"

Aiden, Aspen, and I all leaned forward, trying to catch whatever Oliver said on the other end of the line. Thankfully, we didn't have to wait long.

His features were stern, all business when he ended the call.

"You will not believe this," he muttered and turned to look down the road. I followed his line of sight to where Langston was hauling ass in the opposite direction.

"Now what?" Aiden grumbled. "I swear, if anyone else was stabbed, it wasn't because of us."

Brandon shot Aiden a dull look. "Liam caught someone breaking into Caroline's cabin and called Oliver after he had the bastard hog-tied."

A huffed laugh escaped me. Of course our cowboy hog-tied the dumb asshole who—

"Wait, did you say Caroline's?" I stood straight and started down the steps. "Who the fuck was breaking into her cabin, and why?"

Brandon fell into line beside me as we hurried down the road.

"You can't kill him until we get some answers," Brandon stated, though the way he popped his knuckles and stretched out his thick neck told me that was a warning to himself too.

My heart dropped at his tone. "Who broke the fuck in, Brandon?"

"Jasper. Jasper Cain."

I cracked my knuckles one by one. "Then let's go find out

why he was in Caroline's cabin and what he knows about her disappearance."

Hopefully he had information we could use to bring her home.

If not, I was almost certain we'd never see our friend again.

Keep reading for the conclusion to Aiden, Miles and Aspen's story!

Want to know what Jasper was doing in Caroline's cabin? Desperate to know what happened to her and the other missing women?
Find out in book 2, Claiming Ours, releasing fall 2025!

EPILOGUE

ASPEN

One year later

The phone vibrating on the bedside table had me groaning as I rolled over, blindly reaching over Aiden's bare chest. He grumbled something about it being too early and rolled over, giving me his back. Fingers tapping across the hard wood, searching for the annoying device, I blew a few rogue hairs off my face.

Finding the phone, I pulled it close and held it to see who needed me at six in the freaking morning. Blinking rapidly, I sighed as I slid my thumb across the screen to answer the call.

"Hey, Juno," I rasped, my voice thick with sleep. "What the hell are you doing up this early?"

"Early bird gets the sales, babe."

I huffed in agreement and leaned back against the headboard. My gaze shifted to Miles on my other side, finding him awake, hazel eyes staring up at me. Reaching over, I ran my fingers through his short hair and down the back of his neck, letting him know I was all good.

"Working on the website again?" I said with a yawn.

"Babe, your pictures are breaking the internet. Everyone wants a high-resolution copy, and that shit takes a lot of bandwidth." My lids fluttered closed. "That along with the number of payments you have coming through meant I needed to upgrade your site and change hosts to make sure there isn't lag time, which means lost sales."

"You're too good to me, Juno."

"Yeah, well, you're paying me, so it's kind of my job. Plus, it's fun. Having creative freedom and this back-end shit is my jam."

"Well, thank you, nonetheless. You're a computer god, and I owe you a night at Dave's as a bonus for all this."

A male voice called her name in the background. "You know I'll never turn down free booze. I gotta run. See you tonight at book club. You're bringing the wine, right?"

"Yep, and I wouldn't miss it. Bye."

The moment the phone fell to the bed, Miles's thick arm wrapped around my waist and slid me down until I was once again lying between him and Aiden. I traced a finger along his scruff-covered jaw.

"I was worried it was your mom again," he said.

Shifting on the soft sheet, I wiggled until my face pressed against his chest and our bodies were sealed together.

"Yeah, well, I highly doubt I'll hear from her again after that ultimatum I gave her. If she can't accept us, the three of us together and our community, then I don't want her in my life." It was true. Without the guys' input or insistence, I'd finally had enough of my mother's old-school rants and lectures and told her to never call again until she was ready to accept us all.

That was two months ago.

Was I sad? Well, yeah, but I didn't regret the decision. Since I cut out her constant accusations of living in sin and going straight to hell for the life I chose, the one that made me happy and where I was obsessively loved by two amazing men, I'd been more settled.

However, that could also be because of the major news I was hiding from the guys.

News that would change our lives forever.

News that would maybe change my mother's view on our relationship if she ever pulled her head out of her ass and reached out so I could tell her.

"What?" Miles said, tone tense.

"What, what?" I replied, fluttering my lashes. Damnit, how did he always know when I was holding something back?

"Aspen," he growled. With a careful tug, he slid me on top of him until I straddled his hips.

"I love waking up this way," Aiden muttered. My hair fanned out as I turned, finding him watching us with a smirk pulling at his lips. "Though I agree with Miles. What's going on, sweetheart?"

I groaned and looked at the ceiling. "How are you guys this perceptive?"

Miles chuckled. "You're easy to read despite what you think, baby girl. Now, out with it. What's going on in that beautiful brain of yours that's had you preoccupied the last couple of days? We've given you time to tell us, but time's up."

Chewing on my lower lip, I flicked my gaze from Aiden to Miles and back again.

"Fine. I have been holding something back from you." Miles's muscles tensed beneath me, and Aiden sat up straight with a concerned look. I shot him a stern expression. "Don't go there, Aiden. It's nothing bad, and it's nothing you did." I bit my lip to conceal my smile. "Well, maybe you did it, but we won't know for another nine months."

Silence encompassed the room, neither of them even breathing as they blinked at me while processing my words.

Aiden was the first to put it together. With a curse so loud I flinched, he leapt up and stood on the bed. "Don't kid me about this, sweetheart." Tears filled my lower lids as my smile grew. "Please, Aspen, please don't be joking."

"I'm not," I whispered, throat tight with emotion.

A wide, warm palm pressed to my lower belly, drawing my gaze to Miles. His hazel eyes were locked on the space beneath his hand.

"You're pregnant?" I nodded. "And you want this? With us?" I nodded again, the motion making the restrained tears flow down my cheeks. "Baby girl," he rasped, "when?"

"I went into town last week and got a few tests. They all came back the same."

"We're going to have a baby!" Aiden yelled, punching his fists into the air.

"Fuck, man, put some pants on so your dick isn't swinging around so early in the fucking morning," Miles grumbled.

"Why are you thinking about pants right now? Our girl is pregnant. We're going to be dads." Aiden paused his frantic rant and stilled. "Shit, I have so much to do." He jumped off the bed, still butt-ass naked. "I'll go get the iPad so we can start ordering..."

I shook my head and turned back to Miles when Aiden disappeared into the other room. "You're happy?" I asked.

"Happy?"

I nodded.

Palming the back of my head, he pulled me down to press a firm kiss to my forehead. "Happy doesn't cover it."

"You're going to be a great dad," I told him, unshed tears constricting my throat.

"And you're going to be the best mom this world has ever seen."

"I've got it," Aiden cheered and leapt onto the bed to lie beside us. "Okay, so first things first. What do you need, sweetheart? For the pregnancy, then we'll move on to baby stuff."

Reaching over, I cupped his jaw in one hand and Miles's in the other.

"I have everything I need right here."

And that was the truth.

For the pregnancy.

For after.

For forever.

Thank you so much for reading!
Ready for more from Anchor Bay? Stay updated on all new releases by signing up for my newsletter: https://bit.ly/
47JZhdu

ALSO BY KENNEDY L. MITCHELL

Anchor Bay: An Alaskan small town suspense, MFM, interconnected standalone series.

Our Chance - Anchor Bay prequel

Forever Theirs - Aiden, Miles, & Aspen

Claiming Ours

Book 3

Book 4

Book 5

In Clear Sight: A Small Town, WITSEC Interconnected Standalone Series

Safe Haven - FREE Prequel

Guarded by the Marshal*

Cherished by the Agent*

Saved by the Officers *

Hidden by the Doctor *

*Now available in Audio!

Protection Series: A Dark Romantic Thriller Interconnected Standalone Series

Mine to Protect *

Mine to Save *

Mine to Guard *

Mine to Keep *

Mine to Hold *

Mine to Love *

Mine to Share

Mine to Shelter

Mine to Shield

*Now available in audio!

SEALs and CIA Series: A Navy SEAL Interconnected Standalone Series

Covert Affair

Covert Vengeance

More Than a Threat Series: A Connected Bodyguard Romantic Suspense Series

More Than a Threat

More Than a Risk

More Than a Hope

More Than a Threat Series Boxset: Complete Series

Power Play Series: A Protector Romantic Suspense Connected Series

Power Games

Power Twist

Power Switch

Power Surge

Power Term

Standalones:

Finding Fate - Dark, Captive Romantic Suspense

Memories of Us - Contemporary, Small Town Romance

ABOUT THE AUTHOR

Kennedy L. Mitchell lives outside Dallas with her husband, son and two very large goldendoodles. She began writing in 2016 and has no plans of stopping.

She would love to hear from you via any of the platforms below or her website www.kennedylmitchell.com You can also stay up to date on future releases through her newsletter or by joining her Facebook readers group - Kennedy's Book Boyfriend Support Group.

Thank you for reading.

facebook.com/KennedyLMitchellBooks

instagram.com/kennedylmitchellbooks

bookbub.com/profile/kennedy-l-mitchell

ACKNOWLEDGMENTS

This series was a labor of love and heartache for sure. I can't say thank you enough to everyone who has helped me along the way in my healing journey. Kristin, Chris and Em, thank you so much for always reading and providing the best feedback as I wrote Forever Theirs. Your feedback and support made this story amazing.

And thank you to my amazing ARC and promo team for all the posts, shares and reviews. Starting a new series is SO HARD and all your effort is greatly appreciated. I couldn't do this without your help!

And of course thank you to my amazing editor and proofreader who make my words make sense - lol.

To you the reader, thank you for giving my new series a chance. I've always loved the idea of a series based in Alaska and I hope you enjoyed the first book in this new series. Hopefully Miles, Aiden and Aspen's story offered you a brief escape from reality and all the heaviness of the world.

9 781962 509237